PRAISE FOR KERRY ANNE KING

Praise for *Other People's Things*

"Woven with suspense, family drama, magic, and just the right touch of romance, *Other People's Things* is an utterly compulsive read. With a compelling cast of characters and a delightfully imaginative plot, readers are taken on a journey of self-discovery as a young woman struggles to embrace her unique gifts and find her place in a world that has already made up its mind about her. King's emotionally honest storytelling and wonderfully flawed protagonist remind us that people aren't always who we think they are—and that some curses might actually be blessings in disguise."
—Barbara Davis, bestselling author of *The Last of the Moon Girls*

Praise for *A Borrowed Life*

"King's fans will love this tale of rejuvenation."
—*Publishers Weekly*

"In this vivid and triumphant tale, a woman loses her controlling husband and discovers she's been tightly contained in a cocoon for decades. Learning who she is, one step at a time like an unsteady toddler, means challenging everything and every relationship in her life—and grappling with surprises that will turn her world upside down. Is she Elizabeth, the tight-laced pastor's wife, or Liz, the thespian who has a point of view all her own? Earthy, unpredictable, and wildly enjoyable."
—Barbara O'Neal, *Wall Street Journal* and *Washington Post* bestselling author of *When We Believed in Mermaids*

"Watching Liz Lightsey come back to life after years of letting her identity slide away is a treat. *A Borrowed Life* shows Kerry Anne King at her empathetic best, writing a tale of passion, meaning, and growth at any age, and leaving this reader touched and delighted!"

—Kelly Harms, *Washington Post* bestselling author of
The Bright Side of Going Dark

"Written by Kerry Anne King with humor and heart, *A Borrowed Life* is the story of Liz, a woman who finds herself at a midlife crossroads and bravely decides to reinvent her life by taking a giant leap outside her comfort zone. At times hilarious and cringe inducing, heartbreakingly sad and bursting with joy, Liz's unpredictable journey will have you gasping at every turn. I loved this book!"

—Loretta Nyhan, bestselling author of *Digging In*

"Kerry Anne King's *A Borrowed Life* is both beautifully written and unflinchingly honest. A cautionary tale about the insidious ways we allow others to keep us small, it's also a lesson on the enormous power of love and friendship, and how the people in our lives can lend us strength as we grow, cheering us on to be our best lives and who we are truly meant to be. This story with its wonderful cast of characters is one that will grab you by the heart and refuse to let go."

—Barbara Davis, Amazon Charts bestselling author of
The Last of the Moon Girls

"Life has a way of coming up with surprises, even for people who know themselves to be settled. In Kerry Anne King's latest wonderful novel, Elizabeth is a mother and dutiful pastor's wife, serving the needs of her family and the church. But when Thomas suddenly dies, Elizabeth embarks on a journey of self-discovery that awakens her to life's joys and losses, risks and magic. With *A Borrowed Life*, King has written a heartrending, page-turning novel that zips along with twists and turns, humor and poignancy, and will have you cheering (and gasping) as

Elizabeth-now-Liz rediscovers the meaning of freedom and creativity and love."

—Maddie Dawson, bestselling author of *Matchmaking for Beginners*

"In *A Borrowed Life* Kerry Anne King cleverly delves into a forty-nine-year-old woman's unexpected coming of age. Newly widowed, after a twenty-six-year marriage to a man who controlled her thoughts and actions, Elizabeth becomes Liz and takes complete charge of her life, exploring her world as never before. Making decisions that bring her happiness, often at the temporary expense of her inflexible adult daughter, Liz discovers life is not linear as she contends with unexpected roadblocks. King's storytelling gifts have us completely engaged until the last page is turned."

—Patricia Sands, author of the bestselling Love in Provence series

Praise for *Everything You Are*

"Hopeful at its heart and sincere to its core, *Everything You Are* is a testament to the power of connection."

—*Booklist*

"*Everything You Are* is a fresh, imaginative story about the power of dreams and our hunger to be who we really are. Kerry Anne King orchestrates a fluid, emotional, and wholly original tale of families, secrets, and the power of our gifts to free us. I loved every magical word."

—Barbara O'Neal, author of *When We Believed in Mermaids*

"Real and raw, King's *Everything You Are* is a gorgeous tale of life told between those lines too often blurred. Love and sorrow, regret and hope are woven into every aspect of the story by music—not just any

music, but the magical kind that leaves both creator and listener, for better or worse, irrevocably changed."
—Terri-Lynne DeFino, author of *The Bar Harbor Retirement Home for Famous Writers (and Their Muses)*

"Writing sensitively about characters struggling to overcome tragedy and loss, Kerry Anne King has delivered a beautiful, soulful novel that hits all the right notes—especially for music lovers. It will leave you with tears in your eyes and sighs of contentment when you reach the satisfying, emotional conclusion. A richly rewarding read."
—Julianne MacLean, *USA Today* bestselling author

Praise for *Whisper Me This*

"Rich in emotions and characters, *Whisper Me This* is a stunning tale of dark secrets, broken memories, and the resilience of the human spirit. The novel quickly pulls the reader onto a roller-coaster ride through grief, mystery, and cryptic journal entries. At the heart of the story is an unforgettable twelve-year-old, who has more sense than most adults, and her mother, Maisey, who is about to discover not only her courage, but the power of her voice. A book club must-read!"
—Barbara Claypole White, bestselling author of *The Perfect Son*

"Moving and emotionally taut, *Whisper Me This* is a gut-wrenching story of a family fractured by abuse and lies . . . and the ultimate sacrifice of a mother's love. King once again proves herself an expert with family drama. A triumph of a book."
—Emily Carpenter, author of *Burying the Honeysuckle Girls* and *The Weight of Lies*

"Kerry Anne King writes with such insight and compassion for human nature, and her latest novel, *Whisper Me This*, is no exception. The families on which the story centers have secrets they've kept through the years out of concern for the damage that might be done if they were exposed. But in the end as the families' lives become intertwined and their secrets come inevitably to light, what is revealed to be the most riveting heart of this book are the gut-wrenching choices that were made in terrifying circumstances. One such choice haunted a mother throughout her lifetime and left behind a legacy of mistrust and confusion and a near-unsolvable mystery. Following the clues is an act of faith that sometimes wavers. There's no guarantee the end will tie up in a neat bow, but the courage of the human spirit, its ability to heal, is persistent and luminous throughout the pages of this very real and emotive story. I loved it."

—Barbara Taylor Sissel, bestselling author of
Crooked Little Lies and *Faultlines*

Praise for *I Wish You Happy*

"Laugh, cry, get angry, but most of all care in this wild ride of emotions delivered by Kerry Anne King. Brilliant prose inhabited by engaging characters makes this a story you cannot put down."

—Patricia Sands, author of the Love in Provence series

"Depicting the depth of human frailty yet framing it within a picture of hope, *I Wish You Happy* pulls you in as you root for the flawed yet intoxicating characters to reach a satisfying conclusion of healing. King's writing is impeccable—and her knowledge and exploration of depression and how it affects those it touches makes this a story that everyone will connect with."

—Kay Bratt, author of *Wish Me Home*

"Kerry Anne King's Rae is a woman caught between the safety of her animal rescue projects and the messy, sometimes terrifying reality of human relationships. You'll never stop rooting for her as she steps into the light, risking everything for real friendship and love in this wistful, delicate, and ultimately triumphant tale."

—Emily Carpenter, author of *Burying the Honeysuckle Girls* and *The Weight of Lies*

"Kerry Anne King explores happiness and depression [and] the concept of saving others versus saving ourselves in this wonderfully written and touching novel populated by real and layered people. If you want to read a book that restores your faith in humanity, pick up *I Wish You Happy*."

—Amulya Malladi, bestselling author of *A House for Happy Mothers* and *The Copenhagen Affair*

"It's the horrible accident that forms the backbone of the plot at the beginning of *I Wish You Happy* that will take your breath and have you turning the pages. The hook has a vivid, ripped-from-the-headlines vibe, one that will have you wondering what you would do, how you would respond in a similar situation. But there are so many other treasures to find in this story as it unfolds. From the warm, deeply human, and relatable characters to the heartbreaking and complex situation they find themselves in, this is a novel to savor, one you will be sorry to see end. Sometimes funny and often very wise and poignant, *I Wish You Happy* is a reading journey you do not want to miss."

—Barbara Taylor Sissel, bestselling author of *Crooked Little Lies* and *Faultlines*

"Kerry Anne King has written a novel that will grab you right from page one and then take you zipping along, breaking your heart and making you laugh, both in equal measure. It's a lovely story about how we save ourselves while we try to save those around us. I loved it!"

—Maddie Dawson, author of six novels, including *The Survivor's Guide to Family Happiness*

Praise for *Closer Home*

"A compelling and heartfelt tale. A must-read that is rich in relatable characters and emotions. Kerry Anne King is one to watch out for!"
—Steena Holmes, *New York Times* and *USA Today* bestselling author

"With social media conferring blistering fame and paparazzi exhibiting the tenacity often required to get a clear picture of our lives, King has created a high-stakes, public stage for her tale of complicated grief. A quick read with emotional depth you won't soon forget."
—Kathryn Craft, author of *The Far End of Happy* and *The Art of Falling*

"*Closer Home* is a story as memorable and meaningful as your favorite song, with a cast of characters so true to life you'll be sorry to let them go."
—Sonja Yoerg, author of *House Broken* and *Middle of Somewhere*

"Kerry Anne King's tale of regret, loss, and love pulled me in, from its intriguing beginning to its oh-so-satisfying conclusion."
—Jackie Bouchard, *USA Today* bestselling author of *House Trained* and *Rescue Me, Maybe*

"King's prose is filled with vitality."
—Ella Carey, author of *Paris Time Capsule* and *The House by the Lake*

OTHER

PEOPLE'S

THINGS

ALSO BY KERRY ANNE KING

Closer Home

I Wish You Happy

Whisper Me This

Everything You Are

A Borrowed Life

OTHER
PEOPLE'S
THINGS

A NOVEL

KERRY ANNE KING

LAKE UNION
PUBLISHING

Published by Lake Union Publishing, Seattle

www.apub.com

Amazon, the Amazon logo, and Lake Union Publishing are trademarks of Amazon.com, Inc., or its affiliates.

ISBN-13: 9781542026239
ISBN-10: 1542026237

Cover design by Shasti O'Leary Soudant

Printed in the United States of America

For my Viking, with thanks for loving me as I am and for venturing into this journey of creative chaos right alongside me

Chapter One

NICOLE

Better than jail.

This is my new mantra, and I've repeated it a gazillion times already this morning. When Roberta shook me awake at the god-awful and ridiculous hour of five a.m.—*this is better than jail.* When I realized that the coffee in the pot was decaf and there was no cream in Mom's house—*this is better than jail.* Now, shivering in the car with a travel mug half full of bitter, zero-zing coffee that has already cooled too much to even warm my hands, the mantra is wearing thin.

Snow is falling in the early-morning darkness, a mesmerizing mosaic in the beam of the headlights. Visibility is nearly zero, and Roberta inches along in silence, white-knuckling the steering wheel, straining toward the windshield as if those few extra inches will offer an advantage. Normally I'd point out that by cruising at the speed of an elderly glacier, she is creating a traffic hazard the polar opposite of traveling too fast.

But for once in my life, I keep my mouth shut. My sister has given me—*me*, Nicole Angelica Marie Wood Brandenburg, jailbird, nutcase, and spectacular failure to launch—a job. This is an act of such beneficence that I'm indebted to her through at least the next three reincarnations, so I need to keep my mouth shut and try to be civil. Since I'm utterly incapable of really keeping snark to myself, I text my best—and only—friend, Ash, instead.

Nicole: OMG! Send help.

Ash: LOL. Housecleaning is that bad?

Nicole: We have entered a cautious driver time warp and will never reach the house. If we don't make it out, you get my wedding ring.

Ash: 😨 Don't you inflict that on me. Bad Karma.

Nicole: Sell it.

Ash: If it's real.

Nicole: Ha. Very funny.

"Here we go," Roberta says, finally easing her well-worn Subaru hatchback into a white expanse of driveway marked by a single set of tire tracks. The neighbors on either side are engaged in snow management, one with a shovel, the other with a snowblower. An exercise in futility, in my opinion, given how fast the flakes are falling.

I hate winter. Five years ago, after Kent and I got married, I started a let's-leave-Spokane-and-move-someplace-warm campaign. I sent him videos of Mexico. Planted flyers about communities in Arizona and California on his desk. Now that I've utterly destroyed my marriage along with my chances of ever having enough money to move out of my mother's house, all exotic locations are out of the question. Winter will be with me forever.

With a sigh, I accept my fate and open my door, shivering as the cold insinuates itself through my thin coat and my thin flesh and right into my bones. My warm winter clothes and my boots are still at Kent's condo, and I am neither going back for them nor asking him to send them to me.

"Nickle." Roberta's voice holds a warning. "Leave your backpack in the car."

"But—"

"You get toilet duty. Scrub the bathrooms and the kitchen floor. And I will check your pockets before we leave. Are we clear?"

"Yes, ma'am." I salute her, slamming the door harder than necessary. Gratitude for this chance to earn a living has not quite quashed my inner rebel, or my annoyance that she still talks to me as if I'm a child. *Better than jail,* I remind myself. Also, I owe Roberta both of my kidneys and my immortal soul. As the owner of Sunny Side Up Cleaning Services, she has taken a huge risk in hiring me, since she has every reason to believe that I'm an incorrigible kleptomaniac. But she's also not stupid, and she's not about to set me loose dusting curios. I'm unlikely to try to stuff a toilet brush or a mop into my back pocket.

Slipping and sliding in the snow, I wrestle the vacuum cleaner and a bucket full of rags and cleaning solutions out of the hatch, leaving Rob to manage her clipboard, a mop, and a duster. Snow cakes between the tops of my sneakers and my socks as I half wade, half skate to the porch like some ludicrous cross between a clown and an ice dancer. Roberta, her feet snug and warm in boots with serious grips on the soles, has the door unlocked by the time I join her on the porch.

Our eyes meet, and my irritation evaporates. Roberta carries a lot of responsibilities on her shoulders, and it's beginning to show. Her hair, short for convenience rather than style, is more gray than brown. There's a permanent furrow in her forehead and lines around her eyes. Her face is kind enough but clearly shows that her life has been mostly hard work and worry, with little time for fun. By the time she was twelve, she was babysitting three younger siblings and helping Mom with meals and housework. Now she runs a busy cleaning business while also managing two teenagers and a husband.

If I were any other new employee, she'd probably have pawned me and my orientation off on somebody else and would be sitting in a warm office right now drinking coffee and taking care of the books. But I am not to be trusted, and she and I both know it.

I swear to myself in that moment that I will not remove any object from this house, or the house of any other client, no matter what I see, or feel, or how strong the temptation. But the instant I cross the threshold, I realize with crystal clarity what a bad idea it is for me to work for a cleaning service. This house is a land mine. Every flat surface is covered with stuff. Figurines. Magazines. Odds and ends of this and that.

Roberta's voice, giving me instructions, drifts farther and farther away. My heart thuds against my ribs; my mouth goes dry. I discipline myself to take three slow, deep breaths, an act of faith that the long line of counselors who have advocated this technique might actually know what they're talking about. Other than a sneeze induced by a floral air freshener, the results are inconclusive, but at least I haven't gone into a full-on panic attack.

Roberta, who knows about my weird compulsion even though she doesn't begin to understand it, sighs. "Please just get to work. We don't have time for your nonsense."

From the relative safety of the doormat, I scope out what I can see of the house. Everything looks reassuringly normal. No twisting or bending or shimmering of the light. No random objects demanding to be picked up and moved. But I know from experience that books are one of the worst offenders, and they are everywhere.

"Come look at this, first." Rob leads me through a house that is cluttered but surprisingly clean. Visible bits of carpet are vacuumed. There's not a speck of dust. The kitchen sink is empty and spotless, a dishcloth folded perfectly in half and hung over the gleaming faucet to dry. A notebook sits on the counter, and Roberta flips it open and points to a precisely written list.

"Most customers have a book like this where they leave special instructions. Mrs. Lane always writes something, so you need to remember to look. No special requests today, so we'll just dust, scrub, and vacuum wherever there's a space to do so. Get a move on. Your toilets are waiting."

4

I stick my tongue out, very mature and professional, take a breath, and venture into the main bathroom. Here, there is no clutter. Spotless floor. Shining toilet bowl. Not so much as a stray hair in the sink. Perfect guest towels in sunshine yellow hang precisely on the rack. Unused decorative hand soaps sit in a dish on the counter. I doubt this bathroom has ever been used, and I find myself wondering if Mrs. Lane is lonely.

Reminding myself that the emotional well-being of a woman I have never met is not my problem, I queue up music on my phone, turn up the volume, and start scrubbing nonexistent soap scum from the bathtub to the accompaniment of the Three Tenors. I've finished the tub and sink and am pumicing the already pristine toilet when Roberta bounces in to check on me.

"What is that caterwauling?" she shouts, to make herself heard above "O Sole Mio." She grabs my phone and shuts off the music. "I don't get why you insist on listening to this. Or why you can't wear earbuds."

I shrug, trying to unstick hair from my cheek with my shoulder. "Helps me focus. Forgot to bring the earbuds."

Rob likes the Beatles and the Bee Gees. Old-school stuff that is easy to listen to and doesn't make you think. My tastes are weird and eclectic, and I'll listen to anything from acid rock to opera, but when I'm feeling anxious, classical is where it's at.

"Try something zippier," Roberta says. "We're not meditating, we're working. Get a move on. We haven't got all day."

"I'm not Mary Poppins," I protest. "Not magic. It takes time to scrub every—"

"You don't have to scrub *every* surface," she says.

I look up at her, Roberta in her mom jeans and oversize T-shirt, with that face that broadcasts *honest and dependable* as clearly as a bat signal. With a shock like the cold of a toilet swirlie, a torment with which I have way too much personal experience, I see in her eyes what she will never say out loud:

"Just wipe everything down with a damp cloth. Spray some air freshener around. No need to waste time doing what has already been done. Mrs. Lane will never know and we can be out of here and on to the next house."

"And I'm the criminal in the family," I say, never able to keep my mouth shut.

"Just hurry, will you?" Roberta turns and stalks away, but I don't miss the fact that she didn't ask, "What are you even talking about?" Which means she knows damn well, and I'm right about what she wants me to do.

And I absolutely and utterly cannot do it. If my job is to scrub this bathroom, I am compelled to scrub this bathroom. Every square inch of it. I won't sleep tonight if I get paid for something I didn't do. Which just highlights how screwed up I am. When I take something that doesn't belong to me, it feels 110 percent right and I sleep like a baby, but I'm incapable of the small dishonesties the rest of the world takes for granted.

Today, I'm not taking anything, I remind myself, no matter what I see or feel, or how many damn books there are in this house. I change up my mantra and run it through my head, over and over and over again.

Don't hurt Rob. Do my job. Stay out of jail.

Everything is fine until I move on to the master bedroom. The bed is neatly made, but the room is crammed with stacks of books and magazines, games and puzzles, plastic craft bins, and other random stuff. A narrow pathway winds through the clutter to the bathroom, which, unlike the guest bathroom, shows signs of frequent and recent use.

Shampoo and conditioner, bodywash, a can of shaving cream, and three razors compete for space in a shower caddy. A hand towel, slightly damp, hangs askew on a hook by the sink. And a shelf stuffed with paperbacks lurks next to the door, waiting to ambush me.

This strikes me as manifestly unfair. There are rules. I mean, sure, keeping a reading book in the bathroom makes total sense, but a shelf crammed full of them? During my almost thirty years, I've relocated a wide variety of objects from one place to another, but books, above all things, are my kryptonite. Why, I don't know, but I do have a theory.

Books absorb energy from readers. Energy doesn't like to stagnate, it wants to move. Ergo, books want to move. And now, on this day where I must not, no matter what, move anything other than dirt and dust, here I am up close and personal with what I most need to avoid.

I deliberately turn my back on the rainbow of colors and textures created by all of those lovely spines. I will not look. I will not touch. Today I am cleaning toilets and scrubbing showers and floors and washing mirrors. I turn the music back on, then don a pair of gloves and get them wet and foamy with cleaning spray to augment my always fragile willpower. As I scrub the shower, I sing along to "Ave Maria," hoping in my heart that maybe the Holy Mother really does exist and will extend some sort of mercy from heaven down to me.

No such luck.

The sensation of wrongness starts at the base of my spine, as it always does, creeping and crawling like a spider, tiny legs whispering upward from one vertebra to the next. I slap at it, soapy glove and all, even though I know nothing is there, and mutter under my breath, "Do my job. Don't hurt Rob. Stay out of jail."

I laser focus on my task. Rinse the shower clean. Squeegee the glass. By the time I move on to the sink, the spider sensation has given way to an army of ants running up and down, occasionally stopping to bite. I breathe in, the smell of bleach and chemicals crisping the hair in my nose, burning my sinuses, but that does nothing to intercept the ant parade.

The sink doesn't need scrubbing, and I'm done with it all too fast. When I start on the mirror, I find myself staring at a reflection of the books. I can't read the titles, but I don't need to in order to see which book is causing the problem. There's a blur and shimmer around it, as if I'm looking at it through a heat haze.

Do my job. Don't hurt Rob. Stay out of jail. But I need to dust the bookshelf, which puts me directly in the way of temptation. Holding my breath, I whisk my duster over the danger zone, resolved to finish and get my hands safely immersed in a bucket of soapy water as rapidly as possible.

The book that wants to be moved is an old paperback copy of Dante's *Inferno*, the binding creased and broken. Well, that's appropriate, since I'm obviously inhabiting one of the circles of hell. I allow myself to touch the spine once, ever so lightly, and when I draw back my hand, it wants to cling to my fingers like cobwebs. I rub my hand on my jeans, trying to wipe off the lingering sensation, and with an effort of willpower, I manage to pull on my gloves and start scrubbing the floor.

Don't hurt Rob. Do your job. Stay out of jail.

A party of enthusiastic grasshoppers takes up residence in my belly. From long experience, I know that very soon they will begin to gnaw on my stomach lining and I'll feel like I'm being eaten from the inside out. All over a battered old book.

If I took it with me, would Mrs. Lane even notice? And if she did notice, would she know I was the one who walked off with it? Even if she figured it out, nobody is going to send me to jail over an old book with a bent cover and dog-eared pages.

"You not done yet?"

I startle and slop a puddle of water onto the floor as Roberta pokes her head in and huffs an annoyed sigh. "You're gonna have to pick up the pace, Nickle," she shouts, to be heard over my music. "I already did the kitchen floor for you and started packing stuff out. Wipe up that mess and come on. This is done enough."

She vanishes and I hear her footsteps on the stairs.

Which means I am now alone with the enemy. As I peel off my gloves slowly, one finger at a time, I tell myself I will not touch the book. I will certainly not *take* the book. But even as I repeat the words over and over in my head, somehow, the book is in my hands. I scan the first page. Note the words "Property of Tag" scrawled inside the cover. A moment later, it's tucked into the waistband of my jeans at the small of my back, my sweatshirt tugged down to cover it.

When I get downstairs, Roberta is already out the door. I put on my coat, which provides extra concealment for my contraband. Then I lug out the bucket and dump it in the snow, well away from the house. Tuck my tools into the open hatch of the car. The motor is running, the stink of exhaust sharp in the back of my throat.

"Thought you were going to search me?" I say, sliding awkwardly into the front seat beside my sister, the book stiff as a brace on my lower back.

She gives me the side-eye as she backs out of the driveway.

"Did you steal something?"

"Nope."

It doesn't feel like a lie. It never does.

Chapter Two

HAWK

I'm wakened by the sound of goodbye.

Even in my own bed, some part of me is always listening into the dark for the first subtle sounds that mean conflict and danger. Here, in a still-unfamiliar apartment, I've barely skimmed the surface of sleep, dipping under briefly and then waking again, over and over while the night dragged by. So when the mattress beside me dips, followed by the faint rustling of fabric against skin, I don't even need to put out my hand to know that Mickey is no longer curled in the bed beside me.

The bedside clock reads not quite five a.m., and she's not an early riser. I tell myself maybe she's just gone to the bathroom. That she'll return, her skin cool from the night air, and snuggle up against me so I can warm her. But in my heart, I know better, and after a few minutes, I get out of bed, pull on my jeans and T-shirt, and go in search of her.

I find her in the kitchen, waiting for the sputtering coffeepot to fill. When she hears my footsteps, she startles and half turns toward me, one hand clutching the edges of her dressing gown together at her breast. Her eyes are wide, fixed on mine, her body poised like a deer, ready to flee. I hate the way she's looking at me, fearful and cautious, as if one wrong move will send me into a fury that ends in blows and bruises.

It doesn't matter that I've never struck her, never even raised my voice to her. Ever since we met, I've told myself she'll relax when she gets to know me. That I can erase her memory of unpredictable fists with soft words and gentleness. Last night, she flinched when I reached out to touch her face. We both pretended it hadn't happened, but I saw her wiping away tears when she thought I wasn't looking.

No matter how hard I try to avoid the tendency, I seem to gravitate toward damaged women, a by-product of my childhood, if I believe the self-help book I read once. I consciously make a point of dating women who are, on the surface, confident and well adjusted and secure, but inevitably, a few dates in, when we reach the stage of kisses and confidences, they tell me about the boyfriend or the husband or the father or the stranger who instilled in them a fear so permanently ingrained, it's become a fiber of their being.

I see it in their eyes, the way they cross their arms over their bellies to protect the soft center, the way they watch my hands and flinch at sudden movements. My appearance doesn't help matters any. I'm six foot four, two hundred pounds, my features hard angled and irregular. Nobody, not even my mother, has ever referred to me as handsome, and one of my girlfriends once summoned the courage to tell me I look fierce.

I'd hoped things would be different with Mickey, but then I always hope.

"Hey, Mick." I soften my voice, drop my shoulders, make myself look as small as I can. "Couldn't sleep?"

"I can't," she begins. "I thought I could. I wanted . . ." She stops, her face pleading with me to read the words she doesn't want to say. Tears track silently down her cheeks. She's not talking about sleep.

"Okay," I say as gently as I can. "It's okay."

"It's not you," she whispers. "You've been wonderful." Her face contorts with an effort to hold back the tears, but they keep on falling.

"Maybe it's just going to take more time." I hate the pleading note in my voice. It reminds me too much of the skinny, dorky, awkward teenager that I haven't quite succeeded in leaving behind. I want to circle Mickey in my arms, comfort her, but I stay where I am, helpless and clumsy and vaguely guilty for the sins of all mankind.

"A lot more time," she says, her voice high and squeaky. "Maybe more than this lifetime. I'm sorry, Hawk."

"Me, too," I say. "I'll go now. Call me sometime."

She nods but doesn't try to stop me. So that's that, then. She won't call. This relationship is over almost before it began. How long this time? One month? Two? Somewhere in between, I think. Make it six weeks and call it even. As I let myself out the front door, ensuring it's locked behind me, I feel regret and loss but not heartbreak. I wasn't in love. I'm not sure love is something I even believe in.

Both personal experience and my work as a private investigator weigh heavily against the idea that two people can fall in love without irreparably damaging each other in the process. My parents' marriage was an unmitigated disaster that very nearly killed my mother. She's compensated by getting a law degree and building a practice that specializes in helping women get clear of domestic violence.

When I went to college I majored in political science, thinking I would also go to law school and join her in her practice, but it quickly became clear that law wasn't for me. And then I thought I'd go into law enforcement, inspired by my aunt, who has recently worked her way up to detective. But listening to her talk about the inside politics, the unwritten codes, the constant injustices and inequities she has to deal with, I sidestepped and got my PI license instead.

According to the ads I run, Hawkeye Private Investigation Services specializes in locating missing persons, but in reality, I do a lot of work for Mom, much of it pro bono. My aunt hires me to pursue investigations that she either doesn't have time for or can't legally get into. And the rest of my time is mostly spent gathering proof of infidelity for people who believe their partner is cheating. On all counts, my work does not lend itself to the development of a healthy romance.

It's snowing, and my Jeep is covered two inches deep. A pervasive sadness makes the cold feel colder, the winter dark of early morning even darker. By the time I brush off the snow and scrape the windows, I'm damp and shivering, but I don't want to go home. Since I'm awake, I might as well use the time to catch up on email and some of the other business details I tend to neglect. Starbucks is close, open, and has Wi-Fi, three things in its favor, so I set myself up in a corner space with a latte and three breakfast sandwiches and get to work.

I've barely started when my phone rings. Unknown number, and it's damned early, but neither of these things is uncommon in my line of work. I glance around the shop, which is still mostly deserted at this hour, and decide to risk picking up. Confidentiality is important, but I'm staying right here where it's warm and toasty until I know what I'm dealing with.

The voice on the line is male, authoritative, and superior. "Hawk? This is Kent Brandenburg. I need you to clear your schedule and do something for me."

His tone rubs me the wrong way. I'm not in any frame of mind to tolerate some guy ordering me around. "Sorry, my caseload is full," I lie, my thumb already on disconnect. But his name tugs at my memory, and I hesitate, just long enough for him to say, "You've done work for our firm before. Findlay, Strachey, and Lytle. This is a matter of some . . . delicacy, and I trust your discretion. You'll be very well paid for your time."

The implication, of course, is that whatever he needs me for is more important than anything else I've got going on. I vaguely remember meeting Kent Brandenburg. I disliked him. Too handsome, too well dressed, exuding privilege from every pore.

Again, my thumb hovers over disconnect. Again, I hesitate. It's good for both my business and my clients for me to be on good terms with the law firms. Spokane is a small city and word gets around. Not to mention that the last thing in the world that I want to face today is the infidelity case I'm scheduled to work on.

"I'm listening," I say, getting up and heading outside, where we can talk without the risk of being overheard.

"Here's the thing." It's Kent's turn to hesitate, and I take advantage of the pause to get first one arm and then the other into my jacket.

He draws an audible breath and launches in. "I need to keep this quiet, and I need to keep it from the rest of the firm, so I don't want to call in law enforcement. My wife is a kleptomaniac. Inconsequential things, usually, but this time she's walked off with company money, and I need to get it back before it's missed."

This gets my attention. A theft investigation would be a welcome break from delving into the detritus of twisted and broken human relationships.

"How much money?" I ask.

"Twenty thousand."

I whistle. "And when did she take it?"

"Approximately two weeks ago."

"Approximately? Mr. Brandenburg, do you have proof that it was your wife who took this money?" All of my clients lie to me, either inadvertently or deliberately, and I've caught a whiff of deliberate dishonesty, which is a red flag.

Brandenburg laughs. "I know she did it. She didn't even deny it when I confronted her. But she wouldn't tell me what she'd done with the money."

"And you want me to find it?"

Red flags have now become warning flares. This guy might be an attorney at a respected firm, but in addition to being condescending as hell, he's also either delusional or firmly camped out in denial. It's now my job to tell him this without pissing him off. Last thing I need is some big-shot attorney bad-mouthing me and my business to his colleagues because I turned him down.

"Mr. Brandenburg, I have to tell you that I'm afraid that money is long gone. She's most probably spent it—"

"I don't think so."

"You think she's stashed it somewhere?"

"Temporarily, yes," he says. "Here's the thing about my wife. When she steals something, she doesn't collect it or keep it, she moves it. Calls it 'relocating.'"

I can practically hear the air quotes he's making around the word, his voice dripping with scorn.

"And you think she has relocated this money?" I ask, interested despite my misgivings.

"Either that, or she's still waiting to do so. She claims that she gets a feeling about where an object wants to be. Until the universe speaks, she'll keep it with her. That's what she says. Not that you can believe somebody like that, so maybe you're right and she'll just spend it. Hell if I know."

I am officially intrigued. Plus, I'm short on funds and I have bills coming due. My last two clients were broke themselves and haven't paid me yet. Brandenburg, on the other hand, should have absolutely no problem paying up.

Still, I'm used to listening to my gut, and I hold on to caution. "I'm not sure that I'm clear on what you want me to do."

"Just watch her. You don't need to catch her in the act or anything, just let me know where she goes and who she's with. I'll pay you two hundred a day, plus a five-thousand-dollar bonus if you locate the missing money."

"All right, I'll do it," I hear myself say. "I'll need some details. Name, birth date, Social Security number. Current location. Anything you know about her daily routine."

"Fantastic. I'll email you. We're separated, but according to the family grapevine, she's apparently started working with her sister, so Roberta will have eyes on her all day. That will give you time to get up to speed."

I give him my email address and go back inside to await further information. My latte has gone cold, and I order another, along with a couple of chocolate muffins, and settle in to do my homework.

Nicole Brandenburg's rap sheet is extensive, a long list of shoplifting and petty theft charges and convictions that stretch all the way back to a sealed juvenile record I can't access. The objects she is known to have stolen range from books to bicycles, yard art to garden tools, with any number of random items in between. Most of it has little cash or resale value, so stealing a large amount of money is a first for her, at least as far as the record goes. Who knows what she's gotten away with?

I'm thorough with my background checks, so I go on to investigate the rest of her family. All of them—Mom, three older siblings, deceased father—are squeaky clean. No 911 calls for domestic violence, everybody's taxes have been paid on time, there's barely a handful of speeding tickets between them. Her brother, Warner, is a high school history teacher. Her sister Brina, a financial planner with Edward Jones. And Roberta, the oldest, owns and operates a housecleaning business, Sunny Side Up.

Nicole's employment history, on the other hand, is a series of short-term, dead-end jobs. Unlike her siblings, who all have college degrees, she dropped out of high school and only recently acquired a GED. Her sister's decision to let her help clean houses shows either terrible judgment or a strong family connection, or maybe both.

With the family all accounted for, I check out Kent Brandenburg. I always investigate my clients, ever since the case where the guy who hired me was trying to locate his ex so he could kill her for leaving him. What I find about Kent Darryl Whitmer Brandenburg III doesn't make me like him any better, but there's also no obvious reason not to take the case. He's a golden boy, the only son of an investment capitalist and a plastic surgeon. He grew up in New York, and both of his parents still live there. He went to a fancy prep school and has a law degree from Harvard. Now he's an up-and-coming criminal attorney.

Of course, up and coming in a small city like Spokane might be the equivalent of down and out somewhere like New York City. What is Kent doing here, all the way across the country, away from his old-money family? And why would he marry an uneducated woman with an extensive legal record? Something is off, and it's not just that I don't like the guy. On the other hand, his legal record is clean, and he's offered me more pay for a week's work than I'm looking to make in a month, not to mention the bonus if I find the missing money.

Besides, from the sounds of things, Nicole is a petty thief who has upped her game, and I'll be doing society a favor by bringing her to justice.

I shake off my uneasiness. In the PI business, everybody has an ulterior motive. If something seems really off, I can bail at any time. Packing up my mobile office, I check the time and decide I can still get in some work on another case. Brandenburg has not only emailed me all of his wife's identifiers, he's given me access to a location tracker app he installed on her phone. This invasion of her privacy is another strike against him, but I tell myself it's not unreasonable, given his position and her criminal tendencies, and it will certainly make my job easier.

Chapter Three

NICOLE

Mom has dinner waiting when I let myself into the house, my new guilty secret adding what feels like fifty pounds to my day pack. But once I'm safe in my childhood home with the aroma of Mom's special secret chicken recipe wafting into the air around me, it's easy to dismiss my nagging worry. The book is such a small thing, really, in the grand scheme of things. Especially compared to the twenty thousand dollars that I fervently wish would make its intentions known so I can unload it.

"How was your day?" Mom asks, aiming for casual, but I'd have to be deaf to miss the note of anxiety in her voice. She's been worrying about me for so many years, and I want more than anything for her to be able to stop. She loves that I'm working with my sister, loves having me live with her so she isn't alone. But she's worried about me and Kent and whatever it is I've done to break up our marriage, and she's worried about what I might do while working for Roberta, and she's even more worried that I'll never figure out some sort of meaningful direction for my life.

"Cleaning was kind of fun." I hang up my coat. Line up my shoes side by side on the mat. Set my day pack with its incriminating secrets up against the wall, along with a shopping bag from Target. Mom hugs me and I hug her back. She feels small and fragile, a reminder that I'm no longer a child but a grown woman who should be taking care of her mother by now, not the other way around.

"What's in the bag?" she asks, avoiding my eyes, and I feel the sliver of suspicion slide between my ribs and into my heart.

"Rob dropped me at Target so I could pick up a few clothes. In case you're wondering, everything in there is bought and paid for. You can check the receipt if you want," I say, burning with unjustified resentment.

"Honey, I don't understand why we don't just get some of your things from the condo. Surely—"

"Not going to happen." My voice is sharper than I mean it to be, and I see a sheen of tears in her eyes before she turns away to hide her face, which makes me feel like an absolute heel.

"Well, anyway, it's lovely to have company for dinner," she says. "I get lonely without your father."

"I'm sorry. I didn't mean to bark." I walk over to her and hug her again, guiltily grateful that my father died believing I finally had my life together. The last time I saw him, a month and two days after my wedding, he'd wrapped his arms around me and I'd pressed my cheek against his chest and listened to his heart beating out a steady, dependable Dad rhythm.

"I'm proud of you," he'd said, kissing the top of my head. A week later, that seemingly dependable heart utterly betrayed him, and he dropped dead in the middle of his accounting office.

Much as he loved me, I know that what he was proud of wasn't really me but the fact that I'd somehow managed to marry Kent. My entire family had fallen under Kent's spell the same way I had, and no wonder. He was a dream come true: smart and ambitious and wealthy, with smoldering good looks and charm piled on top. All of us were surprised that he'd fallen for me.

We met in a cramped conference room where I'd been stashed for safekeeping prior to a court appearance. The memory is vivid, and even here, in my parents' house, I can smell that small room permeated with the body odor of some individual who either had no access to showers or avoided them on principle. It was hot, my T-shirt clinging to my body, damp with my own hopefully non-stinky sweat.

Every nerve in my body was screaming with anxiety. I'd gotten used to my frequent court appearances, but the charges against me were steeper this time around—the bicycle I'd moved was an expensive one; plus I had multiple strikes against me.

Across the table, a case manager, the emissary of my new, high-powered attorney, perched on the edge of a chair, trying to keep her obviously expensive skirt and jacket from touching any contaminated surfaces. She breathed ostentatiously through her mouth, her nose wrinkled in obvious disgust, and absorbed herself in her phone. In the past, I'd been stuck with court-appointed counsel, but this time, because the legal stakes were higher, my dad had paid for a hired gun.

Who was officially late. I fidgeted and worried, afraid that my dad had been suckered by a shyster who was going to drain him of money he couldn't afford to lose in exchange for absolutely nothing.

"Is the illustrious Mr. Brandenburg even going to show up?" I queried. "Or does he just take his money and phone the case in?"

The case manager yawned, not bothering to look up or to stop tapping at her phone. "He'll be here."

As if on cue, the door opened. In hindsight, there should have been dramatic music, but there was no advance warning of what was about to happen. I assumed a casual position, ready to unload a can of snark on the middle-aged, boring, condescending dick I expected. But the man who stood in the doorway was not that person. Yes, he was older than my twenty-five-year-old self but definitely not middle-aged. He exuded competence, confidence, power, money, and charm. And he was gorgeous—a little bit Matthew McConaughey, a little bit Ryan

Gosling—with keen blue eyes, a classic jaw, and sensitive lips. His perfectly tailored suit jacket and trousers revealed a form broad in the shoulders and narrow in the hips.

The case manager stopped texting, her eyes fixed on him adoringly, but he didn't even glance in her direction as he said, dismissively, "You can go, Brenda." He leaned toward me, his eyes gazing deeply into mine as he held out his hand.

"Nicole. I'm Kent. Tell me about the bicycle."

His hand lingered over the shake, fingers brushing mine as he released me and sat down on the other side of the table. My tough-girl persona totally abandoned me. I couldn't think of a single smart-ass thing to say. So I blurted out the whole story, about the bicycle and how it wanted to be moved a few blocks away from where I found it, and how I got caught by an extraordinarily on-the-ball police officer before I could leave the bike where it wanted to be.

Kent listened as if we had all the time in the world. As if we weren't due in court at any moment. He acted like he wasn't paid to be there but had come to help me because there was nowhere else he would rather be.

"Fascinating," he said when I fell silent. "I almost wonder if a jury trial . . ." His voice trailed off as he rubbed his jaw, still gazing at me in a way that made my heart beat a little faster. "No, we'd better not risk it. But I think I can get you a good deal. We'll enter a not-guilty plea today and file for a continuance."

He stood and held out a hand to me, either to help me out of my chair or for me to shake again, or both. I was dazzled by him and bewildered by the action, even more so when he didn't release his grip after lifting me to my feet. His touch, his interest, the faint spice of cologne and aftershave all made me dizzy.

"Wait for me after court," he said, his voice sending little shivers up and down my spine. "So we can talk about your case."

I waited. And then we did talk about my case. In a five-star restaurant. Over a bottle of expensive French wine. After dinner, he took me to his elegant condo and made love to me, and by morning, I was enchanted, entranced, captivated, and infatuated. The fact that such a man was interested in me—a high school dropout with a habit of moving other people's things—inspired something in my soul that was near to devotion. And when my father came to me a few days later, with tears in his eyes, to say that Mr. Brandenburg had waived all fees and taken my case pro bono, my fate was sealed. A few months later, I married the prince and moved into the castle.

If only I were a different kind of me—a me that knew how to play fairy-tale princess and live in a happily ever after. But there's more curse-come-to-call than princess about me. I've blown the castle sky-high along with any hope of happiness with the handsome prince.

Now, standing in my mother's kitchen, I poke around at my emotions to see if I'm feeling any pain yet over this loss. It's been over two weeks but I'm still apparently numb. I feel shame, mostly that I'm about to be thirty and don't have a job or a home or an education or anything, really, besides an extensive counseling and legal history. I feel fear about my future. But where there should be grief and heartbreak, all I feel is relief and a tiny, fragile glimmer of freedom.

Shaking off thoughts of both Kent and today's relocation incident, I go wash up for dinner while Mom pulls chicken out of the oven, enough for the whole family. She's never been able to adapt her recipes since we all grew up and moved out. Which is fine, because my siblings and their kids raid the fridge every time they come by.

Mom also brings out a bottle of wine and two of her special-occasion glasses.

"Are we celebrating something?" I ask as she pours one for each of us.

"You being home," she says.

But I suspect it's much more likely that she's hoping the wine will inspire confidences. So far, I've told her nothing about what happened with me and Kent. I showed up at her door in tears and told her my marriage was over, and that was it. She thinks she wants the details, but I know they will break her heart, and I have no intention of ever telling her, unless she asks, in which case I'll have to spill it all because I never lie. The peace between us depends on my skill at evasion and her desire to avoid conflict.

Hard work has made me ravenous, and I consume two thighs and half a plate full of mashed potatoes, buttery smooth and light, the way only Mom can make them, along with salad and bread. She barely picks at her food, and when she refills my glass, I know the moment is upon us. She sets her fork down. Dabs her lips with the napkin. Folds her hands in her lap. And asks the direct question that I am now required to answer.

"What happened, Nicole? Things seemed to be going so well."

Seemed. A good word, "seemed." *Definition: to give the effect or appearance of being.* My whole relationship with Kent is encapsulated in that phrase. I know she's hoping I'll tell her that we just had a little tiff, that I'll be going back soon and we just needed a few days apart. I take a breath and make a Hail Mary pass at avoiding the whole story. "We're over. That's all you really want to know."

She takes a swallow of wine, then looks me in the eyes and says, "Tell me what you did." Mom loves Kent and she knows me. There's not any question in her mind that our breakup could be his fault. Which, of course, it isn't.

I sigh. "I moved something."

"Like furniture?" she asks, ever hopeful.

"Like money." I can't bear to see the expression on her face, so I watch her hands instead, the way they come up to her heart as if in prayer, the way her body curls inward, like a dying leaf.

"You stole *money*?"

I understand her shock. My encounters with the law have been, up to this point, mostly misdemeanors. Shoplifting, trespassing, minor theft of relatively inexpensive objects. Kent got the charges in the bicycle incident significantly reduced. What I've done this time is more dramatic. There's no point trying to explain to my mother why money in Kent's desk drawer didn't want to be there anymore. I don't understand it myself.

What's even harder to understand is that the money doesn't know where it wants to be. Right after I took it, I hid it in a safety-deposit box. When he discovered it was missing and kicked me out of the condo, I retrieved it first thing and have been carrying it around with me ever since. So far, the money is not in any hurry and is content right where it is.

"Oh, honey," Mom says. "Oh my."

I take a slug from my wine glass, like I'm doing shots rather than having a civilized dinner, and refill again from the bottle.

"But he loves you," she says, bravely, with only a little quaver. "And he knew when he married you that you have this little problem. So he'll forgive you, surely?"

"He almost called the cops right then and there," I tell her, wincing at the memory of the curses and insults he'd shouted at me when he discovered what I'd done. "Says he still will if he ever finds out I've done it again. Or if I don't go to counseling every week. Or if he just happens to feel like it."

We are both silent then, with the shared knowledge that I've never been able to stop before and no counseling in the world is likely to stop me now. Mom makes a helpless little gesture with her hands and lets them flutter down onto the table.

"Well, but . . . maybe if you just gave it back?"

"I can't do that."

"Are you sure?"

"I'm sure."

It takes her longer than usual to gather up the dregs of her optimism, but Mom has been putting a brave face on life since forever, and she's not about to be beaten now.

"Can he really do that? Send you to jail? You're married. What's his is yours and vice versa."

"Not with the prenup I signed. What's his is his, I'm afraid."

She contorts her face into a smile that looks like it hurts. "Where there's smoke, there's fire. If he didn't love you, he wouldn't make all of those threats. It will all turn out fine, you'll see. Your father and I had some big fights, and look how that turned out!"

This is overly optimistic, even for Mom.

She refills her glass and raises it in my direction. "To new beginnings. You've got nowhere to go but up, so up you go!"

It's pointless to argue with her, so we clink glasses, and drink. When her glass is empty, Mom gets ice cream out of the freezer—my favorite, chocolate with a caramel swirl—and we binge-watch *Friends* while we eat the entire quart.

Chapter Four

NICOLE

Wednesday afternoon, after our last house of the day, Roberta drops me off for the mandatory counseling intake Kent set up for me. Rob and I have not discussed what happened to my marriage, but I know Mom has told her and made her swear not to say anything to me. I can tell by the way her lips press together in a thin line of judgment every time she looks at me.

Dr. Travers's office is located on the second floor of a building that also houses medical specialists and upscale massage therapists. There is no receptionist, and only one office door, currently closed. The small waiting room is furnished with three cozy armchairs and an abundance of plants. Soft music plays from an overhead speaker, and the walls are hung with prints depicting serene lakes and forests and mountains. A small fountain splashes in a way I assume is meant to be soothing but just makes me need to pee.

All of this ambiance is meant to put me off my guard, to invite me to relax and be open to sharing confidences with a supposedly trustworthy professional. But I don't want to be comfortable. My preference is for a big, public space with too many clients and not enough therapists, which gives me a much greater chance of slipping through some crack in the system. Here, I am too visible, too exposed.

The door opens, and I get my first look at my new husband-mandated psychologist as he ushers a middle-aged woman, dabbing at tear-wet eyes, out of the inner sanctum. She is little more than a blur in my peripheral vision as I assess the man I consider my opponent.

For some reason, I'd visualized a woman, a benign, mild-mannered person in a skirt and jacket with understated pearls. As it turns out, Dr. Travers is male, dressed in khakis and a casual shirt, and possesses a pair of dangerous x-ray vision eyes.

"You must be Nicole. I'm Dr. Travers, but let's not be that formal. Call me Graham." His voice is professional and warm but has an edge to it—impatience or hunger or maybe just curiosity.

He gestures toward his office. I consider bolting for the exit but have to admit that enduring a one-hour session is probably an improvement over doing hard time in prison. I scan the space, searching for clues as to what sort of therapist Dr. Travers will be. More nature photographs hang on the walls, interspersed with diplomas. There's an antique desk, a little battered rather than perfectly restored. Two softly lit armchairs are set apart from each other at a therapeutic distance. I kick off my shoes and settle into one of them, pulling both feet up to sit lotus style. I have to admit, I like the armchairs. My last counselor's tiny space was furnished with folding chairs, and my butt used to fall asleep during sessions.

Graham—not Dr. Travers, or even Mr. Travers, I remind myself—lowers himself into the other chair and sits looking at me expectantly. I know the move. He wants me to start talking and will use my opener to guide his questions. He's trying to get a read on me. I stare him down with the most insolent expression I can muster.

"I'm trying to figure out which number you are in the great long line of healers who have tried to fix me."

This is actually the truth. There have been so many that I can't come up with a number. Fifty has a nice, round, reasonably accurate feel. The first was when I was six, soon after I'd relocated my first item. Her name was Melody. She, too, was a first-namer, very young, I think now, although she looked old to me then. I loved her flow of long blonde hair, her sweet smile, the games we played together. After Melody, the faces blur together—male, female, every skin tone from palest white through tan and olive and black. Glasses, no glasses. Old, young, bearded, smooth shaven, and everything in between.

Graham doesn't blend in with any of them, and I'm trying to figure out why. He's middle-aged, his dark hair silver at the temples. His face wouldn't stand out in a crowd. All I can think of is that it's something about his eyes. Even though they are penetrating and keen, there's a sadness in them. Cowboy eyes, I decide, the eyes of a man who fled to the range after a personal tragedy and has spent his life sweeping the horizon for signs of danger. I am currently his horizon, and I feel like a mouse who can't find a hole to hide in.

"Do you *need* fixing?" Graham asks. He doesn't try to mirror my posture, doesn't bother to affect a distant and professional persona. He leans forward slightly, those keen eyes looking into and through me. His question doesn't sound rhetorical. He looks like a man who is truly curious about the answer.

"You've read my file. What do you think?"

"Actually, I haven't yet. I prefer to get my first information from you, not from other people's opinions of you."

Well. That's new. And dangerous.

"Pretty sure you're supposed to read it," I tell him, needing a safe buffer of dossiers and paperwork between him and me and the truth. I feel like there's a fist in the soft spot below my ribs. "Also, pretty sure Kent has already filled you in."

He sighs and leans back a little in his chair. "I'll be straight with you. Do you have any idea how many hours it will take me to review all of your records? I don't get paid for what I do when I'm not talking to you. I haven't got the necessary hours to wade through the notes of every head shrink you've ever talked to. Call me lazy."

"So I can talk about whatever I want?"

"Not that lazy," he says, a slight smile tugging at his lips. "How about you start at the beginning."

"'In the beginning God created'? That beginning?"

"How about you tell me about the first time you took something that didn't belong to you."

The fist begins to squeeze. It's hard to breathe.

"How about you go and perform an anatomically impossible sex act?" I don't say it, but I can tell he's read it in my face. Instead of anger, his lips twitch with amusement.

"We could do hypnosis," he suggests. "An age regression. Take you right back and relive the moment with surprisingly little anxiety."

"How about we don't? If you try to mind control me, I'll be out the door so fast it will be like I never came in at all."

"Hypnosis is not mind control, but we will certainly not use it without your consent. Promise."

I have got to shift the trajectory here. Normally I am completely in control of my therapy sessions, revealing only what I want, when I want. I always tell the truth, but I pick and choose which truths I'm going to tell. I'm adept at distractions. This man is as single-minded as Tommy Lee Jones in that movie where he thinks Harrison Ford murdered his wife.

"I moved a book yesterday," I say. "Let's talk about that. Or the money I moved, which is the reason I'm really here."

"How old were you the first time?" Graham persists.

I look at the clock. We have forty minutes left if he follows a fifty-minute schedule, fifty if he's a full-hour kind of guy. There's no reason not to tell him. All he needs to do is open my very first counseling record to read all about it. But I know how counselors work.

They are like interrogators and salespeople. If they can get you to answer one question or buy one product, they've broken the ice. The next one is easier. And before you know it, you're buying the vacuum and all of its attachments, or you're spilling your guts and giving up the secrets of your friends while you're at it.

"Tell you what." He gets up from his chair, and I watch as he opens a cabinet and removes a plain, coil-bound notebook. Black. He also grabs a pen. And then he drops both pen and notebook in my lap.

"Write it down. I'll just sit over here and mind my own business."

"Right. And then you read it. I know that drill. All of my secrets in hard copy form available to incriminate me."

It's like I didn't even say anything.

"I'd like for you to try writing it as if it's a story that happened to somebody else. Something like 'Nicole was twelve the first time—'"

"Six."

"Pardon?"

"I was six."

"Perfect. Write that."

I give him my best laser stare. He returns it. Doesn't even blink. Okay, not a cowboy, then, an alien. People pretty much always blink when I stare them down.

"Suit yourself," he says. "You can talk. Or write. Or we can sit here in silence until our time is up."

"That's cheating," I protest. "I saw that in that Robin Williams movie. *Good Will Hunting.* You can't use a movie therapist's method."

"Worked, didn't it?"

Pointedly, I get up, cross the office, and peruse the certificates hanging on his wall. He's legit. He's got a PhD from the University of Washington. An official Spokane business license. He's a member of the APA.

"Satisfied?" he asks.

"Just making sure you didn't get your license from, like, TV or the internet or something. How come you don't go by your first name?"

"If you had to choose between Theodore and Graham, which one would you go by?" he asks, apparently unruffled.

"Probably neither." I return to my chair, but I can't sit still. I fidget, twiddle my thumbs, jiggle my thigh up and down.

He stares at me. I stare at him. The fist in my chest squeezes a little tighter. I'm going to have a panic attack if I don't do something, so I finally pick up the pen and write the first word.

Nicole.

And then I scratch out my given name and replace it with "Nickle," the name my siblings gave me the day I was born. I look at the clock. At Graham. He looks back at me. I doodle a complicated diagram on the page that is really just a tangled mess of lines and shapes and blots. I am not an artist.

The clock has barely moved.

"This is ridiculous," I say.

"You'll look smashing in an orange jumpsuit," Graham counters. "Orange is the new black, right?"

"Aha! So Kent did tell you everything."

"He told me that you've had multiple arrests and done time for theft, yes. And that you'd recently stolen a lot of money."

I bounce the pen up and down on the page a few times, making a scattering of pinpoint marks. I've never been into journaling; I have far too many secrets that I want to hide from myself.

The clock ticks. Graham waits. I give in and start to write.

Nickle was six and it was a bear.

Just an ordinary stuffed bear. Small, brown, and ragged. One ear was torn, like maybe a dog had dragged it around. Nickle didn't even like bears. The real ones were scary and the stuffed ones were stupid and she never played with either stuffed animals or dolls.

But when she saw it sitting on the table at the Goodwill store with a bunch of other toys, she knew immediately that it didn't belong there. At first, she thought maybe it just needed to be somewhere else in the store. She picked it up by the ragged ear and carried it, casually, by her side, hoping nobody would notice. Only babies played with stuffed animals.

But the bear wanted to move and it made her feel sick to see him stuck. So she carried him all around the store. She tried setting him in other places. With the dishes and cooking things. On a chair in the furniture section. Even laid out flat in the middle of all of the tools.

The bear objected to every one of these places and insisted on leaving the store.

Nickle knew that her mother would object just as strongly to the bear leaving the store as the bear did to being in it, so she tucked him up under her T-shirt and folded her arms over him as if her belly hurt.

Her mother was distracted and didn't notice until they were home and getting out of the car. "Here, Nicole, carry this bag for me, will you, please?"

Nickle stared up at her, arms still pressed against her middle so the bear wouldn't tumble out.

"Does your tummy hurt?"

Nickle shook her head.

"Let me see." Nickle, burning with shame and rebellion, pulled the bear out from under her shirt.

"Did you take this from the store?"

"Yes."

"You stole something from the Goodwill store?"

32

Nickle had been to Sunday school. She was well versed in the Ten Commandments and knew what stealing meant, and it wasn't this. "I didn't steal it."

"You took something for yourself that doesn't belong to you. That is stealing. It's against the law and it makes Jesus unhappy."

Nickle started to cry. People who stole things went to jail and to hell. She was afraid of jail. She didn't want to make Jesus unhappy. She certainly didn't want God to punish her or throw her into hell for stealing.

"It's not stealing," she insisted through her tears. "I didn't take it for me."

"Nicole Angelica Marie Wood. Don't even think about lying to me."

"I'm not." The words were as bitter as her tears. "The bear wanted to go. It didn't want to be there."

"Oh, for God's sake, Nicole. I suppose the bear wanted to live with you?"

"No." She shook her head again, sobbing, with no words to explain the problem. "He doesn't want to be here, either."

"I can't believe I'm having this conversation," her mother said. "Where does the bear want to be?"

"I'm waiting for him to tell me."

Nickle got a spanking, right there in the driveway for all the world to see. Her mother loaded her and the bear right back in the car, and they drove to Goodwill, where she was forced to give the bear back, even though—

"Time's up," Graham interrupts. "I'll take the notebook."
"But I'm in the middle of a sentence."
"It will wait. I have another client."

Graham tugs the notebook out of my hand, gentle but insistent. My heartbeat accelerates. What have I written? Have I revealed too much?

"I'll lock it up until next week. Safe and sound. All right?"

"I guess it will have to be."

But it's not all right. I feel raw and vulnerable. I'm not ready to go back to Mom's. I can't face making small talk about my day or fielding questions about Kent with my defenses down like this. So I wander around downtown, my feet growing numb in my worn sneakers, trying to walk off my anxiety. It's not working, and the clandestine money in my backpack suddenly wakes up and starts demanding attention. Other items are talking to me, as well, as if my therapy session has opened me wider to the energy of inanimate objects instead of helping me change my ways.

I don't dare walk into any shops to get a hot drink or warm my feet and hands, because I'm certain I'm going to find things that want to be moved. A discarded hair tie finds its way into my pocket despite an inner voice telling me in no uncertain terms that clearly I am deranged to think that such a small, unimportant, and dirty object needs any attention from me.

Lost in memories, only half aware of my surroundings, I look up to see that my feet have carried me to the downtown Goodwill. It's not the first time I've ended up here, loitering on the sidewalk, but I never go in. Why I come here, I don't know, but maybe it's the same sort of need that drives a criminal to revisit the scene of a crime. Except that I don't really believe that moving the bear was a crime.

A small but indomitable voice deep inside me insists that my family and Graham and the legal system are all wrong. I'm not a thief, and what I do has nothing to do with trauma. There's a reason for it all. If Mom hadn't made me take the bear back, maybe . . .

No, no, no. I will not think about the bear, or about what happened later that day. But trying not to think about something just makes the unwanted thought bigger and more powerful. It's this store that's doing it. Time to move on. But just as I turn to go, a panhandler steps into my path.

"Sorry, I don't have any change," I tell him before he even asks. I'm not scared of him; I did time on the streets, and his greasy hair and tangled beard don't bother me. Even the way he's muttering to himself and rolling his eyes, clearly either high or crazy, doesn't freak me out. But that doesn't mean I want him to get up close and personal with me, mostly because of the wad of bills stashed in my backpack.

His nostrils flare, as if he can smell Kent's money on me, the way I can smell the streets on him. "Come on now," he wheedles. "No money on you at all?" His lips are chapped, his mouth full of broken brown teeth.

The honest answer to this question can only lead to trouble. If it were up to me, I'd be happy to give him the money. Twenty thousand bucks would be a life changer for a man like this. It would buy him food, some warmer clothes, a place to sleep. But the Object Relocation Program doesn't work like that. I don't get to decide what I pick up or where it goes, and Kent's money has absolutely no inclination to be transferred to this man's pockets.

"Hey!" A shout breaks the panhandler's fixation on me, and both of us turn to watch the man striding up the sidewalk toward us. He looks like one of those TV wrestlers—tall and seriously built, with a crooked nose and hard-angled face. He slows his pace as he approaches, holding out something in his hand. "Here. Take this and go get yourself something to eat."

The street guy stares at the offered McDonald's gift certificate with disdain. "Money's better," he mutters.

"Take what you can get," my rescuer suggests, his voice softer than either his face or his words. "The lady's not giving you any money, and neither am I."

"Fuck you." The street guy bares his teeth in a snarl but takes the slip of paper anyway, and goes off, muttering.

According to social convention, this is where I should say thank you to the stranger for intervening, but I'm irritated that he assumed I was in danger and needed help. So I look up—way up, the guy is seriously tall—and say, "Thanks, but I had it all under control."

Instead of taking offense at my ingratitude and outright rudeness, his face warms into an amused smile. His eyes are dramatic, the color and intensity of a hawk's, and a jolt of recognition goes through me, as if he's a lost object I've been searching for and finally found in an unexpected place.

"Since I seem to be in the business of offering unneeded assistance, let me get the door for you." His voice doesn't match his face or his eyes. There's a hint of Southern in it, and it makes me think of warm nights and fireflies and skies full of stars.

"Are you going in?" he asks. "We seem to have created a wind tunnel."

I realize with a flush of embarrassment that I've been staring for way too long. Snow swirls around my feet and through the door he's holding open. A woman inside glares at us, pulling her coat more closely around her body. Warmth and something more reach out to me, draw me into a place I've revisited a thousand times in my mind. It smells the same, I think, as I step inside, like old clothes and musty carpet. But it feels different.

There's an imbalance in the energy, something missing. Something wanted. And I understand that Kent's money wants to be somewhere in this store. I don't know where yet, but I know the game. I'll wander the aisles, searching for the spot that feels just right while pretending that I'm shopping.

I've been worrying about the money for days, and can't wait to be rid of it. What if Mom goes through my things and finds my stash? What if Kent changes his mind and gets a search warrant and sends the cops in to search Mom's house? Worse even than the arrest that would inevitably follow is the crushing anxiety that hits me when I can't complete a relocation. The last time it happened, I experienced weeks of panic attacks and nightmares filled with disasters and catastrophes.

So I can't wait to get on with my mission, but my would-be Good Samaritan has followed me into the store. His body language and the way he scans everything and everybody as he enters makes me think he's a cop. Undercover, given the long black hair tied back in a tail and the gold loops in his earlobes. I wonder who he's following, and then wonder whether it might be me.

Paranoia, I tell myself. Kent already knows I have the money. An undercover cop would be a waste of resources. Still, this guy is sharp and seems to see everything. If he happens to notice me leaving twenty thousand dollars lying around in the store somewhere, he's going to have questions that I'm not going to want to answer. Questions like: "Is that your money?" And: "Where did you get it?" Which, since I struggle with even the smallest of white lies, would not go well for me.

Fine. I like a good challenge, and I've had years of practice at both picking up and returning items. No problem. I've got this.

Chapter Five

HAWK

My cover is blown. Now that I've acted like I planned to go into the store all along, I follow Nicole in, cursing myself for being an idiot. I'm not exactly inconspicuous at the best of times, and now that she has had a good look at me, it's going to be almost impossible to keep her under surveillance without her knowing something is up. Me and my hero complex, rushing in to save a woman who didn't need saving and blowing apart an entire operation.

Worse, now that I've met her face to face, my objectivity is compromised. I have never met somebody so absolutely and vividly *alive*. And when she looked up at me out of the most luminous gray eyes I have ever seen and informed me that she did not need rescuing, thank you very much, my insides melted like butter on a pancake.

I feel disoriented and dazed, as if I've walked through a portal into an alternate reality where nothing is as it seems. I tell myself that her rap sheet is solid evidence that she's a petty thief. I remind myself that sociopaths make the best criminals and are often charismatic and engaging. Emotions have absolutely nothing to do with my work, and I have a job to do. This is exactly the sort of place for a little shoplifting of the type she seems drawn to. Now that she's seen me, I just need to put on a Broadway-worthy acting performance—man shopping at Goodwill.

Nicole heads directly for housewares and stands there inspecting china as if she's about to buy an entire set and carry it home on foot. I hang out one aisle over, hefting cast-iron frying pans, hoping it looks like I'm inspecting them for some manly purpose, like hunting or camping. I've just exhausted the selection and am moving on to roasting pans when she walks out of the aisle and over to women's clothing.

I shift to where I can keep my eyes on her, pretending to browse a selection of horrifyingly ugly cookie jars. A deformed squirrel with an acorn for a lid. A rosy-cheeked Mrs. Claus whose entire head lifts off, as if she's been decapitated. Nicole shuffles hangers in the coat department while I pretend to be fascinated by a pumpkin-shaped jar with a paint job that makes it look scabrous and diseased. My spidey senses go on full alert when she shrugs out of her day pack and drops it at her feet, then peels off her coat as well. She might just be trying on a jacket, but my gut tells me that either she's about to steal something or she's found a place to move Kent's money and I'm about to earn my bonus.

I watch her scope out the store, her gaze pausing on one person after another. Me, checking out cookie jars. The cashier, focused on a customer. The elderly woman puzzling over the comparative merits of two nearly identical casserole dishes. The frazzled young mother obviously overwhelmed by the crying baby and rambunctious toddler riding in her shopping cart.

Apparently satisfied that the coast is clear, Nicole removes a jacket from a hanger and pulls it on. It's a puffy down number, black, way too small. It pulls so tight across her shoulders that her arms stick out, zombie-like, an inch of tattooed wrist emerging from the cuffs. With obvious effort, she zips it up, then twists from one side to the other as if testing the clearly inappropriate fit.

The mother, making soothing noises to the baby and throwing out ineffective bribes at the toddler, rolls her cart up into the coat aisle.

When she reaches out to shift the hangers, the toddler makes a dive over the side of the cart to freedom. The whole cart rocks, in danger of going over, baby and toddler and all. It's too far and happening too fast; there's no way I can get there in time to avert the disaster. But Nicole's hand flashes out just in the nick of time. She steadies the cart while the woman swings around and snags the young troublemaker by his collar.

"Sit down, you little monkey," she scolds. "That's it. No candy bar for you." The threat sounds tired and threadbare, and the kid doesn't even blink.

"Wanna look at toys," he whines, squirming in her grasp.

"In a minute." She smiles wanly at Nicole. "Thanks for the rescue. I should know better than to try to take them shopping."

"No problem. Looks like you've got your hands full."

"No kidding. I need, like, eight arms, and even that wouldn't be enough." She laughs, looking through the selection of coats with one hand while holding on to her rambunctious offspring with the other. "Not much to choose from here, is there?"

Nicole unzips the Michelin Man jacket. "Here, try this one."

The woman eyes the coat appraisingly. "Don't you want it?"

"Way too small for me. Super warm, though. Bet it fits you perfectly."

Nicole angles her body away from me. I can't see her hands, but I can see her arms moving, as if she's adjusting her clothing before she peels off the jacket and holds it out to the other woman.

"I'll keep an eye on monkey boy here while you try it on," she says. I watch her hold the cart steady, making faces at the baby and the toddler. Both of them are intrigued by the stranger and take a break from crying and whining.

"That fits perfectly," Nicole says, radiating delight. "You're going to buy it, right?"

"Maybe." The woman takes off the jacket and stands there, brow puckered, looking at the price tag.

"Cheaper than the medical bills if you catch a cold," Nicole urges.

"Don't even say those words." The woman crosses herself, laughing, but her eyes remain bleak. "I can't." She shakes her head, reaching for the empty hanger.

Nicole intercepts. "Well, if you're not going to buy it, I guess I will after all." The jacket in one arm, she scoops up her backpack with the other and beelines for checkout. The cashier has just finished with another customer and the transaction is swift. Nicole pays cash and stands waiting for change as the mother picks out a candy bar for her son, despite the fact that he doesn't deserve it, and gets in line.

I carry over the pumpkin cookie jar and join the queue, keeping my eyes on Nicole. None of her behavior today fits with either her rap sheet or what Kent has told me about her. She glances in my direction and catches me staring. Her eyebrows go up as she sees the cookie jar, and when she looks at me again, I wonder if I'm imagining the challenge in her eyes.

Purchase complete, she turns back to the woman behind her and drops the bag with the jacket into the cart where the toddler latches on to it. "Stay warm," she says with a blinding smile, and is out the door before anybody has time to react.

The young mom looks shell-shocked. "Wow," she says to the man behind the counter. "I can't accept that."

"You wanna re-donate it?" He looks like a million miles of hard road himself, but his voice is kind. "Look, keep it, and just pay it forward or whatever." He gives her change for the candy bar, which the kid is already smearing all over his face.

"I guess," she says. "God knows I sure could use it."

She picks up the jacket and puts it on. I hold my breath as she shoves her hands into the pockets, waiting for a puzzled look when she encounters a thick stack of hundred-dollar bills. It doesn't happen. Her hands emerge as empty as they went in. She hugs herself, smiling a little, snuggling her chin down into the warmth before rolling the cart outside.

Making an excuse to the cashier, I abandon my pumpkin monstrosity and follow, restraining myself from offering to help her wrangle the kids. I watch her buckle them into the back seat of an ancient car. The tires are bare, the fenders rusting. When she tries to start the engine, it fails to catch, and I can see her lips moving as she coaxes and pleads until it finally grumbles to life on the fourth attempt. There is a knocking sound that does not bode well, and those tires are not safe for any kind of road, especially not packed snow and ice.

Hours later, after I've driven home and eaten dinner, I still can't shake my mood. What if Kent is full of shit and I'm working for the wrong side on this case? As a reality check, I go through Nicole's record again. So many thefts, beginning long before she met her husband. No, Kent isn't trying to frame or gaslight her. She has done these things. One act of kindness doesn't even the score. Maybe it wasn't even an act of kindness.

She could even be working with the woman she gave the jacket to. Much as I'd love to believe in selflessness and goodness, it's far more probable that some kind of scheme went down right under my nose. I've got the license plate number from the beat-up old car. I'll find the owner and where she lives and keep my eyes open. I could use that five thousand bucks.

Chapter Six

NICOLE

Never has TGIF held quite so much meaning. Not only have I made it through the week without getting into trouble, Kent's money has moved on, and couldn't have found a better place to be. Pulling off the transfer right in front of the big man with the all-seeing eyes was a total adrenaline rush. Lucky for me, the jacket had an inside breast pocket. I keep imagining the moment when that woman discovers the money, along with the sticky note I had tucked into the envelope long ago that says, *Yes, this is for you.* Her conscience will be easy, and she won't have to worry about giving it back.

Of course, I still carry the weight of the paperback I lifted from Mrs. Lane's house, but compared to all that cash the transgression is so small it doesn't even move the needle. Mrs. Lane hasn't called to complain and has probably not even noticed. I just have to get through this one last day of cleaning houses, and I'll find a way to celebrate. Treat myself to a movie, or better yet, see if Ash can get a babysitter and take her with me. It's been ages since we've done something fun together.

Is she stupid? the Fates whisper. *How does she never, ever learn?* They settle in for their big moment, eating popcorn and swigging boxed wine while they wait for me to spring the trap.

Our last house of the day is located on South Hill and is the highest-paying job on Roberta's roster.

"Her name is Andrea Lester," Rob tells me as we drive up to a beautifully landscaped home. "Pharmacist and Ice Queen. Do not call her Ms. Lester, she hates that. It's just Andrea. She is ultra-demanding and will notice and complain about any little thing not done to her specifications."

"She lives here alone?"

Rob snorts. "Don't think she could get along with anybody."

I figure the house could easily accommodate a family of five, plus a live-in housekeeper and a couple of dogs, if they were fluffy and stylishly groomed and dressed in little sweaters. This is certainly not the sort of house where a mutt would be welcome.

"This was an amazing score for us," Rob admonishes as we get out of the car. "Andrea pays premium price. Don't blow it."

I consider pointing out that I've never been the one cutting corners, that I scrub where Roberta only rinses, polish where she only swipes, but for once I keep my mouth shut. Which is a good thing, because the minute the door opens, while Rob is occupied with punching in the code for an alarm system, I'm hit with a sensation that can only mean trouble.

It's not the smell of sadness and secrets that overpowers the subtle fragrance wafting from an atomizer near the door; it's something darker that lifts the hair on the nape of my neck. I know, beyond the shadow of any doubt, that if I walk into this house right now, something is going to happen and my sister will not like it at all.

I bounce right back out onto the porch, swallowing down the stirring of compulsion.

"What are you doing?" Rob glares at me. "This is a big house. It pays, but we still don't have all day. There are three bathrooms to clean, plus tons of vacuuming and hardwood floors that need damp mopping.

You'll need to do all that, because there are a couple of special-request items."

"You don't want me inside this house," I protest. "Trust me."

Her face takes on a martyred, patient expression. "It's just like every other house we do, only we get paid more. Use the cleaners under the sinks—she has her own and prefers them. I need you. Don't let me down now."

Don't hurt Rob. Do your job. Stay out of jail.

The mantra isn't working. Really, it's just a bunch of bullshit. *Run away,* I warn myself. *Do not cross the threshold.*

But between Roberta's insistence and whatever it is inside this house that wants my attention, I might as well be a tiny spacecraft at the mercy of a powerful tractor beam. I walk through the door. I take off my shoes and set them on the mat. Rob gives me a tour, and the whole time I'm on high alert, waiting for the object-relocation booby-trap moment that is going to mess up everything.

It doesn't come. The rooms are sleek and modern, all uncluttered, understated elegance. No bookshelves to be seen, no random objects signaling a desire to be moved. I dare to hope that maybe I was wrong. I plug in my earbuds, shove my phone in my pocket, and drown out my lingering uneasiness with the triumphant swells of Beethoven's Fifth Symphony.

Two hours later, as I pack up my cleaning supplies, relief and gratitude flow through me. I'm actually humming to myself when an electric jolt hits me so hard I skid to a halt, overbalancing and nearly falling on my ass right in the middle of the living room.

There might as well be a big red *X* in the middle of the coffee table, along with a sign that reads, *The Book Goes Here.*

I won't do it. Actually, I *can't* do it. The book is in my pack, which is in the car. The car is locked; the keys are in Roberta's pocket. Once I'm out of this house, I will make up reasons never to come back, no matter how miserable and wretched the book makes me.

Wait for it, one of the Fates whispers to her sisters, stuffing her mouth with popcorn. *This is the good part!*

"Hey, Nickle!" Roberta calls from the kitchen. "Can you run out to the car and get an extra can of oven cleaner? Andrea's out."

"I thought we only use her cleaners," I protest.

"She'll never know. Hurry up! I've already got my head and hands in this oven. Come grab the keys."

Roberta's been tracking my progress, I know, and is well aware that I am no longer scrubbing toilets. I have no valid excuse not to go.

I consider telling her the truth. "Rob," I could say. "I'm suffering temptation, and if I go out to the car now, I'm going to sneak in a book that I took from Mrs. Lane's house and leave it in Andrea's living room."

If I do this, Roberta will stop me. She'll also throw a fit, and I'll get a massive lecture about how I really need to grow up and just control myself, for God's sake. Disappointment will ooze through it all. And then she'll have doubts about whether I really should be coming into her houses, and instead of being rewarded for bravery and honesty, I'll be symbolically drawn and quartered, and then fired, and nobody else is ever going to give me a job.

I go into the kitchen and dig the keys out of Rob's pocket and say nothing. I fight with myself all the way out to the car. As I unzip my pack, I tell myself I will not take the book out of it. As I tuck the book into the back of my jeans and yank my sweatshirt down over it, I tell myself that I will not take it into the house. As I hand my sister the can of oven spray, I tell myself I will walk right out the door and put that book back in my bag.

"Thanks, Nickle. You're the best," Roberta says. "You're getting faster every day. Thanks for trying so hard."

My eyes fill with tears.

Don't hurt Rob. Do your job. Stay out of jail.

I walk out of the kitchen, meaning to march straight back to the car. But instead I find myself in the living room. I set the book in the middle of the coffee table, next to the Oriental vase full of flowers and the slick coffee table book, *Wines of the World.*

The house sighs, and eases, an overwhelming emptiness subsiding into a quiet melancholy.

It's only a book, I tell myself as Roberta sets the alarm and we let ourselves out of the front door. *What's the worst that can happen?* But, of course, it's not just a book. It's a tiny piece of fate, relocated by my own hands, and the dominos are about to topple.

Chapter Seven

ANDREA

My career as a pharmacist was born out of a need to understand my own misfiring brain. Studying psychology was out, because I had absolutely no intention of dealing with my own emotions, let alone anybody else's. And I wasn't about to endure medical school so I could get into psychiatry. So I settled on a cut-and-dried profession that I believed would have low contact with patients, leave out uncomfortable emotions, and shed some light on the effects of chemicals on the brain.

Reality, of course, turned out to be very different than what I'd imagined. My contact with patients, for instance, is much higher than I'd anticipated. Some days it seems I'm forever reassuring anxious people worried about drug interactions or side effects, counseling patients about what to expect or watch out for from a new medication, and taking calls from overworked nurses and busy doctors.

Even so, my job is the best part of my life. It keeps my brain occupied solving problems, so it isn't constantly wandering off down rabbit holes of anxiety. It gives me a place to be and a meaningful thing to do. So I'm not exactly pleased when Frank shows up early for his evening shift, especially when he acts as if he's offering me some sort of priceless gift by doing so. I would have welcomed tardiness on his part, or even a call that began with "I'm so terribly sorry," and ended with "I know this is above and beyond any call of duty, but could you possibly cover all of the shifts for the entire weekend?"

Instead, here is Frank, inserting his paunch and his insinuating smile into my personal space. I try to ignore him, reaching for the next prescription to be filled, but he snatches the paper from my hands and holds it above his head, as if this is a game of keep-away.

"Uh, uh, uh," he says, wagging the finger of his free hand in front of my nose. "I've got this. I'm sure you must have plans." He brings the handwritten piece of paper up closer to his face and makes an elaborate show of crossing his eyes in an attempt to read it. "Docs, am I right? Do they teach a class on how to write illegibly?"

Every word that rises to my lips is sharp and repressive. If I speak any of them, I will be forced to apologize later. Yes, I find him annoying, but other than his penchant for bathing in cheap cologne, a tacky comb-over, and a tendency to breathe loudly and talk incessantly, there's no harm in him. He hasn't done anything but try to be nice. So I contort my face into a caricature of a smile and step back from the counter.

"Anything fun planned?" he asks, pulling up the patient profile on the computer.

"Barrel of monkeys, like always," I say, not about to confess that my only plan involves going home, petting Sylvester, indulging in a single cocktail, and spending the rest of the weekend working through an online training for continuing-education credits. Plans require social connections. Social connections mean interpersonal relationships. Interpersonal relationships mean, sooner or later, triggers and panic attacks and the risk of discovery and the need to move yet again.

After all these years and far too many relocations, I know better than to get close to my coworkers. I slipped up at my last job in Seattle, but I won't do it again. Five years in one place and I'd begun to relax, enough that I broke my own rules and joined everybody one evening for drinks. They started asking questions about family that cut way too close to the bone. "Where did you grow up? Do you have any kids?" I lied about all of it but was afraid they'd find me out.

Paranoia crept in. I was always looking over my shoulder and startling at shadows. Every time I heard a siren or saw a cop, my hands would start to shake. My panic attacks intensified in frequency and severity. One day, a mother came to the pharmacy counter carrying a baby, and that's all it took to send me into a full-on meltdown. I claimed a sudden-onset GI upset as an excuse for running to the bathroom and took a couple of days off.

And then, as I always do when this happens, I gave notice, moved, and started over.

I'm tired of moving. I need to be smarter, more vigilant, up the ante on my anti-panic routines. I want to stay here. Spokane is quieter than Seattle, smaller, with less traffic. My new house is wonderful, so much more spacious than the cramped condo I was living in. It's so spacious, in fact, that I'm vaguely horrified, because one middle-aged woman and an elderly cat cannot possibly require three bedrooms, three baths, a study, and an exercise room.

But I can afford it. I've made a good salary for years with only myself and Sylvester to spend it on, and I've been lucky with my investments. And since I never voluntarily go anywhere other than work and the grocery store, it's nice to have rooms to move in and out of for a change of scenery. The views of the river here are stunning, and in the summer I'll have my very own backyard with flowers and grass to tend. Besides, Sylvester has fallen in love with the windowsills. He follows the sun from one window to another, lounging luxuriously, and I figure one of us ought to be happy in this lifetime.

When I step outside the pharmacy, it's already dark and snowing heavily. Snow is the one thing I don't like about Spokane. In Seattle, it was a rare occurrence. Here, it's been almost constant since late November. The parking lot is slippery and I shuffle to my car, slow and careful. Last thing I need is to fall and break or sprain or otherwise damage something, because hospitals are right at the top of my Places to Avoid List. I drive cautiously, keeping a wide space between my bumper and the car in front, breathing slowly to head off the anxiety activation sequence. I can do this. Hands relaxed on the steering wheel instead of gripping. Shoulders down. Exhale longer than inhale.

When I turn into my own street, I breathe a sigh of relief, even as I begin the usual safety scan for pedestrians who don't belong or cars that seem out of place. All is perfectly normal. Lights glow behind the drapes in my neighbors' windows. Christmas lights still light up some of the yards in festive colors.

My hands are steady as I key the double locks on my front door, then disable and reset the alarm. A light, clean fragrance lets me know the cleaning service has come and gone. It's such a luxury to pay somebody else to do the scrubbing and the vacuuming, a gift I've given myself for having to pull up the stakes and move.

Initiating what I think of as the coming-home protocol, I begin a walk through the house to be sure that all is in order. The entryway and kitchen are shining. Sunny Side Up really does do a beautiful job of cleaning. Maybe I'll pop on Yelp and leave a review later this evening.

A tiny whisper of anxiety touches my mind as I realize I haven't seen Sylvester. Usually, he meets me at the door, meowing and shedding all over my legs.

"Sylvester?"

Silence answers. The back of my neck prickles, as if somebody is staring at me from behind. Heart rate rising, I glance over my shoulder, but of course nobody is there. I've locked the door and set the alarm. Blood whooshes in my ears, and I work to control my breathing as I move through the house, turning on lights as I go.

Sylvester is in the living room, laid out over the back of the sofa like a decorative throw. He blinks sleepy green eyes and utters a lazy meow. "There you are. I was worried." I pick him up and cuddle him against my chest, evoking purrs as I rub under his chin and behind his ears.

He's shed all over the white sofa, of course, but that's what my handheld vacuum is for. I sit down with the cat in my lap, taking the weight off feet weary from long hours of standing.

That's when I see it—a dog-eared, broken-backed, battered paperback sitting on the coffee table next to *Wines of the World*. My heart lurches. My mouth goes dry. I don't need to read the title to know that it's a copy of Dante's *Inferno*—the cover is indelibly engraved in my memory.

I close my eyes, but I can still see Tag sitting behind his desk, the book in his hands.

"I'm trying to study," he says, marking his place with one finger. "So I can finish this degree and earn a living for us. It's not like I'm reading for fun."

"I had to drop out of school," I shout. "So maybe you could do that, too, and then you could actually help me."

"Andi. Be reasonable."

"How's this for reasonable? Get your nose out of that goddamn book and take care of the kid for half a minute!" I snatch the book out of his hands, draw back my arm, and hurl it at the wall. It makes a satisfying thud before bouncing off and landing on the floor, pages splayed and bent.

"You are insane!" Tag shouts, running to rescue the damaged volume.

The last word echoes, amplifies, until it's louder than the wailing of the baby. Insane, insane, insane.

Sylvester meows and squirms in my too-tight grip. With a gasp, I move back into the now, murmuring an apology to the cat. He leaps down from my lap and sits on the floor across the room, gazing at me reproachfully. Digging my fingernails into my palms until it hurts, I start counting backward from one hundred. By the time I get to fifty, I'm calm enough to think.

Obviously, the book didn't get here by itself. Since nobody has been in the house except the cleaner, Roberta must have brought it in. I met with her before hiring her company, and we agreed to a premium price in exchange for her promise that she would be the only one to clean my house. So logic says it has to be her, but the idea of that comfortable, practical woman sitting down on my couch to immerse herself in a reading of the *Inferno* doesn't fit.

I know I'm being absolutely ridiculous. This intrusive object on my coffee table is not radioactive or explosive, it's just a harmless copy of a classic that millions of people have read. Maybe Roberta is taking a class. The probability that this is Tag's copy is a million to one. My thoughts are illogical, driven by anxiety and fueled by paranoia.

But my body doesn't buy my logic. My mouth is so dry, I can barely swallow. I know that the only way to deal with my fear is to confront it head-on, but I sit staring at the book for a ridiculous amount of time before I finally pick it up and open it, fully expecting that the inside of the cover will be blank, proof that I have nothing to be afraid of.

Only, it isn't blank. *Property of Tag* is scrawled there in a bold black cursive, once as familiar as my own.

Impossible.

The moment is surreal, as if another woman is sitting here, not me. The house, the book, even the cat, suddenly seem like a bizarre dream sequence. It's been thirty years since my one and only breakdown. I'm not crazy. There has to be a logical explanation.

Carrying the book into my study, I wake up the computer and pull up the security-camera feed. It only records when there is motion at the door, so there's not much to review. I watch myself leave for work in the morning, triple-checking the locks before walking to my car. Two women carrying cleaning supplies go in and out. One is Roberta. The other is taller, thinner, dark haired, her face hidden by a ball cap.

Anger follows hard on the heels of my fear. Roberta has betrayed my trust. I still don't know why either of them would bring in Tag's book. Unless he's found me, somehow, and is using them to deliver a message. If that's the case, then my past has finally caught up with me. The cops could be showing up at any moment.

I have to know. I locate Sunny Side Up in my contacts and hit dial. But it's Friday, it's late, and all I get is a voice mail. Slamming down the phone in frustration, I try to find another method to rein in my thoughts. Over the years, I've learned to examine them carefully, subjecting them to a sort of Snopes fact-checking.

If Tag has found me, surely he'd come here himself, rather than conning Roberta's cleaning company into bringing in that old copy of the *Inferno*. And if he knows where I am and what I've done, then he'd notify the police and they'd come and arrest me. The incident with the book has to be some sort of bizarre happenstance.

But I can't let the idea go. I press the palms of my hands against my eyeballs until I see spots. I count out ten deep breaths and check inside the cover again, hoping to find it blank. Tag's handwriting is still there.

I can feel myself sliding into a place of altered reality, with a creepy-crawly feeling of suspecting everything and everybody, of not being able to trust my own brain. Somehow I have to arrest the descent. I pace the office, counting my steps, twelve paces one way, twelve paces back, forcing myself to look anywhere but at the book.

Little by little, I start to get a grip. I have a protocol for severe anxiety. I have a protocol for everything. I can't throw the book away in case I need it as proof that this moment is real and not part of some fractured-reality delusion, but I also don't want to look at it. Finally I shove it into a desk drawer where it's out of sight.

I keep an emergency sedative on hand, just in case, even though it's been weeks since my last panic attack. My dose is supposed to be one tab of lorazepam, but I take two. I drink a full glass of water, counting each swallow. Count ten deep breaths. Then I change into workout clothes and do five miles on the treadmill, forcing my body to the edge of its limits.

By the time I'm done, I'm reasonably calm and have a plan. On Monday, I'll call Sunny Side Up and ask what happened. Roberta will almost certainly tell me that they picked the book up at some second-hand store, that one of them was reading it when she was supposed to be working, and forgot to take it away with her. I'll fire her for breaking the terms of our agreement. And then I'll throw the thrice-damned book in the trash and be done with this.

Chapter Eight

NICOLE

On Monday morning, I walk into Mrs. Lane's house chock-full of hope and misplaced confidence. Surely if the woman were going to complain, she would have done so by now. Today nothing else will want moving, and I'll do my job and make my sister happy. I want, more than anything, to be worthy of the trust she's placed in me.

But as soon as I step into the kitchen, I know my luck has run out. Rob stands statue still, head bent, hands braced on the counter, the instruction notebook open in front of her. *Here we go*, the Fates whisper as I join her at the counter. *This is where the fun begins.*

The note is written in purple ink, in a cursive script so regular and perfect it could be a computer font, and the tone is informal and friendly.

> *Sunny Side Up—please help if you can. I must be losing my mind! I was in the middle of reading Dante's Inferno. Do not ask me why, though I will say I'm fascinated by the medieval portrayals of hell. Anyway, I'm almost certain it was in the house somewhere, and I cannot for the life of me figure where I might have left it. I even*

checked the freezer—I did put a book in there once while bemused by my thoughts. If you notice it while cleaning, please leave it here on the counter for me. I do hope I'm not coming down with a case of dementia.

I take a step back, bracing myself for Roberta's outrage. She used to slap me, sometimes, when we were kids, and I half expect she'll do that now. But she only turns to look at me, and the contempt distorting her usually pleasant features is worse than a blow.

"What. Did. You. Do?" She bites off each word with a sharp snap of her teeth.

"I love how you assume that I took it. Just like that. Mrs. Lane as much as admitted she's got a short-term memory problem, and you think that—"

"Did you?"

"Did I what?" I take another step backward.

Rob follows. "Did you take the book?"

Again, I ease backward, out of reach of her hands, although I can never go far enough to escape the disdain and betrayal in her eyes. "Easy, Rob. It's just an old—"

"Put it back. Now."

"I'll get her another copy. I'll put it back exactly—"

"Are you insane? She'll know it's not the same book! You'll get the one you stole and put it back. Immediately."

"I can't."

Silence hangs between us as the impact of my words settles in.

Roberta's expression morphs into horror. "You moved it somewhere! Please tell me you didn't put it in another client's house."

I'd like to lie. I'd love to lie. But I won't. I never do. I bite my lip and try to meet Roberta's eyes. "It's not a huge deal, Rob. It's just a beat-up old paperback."

"Which one, Nicole? Which house did you put it in?"

Her phone rings. I take a breath, hoping I've won a reprieve. She'll take the call, calm down, and we can discuss my behavior rationally. She turns her back on me to answer, but I don't need to see her face to see how screwed I am. The words tell me everything.

"Andrea," Roberta says. "What can I— Oh dear. I'm so sorry— If you would let me explain— I can understand how upset you must be. Yes, I know, but I was training my— She must have— No, it wasn't meant to be a prank— Yes, I see."

The storm is about to break and I have no place to hide. I am the betrayer, the meddler, the family black sheep. I've done it again and I know I'll do it forever. What is wrong with me that the needs of random, insensate objects like books outweigh the needs and rights of the people I love?

Roberta lowers the phone to her side. Her voice is quiet now, cold as the heart of winter. "How could you?"

"I'm sorry."

"You're always sorry. And now you've lost me Andrea's house."

"It was just a book," I plead. "Who gets mad about a book?"

"You know what? I'm done." Roberta points toward the door. "Get out."

"Let me help you clean the house first. I'll—"

"Get out!" she shouts. "I should have known better. You have no consideration for anybody but yourself. You'll ruin my business! What else have you taken?"

"Nothing. It was just one stupid old book! I swear! Please, let me help finish this house."

"No. You are done. I want you out of here this instant!"

"But you're my ride," I plead. "It's like twenty minutes to a bus stop." I'm hoping that once she calms down, I can apologize. Appease her, find a way to make it up.

Roberta isn't having it. "Get a cab. Walk all the way home for all I care. I don't want you in my car. I don't want to see your face anywhere near me. This is literally freaking the end."

Rob never swears. "Freaking" is a word at the furthest extent of her vocabulary. I put my shoes and coat on in silence. She watches me, as intent as a guard, as if I'm going to snatch up something from the entryway—the shoe rack, say, or the mirror—and try to run off with it.

"I need my day pack."

"Oh, for the love of Pete." She stuffs her feet into her boots and accompanies me out to the car, observing me grab my pack from the back seat, locking the car door behind me.

"Rob, please, I—"

She holds up a hand. "Don't talk to me." Then she turns and tries to march into the house, only the driveway is slippery and she looks more like she's doing a tap dance slide and shuffle than a military march. I know this will only make her madder. I turn away so when she checks over her shoulder she won't know that I witnessed the failure of her grand display of anger.

~

My emotions are all over the place, a cocktail of shame and fear and an anger I have no right to feel. Roberta will never forgive me for this. And she'll tell Mom, who will be disappointed, which is worse than angry. And she'll tell Warner and Brina, and my whole family will have gossip sessions about how Nickle has fucked up again. One of them will surely tell Kent, who informed me clearly that if I move so much as a toothpick, he'll be morally and ethically required to take legal action to prevent me from harming others.

I don't want to face any of them. I also have nowhere else to go. It's cold and I can't just stand around on the street, so I trudge to the nearest bus stop and ride the route, no particular destination in mind, wallowing in my disgrace. Eventually I stop feeling sorry for myself long enough to make a plan. If by some lucky chance Kent doesn't press charges, I'm going to need a job, and if I'm going to need a job, I'd better start looking.

The search goes about as well as I expect it will, which means not well at all. My job prospects are never good. I'm unskilled. I have a record. At Kent's insistence, I did get my GED after we got married, but my whole work and education history screams loser. I don't even have a current food handler's card, which rules out fast-food outlets until I take the class, and I end up applying to be a dishwasher at a Mexican restaurant, a night stocker at Costco and Walmart, a janitor.

By the end of the day, I'm exhausted and demoralized. The last thing in the world I want to do is go back to Mom's, but all of my earthly belongings, meaning the few possessions I took with me from Kent's that truly belong to me and weren't bought with his money, are there. Besides, where else would I go?

I remember a Robert Frost poem that said something like "home is where, when you go there, they have to take you in." My mother will welcome me back, over and over and over again, but I'm sick to death of this pattern and hate myself for doing this to her. It's late when I get off at the bus stop. I'm hungry and tired and wretched, and I still have five blocks to walk on an icy sidewalk, directly into a freezing wind.

Shivering with cold and misery, I pick up my pace when I see the lights of home, imagining the dinner and hot bath that wait on the other side of my mother's disappointment. But I stop dead in my tracks when I reach the driveway. Shit. Way too many cars. Rob's Subaru. Warner's minivan. Brina's Prius. And, the frosting on a total shit cake, Kent's shiny new BMW.

My heart jolts painfully, as if I've been run through with an electric current. Christmas is long over and it's not anybody's birthday. Something awful must have happened. Maybe Roberta told Mom what

I've done and she had a heart attack or a stroke or something. Only, in that case, they'd all be at the hospital. Unless she died. There's no other reason they'd all be here like this.

I start to run, or try to, but my feet keep losing traction on slippery patches and slowing me down. I make it up the driveway. Climb the two steps onto the porch. I wrench the door open, the words "Oh my God, what happened?" on my tongue, but I never speak them. My eyes and brain put the pieces together, and I know the truth.

I'm what happened.

Roberta, stiff with outrage, sits in Mom's armchair. Warner has taken the center of the couch, with his wife, Betts, on one side and Mom on the other. Mom looks small and old, her face red and swollen from crying, and she can't find a smile for me, although she still makes a valiant effort that comes across more like a grimace of pain. Brina sprawls on the floor, looking annoyed and sulky. Kent, dressed in his usual power suit and tie, occupies my father's recliner.

All of them are as one. A united front, ganging up on me, the outcast weird girl who doesn't belong. Rebellion, my old friend, heats in my belly.

"What's up? Are we having a party?"

An old childhood game and song come into my head. "The Farmer in the Dell." And I flash back to kindergarten and the first time I played, and how it felt to stand alone in the middle while the other kids circled around me, holding hands, singing, "The cheese stands alone."

I am the cheese. Not the big cheese, but the stinky cheese.

This thought strikes me as weirdly ridiculous, and I snort an ill-timed laugh.

"You think this is funny?" Kent demands.

"I'm not sure exactly what *this* is," I retort, which is as close to a lie as I can get. Because I'm pretty sure this is a family tribunal and I've already been tried, judged, and convicted.

"Oh, for God's sake!" Roberta leans forward to get up. "I knew better than to show up for this. I can't be in the same room with her."

"Please, Roberta." Mom's voice breaks and she covers her mouth with both hands. Warner puts an arm around her shoulders and glares at me. Roberta stays in her chair, but she's perched on the edge, ready to bolt. Brina rolls her eyes and starts playing with her phone, looking more like a teenager than her thirty-two-year-old self.

"Do I sit?" I ask into the cavernous silence. "Or are there handcuffs, or maybe a pillory?"

"Cut the drama," Brina says. "I, for one, don't give a rat's ass whether you sit or stand on your head."

Turning my back, I take off my shoes. Hang my coat in the closet. Buy myself a moment to pull myself together. Despite Brina's words, there is an empty chair that they obviously expect me to sit on. Wooden and hard, dragged down from the attic, maybe, because I can't place where it belongs in the house. It is set directly facing the rest of them.

"You all have been watching too much reality TV. I'll be in my room. Let me know when the movie and the popcorn are ready."

But as I stalk past Kent, he snags my wrist in an iron grip. "I'd suggest you sit."

My gaze snaps to his. There's no softness in his face. No give. I can see in his eyes that he knows he's hurting me; he squeezes a little harder. I bend my knees and twist, hard, breaking his grip at the place where thumb and fingers meet. But his words and his threat are stronger bonds.

"I'm going to counseling," I tell him. "Like you said."

"That was only half of the agreement. Sit down."

My pride, the only thing I have left, struggles against the direct command, but I really have no option. *I will not let them break me,* I promise myself, tilting my chin up and pretending I'm not shattering into a gazillion little pieces inside as I bend my knees and sit in the designated chair. Defiance. That's what they will see, what they have always seen. If I tell them what I really feel, that I'm as squashed and hopeless as gum under their collective shoes, then they will pity me, which is even worse. So I won't cry. I won't tell them how I feel. I'll listen to what they need to tell me and then . . . and then . . .

I can't come up with an "and then." I'm as sick of my shit as they are, but I can't see an end to it.

Mom speaks first, her voice the most dangerous to my composure. "Honey, we just want to help you. You can't go on this way."

"And you need to understand the impact of your behavior on everybody around you," Kent adds in a sanctimonious tone. As if I don't know already know how much my actions hurt my family, as if I'm so self-centered and oblivious that I don't even care.

"Wow. Did you prepare the sackcloth and ashes?" I ask him with all of the sarcasm I can muster. "Maybe a whip? You could all take turns—"

"I told you this was pointless," Roberta cuts in. "She's lost me my best customer—could cost me my entire business if word of this gets out. One review on Yelp even hinting that one of my workers stole something, and I'm finished. Does Nicole care about that? Of course not. Can't believe I was stupid enough to trust her again."

I want to wrap both arms around my head to cover my ears, close my eyes tight shut, and scream.

"Easy," Warner says. I've always been closer to him than either of my sisters. He's more like Mom than the rest of us, kind and easygoing. "The purpose of this meeting is to tell Nickle how we feel so we can help her. Let's avoid direct attacks."

"Ignored," Brina says. "Inconsequential. That's how I feel. You get all of the attention. You always did. And here we are again! Me? I never got in any trouble. Got good grades, went to college, got a fantastic job. Does anybody notice? No. It's always about you. Maybe I should start lifting eye shadow from Walmart and somebody in this family would know I'm alive."

Her expression, her tone, are pure venom.

Tears well up, despite all of my years of practice at holding them back. "I've never moved anything from Walmart," I mutter in self-defense. I can barely hear myself, but Brina's got ears like a cat.

"Why can't you ever just admit that you steal shit? It's not 'moving' or 'relocating' or whatever you want to call it." She makes air quotes around the words. "Call it what it is. Stealing. Theft. My God, you're pitiful."

Mom has tears rolling down her face. "Girls!" she pleads. "Stop this."

"That right there is the problem, Mom." Warner pats her shoulder as he says it, softening his pronouncement. "You've always been protective of Nicole. We all have. Because of what happened. But that's not working. She needs to face consequences. Grow up."

Warner's words hurt more than anybody else's, and I lash out at him in an attempt to hold back a flood of humiliating tears. "You're overprotective of me, so you ambush me? Since we're all talking about feelings, I gotta say, I'm not feeling very loved right about now."

"It's not an ambush, Nicole. An intervention is designed to—"

"Spare me."

"Nickle. You know we all love you."

Brina and Rob make simultaneous snorting noises. Kent leans forward in his chair, his eyes hot and hungry.

Warner presses on. "We wouldn't be so angry if we didn't love you. But this behavior is an addiction. Like heroin or cocaine. And it's tearing us all apart. We did overprotect you after what happened. We didn't any of us know what to do about that. How do you treat a little kid who has just seen—"

"Don't." I put my hands over my ears and hum, like I am six again, giving credence to the family consensus that I have failed to grow up.

Warner plows ahead. "Seen a man blow his brains out—"

Blood. Bone. Wads of hair on the table, on the wall . . .

"Stop it! Just stop! You win, you all win. I'm sorry, I'm sorry, I'm sorry."

I'm weeping as if I am truly six, as if I haven't learned control over my emotions and how to keep all of this mess quiet and at bay. My body is shaking, teeth chattering, sobs pouring out of me. I have no control. I am powerless.

"See?" Brina says. "Here we are again. Center of attention."

"Oh shit," Warner says. "What a disaster."

"Nicole. I'm sorry. This was a bad idea." Mom is beside me, her arms around me, but I can't feel them. She might as well be a ghost for all of the comfort she can give me.

"Nicole is great at deflecting responsibility with histrionics. Don't let her fool you." Kent's voice is as cold as ice.

I can't stay here, weeping, while my mother tries to fix things. Gently, I pull out of her arms and stumble out of the room, tear blind, moving mostly by memory. Behind the locked door of my childhood bedroom, I throw myself face-first on the bed and give way to grief and shame and hopelessness. How many times have I soaked this very same comforter with my tears?

My marriage to Kent was supposed to be my way out, but I've blown that wide open. The truth is, my family is right. I am the one who needs to change. And I do need to grow up. Which means getting a job and standing on my own two feet and actually working on my shit in counseling and figuring out how to stop moving things.

Another thought zings into me like an arrow from on high. As long as I stay here, nothing is going to change. It's time to do something radical and drastic. And the only thing I can think of is to run away from home, which isn't a grown-up thing to do at all.

Still. I can't stay here. I drag my backpack out of the closet. Not the day pack I carry in place of a purse but the full-size hiker's pack that I bought before I ran away the first time, when I was sixteen and already tired of trying to conform to a world that had no place for me. I stuff it full of clothes, clean and dirty, along with my other few belongings, and then send a text to Ash, the one person in the world who might still take me in.

Chapter Nine

NICOLE

Nicole: You home?

   Ash: Yes

Nicole: Coming over

   Ash: ...

   Ash: To what do I owe this honor?

I don't blame her for the snark; I've earned it. In the six months she's lived in her current apartment, I have never once been over to visit, even though she is my 'til-death-do-us-part soul sister and possibly the only person on the planet who accepts me as I am.

The two of us arrived for our first go-round in juvenile detention on the same day and instantly teamed up, even though on the surface we couldn't have been more different. She was a ragged, feisty waif of a girl, fresh off the street after running away from her third group-home placement in as many months. Thin and bedraggled and tiny—Ash is five foot one and buys most of her clothes off the kids' rack—she had an uncanny ability to read people's deepest insecurities. On that first day, I saw her reduce a swaggering long-timer mean girl to tears with a few well-chosen words.

I was soft as butter, white, middle-class, and well loved, despite my many transgressions. Ash is a blend of Chinese and some brand of white. Her mother died when she was ten. Nobody knew who her father was. She'd been in and out of foster homes and group homes, and our childhoods couldn't have been more different. But something clicked, and our bond kept us tight right up until five years ago when Kent first came between us.

While my family had fallen instantly and completely under his spell, Ash hated him before she laid eyes on him. I texted her the morning after I first slept with him, raving about how hot and gorgeous and sexy and wonderful he was. And she texted back: You went home with your lawyer? Seriously? WTAF Nickle?

Which kind of put a damper on things. I was pissed at her for throwing cold water on my newborn infatuation, even more so because somewhere deep down inside, I knew she had a point. Besotted as I was, I still knew attorneys were supposed to have a code of ethics that frowned on them having sex with their clients. I told myself that his willingness to bend the rules in order to be with me was another reason to love him.

Kent and I spent so much time together at first that I barely missed Ash. We went out every evening. There were romantic dinners at expensive restaurants. Movies. Leisurely walks by the river. He bought me extravagant gifts and took me shopping for clothes at stores I wouldn't have dreamed of entering on my own. During the three months before he asked me to marry him—down on one knee, with a diamond ring in his hand—I wasn't tempted to move an object even once.

After the engagement, though, Kent got busy with a big case, working late most evenings and leaving me to my own devices, so I tried to patch things up with Ash. I figured now that the relationship was official, she would realize there was no use protesting and come around. When I called, she answered on the first ring and said, before I could get a word in, "I'm sorry. Okay? I miss you. If hanging out with you means hanging out with some lame-ass attorney, I can do that. I promise to be nice."

"Good," I said. "Because we're getting married!"

A long silence followed. "Already?" she finally asked. "Before I've even met him?"

"It's been a whirlwind; everything happened so fast. I didn't know he was going to propose! I could hardly tell him I couldn't answer until I checked with my friend."

Ash sniffed. "Sounds like a total asswipe to me."

"You're just jealous."

"You'd better believe I'm jealous. I've been supplanted!"

"What do you expect? *You* aren't buying me diamonds."

"Just fix it, Nickle. I guess I need to meet him."

Later, when I told Kent that I needed him to meet my best friend, he'd teased, "Am I not enough for you?" Then he kissed me until I forgot all about Ash and everything and everybody else. An hour later, snuggled up to him in bed, I brought the topic up again.

"Seriously, Kent. Ash is important to me. We've been through a lot together. Maybe we could just meet for coffee? Or lunch, even, if you've got time."

"No," he said, running a hand up my arm, onto my shoulder, then down to stroke my breast. "If she's that important to you, we'll take her out for a nice dinner."

His hand made it hard to focus, and I shoved it away, laughing and sitting up to evade his caresses. "Nice dinners aren't exactly Ash's and my thing. She might be more comfortable—"

"But nice dinners are *our* thing," he'd said, drawing me back down beside him and trailing his fingers down the center of my belly. "Trust me. There is not a woman on the planet who doesn't want to be wined and dined."

I had my doubts, but I didn't want to argue, so I let him make love to me again, and then I let him make a reservation at Anthony's right by the window where we could look out on the river and the falls. When the night of the dinner arrived, he dressed in a sports coat and jeans that made him look like a movie star attempting to go casual. He picked out a soft silk blouse for me, with long sleeves that covered my tattoos, along with a pencil skirt and a pair of black shoes with alarmingly high heels for a woman accustomed to wearing nothing but sneakers. He also insisted that I wear my diamonds. All of them—dangling from my ears, around my throat, flashing fire on my finger.

The heels and the tight skirt rendered me incapable of walking in a straight line on my own, forcing me to cling to Kent's arm for balance. I felt stiff and unnatural and nervous about the impending collision of my two worlds, an uneasiness that turned out to be 100 percent justified.

Ash showed up looking exactly like Ash—tiny and gorgeous in jeans and a tank top that highlighted her tattoos, her long black hair pulled back in a ponytail. We stood there staring at each other like strangers. She gave me a stiff, distant hug. When I introduced Kent and he moved in to hug her, she pointedly stepped back and held out her hand instead.

Once we were seated at the table, Kent made a display of ordering appetizers without input from either of us, as well as the most expensive champagne on the list. Then we sat looking at each other across the table. I've never been adept at small talk, and Kent, for some reason, said nothing, just sat there looking vaguely amused, although clearly nothing was funny.

Ash cocked her head to one side and pursed her lips. "You look beautiful," she said to me. And then to Kent: "Did you dress her yourself, Ken? You forgot the tiara."

"It's Kent," he'd corrected.

"Oh, of course, my apologies." And she'd smiled at him, sweetly, with a glance at me that said clearly that her comment was not a slip but a deliberate Ken and Barbie reference. I'd listened to enough Barbie-doll rants from her to understand exactly what she meant.

It was all downhill from there. After Ash went home, before dessert and without any proper goodbye, Kent took my hand and patted it comfortingly. "You've outgrown her," he said. "Don't be sad. You've moved on."

Ash called the next day to tell me straight up that Kent was pretentious and condescending and that he was trying to change me. And I said maybe I wanted to change, and then she said that because she loved me, she'd keep her mouth shut. She came to my wedding but refused to be my maid of honor, which was just as well because Kent didn't want her to be. And then a couple of years ago, she hooked up with a total loser who bailed right after she discovered she was pregnant, and between Kent and that disaster, we've seen precious little of each other.

For the last few months, Ash has been immersed in diapers and feedings and working two minimum-wage jobs to pay the bills. I've offered to help out with the finances, not that I've ever had much money of my own. Kent bought me everything I asked for, and more—but I had to ask. I've never had access to the bank accounts. Ash said she didn't need charity money, which hurt my feelings and pissed me off.

All in all, I have never been to Ash's current apartment, and the closer I get, the more uneasy I become. At every bus stop, as one batch of people gets off and a new batch gets on, faces look wearier and harder around the edges. I hunch into myself and go small, the way I learned to do first in juvie and then in jail.

A clump of teenage boys watches as I get off the bus alone. One of them whistles, and the others jostle and laugh, passing around a joint and inhaling deeply. I keep my footsteps even and brisk, my eyes fixed on my destination, looking as much as possible as if I know exactly where I'm going. A homeless dude hits me up for change, and I want to give him some, but it would be stupid to pull out money and I make myself ignore him.

By the time I reach the apartment building, my heart is thudding in my ears and my skin is crawling with the effort to grow extra eyes and defensive mechanisms. I buzz for entry, relieved to hear Ash's familiar voice through the building intercom. "That you, Nickle?"

"Hurry it up, would you? Things are kinda sketch out here." The boys from the bus stop have followed me, or maybe they were headed this direction in the first place. Fear is messing up my perception, and even the old woman pushing a grocery cart on the other side of the street appears dangerous.

The door buzzes and clicks, and I duck inside, making sure it's firmly locked behind me. The lobby is old and smells like mildew, but it's clean and decently repaired. A row of locked mailboxes lines one wall. The carpet is old and threadbare but vacuumed and mended. I walk down the hallway and find Ash waiting for me, standing in her open door.

I pause, unsure about my reception, but she wraps her arms around me in a sharp-angled, bony hug that is both loving and fierce, and pulls me into the apartment, kicking the door shut behind us.

When she releases me, she takes a minute to lock and bolt the door, then looks me over deliberately, head to toe. "You look great."

"I look like shit. You, on the other hand—"

"Look like shit." This is an exaggeration because Ash is beautiful all the time, but she does look a little bedraggled. Her golden-brown eyes are red and swollen, her silky black hair swept up in a messy bun.

"You look like you again, anyway," she says. We laugh and hug again, and then Ash bends her elbow and swivels her hand palm out so I can see the little blue star tattooed on the inner side of her wrist. I repeat the move, revealing my own little blue star. We press our identical tattoos together and recite, "May the stars align," as if we're still sixteen instead of approaching thirty and dealing with serious adult problems.

"What's going on?" we ask at exactly the same moment.

"You first," I say.

"How long do you have?" She gives me a wan smile, but then her eyes land on my fully loaded backpack and a furrow appears in her forehead. Looking around the apartment, I see her concern. It's tiny and already cramped with her and the baby.

"I just need to crash for a night," I hasten to reassure her, a sinking feeling in my belly. Ash was my only plan, and I don't know what else I'm going to do. "Had to get out of the house. Please tell me nothing is wrong with the baby?"

Ash isn't given to tears, so I know whatever is bothering her is no small thing.

"Arya? She's perfect, only . . ." Ash makes a strangled sound and presses her hand over her mouth. Tears spill down her cheeks. She dashes them away. Takes a breath. "All right, you asked for it. I'd offer you a drink, but booze isn't in the budget." She walks the few steps from the door to a well-worn sofa and sinks into it, drawing her knees up toward her chest and wrapping her arms around them. This is her emotional-defense pose, the way she sits when she's sad and scared.

I shrug out of my backpack and lean it up by the door, then plop down cross-legged on the floor, facing her. "Spill."

"I'm in trouble, Nickle. I work nights, and I'm due at work in, like, two hours, and my babysitter just quit this evening. I already missed a shift last week because Arya was sick, and they said if I skipped again, I'm fired."

"Hey, you'll find another job," I say easily, because it's true. Ash has always had a job, even when we were teenagers and in trouble most of the time.

She wipes her eyes and shakes her head. "I don't have time for that. Not enough money for rent and utilities and all as it is."

"I don't suppose Bozo is helping much."

"He said he's not paying child support unless I let him see Arya, and I said fuck that. She doesn't need him in her life. It's not like he actually wants to see her; he just wants to be a pain in my ass."

"Doesn't he kind of have to pay up?"

"He's mostly unemployed. So any money I get from him isn't going to be worth the risk of him insisting on visitation."

She gives way to full-body weeping that feels like it's tearing my own heart loose from my chest. I put my hand on her shoulder and let her cry, surveying the cramped apartment. The living area and kitchen are all one small space, clean but packed full of a playpen and other baby paraphernalia like diapers and blankets. There are two closed doors, one probably a bedroom and one a bath.

My phone buzzes with an incoming call from Mom, which I ignore. And then a text. I tell myself I'm not going to answer. I left her a note. It's not like I just vanished. But guilt surges, as it always does, and I end up tapping in, one-handed: Safe at Ash's. Staying here tonight.

You'll be home tomorrow, right? she sends back, and I answer, I'm not sure. Call you in the morning.

Ash's weeping subsides into sniffles, and I hand her the box of tissues sharing space on a cluttered end table with a teething ring and an empty bottle. She blows her nose. Most of her face still buried in her knees, she peers up at me with those big, sad eyes and then hides them again. "Sorry." Her voice is muffled. "I didn't mean to go on like that. Obviously things are not so awesome with you, either." Her gaze cuts to my backpack again.

"I ran away from home."

She looks confused. "But you already left Kent's."

"Right. And now I'm leaving Mom's."

"What happened?"

"I moved something from one of the houses I was cleaning with Roberta."

"Oh, Nickle. You didn't." Ash's expression is all horrified fascination, like she's driving by a car wreck on the freeway and hoping for survivors. "What was it this time? Not something like with Kent?"

Ash was the first person I called after Kent threw me out, even before I called my mother and told her I was coming home. I needed her to tell me that Kent was a jerk anyway, that everything would be okay. She did that, and more, and we've been in contact more over the last two weeks than in the last year.

"Just a stupid old book. But tonight my whole family and Kent staged an intervention to show me the callous evil of my ways. I can't stay there, Ash. It's breaking my mom. I can't bear to even look at her."

Ash laughs, a little raggedly, and hugs me. "I always thought we'd have it figured out by now, you and me."

"I thought I did have it figured out," I say.

"Ha. You went so far in the wrong direction, you warped into another reality." She hugs me again, to make sure I don't get mad.

I hug her back. "Listen, Ash, why don't I watch Arya tonight, so you can go to work? And then, maybe I could stay here while I figure out what to do with my life, and keep watching her for you." I hold my breath, hoping she'll go for it.

Her eyebrows go up. "What do you know about babies, Nicole?"

"How hard could it be?"

"Oh. My. God. That right there is why this would never work. You have no idea. Do you have money? I can't afford to feed you."

"I'll learn. Ash, I swear. Give me a chance. I'm looking for a job, and, hey—I'll sell my diamonds. That should buy us a bunch of time. Maybe even a car. You need somebody to help with Arya. I need to be independent. I'm going to go to counseling, even. We can do this together."

At least she's thinking about it. I can see the wheels turning. Back before Kent, there would have been no question. The enormity of the distance I've allowed to grow between us strikes me with an onslaught of grief and loss. Ash was always my person, the only one I'd ever met who accepted my compulsion to move objects around without judgment.

She never called me a thief. She supported me when things blew up in my face.

"Come on, Ash," I plead. "It's perfect. I'll stay with your kiddo while you work and while you're sleeping, and I'll sell the diamonds and find an early evening job. That way, we can share the bed without, you know, sharing the bed, and somebody will always be with the baby."

She still looks skeptical. "You know I love you, Nickle. But you and jobs . . . not to mention babies . . ."

We both sigh at the same moment, and then we start to laugh, and in a minute, we are crying and hugging each other and both talking at once.

"I'm so sorry," I sob.

"I missed you so much," Ash says.

After a long minute, she wipes her eyes and levels a serious gaze at me. "If you're serious—"

"Dead serious," I say, even though the sudden reality of taking care of a baby terrifies me. "What do I do?"

A questioning sound comes from the bedroom, followed by a wail that rises in intensity at an alarming rate.

"Mama's here, baby," Ash calls in a voice I've never heard from her before. She pads into the bedroom, and the racket stops midhowl as if somebody has turned off the volume. A minute later, Ash emerges with Arya in her arms. In the time since I've last seen her, a couple of months, at least, she's changed from a baby doll to a small person.

"Oh my God. She's grown so much!"

"That happens with babies," Ash says a little sarcastically. "She's sitting up by herself. And crawling. And into everything."

Arya's big brown eyes gaze at me solemnly. There are tear streaks on her cheeks and slobber on her chin. One tiny, perfect hand rests on the soft junction between Ash's neck and shoulder, the other is stuffed into her mouth. My heart contracts in a spasm of fear. What if she doesn't like me?

"This is Nickle, remember?" Ash says to the baby, whose gaze shifts to her mother's face and then back to mine. "What do you think?"

Arya gurgles something incomprehensible, and Ash laughs. "I think you're absolutely right."

"Hey," I protest. "No talking about me in whatever language that is. No fair."

Ash laughs. "Come here, new babysitter. Lesson one. How to hold a baby."

"You're kidding, right?" I get to my feet with trepidation, unnerved by the silent interrogation I'm still undergoing. Approaching Arya feels like standing for sentencing in a courtroom.

"Well, Arya," I say, both of us still contemplating each other. "I understand your reservations and suggest a trial. We will reevaluate in the morning. Deal?"

And then the magic happens. She smiles. Her eyes light up. Her slobbery hand waves in the air. Her legs kick and she makes a crowing sound that hits me like the embodiment of the pure joy of the universe. Ash holds her out toward me, and I take her into my arms and settle her onto my hip. Her body is unexpectedly sturdy. She doesn't nestle into me like she did with Ash, but she doesn't fight me or start bawling, either. I smile at her and she smiles back, that same utterly gleeful slobbery smile.

"Hmmm," Ash says. "That went better than expected. I think she likes you."

"You think?"

"God, Nicole, you look like you've been zapped by God Almighty Himself. She's just a baby, not an angel from on high. Let me show you how to change a diaper and fix a bottle."

Ash gives me a crash course on diapers and bottles and spit-up. She says if I survive the first night, she'll teach me about baths and baby food. By the time she leaves for work, I've changed a diaper and prepared a bottle. Arya is old enough to hold it by herself and doesn't need burping. Plus, she usually sleeps through the night and is already sound asleep in a portable crib by Ash's bed.

"If she wakes up and cries, just change her diaper and put her back down. I'm not supposed to answer my phone, but I will. So call if you need me." Ash lingers by the door, clearly uneasy about leaving the two of us alone.

"It's good," I say. "I swear to God, Ash, I'll die before I let something bad happen to her."

"Nobody is doubting your intentions," Ash says, which isn't exactly a vote of confidence. "If she's up, you have to watch her every second. She crawls everywhere and is into everything."

"I swear, I will not take my eyes off of her even to blink."

Ash thinks about this, then finally smiles and holds up her star. I press my wrist against hers. "The stars align," we intone, and she hugs me. "Thank you."

At first, I think this will all be easy. Arya sleeps all night, and so do I. And then Ash comes home, feeds Arya breakfast, and collapses into bed. And I quickly discover that entertaining a baby is hard work, especially in a tiny apartment when somebody is trying to sleep on the other side of a flimsy door. It's too cold to take her out for a walk, and she's too little to watch TV, and by the time Ash reemerges from the bedroom, yawning and bleary eyed, I feel like I need to get out of the apartment or scream.

Even so, the idea of getting back out there job hunting is not appealing. At all. Still. I shower and get dressed, and just as I'm about to head out, my cell buzzes. Probably Mom again. I haven't called her yet, but I did text her again this morning.

But it's not Mom. It's a reminder alert that I set weeks ago. *Writing class starts, 4 p.m.*

"What?" Ash asks.

"Nothing." I shove the phone into my jeans pocket.

"Your face didn't look like nothing."

"Oh, okay, fine. Don't laugh. I was going to start a college class tonight."

"You? High-school-dropout, I-hate-school Nickle?"

"Crazy, right? Well. It was Kent's idea. I'm obviously not going now." I put on my shoes and sling my day pack over my shoulder.

"Wait," Ash says, processing. "Maybe you should."

I give her a withering stare. "Yeah, no. I was only going because Kent was pushing. He was on another 'you need to make something of yourself' kick. I got tired of arguing, so I signed up."

"Can't believe I'm agreeing with that asshole on anything, but he has a point. Better education, better job. If I had time and money, I would totally take a class."

"Maybe you should take this one, then." My voice is sharper than I mean it to be, and I dial it back at once. "Sorry. But it's not the sort of class that's going to help me get a job."

"What is it?"

"Creative writing." I expect her to laugh and agree with me that it's a stupid class for me to take.

Instead, she says, "Please tell me that pissed him off."

I grin, feeling like my old self for half a minute. "It did! He was thinking business or marketing or maybe art history, so I could fit in at the snob fests he dragged me to."

"Why a writing class, though?" she persists.

"Because there wasn't a Pole Dancing 101?"

She snorts, and I add tentatively, "If I tell you something, do you promise not to laugh?"

Ash presses both hands over her heart. "I solemnly swear."

"Okay. Well." Even though it's just Ash, I feel the heat rising to my face and lower my eyes so I won't see her skepticism. "I wanted to be a writer. When I was younger. Before I dropped out of school and everything. And when I saw the class . . . I thought, maybe . . . Anyway. It was a stupid idea."

"I think you should go," Ash says.

"Seriously? If I'm going to take a class, don't you think I should take something useful? I have zero skills."

"Are you kidding? You are the best object mover ever." Only Ash could say something like that and make me still feel loved. But then she goes all serious and says, "Think about it. The class is already paid for. *Kent* paid for it. You should get whatever money you can out of him."

"You mean besides the twenty grand?"

"You deserve every penny of that and more for putting up with his shit."

"You do know I didn't keep that, right?"

We stare at each other in an uneasy silence as I brace myself either for questions about what I did do with the money, or for a tirade about everything that is wrong with Kent and my stupidity in marrying him. Instead, Ash asks, very gently, "Why did he marry you, Nickle? Have you ever asked yourself that?"

I have. About half a million times. I even asked him once, when I'd failed as usual to live up to his expectations. "What did you marry me for, then?" I'd shouted, on the brink of tears. He'd just smiled, an infuriating, condescending, secretive sort of smile, and walked out of the room without even bothering to tell me the lie that he loved me.

"I don't know," I whisper now. It's a question I didn't think to ask until it was way too late.

Chapter Ten

HAWK

Mom hasn't told me what to do since she informed me on my eighteenth birthday that I was now a grown man who could make his own decisions and face the consequences. But when I ask for advice, she gives it to me right between the eyes, no flinching. "You're enmeshed," she says. "You have to get off this case."

She's right. I know she's right, even though I don't want to listen. The last week of surveillance on Nicole Brandenburg has proven that. For one thing, I feel like a stalker and have been completely unable to tap into my usual professional mindset. Rather than objectively following her and reporting on what I see, I find myself willing her to stick to the straight and narrow. I catch myself fantasizing about taking her out for coffee and saying things that elicit a smile, about looking into her eyes and feeling that warm, melting sensation all over again.

If I take myself off the case, I'll never see her again.

"It's great money," I say, grabbing a slice of pizza as an excuse to avoid my mother's searching eyes. For once in my life, I'm actually not hungry.

"But you're not really earning it, are you?" She cuts her pizza slice up into neat, symmetrical bites with her knife and fork while I use my hands. "You said you've held back information from the man who hired you."

"I'm not sure the information is relevant. I'm still watching." Pizza Hut pan pizzas are my absolute favorite, but the gooey cheese feels like old gum in my mouth, rubbery and tasteless.

"Is it your job to decide whether it's relevant?" Mom asks.

Another logical, valid question.

"My gut tells me something is wrong with the story." I drop the pizza on my plate and wipe my hands on a napkin. "It's not clear-cut. He's not the good guy. She's not the callous criminal he makes her out to be."

"Or, your feelings are in the way. You told me about her rap sheet. Is it possible she's an extraordinarily charming sociopath?"

Which is pretty much what Kent said when I let him know my cover was compromised. I called him up the day of the Goodwill incident, rather than sending in the usual email report, and told him I couldn't effectively follow Nicole anymore and he'd be better served to hire another PI.

"She got to you, didn't she?" he'd said. "Those eyes, right? The innocent act. Because, trust me, that's what it is, an act. If you can't get close to her anymore, don't. Just keep track of where she goes and who she talks to, and keep me updated."

That's when I should have told him about the jacket. I should have given him the other woman's name, Kara McInnelly, and her address. I didn't. Nor did I call him yesterday when Kara showed up to her minimum-wage nursing home job driving a newly purchased, roadworthy vehicle and I knew I'd blown my shot at that five-thousand-dollar bonus.

When I did text him to mention that Nicole appeared to have had a fight with Roberta and spent the rest of the day going in and out of a wide range of businesses, he responded, briefly, that he already knew and now needed my eyes on Nicole more than ever.

Mom blots her lips with a napkin. "Listen. You know what I think? You're conflicted. This Kent person has privilege and power and money. This Nicole does not, and that's skewing your judgment. Focus on what you do know and what you can do. I have a client who needs a protection detail. She's left her husband and she's worried he'll try to kill her. Why don't you stake out her place instead? Step away for a bit. Get your head straight."

"I'm being paid well for this," I begin, then break off. We both know that most of Mom's clients don't have money. A lot of what we do is pro bono. The thin white scar on Mom's cheek and the wheelchair she's sitting in are a constant reminder of why we both do the work we do. Picking up a case that pays well every now and then is important, but not at the cost of my conscience and my soul.

Mom's smile warms her thin face, and she pats my hand. "You're a good man, so the world is hard for you. You'll do the right thing. You start that class tonight, yes?"

"If I go." I look down at the pizza on my plate, the cheese now congealed. "I need to get some work done."

The teenage server comes over and asks, "Did you want a box?"

"Yes, please," Mom says. Then she leans forward a little. "Go to your class. Do something that is creative and involves people who are not criminals or victims. Okay? Then step away from the Brandenburg case and do this job for me. The client I want you to watch out for is employed and paying."

~

I take half of my mother's advice. I let Kent know I'm taking today and this evening off. He's unhappy enough about it that I suspect he might just fire me, which is fine. And then I go to the writing class that I've been both excited about and dreading ever since I signed up.

It's probably some sort of cliché that I spend my free time writing terrible detective novels about a gumshoe who has a weakness for vulnerable women. To date, there are five completed manuscripts languishing in my desk. It was actually Mickey who said maybe they weren't as bad as I thought, and the best way to get better at something is to take a class.

I'd meant to be early so I could grab myself an aisle seat and stretch out my long legs, but just my luck, I got stuck behind a fender bender on Division, and by the time I arrive at the classroom, the professor is already talking. When he sees me in the doorway he stops, midsentence, and waves me in. "If you're here for creative writing, you're in the right place. Come on in and have a seat."

My inner nerd, never quite convinced that I'm not still bully fodder, cringes at the attention as heads swivel to check out the newcomer. All of the aisle seats are taken, but there's an empty seat in the back, right next to a woman with a familiar mane of hair in a shade somewhere between dark brown and auburn. I have memorized that fall of hair, the line of that back, can almost read her mood by the set of her shoulders. When she turns her head to look up at me, eyes widening in recognition, my heart does a complicated set of acrobatics before settling into an accelerated rhythm.

As I slide into the seat beside her, time slows and expands. I feel like I've slipped through a portal into an altered reality. What twist of fate has put us here, in this classroom, side by side?

Nicole makes room for me, scooting her chair toward the aisle, shifting her laptop, and I pull out my own things as the professor resumes his speech.

"Let's get to know each other. We'll be sharing a lot in this group, and by the time we're done, you will understand things about each other that your families and friends do not. Since this is a writing class, we'll do this through writing prompts. Take out your notebook and a pen."

"Can we use laptops?" someone asks.

"Not this time. I want you to get a feel for the different modes of writing. You will discover that pen to paper hits different creative triggers than fingers to keyboard. For now, let's go with pen and paper. I'll give you five minutes for a freewriting activity. Write down the following prompt: 'If I were to die tomorrow, I . . .'"

Nicole whispers, "Hey, can I borrow a sheet of paper?"

Who comes to a writing class without paper? I don't ask it out loud, but she reads my face and shrugs. "Wasn't planning to come until, like, an hour ago. I'm totally unprepared." This non-explanation takes my curiosity about her to a whole new level.

I rip a couple of sheets of paper from my notebook as the prof continues. "This is a freewriting activity. The only rule is to keep the pen moving. Do not judge what you have written. Don't try to be perfect. If your mind goes blank, feel free to write 'I have nothing to write' over and over until something comes to mind. You'll be invited to share, but not required to, so don't let the fear of discovery stop you. Ready? Go."

I shove the paper toward Nicole. "Maybe a pen?" she asks, and I draw out one of the three reserves carefully slotted into the pen holders in my backpack and hand it to her. She hesitates, pen poised over the paper, not yet writing. I'm not writing, either, distracted by the slim hand so close to my own, the tattoos spiraling up her arm. I drag my eyes back to my own page, start my own pen moving, and write:

If I were to die tomorrow, that would be okay with me. Hell, who am I kidding? I'd rage against the dying of the light. Give me magic before I leave here, magic beyond the slant of light at sunset, the shimmer of heat on tarmac, the distant burn of stars . . . Give me real love, at least once, however brief . . .

"Time," the prof calls out.

Feet shuffle, chairs slide forward or backward, people stretch and resettle. Nicole keeps writing. Her words are hidden by the fall of her hair, so I try to read the story inked on her arm instead. A hummingbird, a butterfly emerging from a skull instead of a chrysalis. A phrase done in a gothic font and decorated with tiny skulls and flowers: *The curse is come upon me.*

"Now, we'll go around the room," the prof is saying. "Tell us your name, and then share a sentence or two from your work, if you feel comfortable enough to do so. Notice I don't say entirely comfortable—this is meant to stretch you a little. But you may pass, if you wish."

He smiles at a pimply boy in the front row, who can't be more than fifteen. The kid's head bends over his paper and his ears go scarlet. "I'm Chad," he says. He clears his throat, then reads, "If I were to die tomorrow, I think I would miss me."

"Interesting," the prof says, smiling warmly. "I'm going to guess you have a metaphysical mind. Okay. Who is next?"

There is a wide range of responses, some poetic, some very practical, including "Who would buy the breakfast cereal?" from a vivacious woman in the front, who laughs at her own words.

"Okay, you two in the back row," the prof says. "You can't hide forever." Everybody turns in their seats to stare. "You first." He points at me.

I resist the temptation to adjust my weight in the chair or clear my throat. I've had plenty of practice concealing my insecurity, and my voice stays steady as I say, "Hey, everybody, I'm Hawk." And then I glance down at all the poetic magical bits that came out of my pen and know I won't share them with the class. Keeping my eyes on the page, I pretend to read, "If I were to die tomorrow, my novel in progress would at least serve to light the morning fire."

In the wave of laughter that follows, I breathe a sigh of relief. I've kept myself to myself, although possibly not entirely. I'm pretty sure Nicole has been glancing at my paper the same way I've been trying to get a look at hers. She flushes slightly as she reads her words in a clear, steady voice. "If I were to die tomorrow, what would the universe do with all of its misplaced stuff, with other people's things?"

Words of Kent's come back to me: "She claims that she gets a feeling about where an object wants to be. Until the universe speaks, she'll keep it with her." Now I wonder, does she really believe the universe wants her to move stuff? She doesn't come across as delusional any more than she seems sociopathic.

"I suggest that all of you look to your response to this question for a hint as to why you are here and what you might want to write during our time together," the professor says. "We will be working in a creative, open, nonjudgmental space. Forget everything I said about grading and expectations. All ideas are worthy of exploration. Find your voice, find your creative groove, and the rest will take care of itself."

He reads to us then, passages from novels that showcase a strong and interesting author voice, before assigning homework and dismissing the class. Sweat soaks my armpits and my heart speeds up again. Nicole is packing up her laptop. I have about thirty seconds to establish a connection, but my preexisting awkwardness with women is exaggerated about a hundred times over by internal conflict.

My mother is right about me and this case. What I'm feeling is far from objective. I want to unlock Nicole's secrets, one by one, but not for the purposes of locating Kent's missing money. I couldn't give a rat's ass about him at this point. I want to talk to her. I want to ask her out on a date. God help me, I want to see the expression in those eyes just before I kiss her.

She gets up from her chair and shoulders her day pack. I still haven't said anything, so I blurt out the first thing that pops into my head.

"Nice ink." I wince at my own words, which sound like an awkward bar come-on. So I add, "Tennyson lover, are you?" which just sounds nerdy and awkward as hell.

But she stops and turns back toward me, covering the words inked on her arm with her hand. "I was fourteen. I thought it was edgy."

"There are worse things than Tennyson. At least you don't have your boyfriend's name on your neck."

"Because I put it on my ass instead." She grins, those gray eyes lighting up with mischief. I think she's kidding, but the idea of Kent's name tattooed on any part of her body awakens a jealousy I didn't know I was capable of, and certainly have no business feeling.

She points at my own heavily inked forearms, specifically the hawk breaking free from the jaws of a dragon. "So, I was fourteen and succumbed to the pathos of the Lady of Shalott. What's your story?"

"Alcohol and stupidity," I lie. I was sober and completely intentional when I chose the hawk. It's a daily reminder to me that my life doesn't have to be bound by my past. "So, what do you write?"

She shrugs. "Bits and pieces. I probably don't belong in this class. You?"

"I probably don't belong in this class, either." I hesitate, but it's now or never, so I take a breath and dare to say what's on my mind. "Hey, I have an idea. We could form a support and study group, since we're misfits. Meet in a coffee shop or something to do assignments."

Uncertainty crosses her face, and I brace myself for the rejection. Instead, she asks, "Are you a cop?"

Which is so unexpected, I stare at her with my mouth literally hanging open.

"Because that's what I thought you were," she says. "The other day. In Goodwill."

I manage to close my mouth and shake my head. "Nope. Just a regular guy. Who has never, ever been told he looks like a cop."

Nicole tilts her head to one side and looks me over, head to toe and back again. "Obviously, I was thinking undercover. I mean, that hair would never be allowed on the force. Of course, if you are an undercover cop, you wouldn't tell me. Why are you taking this class?"

"Because I want to be a writer?"

"You don't look like a writer."

"I don't look like a cop, either. Besides, what does a writer look like, anyway?"

"Good point. Well. Gotta go. I have a bus to catch." She turns toward the door. I feel something close to panic at the idea of her walking away from me. If she goes now, I'll never see her again. I know now for sure that I'll have to drop the case, but I don't want to lose her.

"So, what about that study group?" I ask.

She pauses, then lifts her shoulders in a shrug. "Things in my life are . . . weird right now. I'm looking for a job. Might have to drop the class."

"Well, then, I could email you assignments and we could meet and go over them. A class of two." I can't believe what I'm saying. I am never this pushy with women. I wait for her to show the signs of fear, the shifted weight, the folded arms, the tightening of the shoulders. It doesn't happen.

"Maybe," she says. "Maybe I'll see you next class, maybe I won't. Thanks for the paper and the pen."

"Wait." I jot down my cell phone number on one of the aforementioned sheets of paper and hand it to her. "Call me. Text me. If you feel like it."

She tucks the folded paper into her pocket and smiles before she turns to go. I watch her until she's out of sight, feeling like all of the light in the room goes with her.

Five minutes later, as I'm getting into my Jeep, my phone buzzes with a text.

Hey, this is Nicole. In case.

In case of what, I wonder, but it doesn't matter. She's trusted me with her number. I stare at it until my screen goes dark, and then I just sit there, for a long time, thinking about nothing and everything and waiting for my head to clear.

Chapter Eleven

NICOLE

I really do mean to work on my problem in counseling, but it's hard to break my deeply ingrained habit of resistance and mistrust. So I show up late, and when Graham asks me how my week has been, I don't tell him that I found a home for Kent's money or that my family staged an intervention and I ran away to Ash's. Instead, I ask, "How confidential is this all, really?" It comes out sounding hostile, more like an accusation than a question, but Graham responds calmly.

"Just because your husband is paying your bill, it does not mean he gets access to your information. If that's what you're worried about."

"Money can buy anything."

Again, Graham doesn't react to my hostility. If anything, there's a sadness in his voice as he answers, "I'm going to guess that you've had previous counselors betray your trust. But I take confidentiality very seriously, Nicole. I would do nothing to compromise either our counseling relationship or my license. Besides the fact that, believe it or not, I do not want to do you any harm and really would like to help you, I'm not about to compromise my ethics or ruin my career for anybody, no matter how much money they might offer in exchange."

That last phrase tells me something I'd only guessed at. "Let me guess," I say. "Kent offered you money in exchange for information."

"Let's just say that I remind all parties of ethical standards, and Kent is well aware that the only way he can access your records is through a subpoena—"

I sag backward into the chair, all of the fight going out of me. "He could totally do that. In a legal capacity, not as my husband. If he decides to send me to prison, he'll use whatever I tell you to help him do it."

"Conflict of interest. The court would never allow it."

I wave that off. "He'll get another lawyer to do it for him."

"Even a subpoena does not mean the court gets all records. Only what I choose to write in my official notes." Graham's eyes meet mine, and there is a promise there, unspoken, that I can choose to accept or reject.

I look for a way to trust what he's offering, and finally say, "Can I have my journal now?"

The shadow of a smile touches his lips, but it doesn't reach his eyes. He looks weary, I think. I shake off an unexpected empathy; the emotional well-being of my counselor is not my problem.

"Before we go back to journaling, it would be helpful to have a game plan, or at the very least a goal," Graham suggests.

"We do," I say brightly. "We're going to work on my trauma. And make me stop moving things."

"Stealing things, you mean."

I shake my head. "I don't steal."

He sighs, the kind of sigh that would go with an eye roll if he weren't a professional. "Nicole. I can't begin to help you until you admit that you have a problem."

I adjust myself in my chair, slipping out of my shoes so I can tuck my feet up under me. "I freely admit that I have a problem. It's just not the problem that you think I have."

"Then perhaps we should define and agree on the problem, as our starting place."

"Fine. Here's the problem. As far back as I can remember, I've had a sense that some objects inhabiting one space really belong in another. I move them. I get accused of stealing. But I'm not stealing. And I really can't help myself."

Graham might as well have a cartoon bubble over his head that reads, *Unbelievable*, but he says, very carefully, "At least you've basically just admitted that you have no power over this . . ."

"Object Relocation Program."

"Object Relocation Program. Right. Are you saying that you did not steal twenty thousand dollars from your husband?"

"I'm saying that I *moved* twenty thousand dollars. Which isn't quite the same as stealing." Before he can say it himself, I add, "And now you're going to tell me I'm using a defense mechanism. Let me guess. Deflecting, right?"

He doesn't take the bait. "Do you want to talk about where you moved the money to, and why you feel it needs to be there?"

"Hell no. That's exactly the sort of information Kent would love to subpoena you for." I can't run the risk of Kent somehow tracing the money to that woman from Goodwill. Obviously, whatever it is that makes me move things around wanted her to have it, and so did I. In fact, imagining the look on her face when she finds the envelope stuffed with hundreds would almost be worth the prison time it might cost me.

"How about this?" Graham suggests. "Let's begin with the possibility, just as a theory, that your relocating of objects has something to do with what happened to you as a child."

My innards twist. My heart picks up its pace. "So you *have* read my records, then."

"Nicole?" Graham's tone is gentle but persistent.

"I'd be willing to consider the possibility that the—event—you mention had an impact on my life. Theoretically, I'd be willing to consider it might be connected to the reason I move things. But there's more to it than that."

"What if we start there, and see what happens?"

I can't answer. I'm locked in a conflict that won't let me fully engage in therapy, no matter how much I want to stop hurting the people I love and to have a normal life. Because I also believe that moving things helps people. The woman from Goodwill isn't the first person to benefit from what I do. What if processing my trauma really is the cure? The idea of entirely letting go of the Object Relocation Program makes me feel small and empty. I don't even know who I would be without it.

"How about I keep writing in the journal and see where it goes?" I finally ask.

Graham doesn't fight me. He gets up, unlocks the cabinet, and brings me my notebook and a pen. "If your writing does lead you to anything emotionally difficult," he says, "you can stop and we'll do some relaxation work. I'd love to teach you meridian tapping to bring down your anxiety. Also, I promise you, if your records are ever subpoenaed, what you write will not be part of what the court receives."

Turning to the first pages I'd written, I reread the last paragraph, unfinished:

> *Nickle got a spanking, right there in the driveway for all the world to see. Her mother loaded her and the bear right back in the car, and they drove to Goodwill, where she was forced to give the bear back, even though—*

I take a breath and press the pen deep into the paper, making a mark that is more paper damage than ink. And then I start to write.

> *—she knew and the bear knew that it didn't belong to this store, or to the little man with the sour breath who took the toy from her reluctant hands and lectured her.*

"The items in this store are here to help people who don't have what you have," he said. "You taking this bear is like taking food away from a little girl who didn't have breakfast or dinner and eating it yourself when you are already full."

Nicole didn't see how this was so. At all. "But I didn't take him for me," she protested.

"It's still stealing." The man's fingers, yellowed at the tips, tightened around the bear's neck and squeezed. "Do you know what happens to people who steal? They go to jail. Do you want to go to jail, little girl?"

Nicole did not. She felt very small. The man scared her. Mom was ashamed of her and she'd already been spanked. So she didn't say that the bear had somewhere to be and it wasn't here. She also didn't say she was sorry. She could be made to give the bear back because everybody was so big, but she couldn't be made to lie.

All she could do was stand there and cry.

Mom took her by the hand and led her back out to the car, where she buried her face in her knees and kept crying. "Nicole," her mother said, stroking her hair. "I know you are not a bad girl. And you aren't going to jail. This is the end of this, okay? Lesson learned."

Nicole didn't see how it could be the end of anything when the bear wanted so much to be somewhere else. So she just kept crying and Mom kept stroking her hair. "I didn't like that man, either, just so you know. Shifty eyed. He's probably a thief himself and that's why he was so mean. You know what? I think I need coffee. You want a hot chocolate? That will make you feel better."

Nicole nodded, just a tiny nod, and put her seat belt on. Mom still loved her. Maybe everything would be okay.

But then they walked through the door into the coffee shop. A bell over the door tinkled. The rich aroma of coffee filled her nose and she breathed in deeply, thinking about the taste of hot chocolate, creamy and rich. She was about to open her mouth to ask, "Can I have marshmallows?" when she felt a crawling sensation on her back.

The room felt different. It sucked at her, empty, hungry, wanting something. And she knew what it wanted.

It was—

"Time's up." Graham's voice shatters the memory the words are building on the page.

I startle, the pen making an ugly scribble. "But I'm in the middle of a sentence."

"Sorry, but I've got another client. It will keep." He holds out his hand and I give him the notebook. "Okay?" he asks.

I check with my inner self. Anxiety coils in my belly, my muscles, but I'm not about to fall apart. "Okay," I say. "See you next week."

I'm not a thief, my child self whispers as I walk out of the office. And, as I always do, I whisper back, *I know.*

Chapter Twelve

Nicole

Are you ready to come home?

Mom has been texting me this question at least once a day. She worries. She'd much rather have me underfoot at her house where she can keep an eye on me than have me living in an admittedly unsavory neighborhood with Ash. I evade a direct answer with Job hunting! and a bunch of starry-eyed smileys, since I can't outright lie and tell her things are going great and I have tons of prospects.

I'm proud of you, Mom sends back, which makes me feel awful. I'm applying for jobs that might have been cause for parental pride when I was sixteen. Shame makes me even more determined. I'll find a job and support myself if it kills me. In the meantime, there are Kent's diamonds, which I certainly don't plan to wear anymore.

When I walk into the jewelry store, two sets of eyes glance up at the sound of a discreet little chime. Both assess and discard me as a valid customer in five seconds flat. The man, seated inside a glass-walled booth, returns his concentration to a microscope he's peering through. The woman watches me intently in a protect-the-inventory way, all the while projecting that while she may be here to serve, she is not here to serve the likes of me.

I know all too well what she sees. Hair that could definitely use a trim, minimal makeup that does little to conceal my worry and fatigue. The jeans and T-shirt that date back to before I married Kent five years ago. Absolutely nothing about me is shouting, *I'm here to buy expensive jewelry.*

Maybe I should have gone to a pawnshop, but I wanted to try the jewelry store first. I need all of the money I can get, and I need a fair deal, which I figure I'm more likely to get here. I walk up to the counter, which forces the woman to acknowledge me, though she clearly conveys her superiority without being outright rude.

"Can I help you?" Her tone indicates that she would happily help me right out the door.

It's not my first encounter with snobs. I can take it.

"I was wondering if you might purchase these from me?" I fumble my tissue-wrapped cache out of the inside pocket of my jacket, where I've stashed it for safekeeping, and lay it on the counter.

The woman's nose wrinkles as though something smells. "There's a pawnshop two blocks down. We deal only in fine jewelry. Diamonds."

"Which is what I have here." I unwrap the package and set the pieces out on the counter, one at a time. The pendant. The ring. The earrings. The diamonds sparkle as they catch the light, the gold gleams softly.

"Are they yours to sell?" The woman's voice is so sweet and cold it gives me the verbal equivalent of brain freeze. It hurts. Before I have a chance to respond, the big guy emerges from the glass booth.

"Thanks, Hazel. I'll take this," he says.

He's got a full-color tat on his left bicep, and the creases around his eyes look like he knows how to laugh, even though he's serious right now. But he looks me in the eyes, and I judge him to be a straight shooter.

"Engagement ring." I move the sparkling gold circle closer to him on the glass counter. "Wedding-day gift." I nudge the pendant and the earrings. "And wedding ring." I add the gold band that Kent put on my finger the day he told God and everybody in the church that he'd love me through sickness and health.

The jeweler picks up the ring and holds it up to the light. "Hmmm," he says, and it's not the good sort of "hmmm" that would mean this is the most beautiful diamond he's seen in ages. He withdraws a small magnifying lens from his pocket, holds it to one eye, and peers carefully through it at the ring. Then he sets it down and picks up the pendant. Hazel glares at me from the other end of the counter, and I surreptitiously flash her my middle finger. Her cheeks flush. Her lips purse.

By the time the jeweler has examined every piece, his expression blank, never saying a word, jagged edges of anxiety are pricking at my skin. His eyes meet mine, then shift downward to the counter. "I'm sorry. I'm not going to be able to help you."

In my peripheral vision, Hazel smiles.

"It's mine," I protest. "I don't know how to prove that to you."

"Who the jewelry belongs to isn't the problem," the jeweler says. "The problem is that these aren't diamonds."

I feel like I've been punched in the belly, and it's all I can do not to double over and start moaning. I stare at him. Then down at the sparkle on the counter. Then up at him again.

"I don't understand."

His expression softens a little. "This husband of yours—"

"About-to-be-ex-husband."

"This about-to-be-ex-husband of yours—he's a stand-up guy? Totally honest?"

There's a lump in my throat that won't let any words out, and the jeweler continues.

"With a jeweler's loupe, it's quite easy to see the difference between an actual diamond and a simulant. Less easy for the untrained eye."

I shake my head. "This can't be happening."

"If you'd like confirmation, I'd be happy to test them for you."

He withdraws a black plastic device from under the counter, not much larger than a pack of cards. "This is a diamond tester. The tip measures thermal conductivity—the amount of heat a stone holds. The value for a diamond is very specific. First, we'll test a real diamond."

He touches the tip to a small diamond in his own wedding band to demonstrate. A small green light shows on one side of the tester, accompanied by a clear high tone. "Real," he says, then picks up my ring.

This time, when he touches the tip to the stone, a red light flicks on and the device emits a low, dull buzz. The sound of disappointment.

"I'm sorry," he says, almost as if he means it. "I can test them all if you like, but the result will be the same."

Still in shock, I stare blankly at the diamonds and then at the diabolical tester. Finally, I manage to ask, "You mean they're worthless?"

"Not worthless, no. Just not what you were expecting. The settings are gold, stamped fourteen karats. I'd need to do an acid test to verify, of course, but if they test out, I can offer you scrap gold value."

Scrap metal. That's all I was ever worth to Kent. All at once, it hurts to breathe.

The jeweler pulls a small calculator from his jacket pocket and begins punching in numbers. "Rough guess without weighing, we're looking at around three hundred dollars."

I work hard to drag my breath in past the block in my throat, and then push it out again.

"That bad?" he asks.

"You have no idea."

"Look. For you, four hundred. Best I can do."

I should say something, but if I open my mouth, a sob is going to come out instead of words, so all I can do is stand there and nod my head.

"It will work out okay," he says. "You'll see."

He pays me in cash, and I tuck it into my pocket and walk out in a fog of disorientation and despair.

I'd meant to go to the writing class, but I'm too demoralized. *Scrap gold.* The words take root in my head, growing into something monstrous. Scrap metal for a scrap person. That's what I am. My theory that what I do helps people, that fate somehow works through me, is utterly ridiculous. Scrap people don't help people. They don't become writers and have happy lives. They steal things and go to jail and have dead-end jobs. That's it. There's nothing else for me.

A text message rolls in much later, after Ash has gone to work and I've taken my self-loathing to bed, the two of us curled up together in a ball of misery. This time, it's not Mom.

Homework assignment: Brainstorm writing topics. Set a timer for fifteen minutes and jot down as many moments from your own life as you can that you could use to write a story.

One simple text message, one student to another, but it totally disrupts my pity party. Who is this guy, anyway? I've never seen a face like his, or eyes like his, hungry and fierce as those tattoos of dragons and raptors and skulls. And a voice that conflicts with all of it, soft and warm as a summer night.

I feel intrigue and fascination and, yes, idiot that I am, attraction. What makes me think a man like Hawk would be interested in a loser like me? Best thing to do would be to just ignore the text altogether. But then another message rolls in.

So, are you coming back to class or did you get a job?

I hesitate, then reply, Maybe and no.

And wait to see what he'll do with that. Will he push me, dismiss me? Instead, he texts back: Let's do the assignment. Now. Got paper? Or do I need to bring you some?

I send him an eye-roll emoji. And then: Hang on a sec. Because I don't actually have a notebook or any kind of paper, or a pen. Ash is organized, though, and it doesn't take long to scrounge up a pen and a small notebook she's been using to keep a running grocery list. I tear out a few sheets, grab a book to serve as a desk, and climb back into bed.

Are you making the paper? Hawk texts. Cutting down the trees? What? I send an upside-down smiley, and then a stopwatch emoji. Ready.

Loser buys us both coffee. Go.

And I do. I start with *the time I moved the bear from Goodwill,* because, hey, I'm already writing that one. I add: *The time my diamonds were fakes. The time I moved Mr. Kennedy's flamingo. Running away from home. The Christmas tree ornament. The Barbie doll swap. The escapade of the twenty thousand dollars. The client's book . . .*

When Hawk texts, Time, I've got forty-five object-relocation-related events staring up at me, and I'm not sure how I feel about that. Yeah, they might be interesting things to write about. They are also evidence of my dysfunction and things to feel guilty and ashamed about.

Hawk reports forty-seven items on his list. You owe me a coffee, he texts. When? After class on Tuesday? Before?

I'll have to let you know.

He doesn't answer my evasion, and I'm not sure if I'm relieved or sorry. Turning out the light, I try to go to sleep, but even in the dark, behind closed eyelids, I keep seeing my list. Hard evidence of objects that I've moved. For the first time ever, I fully realize that every one of them belonged to somebody who must have felt the loss, maybe even felt violated and betrayed, the way I feel about my diamonds being little more than glass.

On the edges of sleep, just before I finally drift into oblivion, I have an idea. Maybe I can find a way to make amends.

Chapter Thirteen

ANDREA

My anxiety lockdown protocol isn't working.

All week I've been walking through a minefield, the smallest things triggering flashbacks and panic. Going to work loaded up on antianxiety pills is out of the question, and the days have been marathons of dragging my mind back to its tasks over and over again. Nights are worse. I know I'm having nightmares, but every time I wake, drenched in sweat, the dream content has skittered away from my consciousness. Waking or sleeping, there is a bitter taste on my tongue, a sensation of grime and shame on my skin.

I blew my one chance to lay this anxiety storm to rest. Last Monday, when I called Sunny Side Up, rather than staying calm and getting the information I needed, I lost my cool. I meant to insist on speaking with the woman who must have brought in Tag's book, but instead I raged at Roberta like a maniac. And after I calmed down and called again to try to set up the conversation I desperately need to have, Roberta told me politely but firmly that the offending party had been dismissed from employment and was unavailable.

So the week has been hell, and the weekend is shaping up to be even worse. My down-to-the-minute schedule of exactly when and how long to exercise, cook, eat, clean, and read up on industry news has done nothing to allay the cycle of worry and fear playing over and over in my head. Sylvester has done his best to comfort me, winding around my ankles, leaping up into my lap every time I sit down, sleeping at my feet. But it's not enough.

I've doubled my dosage on the anxiety meds, which means I'm running far too rapidly through my supply. Monday, I'm going to need to set up an appointment with a new psychiatrist, since Dr. Wells in Seattle won't keep filling for me. I remind myself that I've dealt with anxiety flares before and I can do it again. I just need to tweak the protocol a little.

Since the one thing that seems to be helping is exercise, on Sunday morning I up all of the settings on the treadmill. A faster pace. Steeper terrain. Maybe I can outrun my demons. Breathe. Focus. Transcend.

I'm halfway through mile four when the chiming of the doorbell breaks my focus. My toe catches, jolting me to one side. For an instant, I'm falling, the still-moving track dragging my feet backward as my body continues forward, but I manage to save myself by grabbing the rails, wrenching my left shoulder.

What the hell? My doorbell should absolutely not ring on a Sunday morning, or ever. I haven't made any friends here. Nobody from my past knows where I am.

And yet it chimes again.

Switching off the treadmill, I grab my towel and sprint into my office. The security feed shows a woman shivering on the front doorstep. I recognize the thin coat and the hair. It's the cleaning woman Roberta brought into my house on the day the book showed up.

Magnifying the image, I take a good long look at the face that was hidden by a ball cap on the security feed. The woman is younger than Roberta, no more than thirty, I'd guess, with features that are interesting but not classically beautiful. Her hair is lighter than I'd thought, dark auburn rather than black, and falls loose and unstyled over shoulders hunched against the cold. She chews her lip and fidgets, glancing back toward the street before ringing the doorbell again.

What does that backward glance mean? General concern about staring neighbors, or is she looking for a signal from a partner? I picture Tag sitting in a car, waiting for the opportunity to . . .

Get it together, Andrea. This is your chance for answers.

No time for a long anxiety-control sequence. The woman might leave before I get through it. I squeeze my palms together and count my steps as I move toward the front door, using the numbers to calm my racing thoughts. I draw a deep cleansing breath before turning off the alarm and sliding back the dead bolt.

The woman doesn't waste any time, launching in before the door is all the way open. "I'm Nicole, from Sunny Side Up. Well, formerly from Sunny Side Up. Not anymore. I came to apologize." She clasps her hands together beseechingly. "Please let me explain."

I wrench my gaze away from her eyes, gray and luminous and oddly hypnotic, and scan the street behind her. No strange cars or out-of-place people.

"Talk fast," I say. "I'll give you fifteen seconds."

"The book was my fault," she says. "I'm the one who left it here, so it's not fair to punish Roberta."

"Who really put you up to this?" I demand. Or, at least, I mean to demand. Instead, the question whispers out of me, shaky and small. My legs feel rubbery, much more so than the treadmill can account for. There's a buzzing in my ears.

The woman, Nicole, puts a steadying hand on my arm. "Are you okay? Do you need to sit down?"

"I'm fine," I grind out through clenched teeth, flinching away from her touch. "Tell me who told you to bring—that book—into my house."

She looks bewildered by the question. "Why would anybody do that?"

I glare at her in silence. She takes a step backward, looking over her shoulder again and shifting her weight uneasily before she continues. "It was all me. I brought the book in with me and left it, and it doesn't seem fair to punish Roberta for something I did. Are you sure you're all right?"

"I'm fine," I snap. But clearly I'm not. In fact, I need to sit down. The buzzing in my ears is getting louder.

"It's like this," Nicole says. "Roberta is the best person in the world, and maybe she shouldn't have let me work with her, but that won't happen again. She only did it because I'm her sister, and family is important, right? And I really need a job. But I've been sacked, and I can assure you that neither she nor the rest of her employees will be leaving random items around in your house. Or taking any, for that matter—"

"You took something?"

"From you?" She looks aghast. "No. Nothing. I swear it."

Both of us are shivering in a cold wind that whistles across the porch and in through the open door. A car drives by, slowly, the driver's eyes lingering on us. I feel exposed standing here. Anybody could be watching or listening. Why this woman was in my house makes more sense now; I can understand Roberta trying to help out her flesh and blood. But I still need to know how she came to have Tag's book in her possession, and why, oh why, did she bring it into my house and then leave it there?

I open the door wider and step aside. "You might as well come in."

Nicole hesitates, apparently as uncertain about accepting this invitation as I am about extending it. When she crosses the threshold, it's in one quick movement, eyes closed, as if she's leaping off a cliff rather than stepping into a building. And then she stands there on the mat, hugging herself, shivering a little.

"This way," I say. "Take off your shoes, if you don't mind."

She startles, as if she'd been miles away, and I recognize her anxiety and feel an unexpected tug of empathy.

"Right. Sorry." She kicks off her shoes and follows me into the kitchen.

"Sit." I wave toward a chair in the breakfast nook. Nicole obeys, and I sit across from her, hiding my trembling hands in my lap. My eyes trace the line of her cheek, the fall of her hair, seeking some sort of clue that will explain things, but her face tells me nothing. Color rises in her cheeks as she meets my stare, and her chin lifts.

"You don't look at all like Roberta," I say. "Is she really your sister?"

"Depends on who you ask, I suppose," she answers, with a little grimace. "Or when you ask them."

I feel another tug of empathy, close to kinship. The way she holds her head, the set of her shoulders, reminds me of myself, fresh out of a psych unit and staring down the world with outward defiance while trying to bury my shame and create a new life.

I shake off the emotion, demanding, "Tell me all about the book."

"I . . ." Again, she shivers, even though it's warm here in the kitchen, and she's still wearing her coat. "I have a problem, and this is going to sound insane."

"Somehow I don't doubt that," I say.

"Sometimes . . . an object wants to be moved. And if I don't move it, I . . ." She stops there, glances up at me and then back down at the table.

I prompt her. "What does this have to do with the book?"

Her eyes meet mine. "The book didn't want to be where I found it. It wanted to be here."

I let out a huff of disbelief. "The *book* wanted to be here. Excuse me if I don't buy that one."

Nicole says defiantly, "Believe whatever you want, but it's true." And then she adds, "Now how about you tell me why you're having such a huge meltdown about a stupid book. I mean, it's a *book*. I'm sorry I left it in your perfect house and everything, but I don't see why—"

"Where is he? Where is Tag?" I slam my hand on the table. "Parked out on the street, waiting for you to spring this on me? Where?"

She flinches, her eyes widening, and half rises from her chair. With a supreme effort of will, I rein myself in and lower my voice. "Tell me, and I'll give your sister—if she is your sister—the contract back."

Nicole stares as if I'm the crazy person. "You think somebody else wanted me to put an old book in your house? I found it at another client's place and brought it here. That's the truth. I never lie."

I roll my eyes as if I'm sixteen instead of fifty-one. "Oh good. You're an honest thief."

"I'm not a thief!" she protests. "I just move things. Because they don't want to be where they are and they want to be somewhere else. Look. I'm sorry for any disruption I've caused. I'd be very happy to take the book away with me. And I think you should give Roberta—who is my sister—her job back."

She shoves back her chair, and my anxiety edges toward full-blown panic. She's going to leave me with all of my questions unanswered. The rigmarole she's told me can't be the truth because life doesn't work that way. The book is just too much of a coincidence. Either Tag has something to do with this, or this woman is . . . No. That is impossible. There's no resemblance whatsoever. Just because she doesn't look like her sister doesn't mean—

"The book?" Nicole asks. "If you'll give it to me, I will take it away."

"The book stays with me."

"Will you give Roberta her job back?"

"Not a chance. She broke my rules."

I brace myself for the big reveal, where she'll tell me that Tag has found me. That he knows what I've done. That I'm about to finally meet up with the richly deserved consequences I've eluded for years.

But Nicole just shrugs and heads for the door. "Suit yourself, then. I tried."

I follow her. Surely the other players must be on the porch, waiting. But both the porch and street are empty. No Tag. No uniformed officer waiting to take me into custody, no police car waiting to haul me away.

"Sorry again for all the hassle," Nicole says. I have an irrational impulse to tell her that she needs a warmer coat and should be wearing boots in this kind of weather. But she's an adult, not a child, and I say nothing more as she makes her way carefully down the icy steps and onto the sidewalk. I close the door. Lock it. Reset the alarm.

But locking her out of the house doesn't banish her from my mind. I climb the stairs to my bedroom and withdraw a small wooden box from the top shelf of my closet. Collapsing onto the bed, I open the lid, remove the three photographs tucked inside, and spread them out on the quilt beside me.

The first is of Tag, taken by surprise as he sits at his desk, reading. One hand is in motion, shoving his dark hair back from his forehead. His lips are just beginning to curve into a smile, his eyes shifting from surprise toward laughter.

The second photograph is of my parents, possibly the last picture taken of them before whatever series of mishaps or errors in judgment led to the capsizing of their fishing boat and subsequent drowning the summer I turned eighteen. It is certainly the last picture I took of them, and one of the last times I saw them. They stand together, shoulders not quite touching, faces wearing matching expressions of tolerance over the foolishness of photographs. They are dressed in matching navy-blue windbreakers, their hair cut in the same style by probably the same barber. Mom had no patience for what she called fussiness and frills. Neither of them had ever had much patience for me. I missed them surprisingly little after the first shock of grief had passed.

The last picture is the hardest. It's me, ridiculously young and heavily pregnant and standing sideways to better show off the curve of my belly. My face is alight with hope and love and joy, all emotions that I can only dimly remember, like a fragment of a dream that vanishes on waking. I want to shout a warning to my unconscious young self, but it's far too late for that.

With a sigh, I lay the photos one by one in the box and return it to the shelf. As I'd expected, none of the faces bear any resemblance to that of Nicole. The very idea that my daughter might be alive, that Tag has found her and the two of them have tracked me down and are engaged in some sort of conspiracy of vengeance, is preposterous.

And yet. I can't let it go. Can't let Nicole go. My mental images of my daughter have always been vague and faceless, which made them easier to suppress. Now I see her with breathtaking clarity, wearing ragged jeans and a too-thin coat, shoulders hunched against the coldness of the wind and the world. Maybe she's homeless. Maybe she's lost.

I'm not much for prayer, but I whisper one anyway. "Please. If she's alive, if she's out there somewhere, if she's lost or cold or hurt, please send someone to help her."

And Karma whispers back, *As you do unto someone else's child, so it shall be done unto yours.*

Chapter Fourteen

NICOLE

As soon as I'm out of sight of Andrea's house, I lean up against a telephone pole to breathe and wait for my knees to stop wobbling. Andrea is obviously paranoid, and I'm still freaked out a little by the way her eyes kept looking over my shoulder, as if she really believed I was working with some nefarious person named Tag. The whole thing was a disaster. I've failed to fix things for Roberta. I also didn't get the absolution I was looking for, the reassurance that no real harm was done by me moving that book.

I now have serious doubts about the next stop on the planned trail of reparations that made so much sense this morning, but it's too late to go back now. For one, I've already purchased a replacement copy of the *Inferno* from Barnes & Noble to take to Mrs. Lane, an expenditure I really can't afford. And, I told Ash I was going to do this, and she'll never let me hear the end of it if I say I let two old ladies scare me off. Plus, I've already survived Andrea, so how bad could this be?

My self-talk works up to a point, but when I step onto Mrs. Lane's porch and ring her doorbell, I really hope she won't be home so I can scribble a note and leave the book in her mailbox. Luck is not my friend.

Mrs. Lane responds to the doorbell immediately, almost as if she was expecting me, as wreathed in smiles as if she's known me forever. In my mind, I'd pictured her as a mash-up between my high school librarian and a slobby hoarder with potato chip crumbs on her baggy sweater, but she doesn't bear the slightest resemblance to either. Her comfortably padded body is tucked into a pair of faded blue jeans and a purple caftan with a fringe around the bottom. Gray hair hangs in a loose braid over her shoulder. She's wearing some sort of big green stone around her neck. And she obviously hasn't read any of those online things about what sort of makeup a woman over fifty ought to wear, even though she's got to be pushing seventy.

"Well, hello there!" She sounds genuinely delighted to see me, a total stranger, standing on her porch.

"Hi!" I've utterly forgotten the little speech I'd rehearsed, and this is the only word that presents itself.

"Now where do I know you from?" Her hands ask the question at the same time as her lips. "I can't seem to connect all of the names and faces to each other anymore."

"I'm Nicole, but we haven't actually met."

Her eyebrows climb high in her face and stay there while she looks me over more thoroughly. "Are you sure? You look familiar."

"You've met my sister, so maybe that's it? Roberta? From Sunny Side Up."

I resemble Roberta about as much as a crow resembles a robin, but apparently that's close enough for Mrs. Lane.

"Oh, of course!" She slaps her forehead with one thoroughly beringed hand, and beams at me. Silver bangles jingle at her wrist as she lowers her hand to her side, her expression shifting into a question. "But it's not my cleaning day, and you're not Roberta. What can I do for you?"

I shuffle my feet and hold out the shiny new copy of the *Inferno*. "I'm the one that borrowed your book. I hope you'll accept a replacement copy."

She looks at the book but doesn't touch it, and I blabber on. "I mean, I know it's not the same as the one you had, but I was hoping maybe there wasn't anything particularly special to you about that version? I mean, it all depends where you got it, I know, and if somebody gave it to you, I'm sorry, but—"

"Oh dear," she says, looking alarmed. "You didn't need to spend money on a new copy. Couldn't you . . . I mean, if you're done reading the other one?"

"I gave it to somebody else."

To my absolute surprise, she turns that full-wattage smile on me again. "Oh, you passed it on. That is so wonderful! Did you just love it, then? Does your friend love it, too? How unusual to find a young person who appreciates Dante. And I totally understand how you came to borrow it. You're working, but you get enticed by a cover and you pick the book up just to see what it's about. And then that first incredible page, and you're swept away. Come in, let's talk about books."

Her hand settles on my arm, drawing me into the house.

Curiosity wars with caution. It's not like she's a stranger, I remind myself. Roberta knows her and has been working for her for a while. I've been in the house before. So I let her lead me into the kitchen, which is the polar opposite of Andrea's.

Where hers was cold, stark, and painfully neat, this one is warm and comfortable and redolent of coffee and cookies. Mrs. Lane pours us each a mug from a half-full carafe. "Cream? Sugar?" She searches out a container of half-and-half from the fridge and brings over a bowl of sugar and a spoon. "Or maybe you like flavored? I've got French vanilla and Baileys. Too early for the real Baileys, I guess. I'm just so impressed that somebody from your generation is interested in Dante. Are you an English lit major? Or maybe your thing is philosophy?"

She hands me a mug with a heart and the words *Have You Hugged Your Child Today?* Hers reads, *World's Greatest Social Worker.* This woman is totally nonthreatening, and so lovely that I'm reluctant to tarnish her opinion of me. "So are you a social worker, then?" I point at her mug.

"Forty-five years next month," she says, turning her coffee almost white with French vanilla creamer. "You sure you don't want some?"

"Black is fine." I peer into the still-inky depths of my coffee, hoping to find some sort of magic that will get me out of what I've come to do, but it's just coffee, and I need to tell her the truth. "I haven't actually read it," I confess. "The *Inferno* book."

Mrs. Lane takes a long swallow of her own coffee and leans forward on her elbows, holding her mug in both hands. "You are a bit of a conundrum, my dear. What did you say your name was again?"

"I'm Nicole. Look, Mrs. Lane, I just came to replace the book and—"

"Let's not be so formal. Call me Penelope, but for the love of God, not Penny. I mean, there are worse associations, but Penny Lane? What are the odds? Do you know how many times I've had that song sung at me? I tried to get my husband to take my maiden name, but you know how men are, so I go by Penelope. Now. Tell me why you took the book, then, if it wasn't to read for yourself. It's not like you have a friend who sent you out on a scavenger hunt to locate a copy of the *Inferno*. Or did you? Oh, say you did! That would be so fascinating. I just love it when life gets weird."

She sparkles another smile at me and waits, hands clasped, as if I'm going to tell her some life-altering secret.

I muster a half smile and say, "Awesome. Prepare for life to get weird."

She listens with rapt attention while I tell her about my Object Relocation Program and how it applies, specifically, to her book. I watch her face, dreading the moment when her expression will shift to disappointed, disapproving, or appalled, but she just keeps smiling and nodding.

"What an interesting gift you have," she says when I'm done.

"I . . . What?" I sputter and cough, very nearly spraying a mouthful of coffee everywhere.

"Although I can see it could get you into some sticky places. You move something that belongs to somebody else, and it shifts the course of events. If this were a movie, it's how you'd meet your soul mate."

Okay. I'm two for two on the crazy today. But at least she's a nice kind of crazy, and it's ridiculously easy to confide in her. Maybe because she's a social worker, maybe because I'll never see her again.

"No soul mate for me," I tell her. "It's way more curse than gift, trust me. It lands me in jail, it's causing a divorce, it makes trouble with my family. Roberta's not speaking to me because I moved your book."

"Whyever not? I'm not the least bit upset!"

"The client whose house I moved the book into doesn't feel the same way."

"Oh goodness. Imagine so much fuss over a book! Tell me, has any good ever come from your moving things around?"

Nobody has ever asked me questions like this before. Even Ash, who never condemns me or makes me feel bad, thinks I'm a hapless kleptomaniac with no control over my impulses. "There was the pink flamingo thing," I tell her after a long moment of comfortable silence. She's not pressuring me, not in a hurry, and I feel as close to relaxed as I ever get. "When I was a little kid, I moved one of those plastic flamingos from one neighbor's yard to another, and when he confronted her about stealing it, they ended up going on a date."

"And did that end badly?"

"They've been married for fifteen years. So, I guess not?"

I tell her about some of the other happy outcomes. People who met and bonded over a relocated object and became friends. A woman who discovered her husband was cheating on her when I moved a lipstick from some other woman's purse into her husband's coat pocket during one of Kent's parties. There was weeping on the part of the woman who had been cheated on, and shouting from her husband, and then finally the guilty parties admitted they'd been together. The whole time, I waited in silent terror for somebody to ask how the lipstick got into that pocket in the first place. Nobody ever did, and a few months later, the injured party in the love triangle traded up to a new and better model of husband.

Penelope pats one of my hands in a motherly way.

"Maybe something good will still come of my book that you moved. I'd like to believe so."

"Yeah, I'm not holding my breath. But about that . . ." I pause, wondering if I should ask a question that has just occurred to me. "Could you tell me where you got the book? Do you remember? I can't help feeling like maybe if I find out where the book came from . . . like who owned it last, or whatever . . . if there is some sort of connection, maybe the other client wouldn't be so mad."

For the first time, frown lines crease Penelope's forehead. They have to work hard to be there, I can tell, and I figure she's finally realized what a bizarre conversation this is. But what comes out of her mouth is even further down the rabbit hole.

"Do you think it might be better to just let things work out on their own, instead of meddling? That's always the question. Like when a psychic gets a hit that something bad is about to happen, and when they try to stop it, they actually precipitate the tragedy by trying to intervene. What if your gift is like that?"

I set my cup down and pinch my thigh under the table to make sure I'm not dreaming. "I don't want to *do* anything," I hear my own voice saying. "It's more like . . . research. Like if there really is any sort of connection between whoever owned that book and the woman whose house I moved it to, then I'd know . . . well, that maybe I'm not cursed or crazy. I would like that."

What I'd know, I think, squeezing my hands together between my thighs, is that maybe there's something more to me than a crazy loser jailbird.

Penelope shakes her head. "That makes sense, but I'm sorry. I pick up so many books secondhand, I can't even tell you for sure where that one came from. A library sale, a yard sale, a friend." And then she lights up, all animation again. "What if the connection is between me and this other woman, and not the person the book came from at all? Can you tell me her name?"

I set down my mug and stare at her, wondering if it's possible that anything in my life could be so simple.

"I don't see why I can't tell you that. Her name is Andrea Lester. She's a pharmacist, I think Roberta said."

Penelope thinks for a long moment, then slowly shakes her head. "Nope. Never heard that name, at least not that I remember. Well, it was a fun idea anyway! I would love to be involved; it would feel like living in a story."

I sigh, letting the brief, bright hope leach out of me and the bleakness of reality settle back in. "I should go. Thanks for talking to me."

"Anytime, my dear. Anytime. Come back and talk to me again. And will you let me know if anything comes of this? Here. Let's exchange phone numbers."

"I really don't think anything good is going to come of this one," I tell her as I tap my number into her phone. "But I'll update you."

"You never know, my dear, do you? You just never know."

~

Later that night, when I'm getting ready for bed, my phone rings. Mom, I think, checking in again. Or maybe even Mrs. Lane calling with another crazy idea about my so-called gift. Or Hawk, wanting to talk writing. My heart races a little faster at that thought, but it's an unknown number and I let it go to voice mail.

But then I listen. I always listen, because when you are in the business of moving other people's things around, it's important to be vigilant for impending trouble. I nearly drop the phone in shock when Andrea's voice comes on. "Nicole, please call me. I have a proposition for you."

I can't imagine what she possibly wants, but maybe she's reconsidered my request about giving Roberta the house back. I hit call back, and the phone only rings once before she picks up and says, skipping directly over hello, "Have you found another job yet?"

"I'm not sure what business that is of yours," I answer. "How did you get my number?"

I hear her take a breath and let it out in a whoosh that is probably frustration. "I feel bad that I cost you your job. I got your number from Sunny Side Up."

"I cost myself the job. It's Roberta I wanted you to hire back."

"Roberta will be fine," Andrea says impatiently. "She has plenty of clients. Since you are jobless, you can come clean for me. Be here tomorrow evening. Six o'clock sharp."

"I can't do that."

"So you do have another job?"

"No, but Roberta—"

"Roberta has nothing to do with this. She broke the terms of our agreement by bringing you in. So I'll see you tomorrow?"

"Roberta would never speak to me again," I object, but I'm wavering. Roberta may not ever speak to me again, anyway. And even a few hours a week of work is better than no work at all.

"So, don't tell her," Andrea says.

"I'd never lie to her!"

"Don't lie. Just don't tell her. I'll pay you a hundred and fifty to come in and clean tomorrow."

When I don't answer, she says, as if I've given my consent, "Great. Tomorrow, then. Six o'clock. Don't be late."

She hangs up and leaves me to wrestle with my conscience. I should call her back and tell her no, if only because Roberta is going to have an absolute fit if she finds out about this. On the other hand, I need the money, and Penelope has amped up my curiosity about the book and why it wanted to be moved. I want to know who Tag is, and what his connection is to Andrea. I really want to know whether moving the book will make a difference in her life.

On impulse, I text Penelope.

So, Andrea just called 🙄

She sends a string of star emojis. And?

I'm cleaning her house tomorrow. Apparently. Stay tuned.

More star emojis and a GIF with a unicorn and the word "magic." Then: Breath bated. Update me!

So I don't call Andrea to back out, and I go to sleep knowing I'll be at her house tomorrow at six.

Chapter Fifteen

NICOLE

For once in my life, I'm really trying to be on time, but everything seems to be conspiring against me. Ash slept late, for starters, and when she did wake up, she was grumpy and Arya was fussy. I dropped things and spilled things and now I'm out the door late on the way to the bus. It's been snowing all day, and my boots are still at Kent's. My traction-less sneakers might as well be ice skates on the slippery sidewalk.

Fortunately, my bus is also running a little late, thanks to the snow traffic, and I think maybe I'm going to make it. It's not at the stop yet. I can see it hung up at a red light, both it and me with half a block to go. I am going to make it by the skin of my teeth.

But just as the light changes and the bus begins to move, I feel the telltale prickle at the base of my spine, the one that signals an object demanding my attention. *Damn it, not now.* I accelerate my pace, ignoring the growing compulsion.

A shimmer on the snowbank draws my gaze for a fraction of an instant, and I don't see the patch of ice in front of my feet. My right foot loses traction, and when my left tries to anchor me, it shoots off to the side. For a few seconds, I do the splits, windmilling my arms for balance, but then my right foot skitters farther, and next thing I know, I'm flat on my back.

I lie there, stunned and shaken but not seriously hurt. As I flip over onto my hands and knees, my right hand slips off the sidewalk, and my arm sinks halfway to the elbow in snow. My pinky finger bumps up against the edge of the object that is causing all the fuss. "Really?" I mutter. "You had to drop me in a snowbank? Better be a good one."

I look up at my bus, now at the stop, the doors already closing. Swearing vigorously, I close my fingers around something slick and rectangular, then manage to get my feet under me. With my free hand, I brush as much snow off of my butt and knees as possible, but most of it has already melted and I am now soaked and shivering, pissed off and miserable.

In my hand is a cell phone: wet, muddy, and probably useless. It's in a customized designer phone case that features an endearing picture of a fluffy cat. The screen is shattered. I wouldn't be surprised if someone has accidentally stomped on it with a boot.

Why the phone wants to be rescued, I have no idea, but I drop it in one of the plastic bags I've learned to carry with me for situations exactly like this. And then I stand shivering in the cold wind, waiting for the next bus, which is late. The route takes longer than usual, of course, and the walk from the bus to Andrea's takes forever, and when I finally arrive, it's nearly seven and I can no longer feel my fingers or my toes. My muscles ache from being clenched against the cold.

The door opens before I can ring the bell. Andrea surveys the street behind me, presumably still looking for my nonexistent accomplice, then focuses in on me with a frown.

"You're late."

"There were . . . complications."

"What sort of complications?"

The intensity behind the question reminds me that she might be crazy, but at this point, I don't even care. I'm cold. The house is warm.

I need the money. I want to know what's driving her and why I put the book here.

"Roommate. Roommate's baby. Bus. It's cold, can I come in?"

She steps aside and lets me in. I take off my coat and peel out of my sneakers, looking down in dismay at my socks, which are leaving damp footprints on the hardwood floor. With a sigh, I peel them off too and attempt to dry my bare feet on the doormat.

"All of those things sound more like regular parts of the day than what I could call a complication," Andrea says, staring at my bare feet with obvious distaste. "A little advance planning would render them not a problem."

"Well, in case you hadn't noticed, there was snow, which messed up the bus schedule." Compelled by honesty, I add, "And there was also something that needed attention on the way to the bus."

"What kind of thing?"

"Just an item that wasn't happy to be where it was and wants to be elsewhere."

"And picking up this object required you to roll around in the snow? You're soaked."

"I fell." I stand there, shivering, waiting for her to tell me to get my muddy jeans and bare feet out of her house.

But she's stuck on my relocated object. "This thing you . . . moved. Where did you move it to?"

"It's in my backpack."

"So you stole it."

I flush, even though I'm positive that, this time around, even the law wouldn't find me guilty of stealing. The phone is never going to work again, and nobody would thank me for returning it, even if I knew how to find its owner. Explaining is pointless, but I try anyway. "In this case, the object was buried in a snowbank and is of no use to anybody."

Her head tilts to one side, and she studies me like I'm a painting in a museum—one of those abstract things where heads and body parts are disconnected and you have no idea what the whole thing is supposed to be about. "Are you going to move things from my house, Nicole?"

"I hope not?" I meet her gaze and hold it. "Look. You can ask me before I leave. I never lie."

"Well, you can't work like that. Wait here."

She stalks off, returning a moment later with dry socks and a pair of sweatpants. "Put these on. You know where the laundry room is? Put your wet things in the dryer. Then meet me in the kitchen.

"You can cook, right?" she demands when I reappear, warmer but awkward in the borrowed garments.

"I can follow a recipe. If you want a five-star chef, I am not that person."

She indicates a recipe for oven-grilled chicken and vegetables that is simple and within my capacity. "Once you've got that underway, you can start on laundry." She gives me detailed instructions about what items to wash together or separately, hot and cold, regular loads, and what to do about delicates. She'd be aghast to know that everything I own goes into the same load and gets the same detergent.

And then, thank God, she leaves me alone instead of hovering over my every move.

I start a load of delicates, hoping I got it right, then go back to the kitchen while they wash, starting the chicken and then prepping meals for tomorrow and feeling grateful that I don't have to eat from this menu. Breakfast is a little jar of oatmeal soaked in plain yogurt and fruit. Lunch is a salad, with fresh made-from-scratch dressing.

I pop in my earbuds so I can keep my mind occupied. Tonight I skip the music and choose an audiobook. I've been listening to the classics, part of the self-improvement project I started while I was living with Kent, and I'm immersed in *The Picture of Dorian Gray* when lights blinking on and off draw my attention from the chopping block to Andrea, who is flipping the switch up and down.

I hate being interrupted in the middle of a book. Irritated, I pull the buds out of my ears, right in midsentence. "What?"

"I was talking to you, and you were oblivious. What are you listening to?"

"Dorian Gray."

"Is that a band?"

"Is it . . ." I stop before something sarcastic escapes me. "It's literature. *The Picture of Dorian Gray.* Have you not—"

"I'm familiar." She steps away from the light switch, carries the electric kettle to the sink, and turns on the filtered water. "It wasn't what I expected from you."

I keep my mouth shut, although it takes some doing, venting my annoyance on innocent carrots on the cutting board.

"My apologies." Andrea switches the kettle on. "I made assumptions based on your appearance."

"Just because I have tattoos doesn't mean I'm stupid," I mutter, the whole keeping-my-mouth-shut plan falling apart.

"I see that. What else are you reading?"

"*Moby Dick* is up next, and then *Tess of the d'Urbervilles.*"

"Skip that one. It's depressing." Andrea pulls down a container of loose tea from one of the cabinets and spoons some into a French press. "Would you like tea? It will help warm you."

"Yes. Thank you." I've never been overly fond of tea, but I still feel chilled to the bone, and the idea of a hot beverage of any kind sounds wonderful.

"So, are you taking a college lit class, then?" Andrea asks.

"Nope, I'm improving my mind on my own time."

She pours steaming water into the press. A fragrant aroma wafts upward, and I sniff, involuntarily impressed.

"Pay attention," she says. "This is gyokuro. It's Japanese, and my favorite. Next time, you'll make it. The kettle has a thermometer. Heat the water to one hundred and sixty degrees, and steep for two minutes, no more, no less." She demonstrates by setting a kitchen timer. "Will you want sugar?"

My brain has gotten so hung up on the words "next time" that I stare blankly at the timer and forget to answer.

"Is that a no?" she persists.

"It's a yes. Sugar, please," I say, just to say something. Returning to the cupboard, she pulls down two glass cups, then resumes her interrogation. "Tell me about yourself. Something besides the fact that you move things."

The timer goes off and I watch as she pours the tea. "Well?" she persists.

I add sugar to my cup and take a sip before giving her the bare-bones basics. "High school dropout. Never made it to college. And then I got married to a guy with money and it didn't seem to matter. But now it does."

She waits, letting her face ask the next question.

"I am no longer married. Well, I still am, technically, but not so as you'd notice. And, as you know, I have pissed . . . I mean, I've angered my sister, quite justifiably, and now I'm living with a friend and scrambling for rent money."

"What about the rest of your family? Do you have more siblings?"

One question at a time, she drags it out of me. Brina's resentment and Warner's disappointment, my father's death and my mother's unflagging and heartbreaking hope that someday I'll change and be better. "They are all normal, functional, well-adjusted people," I finish. "And then there's misfit me."

Andrea's eyes are intense, searching my face for something she can't seem to find. I get up and turn my back, washing my cup at the sink, but I can still feel the burn of her gaze. "Have you searched for your parents?" she asks.

I fumble the teacup, just managing to save it from a disastrous crash. I turn to face her. "I don't understand what you're asking. Like I said, my dad died, and Mom still lives in the house I was born in."

"From some of the things you've said, I thought perhaps you were adopted."

And then, as if she's angry all at once, she gets up and stalks out of the room, leaving me wondering what I could have said to offend her.

My clothes are dry, and I change into them and leave the sweatpants neatly folded on the dryer. Andrea appears just as I'm thinking I'm going to have to shout for her. I am not leaving without my money.

"Did you steal anything?" she demands.

"Not the right question."

She huffs in exasperation. "What is the right question, pray tell?"

"Ask me if I relocated anything."

"Oh my God. Well, did you?"

"No. I did not. Although that statue thing on the credenza in the entryway wants to be in the hall closet with the linens. I suspect that might just be me, though, and not a flaw in the universe."

Something flickers in her eyes that might be close to laughter. Maybe. She's impossible to read. Whatever it is vanishes immediately as she counts out ten twenty-dollar bills and puts them in my hand.

I stare at the money and then up at her in confusion. "This is more than we agreed on."

"Go. I'll see you tomorrow."

"I'm coming back tomorrow?"

"Aren't you?" She looks as surprised as if we've discussed this and agreed. "There's more work to be done. Try not to be late."

I hesitate. Tomorrow is writing class, and another chance to try to figure out the puzzle that is Hawk. If I had a car, I could do both. But if I'm relying on the Spokane bus system, there is no possible way. Which means I have to choose, and the choice is clear. Money I need. Complications I don't. It would take me two full days at a minimum-wage job to make what Andrea just paid me for a couple of hours.

"I'll be here," I tell her.

Dismissed, I walk through the dark to the bus stop, careful where I put my feet. I can feel the pull of muscles in my legs that I wrenched when I fell, and I don't need to repeat that maneuver. The snow has stopped, and the air is crisp and cold and tingles my nose. Above, despite the city lights, I can see an array of stars.

While I wait for my bus, I fire off a text to Penelope.

I think she's crazy. But I'm coming back tomorrow. Also, the universe assigned me another project today.

I'm on the bus before an answer comes in. Curiouser and curiouser. Tell me!

I smile at the *Alice in Wonderland* reference, then text: Just an old phone. Not interesting

Au contraire. Fascinating. Can't wait to see where it wants to be

Riding on her enthusiasm, I let myself believe, just for a minute, that I'm not cursed and maybe she's right that everything will work out after all.

Chapter Sixteen

NICOLE

"I have a theory," I tell Graham as soon as I'm settled into my preferred chair in his office. "About why I do what I do. Want to hear it?"

"I'm listening."

My encounter with Penelope has given me courage, and I dive in. "Well, it's this. What if things have a place and purpose in the world, just like people? Objects have energy, right? So maybe there are places where they are supposed to be, and when they are not in those places, that energy gets . . . I don't know . . . off-balance. Like, they end up in the wrong place at the wrong time, mostly because people don't listen and just manhandle things around where they *think* they should be."

Graham says, "And you take it on yourself to . . . relocate . . . these objects to the place where you think they belong."

"I don't exactly take it on myself. And I don't decide where they go. It's more like I'm . . . commissioned."

Graham is wearing *the look*, the expression I expect from people when I try to explain. "If I follow your line of thinking correctly, you believe that you're helping to right the universe by moving other people's things around. Yes?"

When he says it like that, it sounds crazy, but I still nod.

"Don't you think that's maybe a little grandiose? You deciding, for instance, that your husband's money needed to be moved. I suspect, in his opinion, it belonged right where he left it."

Graham will never understand, but I forge ahead anyway. "If this was about grandiosity, I'd be saying that I know where the things are supposed to go. That I'm calling the shots and pulling the strings. It's not like that. I just get a vibe about where an object is supposed to be and I put it there."

"A vibe?"

I sigh. "A strong vibe. A compulsion. Like my skin is turning inside out and I'm being eaten alive from the inside."

"Nicole." Graham's voice is compassionate, his eyes compelling. "I'd like to propose another theory. The theory that the traumatic event you suffered as a child is at the root of this compulsion. Are you willing to explore that?"

My body does the thing it does whenever anybody brings up that day. I feel melted in the middle, hollow in the bones. So I try an evasion.

"Did I tell you I signed up for a creative writing class?"

"That's a great idea," he says, "but let's get back to the subject."

I stick to my chosen track. "Sadly, I had to drop it already, because I found a job. Sort of. Temporarily. One of the other students wants to meet so we can write together."

"Writing can be very healing. It's also an opportunity to find your voice, to figure out what's going on with you and the world. Which is why you're writing down your story when you come here to see me."

Damn, Graham is good. He's gathered up the threads of my meandering and woven them right back into his therapy plan. He holds out the notebook. "How about we put both theories on the shelf for a bit. Finish what you started writing, about that first time you moved something. How about you write for ten minutes, and then we'll spend the rest of the session learning a tapping technique to bring down any anxiety that revisiting the memories brings up for you."

"Whatever it takes to stay out of jail," I mutter, but I'm already opening the book, my fingers impatiently grasping the pen. A need to finish writing out this story is growing in me, and I don't want to be interrupted again before reaching the end. I scan through my scrawl to find the place where I'd left off:

The room felt different. It sucked at her, empty, hungry, wanting something. And she knew what it wanted. It was—

The pen hovers above the page as the memory comes flooding back, vivid and intense. I can smell the coffee and chocolate and baked goods in the shop. I feel my mother's hand holding mine, the coolness of her fingers, the calluses on her palm. I hear the sound of the espresso shots being pulled, the burr of the milk frother, the hum of conversation. My body feels small, as if I'm a child again, with my face tear streaked and that emptiness in my belly and the heat of shame and that sudden knowing that the world wasn't at all what I'd believed it to be.

—the bear. This room wanted the bear. More than wanted. Demanded. Required. And now here was Nicole, but there was no bear and everything felt so terribly, horribly wrong that she could scarcely breathe.

Her feet stopped moving, and she tugged against her mother's hand, wanting to run back out the door. But there was no escape. The door had closed behind her. Mom's grip was kind but firm as she led Nicole up to the counter to order coffee and a hot chocolate with marshmallows. Nicole squeezed her eyes closed and began counting to one hundred, a feat she'd recently mastered at school.

But even with her eyes closed so she couldn't see the weird shimmering in the air, she could feel the emptiness sucking at her. It originated from one place. And it was so strong that curiosity overcame her fear and she opened her eyes to see where it was coming from.

A man sat at a table by himself, in the darkest corner. He had a paper cup of coffee in front of him, but he wasn't drinking it. He had a wild gray beard and long greasy hair and there were rips in the jacket he was wearing. As if he felt Nicole looking at him, he lifted his head and his gaze met hers.

So sad, was what she thought. Tears started trickling down her cheeks again as he bent his head and stared down at the table.

Nicole's mother handed her a cup of hot chocolate and picked up her own coffee, and then chose a spot at the front of the shop near the window. Nicole was sitting right where she could watch the man. She could see the spot where she would have set the bear if she'd brought it with her. By the cup, where the old man's sad eyes would be staring right at it. But she didn't have the bear, and she felt like her skin was crawling with tiny ants and she couldn't just sit here drinking hot chocolate as if everything was all right. Maybe she should talk to him.

Mom would let her go to the bathroom by herself if she asked, because she was a big girl now. She could walk by the man's table on the way and say, "Mister, I wanted to bring you the bear, but they wouldn't let me."

Nicole thought about this plan as she sipped her hot chocolate and stared at the sad man in the torn jacket who was not drinking his coffee.

Just as she'd made up her mind, as she opened her mouth to tell Mom she needed to pee, the man reached down into his coat pocket and brought out something black and held it up to his head. There was a loud bang and everybody in the shop started screaming. The man's head looked wrong and there was red stuff on the wall beside him, and then Mom picked Nicole up like she was a baby and carried her out of the store and into the car, bumping up against other customers who were also scrambling to get out.

"What happened to the man?" Nicole asked as Mom drove straight for home. "Why are all of the people running? What was the bang?"

Mom was crying, which scared Nicole more than anything else because Mom never cried. And she wouldn't answer Nicole's questions, and every night, for months, when Nicole tried to sleep, she was wakened by that loud bang and the red stuff on the wall and the people screaming—

The pen stops moving. I close my eyes, feeling myself floating away, untethered, like a very small balloon.

"Nicole. Let me show you something." Graham's voice is calm, an anchor, drawing me back into my body, which is heavy with guilt and dread. And now I am weeping, an inconsolable grief rising from that old memory and trying to wash itself away, as if an ocean can be emptied.

Graham walks me through an exercise where I tap pressure points on my head, face, and upper body as he says, "Even though I feel frightened, even though I am sad, I love and accept myself absolutely and completely."

I'm more skeptical about this tapping thing than he is about my new theory, but I do it anyway because I've begun to trust him. And I'm shocked when I actually begin to feel grounded and safe. By the time we're done, I'm me again, firmly back in my body, no longer drifting away into an uncertain sky. I dry my eyes. Blow my nose. Commit to coming back next week. When I leave the office, I'm willing to consider that we could be on the right track. I can see Graham's point that this event might be the root of my compulsive behaviors. Maybe I even made up the bear story after the tragedy happened. I was so little. Other memories from that time are incomplete and skewed. Why not this one?

When I reach the waiting room, my brain stops working and my feet stop moving.

Kent is waiting for me.

Chapter Seventeen

Nicole

As always, Kent looks like he just walked off the cover of *GQ*. His smile is polished and perfect. He's wearing the shirt I bought him for Christmas, the one he said he didn't like and never, ever wore.

"Nicole." My name on his lips is a caress. He puts his arms around me and draws me close, and I don't resist. It feels good to be held, warm and safe and familiar.

"What are you doing here?" I ask, my cheek against the rough tweed of his coat.

"I missed you." He pulls away just enough to cup his hand under my chin and turn my face up to his so he can gaze into my eyes. "Come home. We can work this out."

For a moment, caught off guard, I'm tempted to agree. I could go back to my life in the castle. No more worrying about money or finding a place to live. But then I remember the things he said to me the night he threw me out of our condo, the fake diamonds he passed off as real, the truth that I'm actually relieved rather than heartbroken to not be with him anymore.

I stiffen and start to pull away, but his arm tightens, holding me close.

Graham's voice asks, "Everything okay out here?"

"Everything's fine," Kent says. "I just needed to speak with my wife."

"Nicole?" Graham asks.

"Next week, same time?" I ask, aiming for lightness. I don't want to make a scene here in his office.

Graham's eyes, blue and keen, scan my face. He doesn't look convinced. "See you then," he confirms. I look back over my shoulder as Kent sweeps me out the door and into the street and see that Graham is still watching, his forehead creased in a frown.

I hear Ash's question echoing inside my head: "Why did he marry you, Nickle? Have you ever asked yourself that?" And I remember the look in Kent's eyes at the ill-fated intervention, the way his hand clamped around my wrist like a vise, squeezing until my bones hurt.

"I don't think this is a good idea," I say. My voice is too soft, not at all the sort of emphatic denial I was aiming for, and Kent just holds me tighter.

"It's a great idea," he says. "Let me take you out for lunch, and we'll talk about it."

"It's too late for lunch."

"An early dinner, then. Come on. You know you want to." His tone is melting. His hand slides up my back to the nape of my neck, and he bends to kiss me. I turn my head so that his lips land on my cheek. "I can't. I have a job and I'm going to be late."

"Come on, Nicole. You owe me." His voice holds an edge.

My vision clears, as if I've put on glasses, and the world comes into sharper focus. Kent looks frayed around the edges. The stubble on his jaw is well beyond a five-o'clock shadow. There are bags under his eyes, like he's been drinking too much too often, and his right eyelid twitches.

"I owe you?" My voice rises, despite my intention to keep it level. "Right. I moved your money. And then you said that I was a slut and worse than a loser. If I remember correctly, and I'm pretty sure I do, you said the only thing I was good for was fucking, but only in the dark, and that nobody besides you would even want me for that. Well, you know what? I'm pretty sure some other woman can fill that purpose for you. So if you'll excuse me, I have a bus to catch."

This time, when I try to pull away from him, he lets me go. I walk slowly, head high, trying to look dignified. But then I realize I'm probably already late, so abandoning my pride, I break into an awkward trot, my day pack bouncing wildly.

I hear footsteps and Kent jogs up beside me, smooth and easy. "We're not done talking. Forget the bus. I'll drive you."

My stop comes into view. The bus is already there. I run faster, but it's useless, and I slow to a jog and then stop, defeated, as it pulls out into traffic. Andrea won't put up with me being late twice in one week, which leaves me with only one option.

I turn back to Kent. "Fine. You made me miss the bus. The least you can do is get me to my job."

"Of course. Car's this way." He captures my hand, and I don't resist. I need this ride.

As he starts the engine, he says, "Forget this job, whatever it is. Let me take you home."

"I'm not going to just not show up. She's expecting me." It takes all of the willpower I have to stay civil, to keep from shouting, "I am not going home with you. Ever."

Kent's eyebrows lift as I plug the address into his GPS.

"What are you doing up on South Hill?"

"Housekeeper."

He laughs as he pulls out into traffic. "Does your employer know about you and your . . . tendencies?"

I stiffen. "Of course. I told her straight up."

"Christian type, then? All love and forbearance and trying to save you?" He squeezes my thigh, as if to say that he's joking.

But his words are like tiny splinters in my skin, itching and pricking. When I lived with him, it was always this way. Little barbs of criticism under the guise of jokes or helping me to be a better me.

He rests his hand on the back of my neck. "You don't need to clean houses. Come home, Nickle. I forgive you."

The hand is warm, gentle, but his touch no longer melts me. I want to twitch away, acutely aware of the memory of those fingers squeezing my wrist tighter and tighter. Of the unguarded contempt and hatred I've seen in his eyes.

"What do you really want?" I ask, my belly clenching into a knot.

"I don't know what you mean." He sounds hurt.

"Don't play games with me, Mr. Trial Lawyer. I know you."

He sighs and to my relief withdraws his hand and scrubs at one side of his jaw with his fingernails, as if the beard scruff itches. "All right. Fine. I do want you to come home, but I would think that as an act of atonement on your part, you might return the money."

"I don't have it."

"So get it back."

I turn toward him and let all the bitterness of betrayal into my voice. "You know, I had this thought that all of my diamonds might be worth twenty grand. Maybe I could have sold them and given that money to you. But you know what? They aren't even diamonds!"

He laughs, an ugly, brutal sound that scrapes my nerve endings and twists in my belly. "I never said they were, did I? Like I'd turn you and your thieving hands loose with the real thing."

Of course he'd never said they were real. But he hadn't said they weren't. God, I've been so stupid.

"If that's all I'm worth to you, what did you marry me for?" I blurt out, horrified when my voice breaks. He doesn't bother to answer, and I fall into a memory.

I'm standing at the altar in the wedding dress Kent chose for me. It's so tight in the waist it constricts my breathing. Long sleeves cover the ink on my arms. "I love your tattoos, darling, but so many of my associates are uptight," he'd explained, overriding my objections to the dress. Lace itches my shoulders, my wrists, the tops of my too-exposed breasts. I have a crazy impulse to strip it off, right there in front of God and everybody, and run naked down the aisle to freedom.

It's too late. I've already said "I do." Kent slides a ring onto my finger next to the diamond he put there only three months ago when he asked and I said yes.

You're mine now, *his eyes say.* Signed and sealed and paid for. You belong to me.

With a gasp, I surface from the memory straight into a panic attack. My blood whooshes in my ears. My breath keens in my chest. Frantic, I press the button to roll down my window, but Kent hits override on the driver's side.

"My money, Nicole. Where is it?"

"I don't have it."

"So get it."

"I can't."

"Tell me what you did with it!" He grabs a fistful of my hair and twists until it feels like he's going to rip it off my skull, scalp and all.

"It's already moved," I gasp, my panic rising with the pain and his fury. "Gone. I don't know where it is! There's no way to find it."

"Bitch!" He yanks my head from side to side.

I press my hands against the glass and scream, "Help!"

"Stop it, you crazy bitch!"

I scream louder, beating my fists against the glass.

Kent pulls over and hits the brakes, the car sliding sideways on the slippery street. "You have lost your fucking mind!"

His face is red, his jaw clenched so tightly I think I can hear his teeth grinding. I fumble with the door latch, finally getting it open and staggering up and out of the car. Kent peels off, fishtailing, and I stand there, relieved to be free of him and his car but still in panic mode. My heart is pounding so hard, my whole body vibrates with every beat.

I glance around me, anxiety sharpening my awareness of everything that moves. It's dark already, and long stretches of shadow stretch between the streetlights. A man roots around in a dumpster, talking to himself. Two men approach on the sidewalk across the street. My imagination morphs them into depraved sadists. I can almost see the knives in their pockets and bloodstains on their clothes. Maybe the old street dude has dead body parts in his cart and is disposing of them in the dumpster.

Bits of my trauma story bubble up into my consciousness and then sink again. People screaming. Sirens wailing. Mom's arms squeezing me too tight, her fingers digging into my skull as she tries to press my face into her shoulder and keep me from looking at what used to be a man in the corner.

Get a grip, Nicole.

A vehicle slows and pulls toward my side of the street. I start walking, trying to look confident and purposeful. I have mace but it's in my day pack. No time to fumble it out. The vehicle rolls alongside me, keeping pace. The window lowers. I ignore it, keeping my feet moving.

"Hey," a familiar voice says. "What's a nice girl like you doing in a place like this?"

I don't ask myself what Hawk is doing here. I don't remind myself that serial killers are often charming. All I know is that I'm frightened and he is here, and when he asks, "Can I give you a ride?" I open the door and burrow into the passenger seat, feeling like I've found a place of sanctuary.

Chapter Eighteen

Hawk

Nicole is safe.

Which is good, and all that really matters. But the way she huddles into herself, simultaneously crumpled and defiant, makes me want to hurt Kent. For a moment, I allow myself to imagine the satisfying crunch of a fist to that perfect face. But then I remind myself that violence is not the answer, that accelerating insanely to catch up with that asswipe so I can smash my bumper into the back of his immaculate BMW would be a bad idea on every possible level.

"I know you didn't need rescuing," I say, trying to lighten both Nicole's mood and my own, "but thanks for humoring me."

She wraps her arms around herself, shoulders hunched, shivering visibly. "I had everything completely under control." Her voice breaks on a sob, which does something dangerous to my heart. I literally sit on my right hand to keep from reaching out to pat her shoulder or stroke her hair. She draws in a long, quavering breath and says, her voice blurred with tears, "Do you think you could drive me to work?"

"Just call me Jeeves. Where to, my lady?" I keep my voice as easy as I can, acting as if it's entirely normal that she's just jumped out of a car in the middle of a dark street in an unsavory part of the city. Also that it's entirely normal that I just happened to be driving along right at that exact moment.

She gives me an address, and I tap it into my GPS and pull away from the curb, trying to think of what to say and what not to say. She doesn't know that I know that it was her husband's car she just bailed out of. She doesn't know that until last night, I've been paid to keep her under surveillance. Sooner or later, I'm going to have to tell her, and then she'll stop talking to me and I'll never see her again.

Soon, I promise myself. *Not now. Not yet. Let me get her safely to her destination.*

"You're shivering. Let's get you warm." I turn up the heat, even though I'm wearing a heavy jacket and am far from cold myself, and she rewards me with a little hum of pleasure and an easing of the tension in her body, holding both hands in front of the vents.

But then she shoots me a sideways glance and says, "What a coincidence, you driving along just then. What are the odds?"

"Spokane's not that big," I say, eyes on the road.

"Big enough."

This is my opening. Easy and straightforward. All I need to do is spit out the words "I'm not a cop, but I am a PI. Your husband hired me to watch you and find out what you did with his money."

But I don't. I tell myself it's bad timing and for her own good. She's already jumped out of one car tonight. So I try to turn it into a joke. "You didn't answer my texts. You didn't come to class. You owe me a coffee. What was I to do?"

"So you're *stalking* me?"

"'Stalking' is an ugly word. It's not outside the realm of probability that I happened to be here at the right moment. A happy coincidence."

"Serendipity," she says. "Or the Fates playing games again. Or you are a stalker, and I've just jumped from the car of the devil I know straight into the arms of the devil I don't. Figuratively speaking."

She's got one hand on the door latch, her eyes on me, wariness evident in every line of her body.

"Look," I say, "jumping out of cars in dubious neighborhoods after dark might not be your wisest course of action."

She tightens up again at that, arms wrapping around her body, shoulders rising. "Trust me. It was definitely the right thing to do last time, and I'll do it again if I have to."

"Don't jump. I'll pull over for you. But I ask you to think twice. It's not safe out there."

"Like it's safe in here?"

"Contrary to all appearances, yes."

"Yeah, I think I'll take my chances with the out there," she says. "Guardian angel you are not."

I slow, pulling over toward the curb, digging in my pocket for my PI creds. "Does it help at all if I tell you I have a license for the stalking?"

I stop, as close to a streetlamp as I can get, hand her my creds, and turn on the dome light. She's still poised to bolt, but she accepts my license and stares at it, and then at me.

"Wait. So you're a private investigator? Why on earth . . ." She stops. Her eyes spark with anger. "Goddamn son of a bitch. You're working for Kent."

"*Was*," I say. "*Was* working for Kent. I quit."

"And I should believe anything that comes out of your lips? You were following me that day at Goodwill. And the writing class!" Her fear has been replaced by outright fury. I'd much prefer for her to look at me adoringly, but I'll take rage over fear on a woman's face any day of the week.

"The Goodwill store, yes. The writing class, no. I registered for that a month ago."

"Oh no," she says. "Oh my God. You told him about the woman and the jacket."

"I didn't. I swear he doesn't know."

She has the door open and her seat belt off, ready to bail, but she's still in the vehicle, staring me down. "I guess I can believe that, since he was just trying to get that info from me. Why didn't you tell him?"

"Something seemed off. You didn't match what he said about you. And Kara seemed to really need the cash."

"That's her name? Kara?"

She looks genuinely surprised, and I ask, "So you don't know her, then?"

"How would I know her?"

"I thought maybe the two of you were in it together."

She laughs, half amusement and half bitterness. "If only life were that simple. The money wanted that jacket and so did she. I had nothing to do with any of it; it was all fate." She makes a move to get out, then stops. "Wait. If you quit working for Kent, why were you stalking me just now?"

"Because when I told him I was off the case, he sounded . . . I was worried about you. Bona fide hero complex right here."

I take a breath. She's still in the Jeep. Still listening. I've got one chance to buy a little trust, at least enough trust to get her somewhere safe.

"Please," I say. "Can you close the door? We'll just sit right here and you can jump out at any time. Let me explain."

Her expression shifts, and I can see she's come to a decision. I hold my breath.

"Maybe you can drive while you explain? I don't want to be late."

"Whatever you want," I say, a wave of relief washing over me.

"One minute." She takes a picture of my PI license and taps a few buttons on her phone. "There. I've sent this to my friend, so if I disappear, the cops will know where to start looking. Now you can drive."

I shift into gear and ease out into the street.

"Talk," she says.

"Okay. I'd worked a case with your husband's firm before. When he called and told me you'd stolen money from the company, I thought—"

"He said I what? First of all, I don't steal things, I relocate them. And second, if that was company money, then what the hell was it doing at home in his office drawer, I'd like to know?"

I smack my hand on the steering wheel. "Damn. I knew something was off."

"What else did he tell you?"

I'm way out of line by all professional standards. Kent was my client, right or wrong, and I owe him confidentiality. Ethically, though, and definitely emotionally, I need to have this conversation. And I love seeing Nicole like this, blazing with righteous indignation.

"He said you were a kleptomaniac. He hired me to follow you, tell him where you were and what you were doing. Bonus if I figured out what you'd done with the money and got it back."

"But you didn't tell him about the coat. And the woman I gave it to."

"I didn't. Listen. After I met you, it seemed all wrong and upside down. I didn't believe him, so I—"

"Oh, you should totally believe him," she interrupts. "I mean, I've relocated a ton of things that don't belong to me. And I've been to jail a lot. But I don't do it, like, out of malice. I'd explain, but you'd never understand. Nobody ever does. Well, except maybe Penelope, but she's unusual."

"Your location is on the left," my GPS interrupts, maliciously, I think, as if it knows this is the worst possible timing, and I pull into the driveway of what looks like a show house—immaculate and un-lived-in.

"This your stop?"

"Yep. This is it. Thanks for rescuing me. Again. Although I would have been fine."

"I could wait and give you a ride home. And then you could explain more about relocating things."

"Or not." She's out of the Jeep now, but the door is still open and she bends to look in at me. "How do I know you didn't just make this all up? Or that you're not still working for him?"

"Because of what just happened," I tell her. "Last night, when I said I was off the case, Kent said, 'I guess I'll have to get it out of her myself, one way or another.' And that's why I was worried, and why I kept an eye on you today. Did he hurt you?"

"Not so's you'd notice," she says, but her hand goes to the back of her head, and I imagine him smacking her, or pulling her hair. "I gotta go. Andrea's not a fan of me being late."

I lean across and catch the door before it closes. "At least do this for me, will you? Text me when you leave. And when you get on the bus. And when you get home."

"Kent's an asshole, but I don't think he'd—"

"He's not the only one I'm worried about. There's a woman who went missing yesterday. They found her purse in a dumpster. Not a good time for a woman to be out alone after dark."

She hesitates. "No promises," she says. "But maybe." And then she's walking up the driveway. The door opens before she makes it to the porch, and a woman stands there, looking not at her but at my Jeep, as if she can somehow see me despite the darkness and the glare of my headlights. I wait until they turn and go inside, and still I sit there, watching for signs of danger, until my own common sense tells me I'm acting like a stalker and I force myself to pull out of the driveway and take myself home.

Chapter Nineteen

ANDREA

Damn Nicole. Damn the book. Damn Tag and the memories, and above all, damn my own weakness. Bad enough that I keep inventing cleaning jobs so she'll come back and I can try to get the answers I need, but now here she is, getting dropped off by some unknown person, hidden from me by the dark.

"Who's that?" I demand, as if I have every right to know who she catches rides with.

"Just a guy. His name is Hawk, not Tag, and he doesn't know you. Can I come in?" She brushes past me into the house to take off her shoes. Something is wrong. Behind her bravado, she seems bruised and bedraggled, even though there's not a visible mark on her, other than the mascara smears under eyes that are red from tears.

I want to pepper her with questions. *Are you all right? Did somebody hurt you?*

All of which shouldn't matter to me at all. I hardly know her. Both evidence and logic tell me that she cannot be my daughter, and that she isn't a player in some bizarre game instigated by Tag. His copy of the *Inferno* showing up in my house is just a crazy coincidence. But as hard as I try, I can't explain the way she stirs my own emotions, resurrecting a flurry of sharp-angled memory fragments. Ever since we met, I've felt like a snow globe that has just been shaken.

Fear. Fear of pursuit, fear of myself, fear of Tag. His hands tight on my wrists. His face, distorted like a Picasso. City streets, bewildering and unfamiliar. A series of cheap motels. A hospital, the lights too bright, the sounds jagged. The only constant through it all, the wails of a baby that won't be soothed and an ever-rising panic.

"Are you all right?" Nicole asks.

I shake off the intrusive memory flashes. "I'm fine. Let me show you what I want you to do." Today it's windows. I'd meant to have her come and clean for me just the one time, so I could ask her some questions. But her answers weren't good enough. So I told her to come back the next day, to scrub walls and the insides of kitchen cabinets. This time, I couldn't think of anything I needed done and came up with washing windows.

She glances expressively from the cleaning supplies to the living room picture window and back to me. "Windows. In the winter." Her voice is heavy with sarcasm and disbelief.

"Windows get dirty all year round, not just in the summer. You'll only need to do the insides."

Duh. She's thinking the word, even though she doesn't say it. If I'm going to keep having her come back—if—I'll need to come up with better chores. Rent a steam cleaner and have her do the carpets. Maybe she could even paint some walls. "You don't want to do windows, feel free to leave," I say.

Her hands come up, palms out. "Got it, boss. Whatever you say."

She picks up the window cleaner and a roll of paper towels, and I walk away and take refuge in my study where she won't see that I'm out of control. I press the palms of my hands against my eyes, trying to blot out the images, to stop my brain from its frenzied attempt to assemble disconnected fragments into a meaningful narrative, but it's like trying to stop the world from turning.

A face surfaces. Not Tag, this time, but Ronda. Strained and worried, checking us into a motel. Terrified while I'm curled into a shivering ball of misery. Holding the baby as if she's a bomb about to explode.

And it occurs to me that Ronda is the one person who might help me piece my memories together, who might even know Tag's whereabouts. We were best friends all through high school. We lost touch some when I went off to college, but when I dropped out because of the pregnancy and moved back to Richland, we picked our friendship up right where we'd left off. But I haven't spoken to her in thirty years. I have no idea where she is, or if she's even still alive. If she is, and if I can find her, contacting her means breaking the cover I've now maintained for more than half of my life. A couple of weeks ago, I wouldn't have dreamed of taking the risk, but I need to do something to stop my free fall into insanity.

A tap at the study door jolts my heart into an extra beat, sending adrenaline surging through my body.

"I've brought tea," Nicole's voice calls. "Can I come in?"

I drag in one full breath, and then another. Smooth my hair. The cracks in my facade are forming faster than I can mend them, and I can't seem to hold myself together long enough to answer.

"Andrea?" Nicole sounds tentative, worried. The door nudges open.

Sylvester slips through the opening and trots over to me, meowing around my ankles. I pick him up and set him in my lap, using him both to calm myself and as an excuse to hide my shaking hands.

Nicole sets a tray on the desk. Teapot and two cups. Sugar bowl. Cream.

Digging deep for my usual sarcasm, I say, "Don't tell me. The teapot wanted to be in here instead of in the kitchen."

Nicole flushes. "I thought maybe you'd like some tea." And then, all in a rush: "Actually, I needed tea, but I thought maybe you'd like some, too."

She's washed the mascara off her face, but her eyes are, if anything, more red than when she came in, and there's a wobble in her voice. An unexpected desire washes through me. I want to hug her, to make soothing little noises and stroke her back. I want to tell her that everything will be okay, she can get through this, whatever it is.

But I cannot afford to trade tea and sympathy with Nicole. She's already made too much of an inroad into my life. So I give her a repressive look and say, "Next time, please leave the teapot where it belongs, even if it starts talking to you. Did you get the windows done?"

"I did."

"Well, good. In the future, keep in mind that I'm not paying you to sit around and drink tea."

"So there is a future?" she asks. "You want me back?"

I need to end this. Now. Before I get sucked in any deeper. But instead I hear my voice saying, "I'll see you tomorrow. I'm renting a carpet cleaner and you can do the upstairs."

"I'll be here."

I can see that I've hurt her, and my traitorous heart aches to take back what I've said as she turns and stalks toward the door, back rigid, head held high.

Instead, I ask, "Did you move anything?"

"I did not."

"Come back here so I can pay you."

Stiff as a board, she comes back and stands silent while I count out her money. She folds it, pockets it, and exits my office, still without saying a word. Sylvester in my arms, I follow to let her out, standing in the open doorway to watch until she vanishes into the dark and the fog. Whoever brought her here is apparently not somebody who will take her home.

I lock the door. Set the alarm. Feed Sylvester. And all the while, I carry on an internal debate about Ronda. There's no harm in looking, I tell myself. If I succeed in locating her, there's no need to act on it.

Plus, the chances of finding her are slim. She could be married with a different last name. She could be dead. She could have moved to Florida or out of the country altogether.

When it becomes clear that my brain is not going to quiet until I at least give it a try, I sit down at my desk. "Five minutes," I mutter. "And then I'm letting this go." Since I don't do Facebook or other social media, I type *Ronda Porter Richland* into Google. A variety of sites pop up, hinting that they have found this person and have a range of information, from contact number and address to legal records.

I choose one and click, and it leads me down a rabbit hole of sequential privacy violations I can't afford to take. *All of your information is anonymous and protected,* it declares, but requires me to enter my email address. I create a new Gmail account and type that in. Then it asks for identifying information, which I make up. And then, dangling the promise of answering all of my questions about Ronda Porter, it demands a credit card.

By now, I'm in too deep to back out. So I put in the card number, and a few clicks later, I'm looking at a phone number for a Ronda Porter in Pasco, Washington. There's no picture, but the birth date is right, and Pasco is right across the river from Richland, where we both grew up.

My hands are shaking again as I pick up my phone and dial. What will I say to her after all these years? "Hey, Ronda, how've you been?" As it turns out, I say nothing because voice mail picks up. Her voice on the recording sounds older, hoarser, as if she's spent the last thirty years smoking a pack a day. But it's definitely hers. I hang up without leaving a message.

The call has sent my anxiety skyrocketing. I can feel my heart racing; I can barely catch my breath. What a stupid idea to call. All I've done is throw gasoline on an already blazing fire.

The phone rings. I stare in dismay as the number I just called flashes across the screen. I can't do this. I won't do this. Turning off the ringer,

I shove the phone into my desk drawer and slam it shut. *Damn, damn, damn.* She'll get my voice mail recording. She'll know it's me.

I have got to get myself together so I can think. Drawing on all of my willpower and long years of practice, I engage anxiety lockdown protocol, full alert. Double dose of meds. Exercise. Meditation. It's worked a thousand times before, but today it is not even close to being enough.

Chapter Twenty

NICOLE

Penelope: Anything new?

Nickle: My husband hired a PI who unhired himself and is maybe now my friend

Penelope: Is he dreamy?

Which is exactly the word Ash comes up with that night when I tell her about Hawk.

"Dreamy" isn't even close to the right word for whatever Hawk is. He makes me feel the kind of wide awake you get stepping outside on a cold winter morning. Frosty air crinkling the inside of your nose, your hands and feet tingling with cold, sunlight on snow dazzling your eyes.

"Try bracing," I say to Ash. "Like a north wind. Also, even if he was dreamy, he is—or was—working for Kent. If he's even legit."

"He gave you a card, right?" she queries. "Let's look up his business."

"Don't you have to be at work?"

She glances at the clock. "I've got fifteen minutes. Come on. I wanna see." We sit side by side on the couch with my laptop balanced between us, and Google takes us to HawkeyePI.com. I have to admit that the site looks professional and legit. Ash clicks on the pic of Hawk's face to make it bigger.

"See? Not dreamy," I say.

She grabs the laptop and brings it closer to her own face. "Those eyes, though. And he doesn't look ordinary and boring. Hook me up; I'll date him."

For some reason, that comment grits like sand between my teeth. Ash jabs her elbow into my ribs. "Don't tell me you aren't interested. You're jealous at the very thought. You looked like you smelled rotten eggs just now."

"Just because he has a website doesn't mean—"

"So call Kent, and check on his story."

"You think my *husband*, to whom I am still married, in case you've forgotten, is going to admit he hired a PI to stalk me? Besides, I don't want to talk to Kent again. Ever."

Ash rolls her eyes. "He's an asshole. Granted. But you are a coward."

"You want to talk to him? Be my guest. Date *him* if you like."

She puts her arms around me and laughs when I stay stiff and don't hug her back. "This isn't about Kent. This is about this Hawk guy and the fact that you are scared to give him a chance."

Ash is wrong, or at least partly. The problem isn't really Hawk or Kent, it's me. I can't be trusted with people any more than I can be trusted with their belongings. But Ash is relentless. "Dare you to go out with him. Wait. You'll never do that. So make it this. Go to class tomorrow and talk to him again."

"I have to be at Andrea's by six. Plus, I've already missed two classes and I'm behind."

"Excuses, excuses. You're just chicken." She actually makes clucking noises, and if I didn't love her so much, I'd want to smack her. There's no real reason not to go to the class. Hawk has texted me assignments and Word docs with careful notes. I've read everything and done the exercises. I've experimented with freewriting, and shortlisted the topics I'd like to write about from the list we made earlier.

But. I have enough going on without the class, and I certainly do not need a raptor-eyed private investigator anywhere near me. "Fine, I'm a chicken," I tell her. "Go to work. And be careful."

"Yeah, yeah. Got it. But I am setting my alarm to wake up early tomorrow afternoon so you have no excuse not to be out of here in time to make that class. Four o'clock, right?"

I have no intention of going to the class, I tell myself. In the morning, when Ash stumbles in, exhausted from a hard night, I inform her she should sleep in because I'm staying right here until it's time to go to Andrea's. And still, somehow, at two minutes before four, I find myself standing in the classroom doorway, still carrying on an internal argument with myself.

Just because I'm here doesn't mean I need to talk to Hawk. I certainly don't need to sit beside him. I can leave at any time. The only reason I feel shaky and breathless is because I'm nervous about walking into a classroom. I'm searching the room for the best place to sit, not because I'm looking for long black hair and broad shoulders and . . .

His head turns, as if he's felt me standing there, and an incandescent smile lights his face when he sees me. As I sink into the empty chair beside him, it feels so inevitable, I wonder why I bothered to resist.

"I'd about given up on you," he says, shifting his body toward the aisle to make more room.

"You didn't know I was coming?" I hold my breath for the answer. If he didn't know, then he's no longer tracking my movements.

"I did not."

The professor starts talking, eliminating any further conversation. "How are those short stories coming?" he asks. "Next week we'll be reading them aloud in class." He holds up his hand for silence at the murmur that follows his words. "Come on, people, this is a writing class. If you want your writing to be yours alone, then I suggest you drop the class and keep a journal." He surveys us all, making direct eye

Kerry Anne King

contact with me, and says, "Confession time. Hands up. Who hasn't even started yet?"

I freeze under his gaze, my hands staying right where they are on the table in front of me, even though I haven't written word one. But other hands go up around the room, and a woman near the front says, "Every time I look at that blank page, it's like I forget what words are." Laughter goes around the classroom at that, and I suddenly realize that I'm not the only one.

"So here's what we're doing, then," the professor says. "The rest of this class is devoted to getting words onto that page so it is no longer blank. Any words. You can delete them later if you don't like the first ones to volunteer. Ready? Let's go."

I open a new document on my laptop and stare at the blinking cursor, but don't type. It's not that I can't think of any words, it's that there are too many, a jumble of them clamoring to get onto the page, and I don't have any idea what order I should put them in. Beside me, Hawk is typing away, so absorbed in what he's doing that he doesn't even notice me glancing at his work. The professor looks at me and smiles encouragingly, and I start moving my fingers so it will at least look like I'm working.

> *That flamingo stood on Mr. Kennedy's lawn as if it belonged there, but it was a bird caught in a spell. The whole neighborhood thought it was tacky lawn art, but Nicole knew better . . .*

No, wait. This isn't about me, even though the flamingo thing happened. This is fiction. The girl in this story could be anybody. Maybe she has a magical gift. That would make Penelope happy. I delete *Nicole* and type in *Bethany*, for no other reason than that it's the first name that presents itself for consideration. Then I keep going.

It was under a curse, poor thing, trapped in plastic, unable to move from the lawn where it found itself. Bethany looked into his painted black eyes and felt his fear and frustration. He couldn't fly and he couldn't walk and he wanted, needed to move . . .

Just as it happened in Graham's office, I get caught up in what I'm writing. I forget about the classroom and about Hawk. I'm aware only of my fingers moving on the keys, of thoughts and ideas and feelings matching up with words and flowing out onto my screen.

"Time," the professor calls out.

I blink and look up, feeling like it's impossible that an hour has gone by. A warm glow fills me, a lightness, the same sort of emotional release I get when I've successfully moved an object.

"Remember to save your work," the professor goes on. "Not much in the world sadder than losing an hour of inspiration. Finish those up at home over the weekend, and come in prepared to read on Tuesday."

Feeling dazed, I save the file, but still sit there, not wanting to shatter this moment. When I put my laptop away, I'll be crossing a portal into my usual reality. Walking in the cold and dark to the bus. Deflecting Andrea's intrusive questions.

Beside me, Hawk stretches and stows his laptop in his bag. He grins at me. "Can't wait to hear what you're writing."

That breaks the spell. Writing is one thing. People reading what I've written is something else again. I shiver and close the laptop. "It's just words on a page. Who knows if they even make sense?"

"That's what revision is for," he says. "If they don't make sense, you swap 'em out for other words." He shifts in his chair. Clears his throat. "Listen. If you'd like, we could go over our work together on Sunday before we have to share with the class. Get some feedback, polish it up a little."

When I don't answer, because I don't know what to say, he keeps talking. "You still owe me a coffee. And you could maybe tell me about moving things."

"Relocating. That's what I'm writing," I blurt out. "A woman who relocates objects."

"Cool," he says. "Mine's about a PI. I've written a bunch of crappy novels about him already. That's my big confession. So. About Sunday?"

This is a very bad idea. But Ash is in my head, clucking like a chicken, and it would be awesome to have somebody look at my story before I share it with the class. If I finish it. If I decide to come back. "Fine," I hear myself say, as if from a distance. "When? Where?"

"Say, two o'clock? I'm kind of in love with Forza's, or we could do Starbucks if you'd rather."

"Buses are sketchy on Sunday, so maybe Starbucks."

"Or I could pick you up. Just as a matter of convenience, of course. Not like this is a date or anything."

Again, he shifts in his chair, and it strikes me that he's nervous about asking me. There's a guardedness in his expression, as if he's braced against a blow, which makes me feel more at ease.

"All right," I say. "Pick me up at two. I'm gonna assume that you know where I live."

He flushes, and I laugh as I get to my feet and shoulder my day pack. "See you Sunday."

All evening while I'm cleaning carpets at Andrea's, my head is alternately full of my story and the expression on Hawk's face when he asked me to meet him for a non-date. But then my phone buzzes with a text, and it's Mom, who hates texting. Call as soon as you can.

Which is obviously now, whether Andrea approves or not. I turn off the noisy carpet cleaner and call, demanding, "What's happened? What's wrong?" the instant she answers.

"Nothing's wrong! I just needed to talk to you because I realized we're going to have to celebrate your birthday early this year."

"What? Why? I'm working, can we do this later?" Worry shifts to an off-balance sensation, as if I'm trying to walk on uneven stilts.

"I'm thinking this Sunday. Since you'll be gone over your actual birthday."

"Where am I going to be?" I ask cautiously. If she has knowledge that Kent is sending me to prison, surely she wouldn't sound so chirpy.

"Oh, you don't have to pretend with me. Kent told me all about it."

"About . . ."

"Mexico. And your second honeymoon."

"Mom—"

"A second honeymoon on your birthday is so romantic. Isn't that just like Kent? I knew the two of you would patch things up. I'm so happy for you. Nicole? Are you there?"

"I'm here." I dig my fingernails into the palm of my hand to help me keep my mouth shut. Of all the manipulative moves Kent could make, this totally tops the bullshit heap. "Do you really think a romantic getaway with the man who is divorcing me is a good idea?" I ask.

"He still loves you, honey," Mom says. "In spite of everything. That's the whole point of the second honeymoon. Not getting divorced."

Words do not present themselves. I can't tell Mom that I don't want to be loved "in spite of everything." I want to be loved because of who I am. A ridiculously hopeless want, for someone like me, but I'm holding out for it anyway. Plus, there are still the things Kent said to me the night he locked me out of our condo. And the question that Ash has planted about why a man like him wanted to marry a woman like me in the first place. And the diamonds that are not diamonds, and the fact that I thought he was going to pull a chunk of my hair out by the roots yesterday.

But my family has always believed he hung the moon, and I don't know how to tell my mother any of these things. If I tell her and she doesn't believe me, I think I'll be broken beyond repair. Before I can think of a valid excuse, she sighs. "You'll do what you want, of course. You always do. But I've already told the others we're celebrating your birthday on Sunday."

"Do you really think that's a good idea? Roberta and Brina won't—"

"Honey. It's your birthday. I'll talk to the girls. You've been doing so well, and this is a perfect opportunity for you all to remember how much you love each other. Bring your friend and the baby. That will be lovely."

"I don't know—I have plans."

"I think family is more important than any other plans you may have made."

I'd have to be a monster to argue with that.

Chapter Twenty-One

NICOLE

Nicole: Andrea still crazy. Family dinner tonight
   Penelope: How lovely!
   Nicole: Not so lovely. They all hate me
   Penelope: Oh, it can't be as bad as all that
   Nicole: Now you're the crazy person

~

"You're a saint for coming," I say to Ash as I jiggle Arya, who is fussing because she wants to get down and crawl around on the floor of the bus.

"Hey, it's free cake," Ash says. "And dinner. Not exactly a martyrdom thing."

"Nothing is free. You'll see. This cake is on the front lines of a war zone."

Ash laughs, as if I'm joking. "I've got baby wipes. We can clean up exploding cake. While we're talking war zones, have you called Kent and told him how much you are not going on a second honeymoon? Or how much you did not appreciate the private investigator thing?"

I haven't, and she knows I haven't, so I say nothing and watch the streets go by. The snowbanks are grimy; the whole city looks like a jail. Which is fitting, because we're on our way to an event that feels more like an execution than a celebration. I haven't talked to any of my siblings since the intervention. Maybe Mom has the power to prevent outright bloodshed, but she's delusional if she thinks they will embrace me with open joy and forgiveness just because I happen to be turning thirty.

At some point in this dinner, I will have to tell them that there is no second honeymoon. That my diamonds were fakes. That my husband hired a private investigator to follow me. And Brina will ask what makes me think I deserve real diamonds. Roberta will ask me what I expect when I steal that kind of money. And they will all make me feel horrible for not agreeing to the mythical second honeymoon in Mexico.

"Sooner or later, you have to talk to Kent," Ash says. "Do you think he'll be at the party?"

"Oh my God." I stare at her, aghast. I hadn't even considered this possibility, and I totally should have.

"Don't let him manipulate you," Ash instructs. "And tell your family he's an abusive asshole, for fuck's sake."

"He doesn't. I can't—"

"For a woman who has actually lived on the street, you are so incredibly naive. You do know that abuse doesn't necessarily mean pounding a woman to a pulp, right?"

"He didn't—"

She ticks items off on her fingers. "He was always making you feel like shit about your legal stuff, your education, your appearance. Tell me he wasn't."

"He was just trying to . . . help me be better," I protest, even as memory after memory confirms what Ash has just said. What Kent made me feel, on a regular basis, was ineffective, incompetent, graceless, and worthless, all tangled up in the belief that he somehow loved me anyhow and was doing his best to help me improve.

And he has hurt me. My scalp is still tender when I brush my hair. When I think about him showing up for dinner, I feel an actual jolt of fear, wondering what else he might do to humiliate me in front of my family. Does he still think he can make me get the money back, or is he playing some twisted revenge game?

By the time we're walking up the street to Mom's house, I'm a wreck. The fact that I don't see Kent's car anywhere makes me feel only marginally better. I pause in the driveway, looking at all of the familiar vehicles and thinking maybe I can still escape this. I'll send Ash and Arya in as a peace offering, and make a run for it.

But Mom has been watching for us. She flings the door open while we're still walking up the sidewalk and runs out to wrap me in a hug. "I've missed you so much! Happy early birthday!"

Then she hugs Ash and croons over Arya. "Let's get you all inside where it's warm. Go join the others in the living room. Dinner will be ready in a few minutes."

"Let me help with dinner," I coax as she takes our coats. If I can go into the kitchen, it will let me delay facing the rest of the family.

But Mom's not having it. "No, no. It's your birthday. You take your guest on in and be comfortable." She hugs me again, then trots back to the kitchen. I drag my reluctant feet into the living room. Faces turn our way, not exactly filled with joy and light at the sight of me.

"This is Ash," I say, breaking the silence. "Ash, this is my brother, Warner, and his wife, Betts. And that's Brina, and Roberta's husband, Darryl, and these are all my nieces whose names I know you cannot possibly remember."

Brina doesn't get up from where she's scrolling through her phone in front of the fireplace, but glances up long enough to say, "Hey, Ash. Nice to meet you." She doesn't say anything directly to me, but at least she hasn't launched hostilities. Clearly, Mom has given her the "your father is dead, you need to love each other" speech.

Warner gets up, shakes hands with Ash, and hugs me. "Missed you, Nickle."

"Missed you, too."

Darryl and the kids all say hi to Ash, and everybody falls in love with Arya on sight. She's shy for a minute, hiding her face in Ash's shoulder and peeking out at the assembly, but then gets down on the floor, crawling from one person to another, smiling and flirting with them all between making attempts to get her hands on every breakable item in the room.

The mouthwatering savory aroma of lasagna and garlic bread, my birthday-dinner tradition since as long as I can remember, wafts into the room. I breathe it in and relax a little. Maybe this whole thing won't be as bad as I'd expected. Everybody is making an effort to be civil. Roberta is safely tucked away in the kitchen with Mom, so she's not here to glare at me.

And then the doorbell rings.

Every adult in the room stiffens, like dogs on point. Nobody gets up. Mom doesn't pop out of the kitchen. The bell rings again. Eyes turn in my direction.

"Is somebody going to get that?" I ask, presentiment crawling over my skin.

"Just because it's your birthday doesn't mean you're too old to open the door," Brina grumbles. "You get it."

There's no reason and every reason for me not to do as she says. When the bell rings again and nobody makes a move, I get to my feet. Slowly, like I'm sleepwalking through a nightmare, I move down the hallway and open the door.

Kent stands on the porch, beaming as if he is the gift of the century. "Surprise!" he says. His arms circle my shoulders and he crushes me hard against his chest. Resistance wells up, thick and hot, but I don't struggle, even when he bends his head and kisses me.

"Let me go," I whisper, holding myself stiff while running a whole new mantra through my brain. *Don't struggle. Don't flail, don't twist, don't kick him in the balls. It's your birthday. Make your mother happy.*

Kent laughs and bends down to kiss me again. I turn my face away, and his lips land on my cheek. "I'm powerless before your charms," he says, loudly enough for everybody to hear, even in the next room. He tucks me against his side with an arm clamped around my waist and propels me into the living room, exuding smiles and charm.

Playing to the jury, I think. *And they are already all on his side.*

Brina looks envious. My nieces wonderstruck, lips slightly parted and eyes unabashedly soaking in Kent's undeniable sexiness. Warner and Darryl get up to shake his hand. Ash's eyes meet mine, clearly conveying the message *I told you so.*

Mom bustles in from the kitchen, smiling as if all of her dreams have come true. "Kent, my dear. Your timing is perfect. We are just getting ready to sit down and eat."

He releases me so he can hug her and drop a kiss on her cheek. "It smells delicious, Mom."

Standing here, with all of the people I love looking at us like Kent is the messiah and I'm some dysfunctional stranger, a flash of insight shows me that our relationship has been skewed from the beginning.

Since the day I met him, he's been painting us both the way he wants people to see us, and doing it with such bold and vivid strokes on such a large canvas that I've believed his story, have allowed myself to become a character that he's shaping. In the version of us that Kent is intent on creating, he's a long-suffering hero, attempting without much success to reform me into the polished, sophisticated woman I could become, if only I were not so fatally flawed.

I've felt indebted to him. Grateful for his patience and forbearance. Flashes of memory come at me, rapid fire.

Kent laying out an outfit for me before going out for dinner with high-powered friends, then supervising and offering advice as I do my hair, my makeup. Casually and carelessly mussing both hair and lip-stick in the car with a passionate kiss, not giving me time to repair the damages before joining our dinner party. Laying his hand on my wrist at the table and accidentally sliding my sleeve midway up my forearm, revealing the tattoos he'd previously insisted I conceal. I had never even considered that he might be doing it on purpose, that my humiliation and sense of inadequacy fed some insatiable hunger.

The shift in perspective makes me feel disoriented, as if I'm stand-ing in a dark space erratically lit by a frenetic strobe light. Arya crawls over to me and holds up her arms, babbling, and I scoop her up, grate-fully, and hold her tight, burying my face in her silken hair.

"Well, come and let's have dinner," Mom says. "I'm sure everybody is starving. I know I am."

I carry Arya into the dining room, secure her into the high chair set up for her, and drop into the chair beside it. Ash will sit on the other side. The chair at the end, beside me, has been Warner's ever since my father died. Perfect. At worst, Kent will be seated right across from me, and there's no way for him to sit next to me.

But nobody else is sitting. They all stand around the table, waiting.

Roberta looks at me like I'm a bug she'd step on already if it weren't for the fact that I would make a stain on the carpet.

"Warner, would you say the blessing, please?" Mom asks. Warner bows his head and reaches out his hands to the people on either side of him. My face flushes as I realize my crime; we always stand in a cir-cle and join hands for a blessing when there's a special occasion. As I shove back my chair and get to my feet, my plan falls apart. Kent edges around the table toward me and claims my hand. Brina is jostled into position on my other side. I pray for Warner to be brief. He isn't.

"Our Father, we are so grateful for the love that has gathered us all together . . . ," he begins, and wanders back to the day of my birth, progressing through gratitude for the family, for jobs, and for freedom. Finally he gets around to the food and says amen.

I end up right where I didn't want to be, pinned into a middle chair with Kent on my right and Brina on my left. He rests his arm on the back of the chair, his manspread thigh pressed against mine.

"God, that looks and smells divine," he says, sniffing the air with enthusiasm. "Haven't had a homemade meal since Nicole moved out, and this is a feast."

Now that my blinders are off, I see this is another tale he's spinning, that he's starving and neglected, that I abandoned him. As if the things he said to me that night were never said, as if he hadn't physically dragged me to the door and locked it behind me.

"Maybe you should learn to cook. Men do, you know," Brina says, grabbing a slice of garlic bread and passing the dish to me. Surprised, I flash her a smile of gratitude, but she glares back, making it clear she is scoring a point for womankind in general, certainly not defending me in particular.

"There's always the old grill, am I right?" Darryl asks. "That's what I do, when Rob's out all day cleaning. Poor girl comes home exhausted. You can make pretty much anything on the grill. Course, now the kids are old enough to take a turn in the kitchen."

I spoon food onto my plate so I won't hurt my mother's feelings, or Roberta's, but I eat like a mechanical doll. The lasagna, my favorite food in all the world, is dripping with cheese and sauce and presumably flavor, but it might as well be cardboard. I keep hoping Arya will have a meltdown, and I can be the heroine who spirits her away from the table and entertains her in the other room, but she is perfectly happy with the finger foods placed on her tray.

Conversation ebbs and flows in and out of my awareness. A spark of anger ignites in my belly, growing with every word Kent says, until it feels hot and hungry enough to consume everything and everybody. I wonder if Graham's tapping thing might work on anger and imagine my fingers moving over the pressure points, while in my mind, I run through a script that goes, *Even though I am trapped and my perfect husband is actually a monster, I love and accept myself absolutely and completely.*

It helps just enough to keep me from erupting, a vent for a volcano amping up to blow sky-high.

Until Kent puts an arm around my shoulder, beams around the table, and says, "Catch me up. I'm way out of the loop with family events." He smiles at my nieces in a way that brings a glow to their cheeks and makes me want to stomp on his foot under the table. "Any new conquests, girls?" he teases.

Then his gaze lands on Roberta, and he asks, "How's business?"

The room goes silent. Forks and knives stop moving. Mom looks stricken, Warner serious. The teenagers all suddenly have urgent messages on their phones. Roberta gives me a venomous look and says, "Fine. No thanks to Nicole."

Kent's arm tightens around my shoulder, and he kisses the top of my head. "Our adorable klepto does make a mess, doesn't she? Anything new since the book?"

I inhale sharply as the memory strobe light starts up again. A procession of different restaurants, of different faces with different expressions. And Kent, the only constant, recounting my latest exploits to his friends while I listen in mortification and shame.

Something breaks loose inside me. I shove back my chair with force, sending it crashing to the floor behind me as I scramble to my feet. Arya, startled, begins to wail, but I don't look at her. Don't look at any of them as I blindly flee.

"I'll make sure she's all right," Kent's voice says, and I pick up speed, racing for the bathroom. Before I can get the door shut, he is there, forcing his way in behind me. I lean back against the counter, catching my breath, my rage tearing free from the cage I've tried to trap it in.

"What the hell is wrong with you?" I wrap my arms around my chest, holding myself together, creating a barrier between my body and his.

My mother's voice floats in. "Are you okay in there?"

"She's just catching her breath," Kent calls back. "I'll take care of her."

I hear Mom's footsteps retreating. Kent locks the door. He grabs my wrists in an iron grip, pinning them down at my sides. Presses me back against the counter with his body and bends his head to kiss me. I turn my face away, but he presses me even harder. The edge of the counter digs into my back, and I gasp with pain. He takes the opportunity to press his lips against mine and shove his tongue in my mouth.

I feel his erection hard against me, and another flash of insight hits. He is aroused by my humiliation. He always has been. How could I not have seen this before? How many times has he brought me home after one of those horrible dinner engagements and initiated sex? Sometimes he couldn't wait until we got home, and we did it in the car, parked in an alley or a dark side street. I'd taken it as an indication that he loved me, even though I didn't live up to his standards.

Stupid, stupid, stupid.

He releases one of my wrists, and I can feel him fumbling with the zipper on my jeans. He's going to take me, right here, right now, while the family is gathered at the table for my birthday dinner.

Not this time.

My teeth snap together with his tongue between them. Kent stiffens. He rears his head backward. I feel a tearing sensation, taste the salt of blood.

His eyes are wide, his hand pressed hard against his mouth. Blood dribbles down his chin.

My stomach heaves, and I slide out from between him and the counter and bend over the toilet. It feels weirdly good to vomit, as though I'm purging my body of a poisonous toxin. When I'm finally done, I wipe my mouth with the back of my hand and turn back to Kent.

He's at the sink, rinsing his mouth over and over in a stream of water from the faucet.

"You and I are done." The truth of conviction resonates in my bones. "No reconciliation. No second honeymoon. We are going through with the divorce, and you're going to stop telling lies to my family. And right now, you are sick and need to go home."

He doesn't argue. He doesn't protest when I shove him aside to wash my hands and rinse out my own mouth. Doesn't try to stop me from unlocking the door. When I walk out, he follows. I lead him directly to the front door and hold it open.

Mom appears, then Warner.

"What's going on?" Mom asks.

"Kent isn't feeling well. He's going home."

It's not a lie. His face is drawn with pain, and he looks like he's about to be sick all over the floor.

"Oh no," Mom says. "Was it the food? I can't imagine. Everybody else is fine."

"Preexisting condition," I say. "He'll be fine."

Warner looks uncertainly from Kent to me. "I'll get your coat," he says.

"Do you want a care package? If you wait just a minute, I'll get something ready for you." Mom heads for the kitchen, and I let her go. It will keep her busy and stop her from asking questions.

Ash comes out of the dining room, Arya in her arms, and stands beside me, the backs of her fingers just grazing mine. Arya squirms and reaches for me. I put my arms around her and draw comfort from her sturdy body.

Warner returns with Kent's coat. "I'll walk you out," he says.

"No need," Kent slurs. "Thanks."

"What did you do?" Roberta demands as the door closes behind him. "There's nothing wrong with the food, but he looks like we crammed raw hamburger down his throat."

I swallow hard at the thought of raw hamburger, remember the sickening feeling of Kent's tongue tearing between my teeth, the iron tang of blood in my mouth. Mom comes bustling out of the kitchen with a plate of food covered with tinfoil. "Did he leave already?"

"He really had to go." My voice quavers, not because of Kent, not anymore, but because of the way my family is arrayed against me. I see the judgment in their eyes. It doesn't matter what I try to tell them, they'll side with him, not with me. But Arya snuggles her face into my neck. Ash slips her hand in mine. That allows me to blink back tears, steady my voice, and give them the only part of the truth they'll be able to hear.

"I told him I'm not going home with him and I don't want a second honeymoon. I want to go through with the divorce. He didn't take it well."

"Oh my God," Brina says. "He's gorgeous and he has money and he's willing to put up with *you*, and even that's not good enough? I think *I'm* going to be sick." She turns her back and stomps to the hall closet, rattling hangers while she grabs her coat.

"But there's cake," Mom wails. "We haven't lit the candles yet."

"Confetti cake, right?" Brina shoves her arms into her coat sleeves, pulls up the collar. "I always hated confetti cake. We all do. Nicole's the only one who likes it."

"It's Nicole's birthday," Mom protests, but she sounds uncertain, as if she's been caught in an error of thinking and is afraid to argue her point.

"Sorry. I can't do this." Brina drops an apologetic kiss on Mom's cheek, then slams the door.

Mom's face crumples and she starts wiping tears with the corner of her apron. There are people still sitting at the table waiting for us and she has made my favorite cake. I can't run away this time.

All of this is my fault. I allowed Kent into our lives. I let him demean me, belittle me, drive a deeper wedge between me and my family. I may never be able to clean up the mess I've made, but the least I can do is stick around for cake.

Mom and Roberta clear the dishes in silence. When I try to help, Rob tells me to sit down and stay out of the way. Even the kids are affected by the mood, their conversation drifting off to nothing until we are all sitting there, silent, avoiding each other's eyes. Mom lights the candles on a pink-frosted confection, and when she carries it to the table, everybody sings dutifully, without enthusiasm. The first slice is passed to me, the birthday girl who isn't a girl anymore and is not in the mood for cake.

I take a bite and manage to swallow. "It's beautiful," I say, skirting the margins of truth. "But maybe we could do chocolate next year, if everyone would rather."

"Nonsense," Mom says, her tone brusque to hide her emotions. "It's your birthday. You get confetti cake."

Warner valiantly makes conversation, starting with the Seahawks. Rob's husband and Betts join in, and the three of them keep talking as we all work our way through cake that nobody, except for the kids, is interested in eating.

"Well, that was fascinating," Ash says an hour later when we're finally able to escape. "From a bystander's perspective, anyway. I was horrified but entertained. And suddenly glad that I don't have family."

Her comment coaxes a bitter laugh out of me, and I feel a tiny bit lighter, just enough to explain what happened in the bathroom.

Ash stops walking. "You have got to be kidding."

"I didn't really mean to bite him, my teeth just—"

"Not you, him. He totally deserved that, and I'm glad you took his money."

"We *are* talking twenty thousand dollars."

"Pfft." She rolls back into motion, shifting Arya to the other hip. "What's that amount to him? Your husband is an abusive asshole.

Making trouble between you and your family, forcing sexual behavior on you whether you want it or not. Making you feel small and stupid."

"He'll want revenge for this," I say, dread flooding out the remnants of my anger. "Will you visit me in prison?"

"That's not going to happen. I mean, I would visit you, but you're not going there." Her voice lacks conviction, though, and we walk to the bus in silence.

Chapter Twenty-Two

Hawk

The text message from Nicole rolls in Sunday morning. Sorry, family thing came up. Birthday dinner. Can't meet up today 😣

I ought to have known she'd blow me off at the last minute. Thank God for text messaging, so I can play it cool. I respond with a shrug emoji, following that up with: No worries. Happy Birthday to whomever.

She texts back: Me. Only it's not my birthday.

To which I send an exploding-head emoji, and she returns a crazy face, and that's it.

Obviously, she's made up the whole lame excuse. If there's a family birthday dinner, she would have known about it long before now, especially since the birthday in question is apparently her own. More likely, she didn't want to hang out with me. Or, she's casing a neighborhood garage so she can walk off with a shovel or a rake or wind chimes.

But my instructions to myself to forget about her, to let this all go, fall on deaf and stubborn ears. Late that evening, before I crawl into bed, I text: How was the party? I don't really expect an answer, but one pops up almost immediately.

Nicole: Disastrous.

Hawk: That bad?

Nicole: Seriously. You can't make this shit up.

As if my fingers have a will of their own, I tap in: Let me buy you a piece of b-day cake and you can tell me all about it. Tomorrow? 4 ish? 🎂

God. That sounds too much like I've asked her out on a date. I add: We've got those stories to work on. I promise not to sing Happy Birthday to you in public.

The dots of a reply come up, go away, come up, go away, and then nothing.

I'm about to put my phone away and go to bed when she answers: I like cake

Perfect. I'll pick you up.

I fall asleep asking myself: Why? Why this woman? Do I have no sense of self-preservation at all? She's a thief. Her husband being a jerk doesn't change that. Nothing changes that. What is it that is driving me to know more about her, to spend time with her? For one thing, she's not afraid of me. And she's unpredictable and surprising and unlike anybody I've ever met. When I'm with her, I feel like a wide-eyed child, full of the sense of wonder that was uprooted from my childhood way too early.

On Monday, time is elastic and erratic, stretching and contracting. I'm absorbed with digging into the missing person case I'm working on with the police department, one that could be a matter of life and death, but even so, I arrive at her apartment a good fifteen minutes early. When she emerges from the front door, I feel like the gray skies have parted and the sun is shining directly on me.

All rational thought deserts me when she opens the door and climbs into the passenger seat, and I can't think of anything to say. Finally I settle for "What kind of cake? So I know where to take you?" As if I know all of the menus of all of the restaurants in the city and will choose the perfect place based on her answer.

"Could we maybe have pie?" she asks. "With ice cream?"

"So you *don't* like cake?" I seem to have three hands, four eyes, and zero working tongues. I start driving, even though I have no idea where I'm going, which at least gives me something to do with my extra hands and eyes.

"I had a bad cake experience. At the family birthday," she says. And then, all in a rush: "My roommate is the one who texted you back. About liking cake."

I keep my eyes on the road, working hard to hide the disappointment squeezing my heart. "Did you want me to take you back home?"

"I'm already in the car," she says. "What I'd really like is pie. Plus, you know, writing."

"Well, okay. Birthday pie and writing it is." I do actually know a place that makes great pie, a place that will be conducive to talking and writing, as I promised.

Nicole glances at me when she thinks I'm not looking, and then away. Chews at a fingernail. It makes me feel a little better to know she's as on edge as I am. Finally, she says, "You wanted to know about what I do. The relocating-objects thing."

"When you say it like that, it sounds like you work for a moving company."

Unexpected laughter spills out of her, and she shifts her position to look at me directly. "A cosmic moving company! I love it." But then she sighs and deflates. "Mostly people don't want their things moved, or at least they think they don't. And so I get arrested a lot. Which you already know, because I'm going to assume you've looked up my record."

She keeps her eyes straight ahead, hands clamped together in her lap, her forehead creased, lips pressed together, while I process a number of possible responses and say none of them.

"Are you ever going to say anything?" she asks after the silence has rubbed thin.

"I don't know what to say, therefore I say nothing."

"Most people at this point express rather clearly their opinion that I am a thief and worry that I might steal from them."

"And are you?" I ask. "Going to steal from me?"

"I never steal things; I only move them, which sometimes looks like stealing but never is. Welcome to the world of Nicole, where nothing—and I mean nothing—is ever normal."

"Can we talk about Kent for a minute?" I ask.

Her face darkens. "If we have to."

"What's the status of your relationship?" I have no business asking this question, but I have to know. Will she be going back to him, the way abused women so often do? How emotionally wounded is she?

"Fake diamonds and threats of prison," she answers, which doesn't answer my question at all. I want to shake her until all of the secrets fall out of her. I want to kiss her. I will not, of course, do either. She jolts me out of my thoughts with a question of her own.

"So, is your character a Hawk, too?"

"What?"

"In the stories you're writing. Your character is a PI, you said. Is he you? Or are you him?"

"Hardly. His life is much more interesting. I do a lot of surveillance for people who think their partner is cheating—"

"And for people who think their partner stole money," she interjects.

"That was a first, actually. Mostly I look for dirt on assholes who abuse their wives. My mom has a law practice that specializes in prosecuting those suckers and getting good divorce settlements for the injured parties. Most of what I do is online. In my stories, my character gets to investigate murders and has dangerous close calls and proves himself brave. And here we are."

We're both silent while I park. Silent as we walk into the restaurant. I choose a table at the back where I can keep an eye on the door, because one thing my PI work has done is make me uncomfortable when I can't see all of the exits and who is moving in and out of them. The menus are on the table, and when the waitress comes, Nicole is ready with her order—coffee and pecan pie with ice cream. I order coffee and chocolate cream pie with extra whipped cream.

We make awkward small talk while we wait, but once the pie and a carafe of coffee have been delivered and there's no danger of the waitress coming back anytime soon, I say, "So tell me about the birthday from hell."

Nicole stabs her fork into her pie. "Here's the short version. My siblings have not been talking to me, but my mother thought, for some reason, that a birthday dinner would fix that, and my not-husband was invited because he told them that the two of us are reuniting and he's taking me to Mexico. He . . . tried to kiss me, and I bit him. So. Not a huge success." She forks up a bite of pie and ice cream, watching my face all the while with those big, expressive eyes.

I take a bite of my own pie, mostly to give me time to process. When I've washed it down with coffee, I say, "So you and Kent are going to Mexico—"

She shakes her head vigorously. "We are not. He told my mother that." Her eyes go dark. She shoves the melting ice cream off to the side and makes a little pie dam with a few pieces of crust. "My family loves him. They are completely on his side."

"I see the problem," I say, because I have to say something, even though my heart is still hung up on the bit about kissing and biting and my hope that she and Kent are really through.

"Oh, it gets even better," she says. Her tone is light, but I hear the bitterness that lies beneath it. "My sister owns a housecleaning busi-ness. She hired me, and I moved a book from one client's house into another's. So that client fired Rob and she fired me and then—when I tried to talk said client into forgiving my sister, she hired me instead."

"Your life must be . . . complicated."

She grimaces. "Right?" And then, completely unexpectedly, she grins. "But, hey, Penelope thinks my moving things is a gift."

"And who is Penelope now?" I ask, my head spinning.

"Penelope is the woman who had the book before I moved it. Andrea is the one whose house I moved it to."

I am out of my depth, and it's going to take some time to figure out how to swim in these uncharted waters. "Listen," I say. "I'm hungry. Do you want something else to eat?"

"You're an eat-dessert-first kind of guy?"

"It made sense at the time. Let's get food. And then, if you want, you can tell me all about what you've been moving, or we can talk about the weather or write, or whatever."

"Okay," she says.

"Okay? Awesome." I feel like I've passed some sort of test. We order cheeseburgers and onion rings and then sit looking at each other in a not-quite-awkward silence. I'm not going to risk losing ground by asking more questions, and I wait for her to choose the topic of conversation.

"So what else do you want to know?" she asks, and it's my turn to breathe a sigh of relief that she's opened a door to more questions.

"Penelope. And the bit about how stealing—I mean, moving things—is a gift."

"So here's the story there. After I moved the book from Penelope's house, I took her a new copy and explained what I'd done. She was full of questions and then she proposed the idea that what I do is not a curse but a gift. She suggested I start looking for reasons why the book would want to go to Andrea's house. So far, I got nothing."

I gesture at the tattooed words on her forearm: *The curse is come upon me.* "Was moving things the inspiration for the ink?"

She nods. "I got it done after the second time I went to juvie. Because I couldn't seem to stop myself, and obviously my life was going to be shit because of what I do. But even then, I couldn't help feeling like all the things I moved *needed* moving, you know?"

Our food comes, and we both start eating as if we're famished. It's another thing to love about her. Some women I've dated seem afraid to eat in front of me. Nicole eats with gusto and obvious pleasure.

"And?" I ask, washing down a bite of hamburger goodness with a swallow of Coke. "What do you believe now? Is it a curse or a gift?"

"Depends on when you ask me." She takes a bite of burger and chews thoughtfully, wiping a trickle of grease off her chin. "There are times when I move things and it turns out to be serendipitous. People fell in love, or whatever. Most of the time, it just gets me in trouble. Sometimes I don't know. Like, maybe that woman who got Kent's money really needed it or something."

"I can answer that one for you. That woman is a single mother who was driving a car that should never have been on the streets. She's now driving something roadworthy, and has moved to a better apartment."

"And you didn't tell Kent." She smiles a glorious smile that makes me feel fizzy, like champagne.

I clear my throat and try to ground myself, but logic is a life preserver that is way down the river already, while I'm stranded on a rock in the middle of whitewater rapids.

"What about this book that you moved into this Andrea person's house? What's up with that? It seems to have gotten you a job, at any rate."

She dunks half of an onion ring in ketchup and takes an appreciative bite. "These are perfect," she says, savoring it. "So. The book. Andrea got into a state, like pretty much outright paranoid, about that book. She kept grilling me about this person named Tag, whose name is in the front cover. Like, she actually thought I knew him and that he put me up to bringing the book into her house."

"And?" I'm too intrigued to eat. My life is limited to a very ordinary world where very ordinary people hurt each other in very ordinary ways. But I've always wanted to believe that there's something I'm missing. I crave evidence of mystery and maybe even a little magic. I'm drawn to metaphysical books and fantasy novels. I love to watch shows like *Ghost Hunters*, and I inhaled *The Secret* when I stumbled upon it.

When Nicole talks about moving things, I feel like a door is opening in my mind, one that will lead me into a reality that is richer and wider and much more interesting than the one I've moved through for the thirty-two years of my existence. Also, she has ketchup on her chin, and I have never wanted to kiss a woman more in all my life.

She shrugs in answer to my question. "And nothing, as far as I can tell. I googled the name 'Tag' and got instructions on how to play the game and previews of a movie that has nothing at all to do with Dante or any of the circles of hell."

"I could dig a little," I offer. "Just to see if I can find a connection between the two women, or where the book came from. For fun."

"You have an unusual definition of fun."

"Call it a strong sense of curiosity."

She scrutinizes my face, head angled slightly to the side, hands quiet on the table.

"What?" I say. "You can ask me anything. I'll do my best to answer."

"I just . . ." She pauses. "My shrink thinks me moving things is all trauma related—which is a story I am *not* telling you today. And I kind of hope he's right, because then maybe I could stop moving things and have a life."

"All right," I say. "I can see that. I mean, I'd want for you to be on good terms with your family and not be in and out of jail. But I'm going to admit that I love the idea that there's something mystical about your . . . abilities."

She shoves a flabby onion ring into the remains of the ketchup puddle on her plate and then lays it down. "Since I'm trying to settle this question, I'd like you to dig, if you mean it about wanting to for fun and curiosity, because I do not have money to pay you. Also, if you really do like that sort of thing, might I interest you in the latest item I'm harboring? I hate to ask, but I'm going to get to the bottom of this object-relocation thing if it kills me, and I could use a little help."

Exultation floods through me, but I try to contain it, to look calm and competent and keep my voice level. "Let's be certain nothing kills you, shall we? Let me see what you've got."

Chapter Twenty-Three

NICOLE

I've been waiting my entire life for a man to look at me the way Hawk is looking at me now—actually at *me*, with the sort of interest that implies it wouldn't matter whether I show him a gum wrapper or a diamond. As if I am cool water on a scorching day. As if I'm something he's been searching for and he can't quite believe that he's found.

His eyes make me feel like I'm standing on a mountain at sunrise, with a cold wind blowing me wide awake. His voice makes me think of warm summer nights and fireflies, even though I've never actually even seen fireflies. Sitting here with him, I feel both adventurous and sheltered. I want to trust him. But I can't.

There were so many warning signs with Kent, and I missed every one of them. I thought I loved him and that he loved me, and until I have time to process the cesspool that was our relationship, there is absolutely no way I should be diving into another. Which doesn't stop Hawk's eyes from doing dangerous things to my heart. Most likely he won't look at me that way after I show him the pitiful object stowed away in my day pack, and I won't have to worry about how I feel.

When I set the phone on the table between us, grayish water pooling in the bottom of the bag, Hawk is all avid curiosity, his eyes intent, his lips pressed together at the center. He lifts the phone, using the tips of his fingers and the edges of the bag rather than touching it directly, and turns it over. His brows contract and his eyes dart upward, all sharp intensity and suspicion.

"Where did you get this?" No summer night in that voice now. It cuts through me like a bitter wind.

"I found it. Lying in the street."

He leans forward. "Which street? When? Where?"

The rapid-fire interrogation pins me to my chair. The illusion of being safe and sheltered vanishes. Anger at my own stupidity at trusting him sharpens my voice. "So you're what, now? The Spanish Inquisition?" I reach for the phone and pull it back toward me.

Hawk blinks. "What? Oh. God. I've done it again, haven't I?" His face softens; he reaches across the table. I cover the phone with both hands before he can snatch it back, but instead he rests his fingers lightly on my wrist.

"I'm sorry. I get intense." His face flushes with what looks surprisingly like embarrassment. "That phone . . ." He pauses. Draws in a deep breath. "I've been involved in a missing person case, and that phone . . . I think it might be evidence."

It's my turn to blink. My mouth is open, but no words are coming out.

Hawk now looks like he's the victim of the Inquisition. The color has gone out of his face, and his jaw is clamped so tight, I can see the muscles bunching. He lowers his gaze. Withdraws his hand. Lines up his knife and fork with his plate. When he finally glances back up at me, his eyes are shadowed.

"You're going to hate me, but I need to report this to the detective working the case. And she's going to want to talk to you."

A lump forms in my throat, hot and tight. My mouth goes dry, my palms clammy. I picture the Fates, pausing with popcorn halfway to their open mouths, cackling with hilarity at this turn of events. *You're going to jail one way or another,* they whisper.

"I only found it," I croak. "I swear. I didn't—"

"You're not in any trouble," he says quickly, and I want to believe he means it. "But that phone . . . if I'm right, it belongs to the woman who went missing. It might help us find her. Or at least whoever took her."

My body goes rigid with shock. It takes a moment of concentrated effort to lift my arm, bend my elbow, slide the phone across the table toward him. "Do what you have to."

The tension in his jaw eases, and he takes a breath that makes me think I'm not the only one rendered frozen by this development. "It will be okay, you'll see. Let me check if she'll just meet us here. That would be easier than going down to the station, yes?"

He waits, and I realize he's actually asking for my opinion and permission.

"Yes," I murmur, squeezing my cold hands together under the table, trying to stop the trembling that is setting in at the idea of talking to the police. Most of the cops who've arrested me have been decent enough, but every single one of them carried a gun and handcuffs and had the ability to stuff me in the back of a cop car and take away my freedom.

Hawk shoves back his chair and looks at me. "I'm going to make a quick call. You'll wait here?"

"Okay."

"I'll just be a minute." I watch his retreating back as he navigates the café and steps outside. I scoped out the room when we first came in, like I always do, locating all the exits. I know there's another door. I could zip through it while he's not looking. Make a run for a bus or maybe hail a cab.

But he trusted me to wait here. He knows that I could run out on him if I choose to. But if I can help save a life, or bring a criminal to justice if it's too late for lifesaving, then of course that's what I need to do. So I stay where I am, and Hawk comes back.

"She'll be here in about fifteen," he says. "I guess writing is out of the question."

We sit in a crushing silence, avoiding eye contact. The phone, still in its baggie, dominates the table between us.

"There she is," Hawk says after the longest sixteen minutes and twenty-seven seconds in history. He doesn't need to tell me. The woman standing in the door looks like a cop, even though she's not in uniform. It's the way she stands, the way her eyes check out every face, every detail, in the room.

"It's okay," Hawk says softly. "Trust me, if you can. She's a good person." He holds me steady with his eyes as the woman crosses to us and slides into the seat beside him and punches him in the shoulder.

"Figured you'd at least order me pie."

"Figured we'd let you decide what kind you want," he answers. "Detective Hansen, this is Nicole. Nicole, Detective Hansen."

"My, my. So formal." She fishes the last onion ring off his plate and pops it in her mouth while he waves the waitress over.

"What'll it be, Aunt Joan?"

"Lemon meringue, of course. Is there anything else?"

"Lemon meringue it is," he tells the waitress. "And another chocolate cream for me. More coffee for all of us. Nicole?"

I stare at him, wordless, and shake my head, too unnerved to even think about food. It's stupid, of course, but I've never even thought of cops as human beings, just uniforms and authorities to be avoided. And this woman, so comfortable and easygoing and apparently related to Hawk, doesn't fit my preconceived notions at all.

"Is this it, then?" She reaches for the baggie and slides it toward her, touching only the edges, the way Hawk did. She repeats his moves, examining the phone front and back, and then turns her attention to me.

"Hawk says you found it?"

I nod. "Last week. Monday."

The waitress comes over with pie and coffee. Detective Hansen forks up a bite, makes a little humming sound of appreciation, and points her fork at me. "Where?"

"On Lyons, maybe about one hundred yards from Division. I slipped and fell—the phone was in the snowbank."

"So, that helps to clarify a timeline. It would have to have been there before the snow started." She takes another bite of pie. "This is useful information. We haven't checked out that area at all. Maybe somebody saw something. You never know—we might get lucky. Whoever nabbed our victim might have even grabbed the phone from her and left us a nice fingerprint."

"Wouldn't the water and the snow wash any prints away?" I ask, curiosity beginning to override my fear.

"It can," Hawk answers. "But because fingerprints are oily, they can sometimes be recovered even after an item is submerged for a period of time."

Detective Hansen crams another large bite in her mouth and washes it down with coffee. "Well, I've gotta run. Thanks for the pie, Hawk. Tell your mother hello for me. Nicole, can I get your phone number, just in case I need more information?"

She jots the number down in a little notebook, smiles at both of us, then shoves back her chair and strides out, leaving us, or Hawk, anyway, to pay for her pie.

Post-adrenaline shakiness hits me.

"Hey," Hawk says. "Hey. It's all going to be okay."

The gentleness makes me sniffle, and I wipe my eyes and my nose on my shoulder. "Sorry. I'm not usually a blubberer."

"I'm the one that's sorry," he says. "I wanted to make a great impression so you'd want to hang out with me again, and instead I dragged you into an investigation."

He looks miserable, like he genuinely believes this is his fault.

I can't talk, because I know my voice won't be steady, so I just point at the curse tattoo instead.

"No," he says, laying his warm hand over the words and hiding them from both of our eyes. "Not a curse. You've turned up the first solid clue this case has seen in days. Imagine if we catch the asshole because you picked up this phone. That would be as close to magic as I'm ever going to get in this lifetime."

"You say that like you really mean it." My voice is wobbly, but at least it doesn't go all high and squeaky.

"Of course I mean it. Can I make it up to you? Buy you more pie? The restaurant maybe?"

I laugh, still shaky but feeling steadier every minute. "Could you maybe just drive me to my job again? The bus takes forever, and Andrea hates it when I'm late."

He drives me in a silence that is equal parts comfortable and uneasy. I keep glancing at him and catching him glancing back at me, and then we both pretend we weren't just sneaking a peek. When he parks outside Andrea's, I turn to him and say, "Police interrogation aside, that was the best birthday pie I've ever eaten."

"Because it's the only birthday pie you've ever eaten."

"And because it was with you." I flush, shocked that I've said this out loud, and open the door to flee.

"When's your real birthday? We could try it again. And actually maybe write next time."

I hesitate, then shake my head. "I've had enough birthday fun, thank you. But the woman who is now in possession of the book is named Andrea Lester. You have her address. And if you can find any connection to her, or Penelope Lane, or somebody named Tag, I'd sure love to see what you dig up."

"Wanna help?"

When I say, "Hell yeah, I do," his smile makes me feel like the sun and the moon and all the stars are shining together. And then, to seal the deal, he lays his hand on my arm to hold me back when I start to get out of the Jeep.

"If you've got two minutes, I'd like to remove the tracking software from your phone."

A stab of betrayal kills the warm, fuzzy feeling before it can get properly started. "You put a tracker on my phone?"

"Not me. Kent."

"That bastard! Oh my God!" But the truth is, I'm not really surprised. This is exactly the sort of thing Kent would do. "How long has this been going on?"

Hawk shrugs. "That I can't tell you."

"But you can fix it for me?"

"It's what I live for."

I hand him my phone and wait while he taps the screen. A moment later, he hands it back. "All clear," he says.

"How can I thank you?"

"Just be you." He says it like he means it, and I walk into Andrea's house feeling lighter than I have since the day I first moved Kent's money.

Chapter Twenty-Four

Nicole

Nicole: So, my PI is now digging into the book mystery
  Penelope: See? Magic!
  Nicole: Maybe? Skeptical. I read my story in class last night. The flamingo story I told you about
  Penelope: And?
  Nicole: The class thinks I'm writing fantasy
  Penelope: Some people have no imagination

~

"We have a problem," Graham says as soon as I'm settled in my chair on Wednesday. "Well, not a problem, per se, but a concern we need to address."

I stop in the act of curling my feet up under me and plant them flat on the floor.

"Kent."

Graham nods. "He called and asked me to share information about your treatment."

"And what information does he want, exactly?"

"He would like to know how I am treating your kleptomania and my opinion on your response to treatment."

I hug my arms around my body, picturing Kent feeding on my weakness, reading what I wrote in the notebook. Cold slithers around in my belly.

"What did you tell him?"

"I told him that treatment for kleptomania depends on multiple factors, and that best practice includes a multimodal approach including psychotherapy, prescription therapy, and behavior modification. He then asked how that applied to you specifically, and I told him I wasn't at liberty to divulge treatment information without a signed release."

I should feel comforted by Graham's answer, by knowing that he protected my confidentiality. But I know Kent and I know there's more to come.

"I'm wondering if perhaps we should talk a little about the state of the relationship between the two of you," Graham suggests. "If you are working on your marriage, then it might be helpful to bring your husband into a session."

I stare at him in horror. "And here I thought I was supposed to be the crazy one."

"Nicole," Graham says gently. "It's not at all uncommon to have a spouse or other family member join a session. Healing doesn't happen in isolation, and what affects one half of a partnership affects the other half as well."

"But we're not a partnership. We are getting a divorce. What did you *tell* him?"

"I told him nothing. I reminded him that as an attorney he is well aware of the laws around confidentiality. But I did tell him that I would speak with you and ask whether you wish to sign a release, or have him join us in a session."

"No!" I protest. "Absolutely not."

"You looked friendly together last week when he picked you up. And he says you are going to Mexico—"

"We are not friendly, and we are not going to Mexico!"

Graham blinks, and I realize I've shouted the words at full volume. I take a breath and try to calm down, but too much adrenaline is running through my body to allow me to stay seated. I get up and start pacing the office.

"Maybe you should tell me a little bit about your relationship, so I can understand," Graham suggests.

"Okay, listen to this. Last week when we looked so friendly? He tried to pull my hair out by the roots and I jumped out of his car in the middle of a shitty neighborhood. He told my mother and you and everybody that we're getting back together and going on a second honeymoon, but he didn't ask me first. I told him no. He forced me to kiss him and I bit him and oh my God, this is all so *fucked*."

Retracing my steps to the chair, I sit down and start putting my shoes on, planning to run, but Graham's voice stops me.

"Nicole. Let's talk about this. You are my client. Kent is not. I'm not saying I believe him, or that you need to do this. Obviously, I don't have all of the information. You should never do anything because somebody else is pressuring you to do it."

I remain perched on the edge of the chair, ready to bounce up again. "What Kent wants most right now is his money. And the only reason he's interested in any details of my treatment is because, for some reason, he gets off on me being all broken and shit."

"You don't think he wants you to get better?"

"See? You're on his side. This is pointless."

"I'm not on anybody's side. My job is to help you gain clarity so you can make better life choices. Let me ask you one more thing. Do you love him?"

I consider this question from a dozen different angles before answering. "No. I do not."

"Well, that's clear, then. No release of information, and we don't invite him to a session," Graham says. "Which sounds like the right answer from you but leads us directly into a difficult dilemma. Your husband also said that he will stop paying for your sessions if you don't allow him to be part of the treatment."

A month ago, I would have taken this as fantastic news, the perfect excuse to walk away from another therapist. Now I hear it with cold dismay. "But this is actually helping!"

"Is it?" Graham asks. "Have you stopped moving things?"

"I haven't *relocated* anything that matters. Or at least, I thought it didn't matter until it did."

"So you did move something."

"Well, yes, but—"

"And you didn't tell me. We need to have trust between us, if we're to work together. I need to be able to trust you, as much as you need to be able to trust me. If you don't tell me about stealing things, or if you lie to me—"

"I didn't steal anything. I don't steal. And I never lie. Oh, what's the point of trying to make you understand if I'm not going to be able to work with you anyway?"

"We might be able to work out a payment plan," Graham says. "I believe I can help you."

I get to my feet and put on my jacket. "I believe you *could* have helped me, if Kent hadn't gotten to you. You listened to him. You believed him. You're the psychologist—can't you see what he's doing?"

"We still have half an hour," Graham says. "Come back and sit down and we'll talk about this."

I shake my head, hand already on the doorknob. "Thank you for getting me started writing, and teaching me tapping."

And with that, I'm out of the office and on the street. My skin crawls as if I'm being watched, and I have to hold myself back from running to the bus stop, my eyes darting every direction looking for

Kent or his car. What if he's following me? Or what if he's hired another PI? I think about calling Hawk, asking him for a ride, but I refuse to let Kent turn me into a frightened bunny, running from shadows.

When I get to Andrea's, I'm out of breath, wound up so tight I feel like I might fly apart. I run up the driveway and the steps, wanting a closed door between me and the invisible eyes that might be following me.

But I'm early, so she isn't at the door waiting for me, like she usually is. And when I ring the bell, nobody answers.

Chapter Twenty-Five

ANDREA

This entire day has been a disaster. If I'd had any sense at all, I would have called in sick.

My appointment with a new psychiatrist and the medication changes he's ordered have made things worse, rather than better. Disjointed memories and emotions zip in and out of my brain. Panic hits with no rhyme or reason. This morning I did something I swore I would never do and took my sedative before coming to work. I told myself that the anxiety would make it harder to concentrate than the effects of the meds. But the truth is, either one of those things makes me unsafe.

My job allows for no margin of error; the smallest mistake could kill somebody. But I couldn't bring myself to stay home. I've been living in a constant state of dread, my brain conjuring all sorts of disasters. Tag showing up at my door. The police. Or Ronda, for that matter, maybe recognizing me from my voice mail and tracking me down by my phone number. I'm desperate for the distraction of my usual routine.

Discipline and focus have always had a calming effect on me in the past, but today, every time I've managed to lose myself in the routine, I've been pulled away to deal with something and it took forever to focus in again. The interruptions have been constant and intrusive. Customers who need prescription counseling for new medications, or who are seeking advice. Calls from physicians' offices with urgent prescription orders.

Even worse, it's flu season, and the powers that be have decided pharmacists should give immunizations, causing another disruption to my carefully structured and ordered day. Every time I've had to stop what I'm doing to give an injection, it has required a mighty act of willpower to get myself back on target. Because I'm so distracted, I've added extra safety steps to my usual system, and everything takes longer. Customers have begun complaining about the wait time. The assistants are irritated, with the customers and with me.

By late afternoon, I'm hopelessly behind and everybody is in a bad mood.

Of course, today when I would have welcomed it, Frank doesn't show up early. And fifteen minutes before my shift is over, I'm called to do one more immunization. I'm tempted to make the customer wait for Frank, but according to the tech who signed the patient in, he's in a hurry to be somewhere and can't wait.

I step out to the small booth we use for injections. "Paul Keating?"

"That's me," a young man says. For half a second he looks like Tag, dark hair, glasses, a hesitant smile. I blink and my vision clears and I see that the shape of the face is all wrong and remember that Tag will be older now, over fifty. He's probably bald, or has a tacky comb-over like Frank. If he's even still alive.

"They're making me do it," the patient says. "Work. I managed to weasel out of it so far, but the paperwork caught up with me."

"You'll be fine," I say, on autopilot, pulling up the screening questions. "Can you roll up your sleeve for me?"

"I hate shots," he says. "Passed out last time I had blood drawn."

He unbuttons the cuff of his shirt, makes one precise fold, then loses patience and shoves the fabric up over his bicep. I know I'm staring, caught in a time loop in which this simple act of rolling up a shirtsleeve happens in slow motion and takes forever, and then, just like that, I'm not in the pharmacy, I'm in the old house in Richland.

"I can handle this," Tag says, rolling up first one sleeve and then another. He doesn't sound like he can handle it, but God knows I can't, so I just stand there while he picks up the naked, squalling baby and lowers her into the kitchen sink half filled with warm water. The baby screams. Tag carries on, anyway, gently washing her slippery body.

I'm the mother. I should do it. But I can't. It isn't safe. A staticky image flickers through my mind. My tiny girl drowned—so sad—and the two of us back to our lives, free and untethered and—

"Ma'am?"

The patient's voice jolts me back to the here and now. He fidgets in the chair. A slight sheen of perspiration shines on his upper lip.

Bringing my mind back again to what I'm doing, I ready the syringe, double-checking that what I'm giving is indeed the flu vaccine.

"Maybe I don't need this after all," he says. "Work is requiring it, but who really needs a job, anyway? Or at least that one." He laughs nervously.

"You'll be fine." I clean his arm with alcohol. Plunge in the needle. "All done," I say, businesslike and dry, slapping a bandage over the invisible puncture wound. "How do you feel? Woozy? Dizzy?"

He shakes his head. "Relieved. I'm fine."

"You need to wait for fifteen minutes to make sure you have no reaction," I tell him. "It's our policy. You can have a seat out in front of the pharmacy."

I turn to the computer to document the injection and find myself staring at the screening questions, still unanswered. The flashback drove them clear out of my mind. Until they're answered, I can't document the shot. But if I go out and ask the patient now, he might get freaked out. Staff will notice and know I made a mistake.

I hesitate. Contraindications are incredibly rare. Plus, he's been given the vaccine information sheet, was carrying it with him, in fact. It's his responsibility to read it.

For the first time in my pharmacist career, I make up the patient's answers to the screening questions, and then I go back to the counter to finish what I was working on before I was interrupted. Shame and doom trail behind me. Pharmacy errors happen, more than the trusting public would like to believe. But not to me. I don't allow myself to make mistakes.

Thank God I got through today, no serious harm done. I won't risk it again. It's five o'clock. Frank is finally here. When I get home I'll call my supervisor and ask for tomorrow off.

But, of course, today of all days, traffic is even more backed up than usual. When I finally get home, Nicole is waiting for me, huddled on the doorstep looking like some sort of refugee. "I called you," she says accusingly. "You didn't answer."

"Sue me. My battery is dead." I unlock the door and punch the code on the security system, then go straight to the kitchen and open a bottle of cabernet. I know damn well alcohol doesn't mix with my meds, but I pour a glass anyway and use it to wash down two pills, even though I already took a dose in my car before driving home.

"Everything okay?" Nicole asks, her expressive eyes traveling from my face to the glass in my hand.

I glare at her. "Don't you have some work to do?"

"Anybody ever tell you you're a bitch?" she retorts.

Both of us gasp at the shock of what she's just said. For a long instant, we stare at each other. Then her shoulders sag and she sighs. "There I go, ruining things again. Do you want me to leave now?"

"No, I want you to do your job." A laugh bubbles up inside me, unexpected and inappropriate. "And no. Everybody thinks I'm a bitch, but nobody's had the nerve to say it in years. Give me five." I hold my hand up, and she tentatively raises her own. When I move to slap her palm, I miss, which strikes me as even funnier.

Nicole nearly runs from the kitchen, and I remember that I need to call Jim and ask for time off. I told half the truth about my phone. The battery probably is dead, but that would be because it's still in the drawer where I shoved it right after Ronda tried to call me back. I haven't looked at it since, afraid she's left a message. Afraid that she hasn't.

I don't have a landline, so if I'm going to call my boss, I'll have to plug it in. And then I'll have to dig through my hiring paperwork to find Jim's number, because I've never had to call him before. This all deserves a refill on the wine, so I top off my glass and take a long swallow. The walls won't stay where they belong, and the floor is suddenly uneven, so it takes me a long time to get to my office.

It takes even longer to deal with the phone, because the charging cable doesn't want to fit into the ridiculously tiny little slot. And then I drop the file while I'm pulling it out of the drawer and the papers scatter all over the floor. Once I find the number, I misdial and get some quavery-voiced woman who is much more annoyed by a little wrong number than anybody has a right to be.

Finally, I get it right and my supervisor's voice comes on the line. It seems like a good idea to keep things light, so I lead off with "Jimmy! What's shaking?"

"Who is this?"

"It's Andrea. Listen, I'm sick. Need the rest of the week off. Maybe next week too."

Silence on the other end of the line. Then: "We need to talk about what happened today."

"What happened today?" I ask. Jim can't possibly know what I've done. Nobody has any way of knowing.

"An interesting little incident." Jim does not sound happy. Before I can suggest that he probably could benefit from a glass of wine and a couple of happy pills, he goes on. "We had a complaint. The patient you gave the flu shot to was very worried when he read his vaccine information sheet. Apparently he has a severe egg allergy."

Way too late, I understand that it would be good to be sober for this conversation. But that ship has not only sailed, it has sunk. The only possible option now is to take another drink. So I do, and then I say, "Not to worry. New CDC guidelines, right? Even severe egg allergies are not a contra . . . contra . . ." For some reason, I can't figure out how to say the rest of that word, so I say instead, "He's fine, right? The egg allergy guy?"

"Andrea, are you *drunk*?" Jim's voice is judgmental and reproving.

"Not your business." It's true. I'm home and on my own time. "The guy is okay, right?"

"The *patient* is fine. But," he says, "you never asked him about allergies, or if he's had Epstein-Barr, or any of the questions on the screening survey. And yet, all of those questions are marked 'no' in the system. Would you care to explain that?"

"Are you calling me a liar?"

"How about you call me when you're sober and we'll talk? Do not come to work until you hear from me."

"Jim! Listen to me—" But he's gone and I'm talking to myself.

A tiny, sober fragment of me is worried and upset and tries to deliver a lecture. *Bad Andrea, mixing pills and alcohol. Now look!* I wave it away. I feel better now than I've felt in weeks. All of my anxiety is gone. The memories are quiet. In fact, with all of the dark emotions taking a holiday, everything appears clear and simple.

The book is the cause of my unraveling. Nicole is the cause of the book. I'll throw away the book. Stop hiring Nicole. And then the memories will go away and the anxiety will settle. My world will be ordered and structured and everything will go back to normal.

But as I reach into the drawer and draw out that damned copy of the *Inferno*, I have an unnerving and untethered sensation that there are two of me in this chair. My old self, and the one I've created to survive. I close my eyes, but that just makes things worse. The room keeps moving . . .

I'm in a rocking chair, the baby in my arms, crying, always crying. Her name is Lelia, so lyrical and musical, but somehow it doesn't fit and I always just think of her as "the baby." I try to get her to suck, but she can't seem to latch on and screams louder. I used to have neat, small breasts, and I liked them that way. Now they are a distortion, a caricature, a ridiculous exaggeration. They ache. Milk leaks out of them, and I try again to get the baby to suck, but she doesn't latch and anger swims up out of nowhere.

This is her fault. She's ruined my life. Made me drop out of college. She's responsible for stretch marks and thirty hours of labor, and a strain on my relationship with Tag. The least she could do is drink milk so my breasts don't hurt like this.

Terror wipes out the anger. What is wrong with me that I can feel this way toward a tiny, helpless baby? I'm not fit to be a mother. I don't want to be a mother. Years of life stretch ahead of me, a life where I'll be trapped, responsible. Tag will go back to school and finish his degree. Then he'll get a job and leave me alone with this small alien being, and something horrible will happen . . .

Nicole taps at the study door, dragging me up out of my memory. But I'm still swamped in a horror no amount of alcohol can drown. So much for living better chemically.

"Andrea?" Nicole queries. "I'm going to leave now. Are you sure you're okay?"

I wave the question away and ask my own. "Did you move anything?"

"I did not," Nicole answers.

I don't like the way she's looking at me. "Well, go on, then." I lurch to my feet and cling to the desk while the room spins.

"I could stay."

"Nonsense. I'm fine, fine, fine. Never seen a body drink before?" My hand on the wall helps me navigate the hallway. The open space in the entryway is tricky, but I make it across and arrive triumphant. Something is wrong with the dead bolt, though. I can't get it open, and Nicole has to remind me to disable the alarm. She fixes the jammed bolt with ease.

Out on the doorstep, she lingers, holds out a hand to me. "Are you sure you don't want me to stay?"

"Go home," I tell her, and shut the door in her face. More wine, I decide. At this point, it's the only viable option.

Chapter Twenty-Six

NICOLE

Penelope: How was class?
  Nicole: Can you get addicted to writing?
  Penelope: When can I read? Also, what's new with the Inferno story?
  Nicole: Evidence is in favor of me being cursed
  Penelope: ???
  Nicole: Andrea was totally sloshed last night. I blame the book
  Penelope: Or she's an alcoholic. You know nothing about the woman
  Nicole: Leaning toward the curse.

~

When I get to Andrea's on Thursday, she doesn't answer the doorbell. Again. Annoyance rises. Yesterday, I was early and she was late and I sat on her porch in the cold for what seemed to be forever before she finally showed up. Inconsiderate of her to do it twice in a row. Even if she is paying me ridiculous amounts of money.

Worry picks away at my irritation. I didn't think she was going to make it to the door last night, and she was too wasted to remember to pay me. I picture her passed out, alone, without anybody to cover her or make sure she's still breathing. Anxiety rises as I ring the bell three times, waiting for footsteps that don't come. Maybe she's just hungover. I try calling her, but just like yesterday, the phone goes straight to voice mail. On impulse, I test the doorknob.

When it turns, and the door opens, fear floods me for real. This is so not Andrea, who is obsessed with her locks and her security system and the idea that somebody is watching her. Not only is the door unlocked, the alarm hasn't been set.

"Andrea?" I call. My voice echoes back to me.

Sylvester appears, meowing loudly. When I bend over to pet him, my hand encounters a sticky patch and my fingers come away wet and red. "Are you hurt?" I ask. I run my hands over his body but don't find any injuries.

"Did you get into paint?" He meows again and slinks off down the hallway.

My heart is hammering against my ribs as I move into the house. "Andrea? It's me. Nicole. I thought I'd just let myself in, since . . . Oh my God! Andrea!"

She lies on her side, unmoving, in the middle of a once-pristine white carpet. Now there are splashes of crimson everywhere. A bottle of wine lies beside her, spilled out in a puddle. The bottoms of her bare feet are also red, and I think for a minute she must have stepped in the wine before she fell, but as I take a step forward, my shoes crunch and I see glass fragments under my feet.

"Andrea? Andrea!" She doesn't move, doesn't answer, doesn't even blink. Lowering myself to my knees, I put my hand on her chest. She's breathing, but slowly and far too shallowly. I grab her wrist to check her pulse. At first I can't feel it at all, but then I manage to find a faint, uneven flutter. Her hands are cold and stained with red. The stain is tacky, darker than wine, and I realize with another shock that it's blood, that her feet are also bloody.

Blood all over the tables. Blood on the wall. The old man's head, collapsed, not looking like a head at all . . .

I grab my phone and dial 911. "Hurry," I beg the dispatcher who answers my call. "Please hurry. I think she's dying."

Sylvester sniffs at Andrea, then meows and rubs against my ankles. I pick him up, and I think he's trembling—only, maybe that's just me.

It seems to take forever for the ambulance to show up.

"How much has she had to drink?" one of the uniformed men asks, in a tone that indicates I should have stopped her somehow. "What medications is she on? Does she have any medical conditions? Allergies? Has she taken anything else? Pills, drugs? How did she cut her feet?"

"I don't *know*," I repeat, over and over, feeling judged and found significantly wanting. But it's not my business to know any of this, or to be trying to save her life or to even be here at all.

"Where are you taking her?" I ask as they load her onto a stretcher.

"Sacred Heart."

They wheel her out the door. A brief wailing of sirens outside, and then a vast and oppressive silence descends. My breathing is far too loud. Guilt almost immobilizes me.

My phone buzzes and a message displays.

Hawk: Check in, Nancy Drew.

When we talked in class today, we agreed I should locate the book and smuggle it out with me so he could examine it for clues. He called me Nancy Drew and I'd laughed, but the joke is no longer funny. What if this is my fault because I brought in the book? There's a smear of blood on my hands, maybe from Sylvester, maybe from Andrea or the carpet. I run to the bathroom and scrub for a long time with soap and water as hot as I can stand it.

Hawk, unaware of the disaster, texts again: Hardy Boys to Nancy. Check in, Nancy.

I try to text him back, but my hands are shaking so hard I keep hitting the wrong letters, and autocorrect is not my friend. Finally I just call and his voice comes on at once.

"Complete disaster, Hawk. The ambulance was just here and—"

"Are you okay?"

"Physically, yes. Only, Hawk, she went on a total alcohol bender, and then I think she stepped on broken glass and she . . ." I realize I'm sobbing. I have done more crying in the last few weeks than the rest of my entire life.

"Nicole. It's not your fault," Hawk says.

"How do you know that? She was fine before I brought that stupid book here. I'm cursed. Everywhere I go, bad shit happens."

"Nicole. You don't know that. Listen—"

"Looks like a massacre in here and . . . oh God, Hawk. I hate blood." I look around at the disaster that was once a perfectly ordered house. The paramedics have tracked through the wine and the blood. I need to clean this up, but I can't, I can't. Only, I have to.

The doorbell rings, and I grab on to hope. A friend. A neighbor. A family member. Somebody to take over the responsibility. Whoever it is can go check on Andrea at the hospital. Figure out how to get blood out of carpets.

"Nicole?" Hawk asks.

"Somebody at the door. I'll call you."

I hang up and go to the door, only to find myself face to face with Kent. My brain refuses to process him standing there, and I just gape at him, wordless, while he shoves past me into the entryway.

"We need to talk," he says. "It's important."

"I'm working."

His eyes widen as he looks around. "What did you *do*?"

"Andrea had an accident. I need to clean up. You need to go."

I start thinking about *Criminal Minds*, *Unsolved Mysteries*, every show I've watched or novel I've read where a man murders his wife. Which is crazy. This is Kent we're talking about. He wouldn't risk his position and his reputation, no matter how much he hates me. Still, I back away from him, primed to run.

"Nice place you've landed in." He looks around, and I know he's appreciating the quality of the flooring, the ugly but expensive art. He picks up the hideous little sculpture on the credenza and turns it upside down, looking for the artist's signature. He whistles. "Your employer must make serious bank."

"Kent. You can't be here. Get out, now."

"Stop being a drama queen. I just want to talk. And stop cowering. Do I really seem the type to resort to physical violence?"

"I don't know what type you are anymore. You shouldn't be here. How did you even know I'd be here?"

And then I remember. I am so, so stupid. I told him I was working here. I gave him the address the day he was going to drive me.

I take another step back, remembering his hand twisted in my hair. "I've already told you the money's gone. I can't get it back."

"Goddamn it, Nicole! You have no idea what you've done!" His breathing is ragged. I think about making a run for the bathroom or the study, but he's stronger, faster, and he'd catch me before I got far.

"You've ruined me. You've got to help me." He softens his voice, pleading almost, but I can feel the anger radiating off him.

"Ruined? Now who's the drama queen? Twenty thousand is throw-away money for you." I edge another step backward.

"Fine," he says. "I admit it. I'm broke."

"Oh, come on, Kent."

"Truth," he says. "Bad investments. Overspending. I'm in debt, Nicole. The banks won't lend to me anymore."

"You're kidding, right?"

He shakes his head. "It's been going on for a long time. That's why I bought you the zirconias. Because I couldn't afford the real thing."

"Like I would have cared? I would've rather had something simple and honest. Diamonds aren't that important to me."

"They are important to *me*. That money you stole was important to me."

"Get a loan from your parents."

"They've cut me off."

This actually doesn't surprise me. I've met them only a handful of times since we've been together. His mother is cool and excruciatingly polite, his father driven and perfectionistic. If Kent has embarrassed them, or failed to live up to their expectations, I can totally see them cutting him off.

I edge sideways, closer to the hallway. "Kent. I don't know what to tell you. You make a lot of money. Maybe you need a budget—"

"Stop!" he shouts. "Listen. There are some . . . unsavory people calling in what I owe."

A gasp of shocked laughter escapes me. "Like . . . gangsters? Broken kneecaps and all that?"

A mistake. I see the fury rising, and I'm already running when he lunges toward me. I make it into the bathroom, but he's got his shoulder to the door on the other side. We've done this dance once, and I'm determined not to let it happen again. I fling all of my weight against the door, but it's not enough. The gap widens, slowly, inexorably. I scrabble on the counter and come up with a bottle of hair spray, depressing the button and aiming the nozzle through the widening crack at what I estimate to be Kent's eye level.

I hear a gasp of pain and the pressure on the door eases. Taking advantage of the moment, I slam it shut and lock it.

"Shit!" Kent snarls. "What the hell? You could have blinded me. Open up, now!"

"I'm not stupid, Kent. You want to talk, then talk. If you're so broke, why did you leave all that money lying around in a drawer?"

"It was a bribe," he says after a long pause.

"Who on earth were you bribing? And for what?"

"God, you're stupid. The bribe was for me. I was supposed to use half of it to buy an alibi for a client, and you moved the fucking money and the client is going to kill me if I don't come through. Which is why." Thud. "You." Thud. "Are going to *fix this!*"

The door jumps alarmingly with every thud. I glance around the bathroom desperately for a means of escape, a place to hide, a way to defend myself. No window. No convenient pair of scissors or randomly placed knife. The only weapons I can come up with are the hair spray and a curling iron.

"What exactly do you want me to do?" I ask.

"Since you can't get the money back, you can provide the alibi."

He's lost it. Clearly. I think about calling 911, but I can already picture how that would go. Kent would be all lawyerly and professional when the cops showed up. "Please excuse my wife, Officers. She's excitable and mentally ill . . ."

Kent says, "You're going to testify that you were hanging out with my client—"

"You want me to perjure myself on the stand because *you* took a bribe?"

"No, I want you to perjure yourself because *you* stole my money."

"I won't lie for you, Kent. Send me to prison, if you want to, but I won't do it."

An animal snarl from the other side of the door. "You are nothing but a scumbag jailbird, and you're too good to lie to save my life? Open that door right now, Nicole. Or I swear I will kick it in."

"And then what? You'll beat me into submission? You can't make me do this."

"Oh, I think I'll find a way." His tone makes me shiver, flooding my imagination with images of all the ways a man can hurt a woman.

And that's when, with a flood of relief, I think of Hawk. If I call him, I know he'll come for me. Maybe he'll call the police; they would listen to him. But when I reach for my phone, my back pocket is empty.

I pat my other pocket, feeling like I'm falling off a cliff into the dark. I set my phone down when I went to answer the door. What was I thinking? How stupid could I be?

Clutching the hair spray and the curling iron, I brace myself for the inevitable. I have no doubt that Kent can kick the door down and overpower me, but I won't surrender without a fight.

Chapter Twenty-Seven

HAWK

Things I know about Nicole:

She has an extensive theft record.

She doesn't actually steal things, she relocates them because of some mysterious imbalance in the force.

She doesn't appreciate being rescued.

Things I know about me:

I can never resist rushing in to rescue a woman in distress.

I'm totally infatuated with Nicole.

So even though I know she's not going to welcome me showing up in response to her phone call, I can't help myself. The near panic in her voice when she described the state of Andrea's house has wakened all of my protective instincts. I want to barge in, sweep her into my arms, and carry her off to safety. Since I'm pretty sure that wouldn't go over well, I've formulated an alternate plan. I'll show up to assist with the cleanup but play it super cool and casual. Just a friend come to help with a mundane task.

All of my resolve goes out the window when I see Kent's BMW parked in the driveway. I'm out of the Jeep and on the porch before the engine has stopped ticking. As I reach for the doorknob, a lingering fragment of logical thought cautions that maybe I'm just jealous and about to walk in on a scene I'd do well to avoid. So many abused women go back to the abuser.

But then I hear Kent shouting, "Open that door right now, Nicole. Or I swear I will kick it in."

That does it. I follow the sound past the entryway and into the hall, where Kent stands in front of a closed door, fists clenched, face contorted with fury.

"What the hell is going on here?" I growl.

Kent turns his head toward me, startled, his hands rising, palms out. Recognition floods his features. "Hey, man, take it easy," he says. "This isn't what it seems."

"Maybe you'd care to explain what it is, exactly. Because it looks like trespassing and vandalism and attempted assault from where I stand."

He takes a step toward me, his voice soothing and conciliatory. "This is between me and my wife. I'm afraid she's been up to her old tricks. I'm trying to get her out of here before she steals something else."

"Looks and sounds an awful lot like a man threatening a woman." My anger is rising. I grew up listening to the sounds of fists on flesh, sometimes my mother's, sometimes my own. Any woman being threatened or harmed rouses my personal demons. I want to draw my .38 and shoot him, right between the eyes, but I'd be sorry later. Besides, what good will I be to Nicole if I'm on the run or locked up?

So I settle for looking as big and threatening as possible, and call out, "Hey, Nicole. You okay?"

"I'm okay," her voice answers from behind the door. "Just scared."

"She's playing the drama card," Kent says. "Nicole's got it down to a science. I told you not to let her get to you, man. And now look at you."

"Why don't you step away from the door," I suggest.

He shrugs and complies. "You don't want to get involved," he says. "Leave now, and I won't call the cops and press charges for pointing a weapon at me." He smiles, cool and calculating, as my hand touches my holster, a telltale move that will only confirm his suspicion that I'm carrying.

It's a valid threat. His word against mine. I have absolutely no reason to be here in this house.

"Not a pretty picture," Kent goes on. "You've been stalking my wife and pulled a gun on me in a jealous rage. End of your license and your business, by the time I'm done spinning the story. Walk away now, let me talk to my wife, and all is well."

"Did you want to talk to Kent, Nicole?" I call out.

"We've talked. I've got nothing else to say."

"See?" I say coolly. "She doesn't want to talk. I may have forgotten to mention that after I quit working for you, I started working for Nicole. She's my client now, and under my protection."

"Think twice," Kent threatens. "Both of you."

"I can live with the risk," I answer. "Nicole?"

"Taking my chances," she calls back.

Kent glares at the closed door, then seems to come to a decision and stomps toward me. "Get out of my way," he snarls, and I step aside to let him pass, then follow him to the entryway. Once he's out the door, I throw the dead bolt behind him and turn around to see Nicole at the other end of the hallway.

I want to run to her, sweep her up off the floor, and hold her against my heart. But I stay where I am, doing my best to project a calm and professional persona. "Are you okay?"

"I didn't need rescuing."

"Of course you didn't. I came to help you clean up. First, maybe a cup of tea? Does your employer have a kitchen?"

Nicole moves toward me slowly until she's so close, I can smell shampoo and sweat, can see clearly the fear and grief in her eyes, along with another emotion I can't decipher. "Thank you," she whispers. "I can't believe you came." And then she takes another step forward and rests her forehead against my chest. She's shivering.

All of my resolve crumbles into dust. I put my arms around her to warm her, comfort her, protect her. She draws a deep breath, and as she exhales, I feel the tension go out of her, her body softening against mine. I allow my hands to learn the shape of her shoulders, the curve of her waist, the softness of her hair, and still she doesn't pull away. Do I dare press my cheek against the top of her head, maybe drop a kiss on her hair?

She's vulnerable and I shouldn't take advantage. I'm caught up in my own internal debate when I feel her body begin to tense again. Easing out of my arms, she asks, "You'll really help me clean up? Because I have no idea how to fix this."

"Fear not, fair lady." I bow with an exaggerated flourish. "I have brought the mother lode of hydrogen peroxide, and this is not my first time cleaning up either bloodbaths or wine stains. The door, however, is beyond my powers of repair."

I don't tell her that my mother taught me how to remove the blood—her blood—spilled on carpets and furniture by my father's hands. I need to keep things as light and easy as I can. Instead I say, "About that tea."

She laughs again, a little less shaky than before, and leads the way into the kitchen. She puts the kettle on and I start rummaging through cupboards. "Ah, there we go. Andrea is all about the good stuff, I see. Now. Do you want to tell me what happened with Kent? Are you sure you don't want the police?"

"No cops. They'd never believe . . ." Her voice trails off, and she says, "I never saw you as a tea drinker."

I pause in the act of measuring gyokuro into the press and grin at her. "Don't I look like I know all about the top-shelf varietals? My mother is into the full tea ceremony. Bone china. Cream in a tiny jug. One lump or two. I do confess to having difficulty with the tiny cups."

I pour not-quite-boiling water into the press and set out two large mugs. "Sugar?"

"Yes, please."

"Perfect. I could also do with a shot of whiskey in mine. Don't tell my mother. Utter blasphemy."

I pour tea into the mugs. Nicole circles hers with hands that tremble visibly. She's acting tough but is obviously deeply rattled. And it's no wonder, between finding Andrea half dead on the floor and being threatened by Kent.

"About your husband," I say, very softly. "Did he beat you often?"

She keeps her eyes on her hands. "He doesn't. He hasn't."

"And yet here he is at your employer's house trying to kick down a door."

"Tonight he may have been trying to kill me," she whispers.

"Let me rephrase my question," I say, my simmering rage rising to a boil again. I stuff it down, keep my voice soft. "Did he try to kill you often?"

"This would be the first time. And I did move his money."

I slam my mug down hard enough that a wave of tea sloshes over the edge. "That sounds a lot like 'he only hits me when I do things wrong.'"

She jumps at the sound, and I brace myself to see fear in her eyes but it doesn't appear. Instead, she smiles at me. "You sound like Ash."

"Then Ash is a very smart person."

"I don't handle blood well," Nicole says after a little silence. "And then Kent. He said . . ." Her face twists, pales. She swallows hard, presses both hands over her mouth. Her eyes widen, suddenly desperate.

I see what's coming. I half lift her from the chair and steer her to the sink, holding her hair back as her body heaves and heaves, trying to rid itself of an overload of shock and fear. When she's done, I hand her a damp paper towel to wipe her face. Then I guide her back to the chair, where she huddles, shivering and small, while I go in search of a blanket to wrap around her shoulders.

"Better?"

She nods, picking up her mug of tea and holding it to her face, not drinking yet but breathing in the fragrant steam. "God, I'm sorry," she begins, but I don't let her finish.

"See if you can get a swallow or two into you. It will settle your stomach. And then we need to start cleaning." I'd be happy to do it all myself, but I know the work will be good for her. Physical action, restoring order, doing something proactive to take her out of fear and helplessness.

She takes a tentative sip of tea, and then another. And then she tells me a story that makes me wish I'd shot Kent when I had the opportunity.

"Let me get this straight," I summarize. "He wants you to perjure yourself to put a criminal back on the street, because the money you moved was a bribe? And he's totally broke and in debt?"

She nods. "If I do what he wants, he says he'll leave me alone."

"That's all he wants?"

She misses my sarcasm, and says, "Oh my God. I just realized. If he's broke, he's not going to pay you." And then her eyes fill, and she adds, "Even worse, he'll ruin you. See? I'm cursed. And everybody who comes near me—"

"Don't you dare say that!" She doesn't even flinch at my raised voice and vehement tone; it's not me she's afraid of. "This is not your fault. None of it. He's the person who is causing the harm. Not you."

"But your license, your business—"

"We'll worry about that when we need to. Okay? Drink your tea. We'll clean up. And later, we'll have a strategy session."

She nods, her head bent, face hidden by her hair.

I shove back my chair and carry our mugs to the sink to wash them. Nicole finds gloves and a bucket. I fetch the peroxide and a sack of old rags I also brought with me.

"I hate blood," she says, with a full-body shudder. "I'm starting with the easy part." She begins mopping the muddy footprints in the entryway.

"Blood's just a chemical compound," I tell her, picking up shards of glass and throwing them into a trash bag. "Protein, water, salt. Hemoglobin is fascinating. Did you know it changes color depending on how much oxygen is in it, or how long it's been outside the body? It can help to determine the time of a crime."

"It's supposed to be inside a body. Not . . . spattered all over everywhere."

"First time I saw a crime scene where somebody had been shot, I puked my guts up." I keep my tone conversational, casual. "A bullet really makes a mess."

"I know," she whispers. "When I was a child . . . this old guy shot himself. In a coffee shop."

Her voice is small, head ducked, shoulders curved inward. As though she's ashamed, as if the old man's death was her fault somehow.

I want to fix everything for her. Erase any painful past. But another thing I learned from my mother is that women are incredibly strong and resilient. I wouldn't want to lose my memories, no matter how ugly they are, and I'm assuming Nicole is strong enough to handle hers.

"Bastard," I say. "You want to take yourself out, do it where you're not traumatizing others. If he hadn't already shot himself, somebody should have shot him for being such a selfish prick."

Nicole stops mopping. Her head comes up, and I watch the emotions move over her expressive face. Shock. Surprise. Thoughtfulness. "I never thought of it that way."

"How else could you think of it?" I ask.

Her lips move soundlessly. Then she squares her shoulders and says, unsteadily, "It was the first time I felt the need to move something. And it wanted to be given to him, but Mom stopped me. I always thought . . . if I'd succeeded, he'd still be alive."

"Whoa," I say. "That's a lot to carry around. How old were you?"

"Six."

"Oh, Nicole."

"And now . . . I've moved the book to Andrea, just like it wanted to be. And she . . . So now I just . . ." Her voice breaks, and she bends her head and goes back to mopping.

"What exactly do you think happened?" I ask. My heart feels too big for my body. I can see the pattern, how she's put these pieces together in her mind. I can also see how they don't quite fit, how she's carrying a burden too big for any human to pack around.

She keeps her head bent, keeps mopping. "I don't know. The EMTs were asking about meds. They found bottles of sedatives and sleeping pills, and she'd been drinking . . ."

"Suicide?" I ask.

Finally she stops moving and looks up at me, her face a study in misery. "Andrea's a pharmacist. She knows how much is safe. She knows better than to mix alcohol and pills."

"So you think she tried to kill herself and that it's your fault because you put a book here?"

One shoulder lifts in a half shrug. "I don't know what else to think. She was fine before."

"First of all, you don't know that she was fine. And you don't know that there's any connection between what happened tonight and the book you moved."

"Don't you see, though? There are really two possibilities. Either I'm just a hapless kleptomaniac with really bad luck and this is a random coincidence. Or, when I move things there are major consequences and sometimes people get hurt."

"Listen. The verdict isn't in on what's happening here. I have something to tell you about Andrea."

"You found something?"

"I did. Her name isn't really Andrea Lester."

"It's not?"

"She was born Andreanna Garner. In Richland. So that gives us a place to start digging, if you still want to."

She stops mopping, curiosity overwriting the guilt and worry. "Was there a Tag Garner?"

"Nope. Didn't find a Tag anything. Sounds more like a nickname than a given name, though, don't you think?"

Nicole leans on the mop, considering, then asks, "How do you think she cut her feet?"

"If she was drinking and taking pills like you said, she would have been pretty out of it. I'd guess she dropped a glass and broke it and then she walked in the glass. Maybe she fell down, then, and was just too drunk and drugged to get up."

"Do you think it might have been an accident?"

Her voice is full of hope, and I say, "Entirely possible. Either way, it's not your responsibility."

"Maybe just a little bit my responsibility," she counters. "I mean, if the book was meant to be here, but we don't know why yet and everything is all out of whack, then maybe I am supposed to do something. Do you think?"

"I think we should finish cleaning up, for sure. And then maybe see if we can find out why she changed her name."

I show her how to soak up blood with a dry rag, then pour hydrogen peroxide onto the stain and blot up the foam, over and over until the spot is white again.

A little later, we sit back on our heels and survey our handiwork.

"Wow," she says. "That actually worked. Thank you. I never would have figured it out."

"Oh, I bet you would have. It's probably on Google. Now. Do you think we should get out of here, or find the book and take it with us?"

"If it's still here. She might have gotten rid of it."

"You can't just . . . sense its presence?" I ask, and her expression closes up tight, as if she thinks I'm making fun of her. "I'm serious," I say. "Trying to understand the world according to Nicole."

She hesitates, then finally says, "If it wanted to be moved, I'd know exactly where it was. It doesn't. So, I don't. We'll have to hunt for it."

It doesn't take long. I'm the one who finds it, stuffed upside down in a drawer of Andrea's desk.

"Got it!"

Nicole comes running.

I open the cover to see the scrawled words *Property of Tag*. "This is one battle-scarred volume. You want to take it, or shall I?"

"You. Please."

So I stuff it in a bag and carry it out to my Jeep while she empties the mop water and puts things away. I come back in for the sack of rags and broken glass. "Shall we lock up and go?"

"Wait," she says. "What about the cat?"

"She has a cat?"

Nicole nods. "I mean, what if we lock the door, and she's in the hospital and I can't get back in to feed the cat?"

"Where are her keys?"

So we go back into the house and search for keys, finally finding a spare set in Andrea's desk drawer. Nicole makes sure the cat has food and water, then shoves the keys in her pocket and we go out and lock the door behind us.

"Where to?" I ask as I start the engine and back out of the driveway. "If you need a safe place, you could stay with my mom for a few days."

"Home." She rests her fingertips on my arm, lightly. "I appreciate your offer. Don't think that I don't. But I babysit for Ash." And then, after a pause: "Plus . . . I can't let him make me run and hide, you know?"

"I get that," I say, keeping my eyes on the road. "But will you promise to call me if you need either brawn or brains? Or both. I have people I can recruit for the brains part."

She laughs softly, returning her hand to her lap. "Pretty sure you're one of the smartest people I know. Also, I was going to call you tonight, only the phone didn't make it into the bathroom with me."

"But not because you needed rescuing," I say.

"Definitely not because of that."

I pull into the lot in front of her apartment and put the Jeep in park.

"Do you think Andrea's okay?" she asks. "Will they tell me anything if I call?"

"Let me try." I dial Sacred Heart and ask for the ER. When a frazzled-sounding voice answers, I infuse my voice with as much anxiety as I can. "I'm looking for my sister, I just heard that an ambulance brought her in."

"Name?"

"Andrea Lester. She would have come in a couple hours ago. Overdose and blood loss. Please tell me she's okay."

I hear the tapping of keys. "She's in the ER, sir, but I can't give you any information."

"Please, for the love of God, you have to tell me something."

The voice goes sympathetic and soothing. "I honestly don't know anything, but why don't you come in and talk to her providers yourself?" She gives me a room number, and I thank her and hang up.

"So we still don't know anything?" Nicole asks.

"We do. We know she's alive, and not in a trauma room. My guess is she'll be okay. Nicole. Try not to worry. This wasn't your fault."

"Nickle," she says.

"Pardon?"

"My people call me Nickle." She rests her hand on my arm. "Thank you. For rescuing me even when I didn't need it. I'm sick about Kent threatening to make trouble for you."

"Let me worry about Kent. Right now, I'm walking you to your door. Don't argue. Either I walk with you openly, or I'll have to stalk you again."

She looks like she's going to say something, but changes her mind. Just nods and starts walking, and I fall into step beside her.

There's nothing out of order in the parking lot or the building that I can see. No evidence of Kent or any hired thugs. Nicole stops outside her door, rises up on her tiptoes, rests her hands on my shoulders, and kisses me.

It feels like a moment caught out of time. Our lips meet and cling. My hands settle on her waist as if they belong there. Only an instant, and then she's gone, leaving me standing there with my heart on my lips and the knowledge that for the first time in my life, I have fallen, utterly and irrevocably, in love.

Chapter Twenty-Eight

Nicole

The kiss was impulsive, thoughtless. I never expected it to feel like this—like coming home to a warm fire, like a key fitting into a lock, like two parts of a whole fused together forever.

But my brain gets in on the action, a little late. It could never really work between us. We're on opposite sides of the law, and I'd be horrible for his career. Plus, there's my terrible record with men and the disaster with Kent and I can't trust my own judgment. So I break away and escape into the apartment, dizzy with all of the events of the day. I'm eager to discuss it all with Ash, but the minute I'm inside the door I see her huddled up in a blanket with a box of tissues in her lap, her eyes swollen and red from weeping.

"What's the matter? What's happened?" A new brand of fear grips me. "Is it Arya? Is she okay?"

"Arya's fine." She gulps. "But . . ." A giant sob crashes through her. She draws in a quavering breath, blots her face with tissues, then says, "You have to move out."

I feel like a bird that's hit a window and fallen gasping to the ground. "What? When? Why? What are you talking about?"

"Now. Tonight." She twists her hands together, tears still flowing, but the set of her jaw is all determination. I follow her gaze to see my full-size, battered, time-to-live-on-the-streets backpack leaned up against the wall by the door.

"I don't understand. It's Ash and Nicole, the stars aligned, you and me against the world. What about Arya? What about—"

"That asswipe that used to be your husband called my landlord. Told him you're living here, said you have a record of theft *and* armed robbery. And that you're dealing drugs on the side. Mr. Henderson said if you're not out before tomorrow, he's evicting me and calling CPS to tell them it's not safe for me to have a baby around you and I should know better." Her voice breaks on a sob.

I can't take it in, can't speak or move or do anything.

"I'm sorry, Nickle. I'm so sorry. But Arya . . ." Ash dissolves into weeping again, and I pull myself together. I put my arms around her, and she wraps hers around me and clings to me, her body shaking with sobs.

"Hey, it's okay. It will be okay," I tell her, even though it's not and I don't see how it ever will be. After the initial shock, I realize I'm not even surprised. Kent will want revenge for being thwarted tonight, and he knows the best way to hurt me is through the people that I love. Which means I have to move out. And that I definitely can't see Hawk anymore because I can't let Kent take him down, too.

I detach myself from Ash's arms. "Arya comes first, before everything. Kent is out for my blood, and I want you safely out of the crosshairs."

"You're an amazing human and I love you," Ash sobs. "If it was just me, I'd tell Kent to go fuck himself and we'd just get another place. But Arya—"

"I know, honey. Don't worry about me. I'll be fine. You'll need help with Arya. I'll call Penelope. She'll help you."

"Isn't she the social worker?"

"That's what makes her perfect."

"I can't trust anybody in the system," Ash protests. "You know that."

"Penelope is safe. Trust me." I scribble the number down on the back of a bill lying on the table. "I'll let her know. But you call her. Just talk to her. See for yourself. Promise."

"Fine. I'll call her. But where will you go?"

"I'll figure something out. And it's best if I don't tell you where I am for now." I hug her again, wanting to hug Arya, too, but not sure if I could ever put her down again if I were to pick her up. "Don't call me. I'll check in when all of this settles down."

"I don't want you to go."

"I have to. We both know that. You packed all my shit?"

She nods.

"Well. This is it, then." I look around the apartment, taking in the details for the last time. It no longer looks crowded and dingy. It looks like home. A place where I felt like it was okay to be me.

Another thing in a long list of things that Kent has taken away from me. I turn my back and open the door.

～

Nicole: Shit hit the fan. Can you help my roommate out with her baby?

Penelope: Well of course. But my goodness. What has happened?

Nicole: I'll explain later. Just, can you call Ash? I'll forward her contact info

Penelope: Will do right now. Update me!

～

I do what I always do when I'm in trouble—go home to Mom.

I knock before putting my key in the lock, not wanting to startle her. A shadow moves in front of the curtains and footsteps approach the door. They are measured and heavy, definitely not Mom's. I start to back away, visions of home invaders spiking my adrenaline, but when the door opens, Kent is standing there, smooth and smiling.

"Trouble in paradise?" he asks.

"You bastard," I spit at him.

He shakes his head. "That's not polite. I was hoping you'd be ready to be reasonable. I have something for you."

He holds out a manila envelope, and I take it on autopilot. "Let me talk to Mom."

"You can talk to her when you are ready to see reason."

Panic grips me. Is he capable of harming my mother? No act of horror or revenge seems beyond him now. "What have you done to her? Have you hurt her?" I shout, "Mom? Mom, are you okay?"

She moves up behind Kent. I try to reach for her, but he blocks me. "Now, Mary," he says gently, "remember what we talked about. This is the only way to help Nicole."

He shifts position just enough to let me see the tears pouring down her face.

"Mom. I need to come in. We need to talk."

"This is best for you, honey. The only thing that might help. Maybe if I'd done it years ago you'd be better now."

Kent keeps his voice soft, sympathetic, even. "I told your mother how you stole valuable belongings from your employer. And she's agreed that it's time for tough love."

"But I didn't steal anything. I didn't even move anything! Get out of the way, Kent. This is not your house. I want—"

He closes the door. I beat on it with my fists, as panicked as if all of the monsters of my childhood are pursuing me at once. No answer.

I call Mom from my cell phone, and it goes to voice mail. I steady my voice as much as I can to leave a message.

"I get why you're doing this. I love you, and I'll be okay. But Kent isn't what you think. You know I don't lie; you have to believe me."

Now what? Where do I go, what do I do? I can't stay out here on the porch all night. Lost and adrift like never before in my life, I trudge through snow back toward the bus. I've only traveled a block when my cell rings. My heart lifts. Mom has listened to the message. Believed me. I can sleep in a warm bed and eat Mom food, and we'll figure this out together, as a family.

But it's not Mom. It's Kent.

Rage boils away my grief and fear. "What the hell are you doing? You leave my people alone, do you hear me?"

"Or what?" His voice is calm, reasonable, as if I'm an irrational child throwing a tantrum. "You have no power here, Nicole. It's all on my side. And you're being rather stupid, don't you think? All you need to do is this one little thing for me. Then you can have your life back, such as it is."

"Fuck you."

"We'll talk again when you've learned to be polite." The phone goes silent.

Motion in any direction seems impossible, but I can't stay here, so I walk another block, and then another, trying to think what to do. If I call Warner he might rescue me, but if Kent has gotten to him and he refused to take me in, the way Mom just did, I don't think my heart could take it. There's Penelope, but I can't go there because of Ash and Arya.

Which leaves Hawk. A hero if there ever was one, ready and willing. All I'd have to do is send one text, "Maybe I do need rescuing," and he'd be here in a heartbeat. But I now have absolutely no doubt that

Kent would tear his life apart. I can't do that to him, after everything he's done for me.

So I catch a bus and find a cheap motel. I've got money to rent a room for maybe a week. Then, if Andrea survives, if she still wants me to work after she comes home, maybe I could afford a studio apartment. Huddled under the blanket in my dingy room, looking at walls that might have once been white, breathing in the stink of tobacco and disappointment left by all the down-and-out souls who have been here before me, I finally open the envelope Kent thrust into my hands.

It's a legal document, and for a long minute, I stare at it uncomprehending, thinking maybe he has filed for divorce. And then I recover my ability to read and notice that I'm looking at a subpoena: State of Washington v. Brian Hazleton. A yellow sticky note in Kent's handwriting reads, *Maybe you have no sense of self-preservation, but I know you love your family. I'll be in touch with a date and time for you to come into the office to give your witness statement.*

This is the final blow. There's nothing I can do, no way out of this mess. If I try to report Kent for accepting a bribe, nobody will believe my word against his. And he's already demonstrated his ability to get to my family and my friends.

As if to drive the point home, Roberta texts me:

What is going on???

Nicole: ?? Need a little more info
Roberta: Kent says you're getting set to trash Sunny Side Up

Another message rolls in while I stare at the screen, too shocked and shaken to reply.

Roberta: Nickle? I'm begging you. Sunny Side Up means the house and food and college for the kids . . .

I look at the legal documents in my lap, at the threat written on a cheerful yellow sticky note, and I descend into a despair deeper than anything I've ever known. Kent and I both know that I will do anything, even lie in court if I have to, to protect the people I love, whether they believe in me or not.

Only, in this case, lying also means putting a criminal back on the street. And not just any criminal. I know the name Brian Hazleton, it's been all over the news. He's been accused of gunning down three people in cold blood. How can I ever live with myself if I help set him free so he can kill again?

But how can I ever live with myself if Ash loses Arya, or Roberta loses Sunny Side Up, or Hawk loses his business?

Picking up the phone, I dial Roberta, and as soon as she answers, I say, "I'm going to try to fix this, but just hear me out, okay? It's not me. It's Kent. He's gone off the deep end and—"

"Don't you try to shift the blame. Kent is—"

"A liar, a criminal, and a dangerous narcissist," I break in. "You're not going to want to believe me, Rob, but please listen. I've done nothing to hurt your business—"

"Except for moving that book."

"Right, and I'm sorry, but I never hurt you on purpose. Kent is pressuring me to do something illegal for him. Less you know, the better. Ash and Mom and you and everybody I love are his thumbscrews."

Silence. Then: "Are you still seeing that psychologist?"

"I'm not delusional, damn it. Listen to me. He's at Mom's house now."

"I know. I just talked to him. He said you were going to start posting bad reviews on Yelp." I can hear her outraged breathing, can picture her usually pleasant face tight with anger and disdain.

"You know I would never hurt you on purpose. You have to know that. Please don't leave Mom alone with him."

"Maybe Warner could go over," she says after a long pause. Maybe it's just my imagination, but her voice sounds softened, at least a little.

"Thank you," I breathe, but she's already gone, leaving me alone to wrestle with my impossible choices.

Chapter Twenty-Nine

ANDREA

I drift just below the surface of consciousness, dimly aware that I'm in a hospital. My eyelids are too heavy to open. All of my limbs feel weighted, and my thoughts are blunted and slow. Nurses have been in and out all night, insisting that I roll this way or that, trying to get me to answer a series of annoying questions. They check my blood pressure, monitor my IV. Now somebody is asking questions again, urging me to open my eyes.

"Can you tell me your name?"

"Do you know where you are?"

Cool fingers lift one eyelid at a time and shine a bright light that stabs into my brain. Memories break and splinter.

White halls. Forced medications. Painting at a table in a large sunlit room with heavy screens over the windows. A circle of patients in a group room, a weary nurse urging me to share my feelings. Patients muttering to themselves in the hallway, or sitting and rocking and sometimes exploding into rages that bring staff members running . . .

"Andrea, you need to wake up now." A new voice, authoritative and commanding, drags me toward reality.

I try to sink into oblivion, but a hand holds me back, squeezing my fingers to the point of pain, that irritating female voice reverberating loudly in my hypersensitive skull. "Andrea. I know you can hear me. Open your eyes."

Of course I can hear her. The dead could hear her. My head and both feet throb with the rhythm of my heartbeat, and I can't think why. A memory blip surfaces. I was drinking. I took pills. That accounts for the headache, and the way this woman's voice feels like a corkscrew between my ears. But what happened to my feet? Carefully, I rub my right foot against my left ankle. Both are heavily bandaged.

My eyes fly open, then close again as the light stabs into my poor, tormented brain.

"Andrea."

I squint, attempting to comply with the command while still keeping out the light.

The owner of the irritating and intrusive voice is a middle-aged woman with short graying hair and a no-nonsense face. She wears a white lab coat, a stethoscope draped around her neck. "There you are," she says. "I'm Dr. Billings, and you're in Sacred Heart hospital. What do you remember?"

"Everything," I lie. Careful not to move my head, I search the room with my eyes, trying to figure out what day it is, what part of the hospital this is. Medical or psych? The windows are unbarred. Surely that's a good sign. *Please,* I pray, even though there is no god that I believe in. *Please don't let it be psych. Not again.*

"Suppose you tell me what happened," the doctor says.

"I drank too much."

"And what else?"

The sound of the IV pump grates on my nerves. It's hard to think, and the memory of what happened is entirely missing. Swallowing back nausea, refusing to acknowledge the pain, which is considerable, I find an evasion. "When can I go home?"

"Much of that depends on you," the doctor says. "I'd really like to hear from you what happened."

I'm starting to hate this doctor. She's relentless. I need to be very careful about what I say. "Obviously, I injured my feet," I say with great dignity.

"Good to know your deductive reasoning skills are intact."

Sarcasm. From my doctor. Where did they get this woman, and how is it that some other beleaguered patient hasn't killed her yet?

I touch my feet together, feeling the padding of bandages between them. What did I do? Whatever it is, I need to talk my way out of here. And for the moment, honesty seems like the best policy.

"Fine," I say. "I had a drink. I know better, because I'm on sedatives already, but it was a bad day. I figured I could handle a glass of wine. I guess I was wrong because I don't seem to remember anything."

"You had more than one glass. Your blood alcohol was .24. Also, from looking at the date your prescriptions were filled, it appears that you've taken significantly more of both the antianxiety and sleeping pills than you ought to have."

Goose bumps rise on the skin of my arms as the fear sets in. I see where this is going.

"We'll have someone from psych come in and talk to you," she says, confirming my fears.

I meet her gaze as levelly as I can. "Look. There's no need for psych. I'm already seeing Dr. Magnuson, and I promise to call him and tell him immediately. I had a bad week. My anxiety got away from me, and I took extra pills. Listen, I'm a pharmacist. I know dosing, and yes, I played with my own medications. But if I'd been trying to kill myself, I wouldn't still be here."

A trickle of sweat runs down my back, another between my breasts. A monitor picks up my accelerating heart rate, beeping loudly. There is no way to hide my panic. What if they somehow figure out who I am and discover my past?

"The only reason you are still here is because your cleaning person found you and called an ambulance, so I'm not buying your story," Dr. Billings says. "Psych will be in to talk to you before I can discharge you. Now. About your feet. You've walked on glass and lacerated them both. Eight stitches in the right, six in the left. You'll need to follow up with your regular provider in ten days to get those out. In the meantime, we'll be observing you for at least a few more hours, maybe overnight, depending on how you do. Your respiratory and cardiac function were quite significantly depressed when you came in."

"I really misjudged the alcohol," I say, channeling as much sincerity into my words as possible. "And, believe me, I've learned my lesson. I am definitely not repeating the experiment."

She smiles professionally, in a way that still manages to be irritating. "I'm glad to hear you say that. We will still have mental health come in for a visit before we let you go."

A moment after she leaves, before I've had time to catch my breath and pull myself together, a man slips into my room, closing the door behind him. He's tall, well dressed, good looking. And a total stranger. If he's the crisis person, they're hiring a different caliber of employee than I remember.

"Andrea?" Even though he shapes it as a question, I can see that he knows exactly who I am. He moves with the sort of confidence and privilege that make it abundantly clear he's not with mental health. "My name is Kent Brandenburg. I'm Nicole's husband."

As I take in his expensive suit and shoes, the diamond ring on his manicured hand, I think about Nicole riding the bus and trudging through the snow. I see her thin coat and well-worn clothes, the way she puts up with all of my bullshit to make enough money to live on.

"So you're the asshole," I say.

He moves closer. "Please pardon the intrusion. I've come to warn you about my wife." Now that he's right by the bed, I can see that his tie is askew. He hasn't shaved. His eyes are bloodshot, and there's something seriously wrong with his smile.

"I'm not exactly in the mood for visitors," I tell him. "Go away before I call the nurse."

"You need to hear this, and I promise only to be a moment. I should never have allowed Nicole to worm her way into your life. I knew better. But one always hopes, you know? That a person can change. Or will change, anyway. I don't know if she told you about her . . . problem?"

"You mean that she steals things?"

He sighs. "Yes. Well. About that. She's also a highly accomplished, compulsive liar. I know she was left alone in your home last night, and I'm sorry to report that she stole a valuable object. I'm here to return it."

He reaches into his suit pocket and draws out the sculpture I keep on the credenza in the entryway, the one that Nicole once said wanted to be moved into the hall closet. As he holds it out to me, I see it through her eyes instead of my own—a twisted, tortured figure that radiates shame and guilt and fear. She's right. It's an ugly thing. Which is probably why I bought it so many years ago; it seemed an accurate representation of my inner self, a representation I haven't even tried to grow out of.

"What's your angle?" I demand.

He looks wounded. "Me? An angle? I've come to return your property."

I just glare at him. Finally, he sets my sculpture down on the bedside table and wipes his hands on his pants, as if it has somehow tainted him.

"Fine, I'll be honest with you." He drops his voice, as if he's telling me a secret. "If Nicole has no opportunity to steal from you, I avoid the indignity of seeing my wife behind bars. I'm a high-profile attorney, and it would be bad for my career. I would appreciate it if you wouldn't continue to employ her."

"Thanks for bringing back my property," I tell him. "Now, if you could go?"

"Do we have an understanding, then?"

"I understand you perfectly," I answer. My skin feels crawly as I watch him leave. And absurdly, lying here in the hospital, waiting for psych to come visit and possibly lock me away, instead of being angry at Nicole, I'm worried about her. It must have been terrifying for her to find me lying half dead on the floor. I should call her, but of course I don't have my phone.

Thinking of my phone makes me think of Ronda, which triggers a whole new spiral of memories and anxiety, and by the time mental health shows up, I'm beginning to think that maybe a straitjacket is exactly what I need.

But somehow I manage to hold it together. I explain about my anxiety and the new pills and being stupid enough to drink. And again, I make it clear that I'll call my psychiatrist at once and make another appointment. The kind, weary-looking woman doesn't quite buy my story. In the end, she agrees that I can go home, but only if I have somebody to stay with me. For a long moment, I stare at her in blank dismay, picturing myself behind locked doors on a psych unit.

And then I give her the name of the only human on the face of the planet who might be willing to take care of me. For a price.

Chapter Thirty

NICOLE

I meet with Andrea and a crisis worker in a corner of the waiting room. The only other occupant is an elderly woman in a wheelchair. She's sleeping, her mouth open as she snores gently. Andrea, too, is in a wheelchair, both feet wrapped up in mummy-style bandages. Her face is about three shades too pale, and the skin around her eyes looks bruised and fragile, but her expression is as sharp and irritable as always.

The crisis worker, Melanie, is pleasant but frayed around the edges and seems to be in a hurry. We talked on the phone earlier this morning, and she doesn't waste any time now with small talk.

"Thanks for coming," she says. "I want to make sure you both understand the plan, and get you to each sign this document to acknowledge your responsibilities."

Somehow, signing my name to commit to said responsibilities when they are officially printed on paper is much more anxiety provoking than a verbal agreement over the phone. I initial the conditions one at a time. I'm moving into Andrea's house for the next two weeks. I will keep all of her medications on my person, or locked and under my control, and make sure she only takes them as prescribed. I will remove all alcohol from the house. I will see that Andrea attends counseling appointments. If any of these conditions are broken, or if I believe that Andrea has any intention of self-harm at any time, I promise to call the crisis number provided immediately.

When Andrea called on the hospital phone and asked me to do this, she promised to pay me, and I've been trying to talk myself into just being grateful that I have a place to stay and money coming in. But she doesn't make it easy. "Took you long enough to get here," she says when Melanie has scurried off to another crisis and I'm shoving the wheelchair across a slushy parking lot to where I've parked Andrea's car.

"You're welcome," I retort, infusing all of the sarcasm I can manage into the words. Fetching her car and coming to pick her up has been an ordeal of hours. First, navigating the bus with a full-size backpack stuffed with all my earthly possessions. And then, at the other end of the route, slogging to her house on foot, through snow, my back and shoulders aching. Finally, figuring out how to operate the car, which is a hybrid, when I've never driven one before. All of this on top of the misery of a sleepless night and worry about my hopeless future.

"Oh," Andrea says after she's awkwardly navigated the shift from the wheelchair to the passenger seat and I've stowed the crutches in the back and trekked across the lot and back again to return the chair. "I suppose you expect me to thank you for coming to pick me up, in my own car, and taking me home again, even though I am exorbitantly paying you."

I buckle my seat belt and start the car. "How about this: 'Gee, Nicole, thanks for saving my life and cleaning up my blood and booze, and agreeing to be my babysitter for the next two weeks because I can't be trusted with my own medicine.'"

As soon as I say it, I feel bad. I can see that she's hurting, and maybe she's even embarrassed a little, and hates being rescued just as much as I do. As if in confirmation, she leans her head back, closes her eyes, and says, "Just take me home."

We drive in a difficult silence. When we get to the house and I've parked in the garage and managed to ignore her snide comment about people who can't park straight even if their lives depended upon it, she refuses to let me help her get out of the car. I stand there, helplessly watching her struggle to get out and upright. When I pick up her purse, thinking at least I can carry it for her, she snarls, "Give me that," and drapes it over her shoulder.

I've had stitches and can imagine all too well how much it must hurt to walk with lacerations on the bottoms of both feet, even with the crutches, but she persists in taking a small tour of the ground floor. The living room. Her study, where she opens the desk drawers and must notice the missing book, although she says nothing. The bathroom, and the marks of violence on the door. By the time she finally collapses into a chair in the kitchen, her forehead is beaded with sweat, her breathing labored.

"Are you okay?" I ask, worry outweighing, for a moment, my outrage that she seems to think I might have stolen something while she was in the hospital.

"Hemoglobin is low and everything hurts," she says. "I'll live. Can I have my pain pills now?"

I get her a glass of water, tap two pills out of the bottle that came home with her from the hospital, and watch, hovering, hoping another 911 call is not in my immediate future. But gradually her breathing slows and her color improves from deathly to a marginally healthier shade of pale.

"Sit down, would you?" She slams the empty glass down on the table.

I sit. Her gaze settles on a spot to the left of my head. She clears her throat. "Thank you for cleaning up the blood. And getting me to the hospital. And saving my life. And agreeing to that insane plan."

"That sounded painful," I reply. "Like a chicken bone is lodged in your throat." What is wrong with me? I actually care about Andrea,

God only knows why, and I need any work she'll throw my way. But my capacity to be polite, to pretend what I don't feel, has apparently vanished.

"I'll pay you a bonus for the extra stress and cleanup," she says.

"I don't want a bonus!" I fling my hands up in the air. "Just don't yell at me, maybe, is all I'm asking."

"Now look who's yelling. Do you think maybe you could make us some tea instead of sitting there scowling at me?"

"You told me to sit!"

"And now I'm telling you to make tea. And while you're doing that, maybe you could explain what happened to the bathroom door and my copy of the *Inferno*."

I clamp my jaw shut to block a string of expletives. "I don't want to talk about it."

"Well, I do," she says. "My house. My door. My book, since you gave it to me."

"I'll pay for a new door."

"Maybe your bonus will cover it," she says. "And the book?"

"You flipped out because it was here! I thought maybe it had to do with you trying to kill yourself, so I took it away."

"I did not try to kill myself," she retorts. "That was an accident. If you don't want to talk about what happened to my door, maybe tell me about this." She reaches into her purse, draws out an object, and sets it on the table.

I stare at it, blank and uncomprehending. It's the horrible little sculpture that usually sits on the credenza in the entryway. "You took that with you?" I blurt out, which is obviously a stupid thing to say, because I watched the paramedics roll her out on a gurney, and they certainly didn't stop to pick up a hideous statue on the way out.

Andrea smiles an annoying, knowing sort of smile, and says, "Tell me everything."

"I don't know everything," I protest. "Like, for example, why you—"

"Tell me what you do know."

I can't lie, but I'm a pro at evading. "Well, after you went to the ER, my husband stopped by."

"And he was in my house, why?"

"He wanted to talk."

"Well, that makes everything perfectly clear."

"He wants me to do something I don't want to do. I said no and he got . . . persuasive. Okay?"

"Are you going to make tea while we talk, or not?" she asks.

I mutter under my breath while I get out the tea canister and slam it down on the counter.

"Let me guess," Andrea persists. "You barricaded yourself in the bathroom and he tried to beat the door down, thus the dents."

"More or less. Yes. Awesome sleuthing."

"And then what happened? He got tired of beating on the door and just left?"

I fill the kettle and turn it on, knowing she's going to hate what I say next. "No, a friend of mine came over and encouraged Kent to leave."

"You've had a whole parade of people through the house while I was gone, then. Wonderful. And while you had the opportunity, you stole my sculpture."

I brace my hands on the counter, head bent, breathing. All of my life, people have been seeing me and my actions through some distorted lens and telling me who I am or why I do what I do. My family. The legal system. Lawyers and counselors and especially Kent, who has spent the last five years letting me know how fortunate I am that he puts up with me and is expending time and energy to try to fix me.

The only thing I've done right recently was to save Andrea's life and clean her house and never move one single object that belonged to her, except for the book she was mad about me bringing here in the first place. And now she's accusing me of carelessness and recklessness and outright theft.

I swing around, both hands in the air in mock surrender.

"You win. I took the opportunity of your near death to ask Kent to come over and threaten me, and then my friend Hawk and I had a bloodstain-removal party. Biggest and best house party ever! I topped it off by stealing the ugliest figurine in the entire history of the known world, which has somehow materialized in your handbag. You know what? I don't need your shit. I'm out of here."

"But you told the crisis worker you would stay," Andrea protests.

"Yeah, I did. But I changed my mind. If you want to kill yourself, that's not my problem."

Maybe I'm Kent's stooge and he's pulling my puppet strings and making me dance, but I do not have to tolerate this from Andrea. I'll go back to the motel. I'll find a job. There has to be something I can do.

Andrea's voice follows me as I stalk out of the kitchen. "Nicole. I propose a truce. Come back and make my tea and let's try to not snipe at each other for five minutes."

The kettle chooses that very instant to come to a boil, emitting a high-pitched shriek. I remember that Andrea can't really walk, that she has nobody, that I will feel terribly, horribly guilty if I leave her alone and she winds up dead. Still, my pride burns as I turn and retrace my steps across the kitchen and pour boiling water over the tea leaves. It's way beyond the perfect temperature to make Andrea's highbrow perfect brew, but if she doesn't like it, she can make her own. She says nothing while I carry the press and two cups to the table. She says nothing until I sit.

Only then does she look up at me and try to smile. "First, I did not try to kill myself. It was a mistake."

"If you say so," I mutter, insolent and rude.

"You should also know that your husband came to see me in the hospital."

I groan. "Oh God. What did he want?"

"He *said* that what he wanted was to protect me from you and your stealing. And he brought this"—her hand rests on the sculpture sitting on the table between us—"as evidence that you were stealing from me."

I close my eyes, sinking into darkness. So he's gotten to Andrea, too. I've missed my opportunity to be the one to walk away. Now she gets to rub my nose in my inadequacies and failures and fire me. She won't believe me when I tell her the truth. Nobody ever does.

"Did you move my sculpture, Nicole?" she asks.

Eyes still closed so I don't have to look at the triumph I'm sure she wears on her face, I answer, wearily, "No, I did not."

"I didn't think so," she says.

"Wait, what?" My eyes fly open and I stare at her in disbelief.

"If you'd moved it, it would have been in the hall closet." Her lips curve in a smile that actually hints at a sense of humor. "Your husband had an agenda. I think what he really wanted was for me to fire you. Why would he want that?"

I pour out the tea and lift my cup, breathing in the steam and, with it, maybe just a whiff of hope. "I'd guess he thinks I'm more likely to be compliant with what he wants if I don't have a job."

"What does he want?"

"He wants me to lie for him. In court. An alibi for a murderer." Tears are very close to the surface again, and I'm as sick of crying as I am of being sorry.

Andrea takes a sip of tea and sets down the cup. "God, this is terrible."

A retort rises to my lips, but before I can speak, she laughs, brief and dry. "Make me a proper cup. After that, you can throw away my alcohol and round up all my pills. And then we'll get a bed made up for you."

"All right."

"I do appreciate you being here," she says. "How will your room-mate manage the babysitting?"

"I had to move out."

"Kent again?"

"Kent again."

"Fix the tea. Please. And then tell me what he's doing."

So I do. I don't mean to, but I tell her everything. I tell her about moving Kent's money, and about the birthday dinner, and about the writing class and Penelope and Ash and Mom and Roberta and even Hawk, including why I have to stop talking to him. I finish up with: "So, it's all just completely tangled and hopeless and I'm out of options."

"I think you're overlooking a valuable resource," she says, finishing the last swallow of her tea.

"I am?"

"This Hawk person. He's a private eye, you said."

"Yes, but he—"

She waves a hand at me. "Yeah, yeah. *You* don't like to be rescued but you're trying to rescue *him*. Since you're out of options, maybe you should stop being a martyr and let him make that decision for himself."

My anger sparks again at her words. "I am not a martyr."

Andrea shrugs. "If you say so. But do you really think it's fair for you to choose for him? Doesn't he get any say at all?"

I don't have an answer for this, so I take refuge in clearing the table and washing our cups.

"He might be able to get some dirt on Kent," Andrea persists. "You know what I think? I think you like this Hawk person and you're afraid to get too close."

"Don't you talk to me about fear of relationships!" I snap at her, our brief truce over. "You're so freaked out by the name of this Tag person written on the cover of a book that you ended up in the emergency room from an accidental overdose. Unless you're lying to everybody and you really did it on purpose."

Andrea pales. I didn't think it was possible for her to go any whiter, but she does. She swallows hard. Strokes the hideous sculpture. And says, "Touché. I did not do it on purpose, but I am the last person in the world you should take advice from. If you'll help me up the stairs, I think I'd like to lie down."

Chapter Thirty-One

NICOLE

I help Andrea up to her room and try to make her comfortable, but she's gone back to snarly and sends me off to round up her meds and dump out all of her wine. The whole time I'm working, I alternately wonder about her story and ponder what she said about Hawk. He's texted me several times today, and I haven't responded. But my resolve is wavering, and when he calls, I cave and pick up.

"Nicole. I have news."

"You do? Good news or bad news?"

"Good news. We've got him!"

"I'm sorry, who have we got, exactly?" Maybe he means Kent, and proof of his blackmail.

"The guy," Hawk says. "From the missing person case. His fingerprints were on the phone. And—are you ready? They also found the missing woman."

"Is she . . ." My tongue can't shape the word. I sink down onto the kitchen floor and lean against the island, drawing my knees up against my chest.

"Alive. Traumatized, as you'd expect. But physically okay."

Good news. Awesome news. Big news. Too big, in fact, as dizzying as trying to grasp the concept of eternity or the size of the universe or Einstein's theory of time. I flop backward onto the floor and lie there on the smooth, cold tile, staring up at the ceiling with the phone held to my ear.

"Don't you dare start in on the 'what if I'd shown the phone to Hawk sooner' self-recrimination soundtrack," he warns.

"It's like you know me, or something." My voice is wobbly again. There are so many holes in my tough-girl persona these days, it's almost like it doesn't exist anymore, which leaves me nothing to hide behind.

"Nickle. You had no way of knowing that phone was anything other than trash. Your Object Relocation Program saved a life and caught a bad guy. You don't get to beat yourself up over that."

I try to digest this while reality morphs into new configurations all around me. I start asking myself random questions like "What if I were lying on the ceiling instead of the floor?" I'd have to move, because the light fixture would be right where my head is, and—

"You okay over there?" Hawk asks.

"I think my brain is exploding."

"Is that a good thing or a bad thing?"

"Was the big bang a good thing?"

"A very good thing."

"I'm not so sure." I bend my knees and press my feet against the floor. Focus on a breath, in and out. Good. I still know how to breathe. That's one thing that hasn't changed. Little by little, I'm grounded in my own body again. Breath moves in and out of my lungs. There's a hollowness in my belly that reminds me I didn't eat lunch and might have forgotten breakfast.

"I feel like I've got five jigsaw puzzles dumped out on the table and never had the boxes for any of them," I tell him. "Also, I think I'm hungry."

"I'll take you for dinner. Pizza? Pizza sounds good to me."

And then I remember. Saving a life by relocating an object does not wipe away my legal problems or make Kent go away. "I can't," I say, sitting up, hoping that maybe being upright will restore logic to my brain processes. "We can't."

"I understand," Hawk says, suddenly stiff and formal. "Well, I just wanted to update you on the case and let you know your evidence helped apprehend the criminal."

I can't let him go, not like that. "You don't understand," I tell him. "I can't because of Kent."

"Don't tell me you're still in love with that piece of human excrement," he growls. "Don't. I can't hear it."

"What I was going to tell you," I say, "is that if he finds out I've been eating pizza with you, he'll do what he said, tell everybody you drew a gun on him while you were trespassing at Andrea's. Ruin your business. Maybe get you arrested."

"Well, that definitely rules out pizza," Hawk says. "What about hamburgers? Or Mexican. I could really use a good carne asada right about now."

"It's not a joke, Hawk. He's serious."

"So am I. Listen to me," he says while I flop back down and resume contemplating the wonders of Andrea's ceiling. "We don't let a guy like Kent beat us. We study the problem, we find his weaknesses, and we take him down."

I wish I believed that could happen, that I could wave a magic wand, and poof! Kent is no longer in my life. Better yet, I never met him, never married him. Best of all? He never existed.

"You don't have to go out to eat with me or hang out with me," Hawk says. "But, please, let me put you on my official caseload. And come meet with my mother. Don't know if I mentioned this, but she's an attorney who specializes in taking down dirtbags like Kent. If you won't do it for yourself, do it for humanity. The man cannot be allowed to continue."

Temptation and hope join forces and nudge me into asking, "How much will it cost? For you. For your mom. Because I don't think—"

"Don't be ridiculous. No charge. You get the friends-and-family package. Meaning, free. No strings attached."

"Nothing is ever free," I protest. "Be honest. Why do you want to do this?"

"Because I like you. And I don't like Kent."

"That's it?"

"Okay. I like you a lot. And I really, really don't like Kent. And also I'm really curious about Andrea and the book and can't wait to see how your Object Relocation Program works things out in her life."

"Come on, Hawk. There are always strings."

"All right. I admit it," he says after a silence so long I think maybe he's hung up. "Here are my strings, dangling dangerously out in the open. I want to spend time with you. I want you to be safe. And I really want to believe that there's some mysterious force behind what you do. That you pick up a phone from a snowdrift and we find a killer. That you move a book and Andrea's life shifts for the better."

"Or," I argue, "maybe she's not paranoid and this Tag person really is dangerous. Maybe he hurt her before, and the book triggered PTSD, sent her into a spiral, and—"

"And maybe you're giving her an opportunity to heal from an old wound."

"Are you for real right now?"

"Absolutely. Maybe you're a . . . catalyst. What you do sparks change."

Catalyst.

I turn the word over in my mind. I like the shape of it, the way it hints at the magic Hawk says he's craving. The good kind of magic. So much better than a curse.

"I already lifted fingerprints off the book," Hawk says. "Aunt Joan sent them for analysis, as a favor to me. Do you want me to put a stop on that?"

I hesitate, wrestling with my pride and my conscience and all of my old beliefs.

"Please don't make me stop," Hawk says. "Letting me work on this, and on the problem of Kent, is like you rescuing me. Not the other way around."

I can't help laughing at that. My breath comes a little easier, and the reality feels like maybe it's settling down instead of swirling around my ears. "All right," I hear myself answering. "Yes. Are you sure your mother won't mind?"

"Are you kidding? She lives for this sort of thing. When can I pick you up? If I get you now, you can join us for stew and homemade biscuits."

"I can't. I'm at Andrea's as her crisis person, and to help her until she can walk. I need to feed her. And then she'll need meds and help getting settled for the night."

"After, then," he says. "Hot chocolate and a late-night confab. Put Andrea to bed, and I'll come pick you up. Okay?"

"I need to check with her." I press my palms against the floor. It feels so solid and cold and real, unlike everything else in my world. "But she wanted me to call you, so I'm saying a tentative yes."

Chapter Thirty-Two

NICOLE

Andrea not only has no objection to me leaving once she's settled into bed with Sylvester curled up beside her, but she's maybe a little too enthusiastic about the idea. "Stop hovering and go. Unless you don't trust me."

"Should I trust you?" I ask, imagining how I'll feel if I come back to find her dead. "The crisis person did say not to leave you alone."

"I trusted you," she says, "when you told me you didn't lie. So here's what you should ask before you go. 'Are you planning to kill yourself tonight, Andrea?' And I'll answer honestly."

"Well, are you? Planning to kill yourself tonight?"

"I am not," she says. "I am going to sleep. For the love of God, go away and let me be alone while I do so."

And so it is that Hawk comes to pick me up. He texts me when he leaves home, and again when he arrives. I'm here.

Feeling ridiculously like I'm a teenager sneaking out of the house on an illicit adventure, I disarm and reset the security system and open the door, almost running into Hawk, who is standing on the doorstep waiting for me.

"I could probably walk out to the vehicle safely," I gasp, resisting the urge to throw my arms around him and hold on for dear life.

"Could have just sat out there and honked the horn for you," he says, laughing. "My mother drilled it into me that when you pick somebody up, you go to the door." He opens the passenger door for me and holds it while I climb in, before walking around and settling himself into the driver's seat.

I'm acutely aware of his body, all hard muscle, and the softness of my own. He smells like green grass and sunlight, freedom and safety. Which is ridiculous. People smell like fabric softener and hair-care products and deodorant and maybe cologne. Not like childhood summers and kites soaring in blue skies and north winds and snow. Freedom doesn't have a smell. I want to kiss him again, a real kiss, this time, to smooth my hand over that jutting jawline, to . . .

Get a grip, Nicole. You are not going to do any of those things.

Hawk talks about writing class and the weather as he drives, keeping things light between us, but the closer we get to our destination, the more the tension builds inside me.

"Are you sure about this?" I ask as he pulls into the driveway of an immaculate two-story on a quiet street lined by big old trees. "I mean, it's so late and all." What I really want to say is "What if your mother doesn't like me?" The answer to which should not matter, but does.

Hawk smiles. "Trust me. It will be fine. Aunt Joan was okay, right?"

"Are you kidding? Took me all week to get over that encounter."

"You'll survive."

I follow him up a wide walkway that's been shoveled and de-iced. A wheelchair ramp slants off one side of the porch. Hawk knocks before putting a key in the lock, and calls, "Mom, it's me. I've brought Nicole."

A woman in a sporty-looking wheelchair rolls herself over to greet us at the door.

"Nicole, this is my mother, Janelle Messina," he says. The woman turns her full attention to me, and I search her face for a resemblance to

Hawk. She's petite and fine boned where he is tall and ruggedly built. Her hair is black like his but threaded with silver. Her features are nothing like his, her face oval and delicate, marred by the jagged white line of an old scar that puckers the skin on her left cheekbone. Her eyes are brown but have the same quiet intensity as his, and I feel like I've been searched to the inner recesses of my soul.

"Nice to meet you, Mrs. Messina."

"Welcome," she says. "Call me Janelle. Come in. Let's get started." She swivels the chair pretty much on a dime and rolls off.

"If you don't mind taking off your shoes here, it makes things easier," Hawk says, bending to unlace his boots. "She can manage the vacuum and the mop, but these days she's much more likely to make me do it."

I take off my shoes and follow him into a spacious room that is part kitchen, part eating area. The counters are low and for the most part have no shelving or drawers under them. A panel of windows takes up the entire wall by the dining table, which has chairs only on one side. The entire space is designed for easy wheelchair access.

Janelle is at the counter ladling hot chocolate into mugs from a pot on the stove. "Marshmallows or whipped cream?" she asks. "Also, I'm putting a splash of rum in mine. Yes or no?"

"I'm the designated driver," Hawk says. "Nicole?"

I consider the rum bottle with longing, imagining the warm haze of alcohol settling over me, but this is not the time to relax and let down my guard. I shudder at the thought of hot chocolate with marshmallows, a drink I've not been able to stomach since that horrible day when the old man died.

"Whipped cream, no rum. Thank you."

Janelle sprinkles a handful of tiny marshmallows into one huge stoneware mug and drops a dollop of homemade whipped cream into the other. "Harold, would you take these to the table, please? Nicole, have a seat."

I widen my eyes at Hawk, who ignores me, carrying our mugs over to the table while Janelle manages her own. When I slide into the chair beside him, I whisper, "Harold? Seriously?"

"Just don't," he says, not looking at me.

Janelle takes a sip of her hot chocolate, levels a steadfast gaze on me, and says, "First, you need to hear that you are not responsible for your husband's behavior."

The words feel like a finger pressed directly against a wound I didn't even know existed. I feel the pressure of tears behind my eyes, a knot in my throat.

"None of this would have happened if I hadn't moved his money."

"Money that wasn't his. And now he's going around hurting people you love. Listen to me. *He* is hurting them. You are not. Let me guess. You're telling yourself things like 'If it wasn't for me, none of this would have happened. My family is better off without me.'"

"But don't you see?" I burst out. "They *are* better off without me."

"Bullshit," she says. "And if he wasn't tormenting you and your family, then he'd be tormenting some other woman and her family."

"But some other woman wouldn't have moved the money."

"There would always be something," she says. "Think back to before you moved the money. Maybe he wasn't after your family then, but what about you?"

I flinch away from her words, knowing they are true. A week ago, I would have said he'd never hurt me, but now I see that he has hurt me in so many different ways. Small things. Squeezing my hand or my wrist until it hurt. Brushing out my hair and pulling too hard at the tangles. Once, during sex, he was rough enough to bring me to tears. He'd apologized, after. "You are so damn sexy, I got carried away," he said. "You know I'd never hurt you on purpose."

"You don't need to answer," Janelle continues. "I see it in your face. He's a predator. He thinks you are vulnerable and defenseless. Let's show him that's not true, shall we? But before we dive into this dilemma about your subpoena and his blackmail, tell me, do you want a divorce?"

"Yes. No. I mean, I want a divorce, but I can't . . . I don't have the money to pay for any of this."

"Nicole doesn't like accepting favors," Hawk supplies. "Strings attached, and that sort of thing."

"Well, of course there are strings," Janelle says. "Act like a decent human being. Do not hurt Harold. He's not as tough as he looks."

"Mom!" Hawk protests.

I can't help laughing, he sounds so much like an offended teenager being embarrassed in public by a protective parent.

"So, are we on?" she asks.

I hesitate. "Do you know what you're getting into? How much do you already know?"

"Oh, Harold told me everything." She leans forward on her elbows, her eyes glowing. "It's such a beautiful mess. An asshole husband, your complicated legal situation and the way you relocate objects, and the mystery around this Andrea person on top of everything! I live for cases like this. Don't look so worried, child. Harold swore me to full and complete confidentiality before he would tell me anything. Nothing goes beyond this room without your permission."

"See? I told you. And you already know how I feel." Hawk raises his mug to me, like a toast, and drinks.

I feel as warm and relaxed and safe as if I've been drinking directly from the rum bottle. "Yes," I hear myself saying. "Yes to the divorce, and to taking down Kent, and to solving the mystery of Andrea. Yes to everything."

"Excellent." Janelle smacks the flat of her hand down on the table. "Now that we've got that out of the way, let's get to work. Kent is an attorney with Findlay, Strachey, and Lytle, correct? I'm going to assume you signed a prenup."

"I did. I shouldn't have."

"Nobody ever should sign a prenup, and yet so many people do. I'll need to have a look at that before we file. You should know that even if he doesn't contest, in Washington State, there's a ninety-day waiting period from the time we file until the divorce can be finalized."

"Shit. Really?"

She shrugs. "Nothing to be done about it, except to file as soon as possible. I'm sorry to say that given a prenup and the circumstances, it's improbable that I'll be able to get you alimony or any other financial compensation."

"I don't think there is money to be gotten, prenup or not," I tell her, feeling just a tiny bit better. "He said he's utterly broke and in debt. I just want to be legally free of him."

"Sure as hell hasn't paid me yet," Hawk says.

Janelle makes a note on the yellow legal pad sitting in front of her on the table. "We will also take steps to make sure you're not held responsible for his debts."

"Can that happen?" I stare at her in dismay.

"Can and does," she says. "But I'm good at what I do, so that will be the least of your worries. Now. One more question before we move on to the more pressing problem. Are you safe? He may escalate when we serve him divorce papers."

"He's already escalating," Hawk growls.

I shiver, despite the warm kitchen and the mug cradled in my hands. "Andrea has an alarm system. So as long as I'm in the house, I will be okay."

"And if you leave the house, I go with you," Hawk says.

I open my mouth to argue, but think better of it and say nothing.

Janelle makes a check mark on her pad. "All right. Now. Can I have a look at that subpoena?"

I dig the document out of my day pack and give it to her. She smooths the crumpled pages, scans it quickly, then sets it aside and turns her attention back to me. "Here are your options. If you do not respond and choose not to show up to court, you'll get charged with contempt. A little jail time and a fine, normally. Not the end of the world, given that you already have a record and it wouldn't be your first time in jail.

"But Kent has stacked the deck. He may also choose to press charges for the theft of his money. He could follow through on his threats toward Ash and Roberta and Hawk. Of course, you can tell the court that he told you the money was in his possession illegally—but that won't stop your arrest, and as you know, it will devolve into a case of hearsay, his word against yours."

"I don't like the odds of that."

"Agreed," she says. "Sadly, even though he's the liar, you're the one with the record. Also, he has allies and connections within the court system and you would not get a fair trial. Unfortunately, even if you do testify, you're over a barrel. If you tell the truth, you may not be believed and Kent is very likely to exact vengeance on the people you love. If you tell the story Kent wants you to tell and get caught, that's up to a ten-year prison sentence and a much larger fine. Not to mention you'd be assisting in returning a murderer to the streets."

"So I'm damned if I do and damned if I don't?" I ask.

"Maybe we can quash the subpoena," Hawk says. "Based on his misbehavior."

"That's what I'm thinking," Janelle answers. "But we'll need evidence. Hearsay won't cut it."

"All right, then." Hawk drains his mug and slams it down on the table. "All we need to do is get him to incriminate himself." He touches my wrist with his warm fingers. "No despair, Nicole. We've got three weeks before the court date. We can do this."

"We've done more with less," Janelle says. "Trust us. We will move heaven and earth to make this right."

I find my spirits lifting at her words. She is so fiercely courageous, has come through so much to be where she is and doing what she is doing. I can feel myself drawing strength from her—from the wheel-chair and the scar on her face and the passion in her voice.

"So we have a plan, then," Hawk says.

"We do?"

Hawk shifts his shoulders and smiles in a way that makes me very glad to be on the protected side of him. "I'll dig around and see if I can find any evidence to prove that the money you moved was a bribe. In the meantime, when you get called in for witness preparation, you'll go, and you'll say whatever Kent wants you to say."

"I will? Why?"

"Because I'll put an app on your phone that records it all, and we'll catch Kent out in a lie. Plus, it will keep him from suspecting that we're up to something."

"I can't, though. I'm a terrible liar."

"Think of it as . . . misdirection. Like planning a surprise party, only better."

I shake my head. "I suck at that, too. My sibs would tell you that, if they were talking to me."

Janelle smiles encouragingly. "Have you ever been in a play?"

A small ray of hope breaks on the horizon of my wasteland of despair. I love being onstage. High school drama productions were one place I felt like I belonged. There was a freedom in stepping into the skin of a character, mostly because I got to not be me for a few minutes. Whatever the reason, I was good at it.

"I have, actually. If I was playing a role, I guess it wouldn't be lying, so much."

"There you go!" Hawk says. "You'll be Agent Nickle, going under-cover to unmask the forces of darkness."

His dramatic delivery coaxes a laugh out of me. It feels good to laugh, and I feel lighter, maybe even a little bit hopeful.

"Now that we have that planned out, what about Andrea?" Hawk asks.

"Harold," Janelle says, her tone gently chiding. "Don't you think that's enough for tonight? I, for one, need to get to bed. I have work tomorrow. And Nicole looks exhausted."

"Sorry, Nickle," he says, chastened. "I get carried away when I'm working on something interesting. How about I just show you the lair and then take you home. Well, not home, I guess, but you know what I mean."

"That would be good," I say, curiosity warring with fatigue.

Janelle smiles at me. "Try not to worry. We are on this. If I know Hawk, he'll enlist Joan to lend a hand. We'll get the rat bastard."

"Night, Mom." Hawk bends to kiss her cheek.

"Don't be too late," she admonishes as he leads me along a hallway, then down a flight of stairs. I stand at the bottom taking it all in.

"Quite the setup you have here."

"Isn't it? Really, I'm just a kid with big, fancy toys. Want the tour? You can kick me if I start to wax too geeky about anything."

He shows me computer monitors and security feeds, photo- and sound-analysis stations, a fingerprint booth, an intake and record-keeping system.

"This is amazing," I tell him. "Impressive, really."

"Did you think I had a little fly-by-night operation going?"

"Hey, you downplayed it. Told me you just follow cheating spouses around and research their social media."

"Yeah, I do a lot of that, too." He laughs, then quickly sobers. "Speaking of cheating spouses, there's something you should probably know."

"Kent had other women."

"You don't sound surprised."

I shrug. "There are gorgeous women chasing him all the time. Why wouldn't he give in to that?"

"Because he had you," Hawk says. "Anyway. I hope you don't mind that I did some digging. It will help Mom with the divorce proceedings if there's evidence of unfaithfulness."

"Dig away. I don't need the details, though."

"All right. I'll keep my findings to myself. Well, shall we go? You look half dead on your feet."

"I am. And I should check on Andrea anyway." I turn toward the stairs, but he gestures toward another door. "Let's go this way so we don't disturb Mom. She's a light sleeper. Besides, I usually go in and out this way, gives us both a little more privacy."

As I cross the room, I pass another door, cracked open just enough to let me see a bed and a dresser, and I realize that he not only works in this basement, he lives here.

Hawk drives in silence for a few minutes, then asks, "Well? What do you think?"

"Your mother is lovely."

"She is. What about the rest of it? Does the plan sound good to you?"

"Your name is really Harold?" I ask instead of answering.

He sighs dramatically. "That's what's on the birth certificate, yes. And as you see, Mom insists on calling me by my given name."

"Your name is Harold and you live in your mother's basement." I can't get over these two facts, which alter my initial impressions of him profoundly.

"Are you done?" He shoots a glare in my direction.

"I'm only just beginning."

"You're evading the important issues."

"This *is* important."

"You're not going to let it go, are you?" Hawk asks.

"Hey, you know everything about me and I know nothing about you."

"Well, now you know my name and my living arrangement. Which, by the way, are two pieces of highly privileged information. I'd appreciate it if you keep them to yourself."

I put my hand over my heart. "Scout's honor. Tell me why you go by Hawk instead of Harold. Please?"

"Would *you* go by Harold if you were me?" He drums his fingers on the steering wheel, and I think he's not going to answer me, but finally he says, "My dad was an abusive asshole. Put my mom in that wheelchair when I was ten, and went to prison. For that, and a few other things. I was a skinny, geeky, book-loving kid named Harold whose father was in prison. As you can imagine, school wasn't pretty.

"All through grade school and middle school, kids picked on me. And then I grew. Into my dad, basically. You probably noticed I don't look like my mom. All of a sudden, I was big, strong, and thoroughly pissed off. A bullied kid in an Incredible Hulk body. So you can guess what happened. I beat up some kids pretty badly. My mom opted for tough love. She didn't even try to get my charges dropped or my sentencing reduced. And the day I got released from my time in juvie, she actually took me to visit Dad in prison. I wasn't exactly scared straight, it was more . . . well, I looked at her, so indomitable and strong in that fucking wheelchair. And Dad, with all of that muscle and rage, just seemed pathetic to me. I didn't want to be him. But I didn't want to keep on being Harold, either. That was just asking for trouble. About then, some chick told me I had eyes like a hawk. So. I went with it. Happy now?"

"Hawk. I didn't—"

"So that's why Mom represents abused women. She's passionate about it. And I do a lot of investigative work for her to make sure we get women safe and get the bastards locked up whenever we can."

Emotions crash through me like a storm surge. I'm sorry I forced him into telling me his story. I'm sorry that I teased him. I'm also increasingly aware that I don't want to be just another woman he's on a crusade to protect. When he looks at me, I want him to see *me*. Nickle. Not the jailbird or the screwup or the object relocator. Just me.

"I appreciate your help," I say when he parks in Andrea's driveway.
"You and your mom."

"But?" he asks. "I hear a 'but' in there."

"But I don't like being one of your projects."

"You are so not a project," he says with a fierce intensity that cleaves
through all of my armor. "There is not another woman like you on the
face of this planet. Possibly in the entire unexplored universe."

His eyes blaze with so much passion, I have to look away, blinking
back dark spots as though I've stared too long at the sun. I don't know
what to do or what to say or how to react or even how to begin to
express my reaction, both to his words and the way he's said them. He
turns his head away from me and stares out the windshield.

I rest my hand on his arm and try to find words. "You are . . . I
just . . . I'm glad you're in my world, Hawk. Tell your mom thank you,
again. I guess I have to admit that I do need rescuing this time."

"Don't forget that you're really rescuing me," he says.

At the door, when I turn to say thank you and good night, he
cups my cheek in his big hand and looks deeply into my eyes. I hold
my breath, thinking that surely now he is going to kiss me, but he just
smiles a little. "You'd better go in," he says. "I'll be listening for the dead
bolt. Make sure you set the alarm."

I want to turn my face into his palm and kiss it, but he lowers his
hand and waits while I put my key in the lock. He's still standing on
the porch when I close the door, my own personal bodyguard, watching
over me.

Chapter Thirty-Three

NICOLE

"The toast is burnt."

Andrea has been prickly and impossible ever since she texted me from her room at five a.m. asking for pain and anxiety meds. She complained about how long it took me, bleary eyed and clumsy, to find them, read the labels, and count out the tablets. The water I brought to swallow them with was too warm and she didn't like the glass it was in. When I took it away and returned with ice water, she threw a fit about that. "Nobody asked for ice cubes. Why is it so difficult to just bring cold water? I certainly see why you are not working as a waitress."

I offered to bring her breakfast in bed, but she wasn't having it. "I cut my feet. I am not an invalid." So I helped her navigate the stairs, and she installed herself at the kitchen table with her feet propped up on a chair, to supervise my breakfast making. Now, she wrinkles her nose at a fluffy, perfect omelet, hash browns, and orange juice. And toast. Which is not burnt but a perfect golden brown, dripping with butter. It smells, quite frankly, amazing, and since I've also made breakfast for me, I ignore her and start eating.

Even though she's being impossible, I've been able to keep my cool because now I know her secret. Her pupils are dilated. Her hands are trembling. It's not the pain and it's not addiction, it's straight-up anxiety. I know that feeling myself, all too well, nerve endings lit up with irritation, wanting to scratch my way out of my own skin.

Andrea pokes at her breakfast with a fork, then says, "Just take this whole mess away and bring me granola and milk."

"A waste of perfectly good food," I say, because empathy has its limits. But I take a breath and think about what high anxiety levels do to my own appetite, and carry her plate to the counter. My phone, back at the table beside my own half-eaten breakfast, starts to buzz. Not just a text, an early-morning phone call.

Which kicks in my own adrenaline response. Is Kent up to something? Did something else happen to my family, or to Ash? Is my mom finally returning my calls? I haven't heard from anybody in my family since that call from Roberta and have no idea what is going on. I turn toward the table just as Andrea's hand reaches out toward my phone. I lunge forward but I'm way too slow, and she answers.

"Good morning. Who is this?"

I reach the table and snatch the phone out of her hand. "Hello?"

"Hey," Hawk says, "I thought maybe I had the wrong number."

"Right number, wrong person." I glare at Andrea, then turn my back, angling for a modicum of privacy.

"Can you possibly get away today?" he asks. "I've got a lead."

I glance over my shoulder at Andrea, who is unabashedly listening. "Can't. I'm working."

"Oh yes, you can, too. Give me that phone," Andrea orders. "Let me talk to him."

"I'll call you later." I end the call, and Andrea and I glare at each other.

"Give me that phone," she says, "or you're fired."

"You can't fire me. I'm your crisis plan."

"How do I know you're not talking to Tag and lying to me?"

"What happened to that trust thing?" I ask.

"If you've got nothing to hide, why can't I just talk to him?"

"Because it's an invasion of my privacy?" But I'm moving back toward the table as I say it. I owe her. I'm the one who bumped up her anxiety about Tag by moving that stupid book. "Fine. Go ahead."

She hits redial and says, as soon as he answers, "This is Andrea. Who are you really?"

I can hear the sound of Hawk's voice, but I can't make out the words. Then Andrea answers, "Well, good, then. She needs friends. And you'd be doing me a favor to get her out of my hair today. She hovers. What time? Great. I'll tell her."

She hangs up and sets the phone back down on the table. "Your friend Hawk is picking you up at ten."

"Andrea. I told the crisis person I would—"

"Nobody really expects you to watch me every minute of the day. This gives you lots of time to change my bandages and monitor my mood before you go. And fix me a lunch. He says he'll have you home by dinner."

I take a breath and blow it out through my nose, like a bull getting ready to charge. "Your pills aren't due until eleven."

"You can measure them out and leave them for me. Even if I did take them early, it's not going to kill me, it just means I'll be thoroughly suffering before you give me the next dose at five."

I want to go with Hawk, but I don't feel good about leaving Andrea, or about fudging her medication times. Last night was different. She was already in bed and off to sleep. But at the same time, if Hawk's got something on Kent, then that's something we need to follow up.

"I want to meet this Hawk person," Andrea says. "When he picks you up. Tell him to come in."

I should call Hawk back and tell him I can't go. But I don't, and he rings the doorbell at ten a.m. precisely. All morning, I've been telling myself it's business. Kent is a bad guy and Hawk gets off on taking down bad guys. Nothing personal. No emotional response required. But the minute I open the door and see him standing there, I go tongue tied and weak kneed.

Andrea calls from the living room, "Bring him in here, Nicole."

"She wants to meet you," I say, feeling ridiculously shy and having trouble knowing where to look. "Come on in."

He follows me into the living room, where Andrea is ensconced on the sofa with the TV remote. I've dragged the coffee table over beside her and loaded it up with anything she might need. Her phone. A book. Beverages. A sandwich and snacks. And her eleven a.m. meds in a little dish.

"Oh," Andrea says, looking Hawk up and down. "A big improvement on the previous model."

I flush, but Hawk just smiles.

"I'd like to see your PI license," Andrea says. "Just to make sure you are who you say you are."

Hawk hands it over and she scrutinizes it carefully. "Well, at least that's legit. But now, here's the real question. How do I know you're not investigating *me*?"

I freeze, my eyes darting from Andrea to Hawk. We're caught now. When she finds out that we have, in fact, been investigating her, she'll kick me out and I'll be homeless and unemployed and—

"Should I be?" Hawk asks, smiling widely as if he's just being funny. "Listen. Nicole has told me you're worried about somebody named Tag, and I can assure you that I do not know any such person and am not in his employ. Does that help?"

"I'd like to say it does," Andrea says. "I'd be lying if I said I believe you completely. But if Nicole trusts you, then I guess so do I." She makes a shooing gesture with both hands. "You two run along now. I'm missing an important plot point in my movie."

"I have a question to ask you, first," I begin, but she interrupts.

"No, I am not planning on killing myself today. Make sure you have her home by five, young man."

"Yes, ma'am." Hawk grabs my hand and tugs me toward the door. If he wasn't towing me along, I would turn back and spill the truth. Even when I'm in his Jeep, I want to go back and come clean.

"We should tell her," I say. "That we were investigating her. That we know she changed her name."

"*Are* investigating her," he says. "That's what we're doing today. And no, we should definitely not tell her."

"Oh, Hawk," I say, stricken. "I thought this was a lead on Kent. I can't investigate Andrea anymore. She trusts me."

"Does she really, though?" he counters. "She's hiding something and she's running from something. Maybe what we find out will free her."

"Or make things worse." I chew on my lower lip, racked with indecision.

"Here's what I'd like to do," Hawk says. "I've located an old high school friend of Andrea's in Richland. I was planning on us paying her a visit today to see what she can tell us about Tag. But if you want to call it off, I will."

He doesn't sound pushy or passive-aggressive at all. This is my decision. And I hate making decisions. It was all well and good looking into Andrea's background before I knew her. But now that I know about her anxiety and I'm responsible for her safety, it feels sneaky and underhanded to investigate behind her back. At the same time, what if we can find out something about Tag that will calm her fear and put her at ease? What if she really is in danger and we can protect her?

Besides, I have to admit that I very much want, more than I've wanted anything in a long time, to go on this adventure with Hawk. To delve into the mysteries of the Object Relocation Program. To forget, just for a little while, about Kent and my family and the impossibility of any normal life for myself.

"Do we have time? I have to be back by five."

"Two hours there, two hours back, an hour, tops, for the interview. Shouldn't be a problem."

"Let's do it," I say slowly. "But after today, we either stop or we tell her what we've found. One or the other."

"Agreed." He shifts the Jeep into reverse and backs out of the driveway.

"How did you find this person?" I ask, brimming with curiosity now that I've relegated my uneasy conscience to a time-out corner. "And do you never sleep?"

He laughs. "I can get by on very little for a couple of days if there's a good mystery going on. Andrea is not on social media at all, by the way, which is weird and usually means something like witness protection or hiding from an abusive spouse."

My mouth drops open at that. "Oh my God. Do you think she really is in witness protection? We could be breaking her cover."

"I'm much more inclined to believe in the abusive spouse," he says. "Tag. No record of her ever being married, by the way, but that doesn't mean she doesn't have an obsessive boyfriend. Honestly? I got lucky. I found her birth info and the names of her parents. She was born at Kadlec hospital, in Richland. Her parents drowned in a fishing accident when she was eighteen and—"

"How awful for her!" My heart twists with guilt and sympathy.

"I know," Hawk agrees. "Tragic. Anyway, they were still living in Richland at the time, so I made a guess that she went to high school there. Richland High has their yearbooks online, so I went in and looked for photos. Andrea turned up several times hanging out with another girl, and I found her class photo and her name, and after that, it was easy to track her down."

"Wow. Color me impressed."

"You look exhausted," he says. "Did you sleep?"

"Not so much."

"Close your eyes now and catch a nap," he says. "Let the worry go for a minute. There's absolutely nothing you can do right now."

He's right. I close my eyes and lean my head back, breathing in what I've come to think of as the Hawk smell. I settle into it, letting the motion of the moving vehicle lull me to sleep. I surface with a start when Hawk pulls into a rest stop only a few minutes out from our destination. My mouth is dry, my neck cramped, and when I scrub my face with my hands, I'm appalled to discover a dried trail of saliva on my chin.

Hawk appears oblivious, stepping out of the Jeep to stretch. "Figured you might want a minute to wake up and to use the facilities."

I shuffle into the restroom, where I empty my bladder and then splash cold water on my face in an attempt to get my brain working again. When I come back out, Hawk looks at me as if I'm beautiful and I try to forget that I've been drooling and probably snoring right beside him for hours.

"So how do we do this?" I ask as he parks outside Mama's Kitchen, the small greasy spoon diner where Ronda Porter works as a waitress. It's in Pasco, about nine miles from Richland, and is located directly across the street from a Mexican restaurant that exudes mouthwatering aromas and is packed with customers.

"After we talk to Ronda, maybe we can get some real food," Hawk says, sniffing appreciatively as we cross the parking lot, and making a face as we open the door of the diner and walk into a scent wall of deep-fried potatoes and overcooked bacon.

"What if she's not even here?" I ask. "And why didn't we just call?"

"She'll be here. And we came in person because it's too easy to just hang up a phone if someone asks intrusive questions."

"Is that what we're going to do? Ask intrusive questions?"

"Hush." We seat ourselves in a booth that allows us to observe the whole shabby joint. The faux-leather bench, once bright red, now faded, is sticky to my touch, and I wipe my hands on my jeans and make a face. Whoever wiped down the table, leaving an uneven pattern of wet streaks, has entirely missed a not-quite-dried blob of what I hope is ketchup.

Despite the fact that only one other table is occupied, we wait a good five minutes before a woman emerges from the kitchen, grabs a couple of menus, and approaches our table, surrounded by an aura of cigarettes and perfume. Her hair is bleached and teased. Makeup settles into the lines and creases on a face that has not aged well. Bright-red lipstick feathers into the lines at the top of a thin upper lip.

The name tag says "Ronda." She looks flat and defeated and you can tell life has been a disappointment. "Special today is a cube steak, gravy, baked potato. Get you something to drink?" Her voice is as lifeless as her eyes.

"Coffee," Hawk says. "Cream and sugar. And water for both of us."

She nods and shuffles away, returning a few minutes later with a carafe, a bowl of individual creamers, and two small glasses of tepid water. "You want some time with the menus or is that it?" she asks.

"Actually, Ronda, we're hoping for a little information."

Her head comes up, startled, and her gaze snaps to Hawk's. "About the area?" she asks, obviously wary.

"We want to talk to you about Andreanna Garner," I blurt out, even though I know I should leave the questioning to Hawk. I can't bear to play cat and mouse with this defeated woman, teasing, tormenting, stalking.

She stiffens. "Look, I don't know what you think you know, but I haven't seen Andi in years, or heard word one."

"We're just friends of hers," Hawk says, in his softest voice. He smiles, but if he's trying to look friendly and nonthreatening, it isn't working.

"Friends?" Her eyes dart from him to me, full of questions. She melts, gradually, first her shoulders, then the rigid muscles in her face.

I'm worried she's going to keep going and end up in a puddle on the floor. I slide over and pat the bench beside me.

"Come sit. Like Hawk said, we're just friends of hers, trying to help her out with something."

"She's okay, then?" She shrugs, looks around the nearly empty restaurant, and slides in beside me. There's a mixture of hope and fear in her eyes. I'm not sure which is worse, that or the deadness that it's replaced.

"Alive and well." Hawk gets up and swipes a cup from the neighboring table, then pours out coffee for all of us.

Ronda hesitates, glancing over at the occupied table, where the customers are busy with their phones, their plates still mostly full. She loads up her coffee with three packets of sugar and five containers of cream. Wise move. I can tell just by smelling it that it was bad coffee when it was fresh, and it's now old bad coffee. I stick with water, but Hawk drinks appreciatively, as if he's enjoying a finely made barista special.

"Why are you here?" Ronda's eyes narrow. "You're not cops, are you?"

"Definitely not cops," Hawk says. "But we did lie to you, a little. I'm a private investigator."

Ronda spills her coffee. I reach for napkins as she sets down the cup and tucks her hands under the table out of sight.

"I don't know anything. I already told you. Andi vanished thirty years ago without a word or a trace. Haven't talked to her since."

I rest my hand lightly on her wrist. "You're not going to get in any trouble. And you'll be helping Andi out."

"How about if you tell us about Tag, for starters," Hawk says. "If you know where he is, that would be very helpful."

"I don't know anything."

"Andi lives in Spokane now." Hawk refills her cup. "Changed her name to Andrea Lester."

Ronda's expression shifts to something cold and calculating, edged with fear. "What is this really all about? I had a hang-up call a few days ago. Called back and got voice mail for an Andrea Lester. Figured it was a wrong number!" She slides toward the edge of the booth and gets to her feet. "Whatever it is she told you, I don't know anything."

"Andrea didn't tell us anything," Hawk says, also getting to his feet and looming over her. "She doesn't know we're here. We're really just looking for Tag."

"Why?"

"We want to find him. He might be a danger to her."

Ronda cuts her eyes toward the kitchen, and then back toward Hawk, who is doing absolutely nothing to make himself look small and nonthreatening.

"All right. Listen. I'll tell you this. Last time I saw her, she was heading for Seattle. She said if the cops started looking for her, I should say Tag was beating her."

"And did he?" I ask. "Beat her?"

Ronda blinks and licks her lips. "I wouldn't know, would I? Never saw any marks on her. First time she ever said anything about it. But she was crying when she called. She said, 'If anybody's looking for me, tell them I ran because I was afraid he'd hurt me.' And then I said, 'Oh my God, did he really hit you?' and she said, 'Just tell them that he did, okay? So the cops don't look for me. And for God's sake, Ronda, don't tell anybody.'"

"And Tag?" Hawk asks, relentless.

"Tag seemed so desperate to find her," Ronda goes on. "Tortured, even. He begged me, pleaded with me, to tell him where she'd gone. He went to the cops, but when they talked to me, I did like she said. Told them Tag hit her and she ran. So nobody ever looked for her or the kid, and I never—"

"Wait. What kid?" My voice is way too loud. The other customers look up from their phones, curious.

Ronda's face echoes the shock that is resonating through my body like an electric charge. She blanches dead white. Her eyes stay locked with mine. Again, she licks her lips. I get to my feet and grab her arm. "What kid, Ronda?"

She yanks her arm away. "You know. Her daughter. Listen, it's been nice talking and all, but I'm gonna get in trouble if I don't get back to work."

The restaurant door opens and a group of men comes in, laughing and talking. "Hey, Ronda," one of them calls. "You working today or what?"

She grabs the comment like a life preserver. "Do me a favor, and leave me alone. I got nothing more to say. If Andi wants to talk, tell her to call me back herself."

Straightening her skirt, she pastes on a smile and sways over to the new customers. "You boys want menus? Or just coffee and the special?"

"Depends exactly what's on that special, honey," one of the men says, leering at her.

My feet are glued to the floor. A baby? There's certainly nothing in Andrea's house that would indicate she has ever had a child. No pictures on the walls, or on the dresser in her room.

"Well, we learned something we didn't know," Hawk says, tucking a twenty and a business card under the carafe.

"I wish we hadn't."

"I know." He rests his hand on my lower back and nudges me toward the door. Ronda glances at us sideways as we pass her but continues writing down orders and acts as if we don't exist.

"You okay?" he asks.

"Sure." But I'm not at all okay. An unwelcome idea has squatted right in the middle of my brain, big and black and ugly.

Hawk buckles his seat belt and starts the engine. "Ronda knows a whole lot more than she's saying."

I lean back against the headrest and close my eyes. My brain hurts. My body feels boneless and heavy. In my head, I hear Andrea saying, "I thought perhaps you were adopted."

"Hey," Hawk says. "Hey." His hand settles on my thigh, and I can't resist leaning toward him, resting my head on his shoulder. He puts an arm around me and makes soothing noises. "Unsettling, I know. You still want Mexican?"

"Not hungry." I bury my face in his shirt, and he pulls me in closer, both arms around me now.

"Me, either. Let's go home." But he makes no move to release me.

"We still don't know if Tag is really dangerous or not," I say into his chest.

One of his hands smooths my hair. "Clearly we need to do some more digging. I may be able to access something, although if a missing person report was never actually filed, there's not likely to be anything useful. *If* we keep going," he adds. "Do you still want to stop? Do we tell her what we're doing? What do you want to do?"

What I want to do is step into a time warp and stop before we started. I want to have never moved the book. I want to have not gotten attached to Andrea. I want to be a normal woman who could realistically dream about having a relationship with Hawk.

So many impossible things to want.

"I think we need to stop," I say, extricating myself from his arms and buckling my seat belt. "It's just not right to keep unearthing things, is it? Also, I'm sorry."

"Your call," he says, although I can see the disappointment on his face. "And why are you sorry?"

"Moment of weakness. Collapsing into your arms like a damsel in distress."

"Hey, nothing like a damsel-in-distress moment to light up the life of a wannabe hero." He shifts into gear and is about to pull out of the parking lot when his phone rings.

"Hey, Aunt Joan. What's up?"

He listens for a long moment, says, "Got it. Hang on a sec." He holds the phone away from his ear and turns to look at me. "The fingerprint results are in. Do you want to see them?"

"I . . . God, Hawk. I don't know."

"How about I tell her to just text me the names, and then I'll tell you if you decide you want to. Does that work?"

They're both waiting for me to answer. Hawk, who was trying to help me. And his aunt Joan, who went out of her way to do me a favor. Me, not Hawk, who really has nothing riding on the results of this other than curiosity.

"Okay," I hear myself say, hoarse and croaky.

Hawk ends the call with his aunt. "Probably nothing helpful," he says. "Although I'm a little surprised, honestly, that she got any hits. Your average human doesn't have prints in the database."

I swallow hard, my throat as dry as the Sahara. Hawk's phone dings. "Here we go," he says. "What do you want to do?"

"We've come this far," I answer. "I guess it's a little late to stop now."

He scrolls through his phone. "As expected—yours. Several sets of unknowns, one of them probably Andrea's. Penelope Lane—she's the one you got the book from, right?"

"Wait, what? *Penelope* has a legal record? I've got her helping Ash out with the baby!"

"Easy," Hawk says. "She's a social worker, right? Anybody who works in that field has been printed and background checked, which means they're in the system."

"So that's it? We struck out?" I want this to be true. No more decisions. A dead end. I'll forget all about trying to investigate why the book wanted to be at Andrea's and try to figure out some way to make my family talk to me again.

Are you sure they're your family? an insidious little voice whispers in my head. *How will you ever know if you don't finish this?*

"There's one more name," Hawk says. "Theodore Travers. Aunt Joan found an address while she was at it. He lives in Spokane." He pauses, his face creasing in concern. "Nicole? Are you okay? What is it?"

I've flashed back to my very first day in therapy. Standing in Graham's office, looking at his diploma and hassling him about the pretentiousness of having so many names. Theodore Alfred Graham Travers. Tag.

"I think I'm going to be sick," I whisper.

"Why do I get the feeling you know this person?" he asks.

I turn to face him. "I'm pretty sure Theodore Travers is my shrink."

"So your therapist touched this book at some point. It doesn't mean he's Tag. His fingerprints would be in the system because of his work, just like Penelope's."

"But his initials are T-A-G. And it makes perfect, twisted sense that he'd be somebody I know and trust. I'm cursed, remember?"

"Even if your therapist is Tag, we don't know for sure that he hurt Andrea."

"But she's terrified of him. Look what happened to her, just from seeing his name in a book. He seems so decent. God. I liked him, Hawk. How could I get it so wrong?"

Hawk's face is grim. "We don't know that he hurt her, Nickle. We don't really know anything at all."

Chapter Thirty-Four

ANDREA

This morning, I wanted Nicole to leave. I've lived alone for so long that it's draining to have somebody constantly and ubiquitously present. Hovering. Worrying.

But as soon as she was gone, I missed her and didn't want to be alone. The hours have stretched out in some sort of super-slow time warp. My feet hurt. My anxiety is taking on a life of its own, a constant gnawing, living, evolving beast. If Nicole didn't have my pills, I would give in and take extras, a fact I acknowledge to myself with self-loathing.

I keep looking at the clock. Still only three o'clock. What if something happens to Nicole? What if she's in an accident? Or absconds with my pain and anxiety meds? How well do I know her, anyway? Not at all. Not really. Worry picks up momentum and there's nothing I can do to stop it. I can't exercise, because of my feet. Don't have access to my pills or alcohol. All I can do is fidget and fuss and wait.

The phone rings and I grab it, thinking it's Nicole checking in, but then I see the number flash across my screen. *Unknown caller.*

Indecision swamps me. *Answer. Don't answer. Answer. Don't answer.* Finally my thumb makes the decision for me, and I swipe, and Ronda's voice is in my ear, strident and angry.

"What the actual fuck, Andi?"

"Hello to you, too?"

"You totally vanish off the face of the planet, and then you send a PI after me?"

Her voice shrills in a crescendo, and I hold it away from my ear, scrambling to understand what she's even saying.

"Calm down, would you? I—"

"I will not calm down! After everything I did for you, I cannot believe you would come after me like this."

Since I'm alone in the house, except for the cat, I put the phone on speaker and set it down, partly to spare my eardrums, and partly because my hands are shaking so violently, it's hard to hold on. I feel like I'm drowning, sinking below the surface of a darkness that will steal my breath and my sanity. I need my pills, but Nicole has them. Nicole, who I've trusted and let into my life and who has utterly and devastatingly betrayed me.

"How would I know anything?" Ronda screeches. "I didn't hang out with Tag. I certainly didn't track his whereabouts after you vanished."

"Please," I say, hating the helpless pleading in my voice. "About Tag. About what happened. I need you to tell me—"

"I have to go. I'm supposed to be working." The call ends abruptly. Darkness sucks me under.

Ronda's car, the home base for the last two years of our high school adventures, now feels surreal and unfamiliar. Maybe it's the unshakeable stink of sour milk and diapers that clings to me, overpowering the smell of air freshener and stale cigarettes. Or maybe it's the baby buckled into her carrier in the back seat, an interloper in our old camaraderie.

"You look good," Ronda says.

I know perfectly well how I look, and good isn't it. I've seen myself naked in the mirror, pale and puffy, with garish stretch marks scarring my still-bloated belly and my swollen breasts and flabby thighs. Ronda, on the other hand, looks fabulous. Thin and carefree and young, where I am already old at twenty-one. The ever-present tears start flowing.

"It's temporary." Ronda lights up a smoke. "You want one?"

"Are you kidding? Tag will freak out if he catches a whiff on me. Or the baby. You can't smoke with a baby in the car."

"Shit. Tag needs to chill." But she stabs the cigarette out in the ashtray and starts driving. "Never mind. I've got something else that will make you feel incredible. Food first. What do you want?"

"I dunno. You pick." I slump back in my seat, so immersed in exhaustion and despair that I can't even imagine feeling incredible. Sleep might do it, but even when the baby is actually sleeping and I lie down, my brain races through cycle after cycle of disaster and won't let me sleep. I've been running two thought channels. Channel One, I'm a terrible mother and a danger to the baby. Channel Two, Tag is a critical tyrant and is trying to take the baby away from me. Waking or sleeping, I'm caught in one loop or the other.

Tonight, Tag went off to class and left me home with the baby. I was playing Channel One, afraid to be alone with my child. What if I were to drop her or drown her accidentally? Or shake her or hurt her on purpose? I'd called Ronda in a flood of tears and panic, and she insisted on dragging me out of the house. When I'd reminded her that I had a kid now and couldn't just run off, she'd said, "Bring her along. How hard can that be?" Which was a big old clue that she didn't know thing one about babies.

"Did I tell you Tag's making me go to counseling?" I ask as Ronda drives to an as yet unknown destination. "And that his mother is coming because, as he says, I'm not coping?"

"Asshole," Ronda says. "Like you need any of that shit. Everybody gets the baby blues."

This is more than the blues. A lot more. But I don't tell her that. I'm incapable of making any decisions, so Ronda chooses Taco Time. All through the long months of pregnancy, I've eaten a healthy diet, everything for the sake of this baby who now doesn't appreciate any of it. I am sick to death of vegetables and chicken breast and never want to ever drink milk again so long as I live. When the food comes, I don't wait for Ronda, just start cramming Mexi-Fries into my mouth, savory, salty, crispy. Suck up great gulps of icy, sweet Coke through the straw.

Ronda parks in the darkest corner of the half-deserted lot, takes a bite of her taco, and then rummages around in her purse while she chews, triumphantly coming up with a small pill bottle.

"Hold out your hand." She taps two pink tablets into my palm. "These will change your life."

"I can't. I'm breastfeeding."

"Oh, for fuck's sake, Andi. Lighten up. Tag will never know and it won't hurt anything. It's just ecstasy. It will be out of your system by morning. You deserve this."

The tablets are the same innocent pink as candy hearts. My brain switches onto Channel Two. Tag is out to get me. Always criticizing, never appreciating. He knows how I feel about his mother, and now he's invited her to visit anyway, and the two of them are going to gang up on me.

It's not fair. I've been so good. Dropped out of college. Not a hit of weed or a single drink since the day the pee stick said I was going to be a mother. I even cut out sugar and caffeine, and for what? So Tag can take the baby away from me?

"Come on," Ronda says. "It's only one time."

"Fuck Tag," I say, and tip the pills into my mouth.

"Let's go somewhere," Ronda says after she swallows her own.

"Like where? We've got the baby. It's not like we can party."

"So we go for a drive," she says.

A little voice of reason whispers that this is so not a good idea, but it's deeply buried and I've released all of my decision-making to Ronda, so I say nothing. I close my eyes, drifting a little. Both my mind and the baby are quiet for what seems like the first time since she was born.

And then the pills kick in. A glow of energy and euphoria evaporates all of my self-loathing and guilt. It feels so good, I start laughing, loud and wild, for once not worrying about waking the baby.

Ronda tips her head back and whoops. "Awesome, right?"

"Where has this been all of my life?"

Everything is magic, even the headlights of the oncoming cars. I want this to go on forever. "Let's really go somewhere!" I say. "Road trip! I've been stuck in the house forever."

"What about your kid?"

I wave that away. "No big deal. I'm breastfeeding. We can buy diapers anywhere."

"And clothes," she says. "We'll go shopping. Where should we go?"

"I dunno. Spokane is boring. Seattle?"

"I know!" Ronda squeals. "Let's go to Canada!"

We laugh until we're breathless.

"Are we doing this?" she asks. "Don't you need to get home?"

"We are absolutely doing this!" Some part of my former self nags at me. Tag will worry. This is irresponsible. But Channel Two is coming in even clearer under the influence of the wonderful mood I'm in. I'm a good mother and he's undermining me. Trying to steal our baby's love. Keep me down. But I can do anything and everything. There is no limit to what I can accomplish, or to my love for the small human sleeping in the back seat.

I see the funk I've been in as a small, transitory glitch. Of course I love my baby, more than anything in the world. How could I ever have doubted that?

We stop at a rest stop to pee. To get water to satisfy a raging thirst that Ronda tells me comes with the pills. The baby wakes up and I change her and feed her and then we're flying down the road again, the world alive with love and light and possibility . . .

And there the clarity stops. All I have is a jumble of disjointed and fractured memory blips that jangle and thrum with wrongness.

Staring at the uniformed officer at the border in mute and trembling terror while Ronda calmly tells him we're heading to Vancouver for the weekend and shows him our driver's licenses and the baby's birth certificate. I know in my bones that Tag has called ahead and spoken to the chief of the Canadian RCMP. I'll be arrested for kidnapping. They'll take my baby . . .

Then Ronda asking, over and over again, "What is wrong with you? You're freaking me out!"

And then a cheap motel, where I don't like the way the woman behind the desk looks at us and grow convinced that she's a spy, working for Tag. And then another motel, and the baby crying, always crying, and then nothing, nothing, nothing, until the hospital and the nurses are trying to kill me with poisoned pills and . . .

Sylvester jumps into my lap and butts his head against my chest, bringing me back to reality. I bend my head and bury my face in his fur, his purr comforting and warm. Little by little, I ground in the now. The throbbing in my feet. My blankets on the couch. This room that I decorated. This house that I bought with money I've made from a long career.

There is more than one reason I don't like to think about that time of my life, and part of it is the way my slanted, distorted, twisted reality from that time collides with logic and sanity. There are so many gaps in the narrative. So much that doesn't make sense.

The hospital, at least, gave me perspective and a diagnosis before spitting me back out into the world. Postpartum psychosis, a state I was probably already ramping up to before Ronda gave me ecstasy. Most likely the pills pushed me into a full-blown psychosis that was coming for me anyway. Even so, even knowing that I was crazy, I can never, ever forgive myself for what I did.

And I'm certainly not about to forgive Nicole for dragging her private-eye boyfriend into my personal business. She can report me to the crisis people all she wants. I'll go to the psych ward before I'll let her set foot in my house again.

Chapter Thirty-Five

NICOLE

"You ready?" Hawk asks.

I'm not and I will never be, but we're going to do this anyway. I get out of the Jeep, take a deep breath, and lead the way into the waiting room, which I'm grateful to see is empty. We don't even have time to sit before Graham comes in. I introduce him to Hawk, and the two shake hands, sizing each other up like opponents before a fight.

"Tell me what's happened," Graham says as we all settle into chairs in his office.

He has retreated behind a counselor persona, which makes sense, I guess, given that I've called and asked for an urgent appointment because of a crisis situation. His gaze settles on Hawk, who is silent and watchful and dangerous looking, and then flicks back to me. "If you'd prefer to speak about it alone, your friend can—"

"Hawk stays," I interrupt, understanding the message beneath the words. "He's not a threat to me."

"All right, then." Graham's lips smile, but his eyes do not. I miss the rapport we'd built in sessions, don't like knowing that even if I had all the money in the world, I won't be coming back to him for counseling.

We are about to take a one-way trip across the co-occurring relationship boundary line.

I glance over at Hawk, and he nods, reassuring me that what I'm about to do is for everybody's good. Still, I hesitate.

"Would it be easier to write what you need to tell me?" Graham asks, leaning the slightest bit forward, deliberately displaying an open and receptive posture, inviting my confidence. I'm familiar with the move, and I know that hours of training have drilled it into him and every counselor I've ever seen. Probably he thinks I'm suicidal and is going to use every tool he has to get me to tell him all about it.

Instead of words, I hold out the copy of the *Inferno*.

He looks at it but doesn't take it, his eyes coming back up to meet mine. "What's this about? Doing some philosophical reading?"

"I need to know if this book belongs to you."

"Perhaps we could get to the crisis? I canceled a regular client session so you could come in."

"This is the crisis, Graham. Is the name written in the book yours or not? Are you Tag?"

I see the flicker of recognition in his eyes when I say that name. He looks down at the broken cover and slowly opens it. His forehead furrows. "Yes, I'm Tag. Or I used to be. I don't understand. Where did you get this? Why bring it to me?"

"I move things, remember?" And then I add, very gently, "Do you know a woman named Andreanna Garner?"

His professional persona falls away, revealing a naked hunger. "Andi. Oh my God. Is she alive?"

I'm speechless, but Hawk answers, "You sound surprised."

"God," he says. "Oh my God." He looks dramatically older, frail, as if he's stepped into a time machine and moved twenty years into the future. A terrible hope comes into his eyes. "Surprised doesn't come close. All these years." His hand goes to his heart and rests there as he asks, "And my daughter? Where is Lelia?"

"I don't know anything about your daughter," I say softly. I catch myself searching his face, looking for features that are a match to mine.

"But you know where Andi is? I could talk to her?"

"We know where she is," Hawk rumbles, "but whether you can talk to her or not is another issue."

"She doesn't want to see me," Graham says. "Of course she doesn't, or she'd have looked for me. I can't believe, after all these years, that you found her."

"I didn't find her," I tell him, "the book did."

"One of your relocation projects?" He runs both hands through his hair once, twice, three times. And then he leans forward. "Nicole. You have to tell me where she is. I don't know what she's told you, but this is the truth. She went out one night with a friend and took our baby with her. She never came back. Not a word. And the cops wouldn't even look for her, because . . ." His voice quavers and he stops. Swallows.

"Because Ronda told them she ran from you because you hit her," Hawk says. "So they wouldn't have seen it as a missing person case."

"They treated me like a monster. Nobody would give me the time of day. I told them that she took my daughter, but we weren't married and there was no DNA test, so I couldn't even prove that." Again, he scrubs his hands through his hair. "But how could she be here? So close, and no sign of her? I have a Google alert on her name. I look for her on Facebook, on all of the social media accounts. In the phone books. I even tried one of those find-a-person apps. Nothing."

"She changed her name," I say. "She really didn't want to be found."

"Why would she run away from you?" Hawk asks. "Did you hit her?"

Graham's face crumples. His hand returns to his chest, and rests there. I edge forward in my chair, afraid that we've given him a heart attack. Hawk shakes his head at me, mouthing, "Wait."

Graham draws the back of his hand across his lips. "She might have been afraid of me," he says. "Not for the reasons you think. I never hit her. But I . . . She may have seen me as a threat. I told her she needed to get help. I called my mother to come and stay. Looking back, knowing what I know now, I think she was . . . well, depressed for certain. Maybe dipping into postpartum psychosis and paranoia. I should have handled it better. I can't imagine . . ." His voice breaks, and he buries his face in his hands. "You have to tell me what you know. I'm begging you."

"That's the thing," Hawk goes on, in that carefully measured tone. "We don't *know* anything. Just a lot of conjecture and surmise."

"Where is Andi?" Graham pleads.

The raw desperation in his voice slices my heart wide open, but I draw on all of my willpower. I don't want Andrea to be hurt.

"She was really freaked out when she saw your name in the book. What's the connection?"

"The night before she . . . disappeared . . . we fought. She was a mess. She wouldn't even say the baby's name. She kept calling Lelia 'it' and accusing me of doing nothing and leaving all of the work to her. I'm not proud of this, but I didn't understand it and I blew up. I was studying Dante for a class. She grabbed the book out of my hands and threw it at the wall. I kept the damn thing with me for years. It was torture to look at it, but it felt like a connection to her. A couple of months ago, I decided it was time to let it go. I donated it to a Goodwill store and . . ." His eyes rest on me and he shakes his head. "Unbelievable. You found the book, and the book found her. It's like a miracle."

I'm not so sure about the miracle. I'm not even sure about being a catalyst, the way Hawk says I am. What I see is that I've reopened a lot of wounds. Hawk and Graham both look at me, waiting, and I know it's up to me to decide what happens next.

An expression Ash has always been fond of comes to mind, and I say it out loud. "Well, I guess it's easier to ask for forgiveness than permission."

They're both still staring at me, obviously not understanding what this means, although it's clear to me. If I ask Andrea whether she'll see

Graham and she says no, which I'm certain she will, then it's too late to spring him on her. And if I ask her about the baby, I'm pretty sure she's not going to tell me, which isn't fair to Graham when he's been searching all these years. Also, yes, I need to know what happened to Andrea's daughter. I need to know that she isn't me.

Chapter Thirty-Six

ANDREA

Four fifty-four. Six minutes to five, when taking anxiety and pain meds will finally be sanctioned. Only, I don't have them because I've trusted them to that devious, intrusive, meddling Nicole, who should be back by now. The afternoon has crawled by, my anxiety ratcheting up with every slow tick of the clock. I'm torn between fury that Nicole has dug into my business, worry that something has happened to her, and terror that my guilty secrets have finally caught up with me.

At two minutes after five, I finally hear a vehicle in the driveway. Immediately, I struggle up onto my feet. I have things to say to Nicole, and I am not going to say them sitting down. In fact, I am not going to let her into my house. Yes, she's holding my meds, and yes, I need the help, but I'll manage somehow. I can get more meds. Sleep on the couch so I don't have to navigate the stairs.

She beats me to the door. Before I've cleared the living room and made it to the hallway, I hear the rattle of keys, the beeping of the control panel as she enters the alarm code. And then I'm looking down the hallway to the entryway and I halt so suddenly that I nearly overbalance and crash to the ground, crutches and all.

Nicole is not alone. She's got Hawk with her, which is not surprising. But neither of them matter. I only have eyes for the graying, distinguished-looking man who takes a step forward and holds his hands out as if he can touch me despite the distance between us. "Andi," he says in a strangled voice. "It's really you."

I can't move. I can't speak. The world goes black around the edges, but then Nicole is there, and Hawk.

"She's going to pass out," Nicole says from a distance. I'm scooped up in strong arms and carried.

"Is she all right? Do we need an ambulance?" It's his voice, Tag's, and I know either my past has caught up with me or I've been swept away into psychosis.

"Just shock," Hawk answers as he lowers me onto the sofa. "She was already weak. I think she'll be fine."

Nicole's hand is on my forehead, cool and gentle. "I'll get water. And her pills."

I keep my eyes closed, even though I'm fully conscious, so I don't have to look at Tag, don't have to explain. One more minute. Just one more. But then Nicole is back, calling me.

"Andrea. Can you hear me? I have your meds."

And I know if I keep faking unconsciousness that they will call an ambulance, and I don't want to go back to the hospital and risk the psych unit again. So I blink my eyes open and allow Nicole to lift my head and hold the water glass to my lips. I swallow the pills that she puts in my hand. Then, painfully and with an effort, I lever myself up to sitting and look into a face that has been in my mind every day for the last thirty years, braced for the reproach and contempt I know I deserve.

He's old. That's my very first thought. The once-smooth face is lined, the square jaw softened. But the blue eyes are the same, intent and intelligent. "I've looked for you. Every day. I never stopped," he says.

I should tell him I'm sorry. For disappearing. For everything. But I can't seem to find the words. So I just sit there, waiting for the justified recriminations and reproaches to rain down on my head. Instead, he drops down on his knees beside the couch.

"Andi. I'm so sorry. So terribly, deeply sorry. I was terrified and exhausted and I didn't understand. I handled the situation like a blundering idiot."

The heart I thought I didn't have cracks right down the middle. Hot tears blur my vision. "You're *sorry?*" I croak. "*That's* what you came here to say?"

"I know it's not enough, can never be enough," he says. "But you have to know I never stopped looking for you. I tried everything. Ronda said you'd run because you were afraid of me—"

"Stop," I gasp. "Please. Just stop." I can't bear hearing this from him, not after everything I've done. It's all so wrong, so twisted. I never once considered that *he* would feel guilty, would think that he had done something wrong.

Tag clasps his hands as if I'm God and he's come to pray. "Please, Andi. Forgive me enough to tell me this one thing. Is our daughter . . . is she . . . ?" His voice breaks. He buries his face in his hands, and his shoulders shake with weeping.

And here it is. Now. The moment I've been running from for so long. I swallow. Clear my throat and confess the horrible, unforgivable truth. "I don't know."

Tag draws in a ragged breath and lowers his hands. His skin is the color of old ivory; he looks like he's aged ten years since he walked in the door. "So what, then? You gave her up for adoption?" he asks, misunderstanding.

So I have to say it again. Out loud, instead of over and over in my head. The truth that makes me an unnatural, despicable, horrible human being. I meet his eyes, my heart breaking and breaking over and over again, and say, "No, I didn't put her up for adoption. I'm saying . . . I don't know where she is. I don't know what happened to her. I . . . lost her."

"You can't have just misplaced a baby!"

I force myself to keep my eyes open, to watch the shock and horror take over the face I once loved, to stay in the moment. I deserve this.

"That's exactly what I did. I . . . misplaced her." Sitting up straight, I force myself to keep my eyes on his face while I say the words that have been choking me for more than half my life. "My memory is all fragments. Postpartum psychosis. I had delusions. I remember believing you were trying to take the baby away from me. And I had terrifying thoughts of hurting her, drowning her, dropping her. I couldn't sleep. My thoughts were crazy and distorted. And then Ronda gave me some ecstasy and it put me over the edge.

"We went on a joyride across the border, wound up in Canada, in Vancouver. I only have bits and pieces, all of it like a movie. I remember a motel, and Ronda and the baby, and next thing I was in a psych ward. No baby. No Ronda. When the doctor and nurses asked about my baby—obviously I'd been breastfeeding and recently given birth—I told them she was with her father. I hoped Ronda had taken her home to you. And I couldn't bring myself to even think of anything else. When I got well enough to call Ronda . . ."

I stop for a breath, and to strengthen my resolve. Saying the words out loud makes it so much more true, so much more heinous and monstrous.

"Ronda said . . . she said she'd left me and Lelia alone in the motel room to go get takeout, and when she came back, the baby was gone and I was frantic and talking gibberish. So she took me to the hospital and got me admitted. After that I . . . well, I still didn't say anything to the staff about Lelia being missing. I tried to kill myself with a pair of scissors, but they were dull and it was just a stupid, sordid little gesture.

"Death would have been a kindness, a mercy I didn't deserve. I kept watching the news and reading the paper, waiting for the police to find a tiny body or report an abandoned baby, but there was nothing, always nothing.

"Meds and time and hormone shifts cleared up my psychosis. When I was discharged, a social worker helped me apply to a community college in Seattle and get a loan and Medicaid and find an apartment. That's when I changed my name. I didn't want to get arrested and go to prison for whatever I'd done. But more, I didn't want you to ever find me, Tag. I couldn't face telling you.

"All this time, I've been looking back over my shoulder, expecting the cops to catch up with me, for you to find me. And then Nicole moved that book into my house, and I thought, somehow, you were behind it. That you'd found me, that you knew . . ."

I can't stand the look on his face for another minute. An unbearable pressure is growing in my chest, behind my eyes. Something gives way, a slow surge, a cresting wave of pain and loss, and I am weeping for the first time since I woke up in the psych unit without my child. My grief is an elemental force that might just tear apart whatever is left of me.

And then Nicole is beside me, her arms around me, and for the first time in so many years, I turn into the comfort of an embrace. She, too, is weeping, holding me tight, tight, and I cling to her as if she is my salvation, my only hope of release from the guilt-racked hell I've been living in. Slowly, gradually, the pressure eases. My tears begin to slow, the sobs ease, shaking my body more gently.

My old self-conscious prickles stir. I have an audience. I am showing weakness and emotion to others, to Tag.

Oh, God. Tag. Still here. Still to be dealt with. Gently I push Nicole away and sit up, wiping ineffectually at my face with my hands. Hawk looms over me, and I shrink into myself, only to notice he's holding out a box of tissues with one hand, stroking Nicole's hair with the other. Tag, across the room in a chair, is a blur through my tear-blinded eyes.

I grab a handful of tissues and mop my face, aware of Nicole doing the same thing beside me. A silence grows, so vast and devastating, I don't think it can ever be broken. There are no words for this. There never will be.

Tag is the one who finally speaks. "I'd like to be able to say that I understand, and that I forgive you."

"But you can't," I say wearily. "How could you?"

"If you were a client, it would be easy. But I've spent my whole life looking for you. For her. And here you are . . ." He mops his face with his sleeve. "Never even thought to look in Canada." He gets to his feet. "I can't—I need to go. Hawk. Please, can we?"

"Of course," the big man says. "Nicole?"

"Staying. Unless Andrea wants to kick me out."

I'd forgotten that I'd planned to do exactly that. My anger at her is a distant thing now, petty and small. "Seems like I still need a little help," I say. "If you're willing to stay."

Tag heads for the door without stopping to look back, but Hawk lingers a moment, drawing Nicole toward him by one hand and cupping her chin with the other.

"You're a catalyst," he says. "Remember that."

And then he, too, is gone and it's just me and Nicole, uneasy now with so much unspoken between us. "What's all that about being a catalyst?" I ask as a starting point.

She draws the back of her arm across her eyes and blows her nose before she answers. "That's what Hawk wants to believe about my meddling. When I move things, like that book, and stuff happens, like this . . . he wants to think it needs to happen. So it's not my fault, really, if the world gets turned upside down. I'm just the spark that ignited what was going to burn up at some point anyway."

"So you're a Universal Shit Disturber," I comment drily, and she laughs at that. Then sobs. Then blows her nose again.

"I'm sorry I went behind your back," she says. "I shouldn't have. I told Hawk we needed to stop, and then Ronda let slip that you'd had a baby, and . . . I couldn't."

"Why?" She was going to say something else, I'm sure of it. Something that matters. "Why didn't you stop?"

"I was curious. And I was worried about your safety. I thought maybe Tag was an abuser and you'd been running from him." She draws in a deep breath, squares her shoulders, and turns to face me. "Okay. Here's the selfish, self-serving, pathetic truth. I thought, maybe, what if that lost baby turned out to be me?"

I want to hug her again. I want to wipe away the tears that are rolling down her face again. I want to believe that it could be that simple, that magical, that the relocated book would bring my long-lost baby back to me safe. But I can't believe it, and I can't reach out to her because I've lived too long behind these walls I've erected and don't know how to let myself be close to anybody.

"You said you weren't adopted." My tone is harsh, and I want to take the words back and soften them.

"Brina used to tell me I was when we were little," she whispers. "I never really believed it, but . . . I'm so not like them, you know? You've met Roberta. They're all so . . . normal. And I'm . . . me." She tries to laugh, but it's a sadder sound than her sobbing was. "They're all sick to death of me. Nobody's even talking to me anymore. So when you asked me if I was adopted . . . yeah. It got me wondering."

"You don't look like me. Or Tag." I resist the fluttering wings of hope, such a foreign sensation.

"I don't look like my parents, either."

"Birthday?" I ask, my throat so dry, the word is barely audible.

"Tomorrow, actually. I'd forgotten. We celebrated early."

"There you go. Not you. Lelia's birthday is in June. The seventh."

Nicole shrugs and tries for a smile. "Well, then. Not me. I'm likely a changeling, like in the fairy tales. The real Nicole stolen away at birth, and a cursed look-alike put in her place."

The fledgling feeling of concern and care for somebody else flares a little brighter, and I carefully pick through a flurry of thoughts and emotions for the right words. "Hawk is right" is what I settle for. "About you being a catalyst. It's better to have this see the light of day. And only fair for Tag to finally know the truth."

Thank you, I whisper in my mind, but I can't bring myself to say out loud, taking cover in my old and familiar persona, threadbare as it is. "Now, if you're done emoting all over the place, would you possibly make me a cup of tea?"

Nicole deflates like a balloon, all the tension going out of her in a single long exhalation. There is still so much that is unspoken, but I see that it's easier for both of us to assume our usual roles. "Yes, ma'am," she says, stalking out of the room.

I lean my head back against the couch cushions, exhausted, but with an idea percolating in my mind. I owe Nicole a debt of gratitude, and I think, maybe, I see a way to pay it.

Chapter Thirty-Seven

NICOLE

When I first started working for Andrea, she was all bristles and sharp edges and rigid demands. Something major has shifted, both with her and between us. She's still sarcastic and abrasive, but softer, as if the mannerisms are just a habit and her heart isn't in it. Often, tears will start pouring silently down her face for no apparent reason, and she just sits and lets them flow, not trying to hide them or brush them away.

Hawk has suggested to her, and to Graham—separately, since they are not speaking to each other—that they register with some DNA profile sites like 23andMe, so that if Lelia is alive out there somewhere and looking for her parents, maybe they'll find her, and they've both agreed.

As for me, I'm a mess. Maybe I'm not Andrea and Graham's lost child, but that doesn't change my alienation from my own family. Mom still hasn't called. I've tried her phone repeatedly, but it always goes to voice mail, and I won't leave a message or send a text because I keep imagining Kent gloating over it. Roberta has dutifully replied to the texts I've sent her, letting me know that Mom is well, but that's it.

Even Penelope and I are taking a texting break, just to be sure Kent can't follow the trail and find a way to get to Ash.

As for Hawk—I've given up pretending that I haven't fallen for him because even I can't keep up that level of denial. He's in my thoughts all the time. Whenever he's near me, my senses are so full of him that I can't think straight. But he's been distant. Polite, professional, friendly. And I've hardly seen him. He's working on my case, he says, trying to dig up something on Kent that his mother can use to quash my subpoena.

Today is my day to go in for witness preparation, and we've still got nothing.

"You've got this," Andrea says while I'm pacing, waiting for Hawk to show up to give me a ride.

I shake my head, dangerously close to tears. "I don't think I can do it."

"Stop playing the victim, Nicole," she snaps. "It doesn't suit you."

"Go to hell," I hurl at her, and she laughs, the most genuine laughter I've ever heard from her.

"See? This right here? That's who you are. Kent wants you to think you're a victim. But you're not. You're the sort of woman who shows up at the door of a crazy bitch to try to make things right for your sister. You fight back to protect your people."

I like the story she's weaving, but it doesn't quite feel true. "You've got the wrong idea of me," I say.

"No, I don't," she answers quietly. "Who's the woman who bit that motherfucker? Who refused to tell him where she moved the money that would have made this all go away? Who is going to do everything she can to protect the family who doesn't appreciate her and isn't talking to her? You are. You're a rock star, Nicole. And don't you forget it."

"Damn it, you're going to make me cry." I dab at my eyes, my heart full to overflowing with this vision of myself she's painted, with knowing that she sees me this way.

She laughs again. "Here's your Hawk. Go get him, tiger."

I bend down and hug her impulsively, and her arms go around my shoulders, a little stiff, but comforting for all that. "Go on, now," she says, and I do.

Hawk is waiting at the door. He smiles, but it doesn't reach his eyes. "Ready?" he asks.

"As I'll ever be."

We drive to the law firm in silence, arriving ten minutes before four, when I'm supposed to meet Kent. Hawk parks a block away, where we are unlikely to be seen. We've agreed it's best not to rub Kent's nose in the fact that we are working together, even though it's a pretty sure thing that he knows we're hanging out. Hawk turns to me, his eyes searching mine.

"You know what to do?"

I nod. "Got it. But I'm terrified."

"*You?* Never. You are the intrepid Nickle, fearlessly penetrating the headquarters of evil. Let me see your phone."

I hand it over and watch as he activates an app he built and installed earlier. It will run invisibly in the background, recording all conversation until it is turned off. "I'm also taking myself and Mom out of your contacts and deleting our chats," he says. "Just as a precaution. You've got my number memorized."

I nod, afraid to trust my voice.

"I won't be far. Call if you need me."

"What if I don't go?" I say. "What if I get on a plane to Mexico or somewhere?"

Hawk doesn't bat an eyelash. "If that's what you want to do, you know I'll help you."

Temptation beckons. I can almost hear the ocean surf, feel the soft, warm air. But I can't imagine feeling peace leaving the people I love behind to be tormented by the man I so stupidly married. I say, "Maybe we could go together. After."

"It's a deal," he says.

I open my door and get out of the Jeep. "Agent Nickle going dark," I say with a salute. I don't look back, afraid I'll chicken out and run back to Hawk for safety. Halfway down the block, I see Kent come out of the building, looking for me. His once perfectly tailored suit hangs on him. His face is thin and gaunt. There are new gray threads in his hair, which needs a trim, and he's got some sort of blemish on his upper lip.

"Thank you for doing this," he says, smiling.

"Just so we're clear," I retort, "this is not some favor I'm doing for you or your scumbag client." He opens his mouth, but I hold up my hand to stop him. "I'm here because of the subpoena. I want your word, not that it's worth anything, that if I do this, you won't contest the divorce and you'll stop blackmailing my friends and family. Oh, and you won't press charges about the money."

"Can we get on with this?" he growls. "Timothy is waiting."

"I want you to say it all. The whole thing."

He twitches, like he wants to hit me but knows he can't. "Fine. I'll sign the divorce papers and I'll stay away from your family and I won't press charges against you. Are you happy now?"

I shrug. "Happy is not the word for what I am. I don't know why you're making me do this. I'm not a very good liar, Kent."

He huffs out a breath of disbelief. "You? You are a brilliant liar. A virtuoso, really. All of those tales you spin about why you move things, and how it doesn't count as stealing? It's genius. The jury will love you." He glances around him and lowers his voice. "Here's your story. You and my client had a fling in high school, but it fell apart when you dropped out. You bumped into each other last year in a Starbucks and caught up over coffee. Make a point that it was sometime after Christmas, early in January. Make sure to look like you're trying to remember the date, it will be more realistic that way."

"And if somebody fact-checks and finds out we've never actually met?"

"You did go to the same high school. That's the only fact they can check. You can be delightfully uncertain about which Starbucks it was and the actual day. And then you'll tell them that the two of you emailed and texted, and when your husband left town for a legal convention, you took advantage of the situation and met for dinner. Which led to dancing and then you went home with him and stayed the night. You were with him from six o'clock that evening until the next morning. Act like you don't really remember the date, and when pressed, you can let Timothy help you figure it out, because he and I went to the conference together."

When he's done, I stare at him in silence, trying to remember how I thought I loved him. How I thought he was so sexy and desirable. Compared to Hawk, he's pale and washed out, a malevolent shadow.

"Do you need to hear it again?" he asks. "You don't look like you were paying attention."

"I heard it perfectly," I reply. "Not only am I going to lie about knowing this murdering scumbag, I'm going to say that I cheated on you. In a court of law. Which you can then use against me in the divorce."

"I won't." He flushes, but that thing on his lip doesn't change color. I wonder what it is, whether maybe somebody else bit him, and then I look closer and see that it's a cold sore. I almost laugh. Cold sores and gray hairs and an imperfectly fitting suit. Maybe Karma is real after all.

"Does Timothy know?" I ask. "That I'm basically lying my ass off?"

Kent's eyes narrow. Little white dents form in his nostrils. "If you hint, breathe a word, so much as roll your eyes . . ."

"Got it. Your boss doesn't know that you're suborning perjury." I turn my back again and start walking, smiling to myself. This conversation has recorded on my phone. I'll give it to Janelle, and she can quash the subpoena and I won't have to testify in court after all.

Kent falls in beside me. "Let me see your phone."

"No."

"I don't trust you. You could be recording this."

Hawk prepped me for this possibility. Assured me there's no way Kent will see the invisible app. I'm supposed to pretend to resist and then give in.

Kent grabs my wrist, and I say, loudly and deliberately, "Let go. You're hurting me."

Heads turn toward us. A man and a woman slow their steps.

Kent releases me at once, smiling in a way that looks painful, holding the pose until everybody decides we are okay and moves on. "Let me see the fucking phone," he growls.

"Fine. Here."

I watch while he scrolls through the apps, holding my breath. "Happy now?" I ask when he stops.

"Not particularly." He shoves the phone in his pocket.

"Give me back my phone."

"Not going to happen. Like I said, I don't trust you. You've probably still got Hawk working with you, and I'm not taking chances. Now hurry up, we're going to be late."

I plant my feet right where I am, and lower my voice. "I am not entering that building until you give me back my phone."

Kent shrugs. "You want to make your court appearance without any witness prep? Be my guest." He starts walking, and calls back over his shoulder, "Also, I have Ash's landlord on speed dial. Seems like I heard you moved back in and there's a steady stream of drug seekers going in and out of the building."

"You bastard."

He keeps walking, not even turning around to see if I'm going to follow. He knows me. He knows he can make me do anything if he threatens Ash and the baby.

∼

The lobby of Findlay, Strachey, and Lytle, Attorneys at Law, is light-years away from the public defenders' offices I've spent so much time in. Everything, from the gold-lettered door sign to the clean, fashionable furnishings and the cozy little kitchenette offering a selection of Keurig coffee and refrigerated beverages, speaks to a high-end clientele. I've been here once or twice to meet Kent for lunch, but never felt anywhere close to comfortable.

Karen, the receptionist, is dressed in a skirt and jacket, blonde hair up in a classic twist. Earrings identical to the ones I sold dangle from her ears. She also has a cold sore that is a mirror image of Kent's. Neither of these things surprises me. I met her once in the hallway of our condo, leaving as I was coming in. On that occasion, she looked somewhat less put together, a little rumpled and mussed, and even then I didn't believe her story that she'd come by for an emergency confab about a client.

She looks up now from her computer screen with a prepasted smile and sort of freezes that way when she sees me and Kent together. "Nicole," she says, glancing down at her computer and back at me. "You're the four o'clock?"

"Yepper." She knows my face, of course, but wouldn't have recognized my maiden name, which I've reverted to without waiting for the divorce.

"Take care of her, would you, Karen?" Kent says, and vanishes through a door into the inner sanctum. Karen swallows and realigns her features into an expression of unconcern. "Timothy is running a few minutes late, but he'll be right with you. Please feel free to get yourself a beverage."

I walk over to the fridge and survey the contents. Nothing appeals to me, but it would help to have something to do with my hands. I skip the Perrier in favor of a Coke. And then I sip it slowly while Kent's mistress and I trade glances and pretend not to look at each other. It keeps me from fidgeting. By the time her phone buzzes and she looks up to say, "Timothy will see you now," I've decided I have no hard feelings and almost feel a sense of kinship with her. I think about telling her that her diamonds are probably fakes but decide against it. Let her believe while she can.

Timothy's windowed office is all understated luxury. A beautiful desk. Inviting chairs. Original, tastefully framed watercolors. There is money in this room, but it is not epitomized by Timothy Lytle. He's a small man, middle-aged and balding. His suit coat doesn't meet over his paunch, and his tie is slightly crooked. He takes both of my hands and kisses my cheek. "Nicole, thanks so much for coming in."

Kent stands beside the desk, his eyes a challenge. I turn away from him and back to Timothy.

"Not like I have much choice in the matter," I say, rude and abrasive. Kent can drag me in here, but the smiling, socially conscious facade he expects from me is one lie I am not telling today.

Timothy gives me an apologetic smile. "I understand your reluctance, but I'm still glad you are here. This will all be over before you know it, and you'll be back to life as usual. Please, have a seat."

He gestures toward two leather chairs, and I sit on one. Timothy assumes a barricaded position behind his desk, a yellow notepad and a small recording device in front of him. He makes a short notation, as if he's had an idea he needed to jot down, and keeps his eyes on the paper as he says, "First, I do understand that there is a difficulty between you and Kent at this time, and why you would be reluctant to be entangled in one of his cases. Let me reassure you that I will be the one questioning you in court. Kent will be in the courtroom, however, as my second chair, so it's best if you make peace with his presence now."

His gaze comes up, on cue, searching my face earnestly for my response.

My imagination paints a clear picture of me sitting in the witness box, looking down at Kent's self-satisfied smirk. "I can handle Kent," I say calmly, and as the words leave my lips, I realize that I actually mean them.

"Good, good. He has been forbidden to speak to you without permission, so you can consider him window dressing for the moment. Sit down, Kent, and look less threatening."

Kent's jaw clamps tight as he lowers himself stiffly into the chair beside me.

Timothy says, "Now, let's hear, in your own words first, how you came to know the defendant, and what the two of you were doing when these terrible murders occurred. We'll walk through that several times, and then I'll ask you some questions and we'll see what we need to do from there. All right?"

I stare at him, my jaw locked, my stomach sloshing dangerously. I remind myself that I'm acting in a play, doing this for the good of the people I love. *I am the fearless Agent Nickle, breaching the headquarters of evil in the pursuit of ultimate justice.* Looking straight into Timothy's eyes, I deliver the story that Kent prepared for me, embellishing the bit about my attraction to Brian, as if I'd been the one to truly cheat on Kent instead of the other way around.

"That was perfect," Timothy says, smiling happily. "The jury will warm right up to you. Yes, you made a mistake, but they'll see that you were a neglected wife, lonely, and how you were taken advantage of and manipulated. So they will be sympathetic to you, and they will want to believe you."

"So that's it? I'm done?" Relief flows through me. That wasn't so bad, apart from Kent grabbing my phone and all the evidence against him recorded on it.

I'm half up out of my chair when Timothy says, "Not quite. We're going to let Kent cross-examine you now, as if he's the prosecutor." He holds up a conciliatory hand before I can object. "I know, it's not fair, but if you can handle Kent hammering at you, you'll have no trouble with the prosecutor. All right?"

"And if it's not all right?"

"I'd ask that you trust me," Timothy says.

I shrug, and sit back down.

Kent circles to the back of the desk and starts hammering me with questions. He's clearly enjoying this opportunity to harass me, but to my surprise, I'm not afraid of him. I answer decisively, consistently, embellishing the story he made up to make it more believable.

"Excellent, excellent." Timothy claps his hands. "That's enough. You didn't let him rattle you one bit."

Kent is not so pleased. I know that tightness in his jaw, the way his lips press together. If he could, he'd grab my shoulders and shake a little fear into me. I smile at him, rubbing it in, knowing he doesn't dare lose his cool in front of his boss.

"We'll meet briefly on the morning of your testimony to refresh," Timothy says. "In the meantime, I'll get Karen to give you a tour—"

"Kent did tell you that I'm already on a first-name basis with courtrooms, right? We can probably skip the tour."

"That's one of the things that makes you such a wonderful witness. You're believable. A perfectly upstanding citizen wouldn't be as likely to have formed an alliance with Brian. But here you are. Good-hearted, honest, only you have this little problem with sticky fingers and infidelity. The prosecutor will pick at that, just as Kent did, but you'll handle it brilliantly. There's just one thing . . ."

He leans back and looks me over from head to toe, the way a man inspects a car he's thinking about buying. "Let's discuss your appearance. We want you to present as neat, law abiding, and believable, but not too fancy, if you know what I mean."

"I don't do fancy. I own jeans and T-shirts. What I'm wearing now is the best you are going to get."

"You have clothes at the condo," Kent says. "I can bring—"

"No. I am not letting you dress me anymore."

Kent bristles. "Don't be—"

Timothy smoothly blocks our impending squabble. "I'll have my case manager take you shopping. Nothing too much—just some tasteful slacks, or maybe a skirt. A long-sleeved blouse to cover those tattoos. And we'll do something with your hair, of course, and your makeup."

I don't bother to object to any of this. I've been in court enough times to understand the importance of window dressing. It's all part of the game. Even my court-appointed attorneys told me what to wear and what expression they wanted to see on my face. And in those cases, there was never a jury involved, just a judge and a plea deal.

"All right, then," Timothy says. "That's settled. Come and talk to Karen, so you can set up a time to go shopping."

I hesitate. Really? Shopping with Karen? But that's nothing compared to all of the other things I've done lately. I am a spy on a mission of discovery. Shopping with my husband's mistress is just another part of a game.

Chapter Thirty-Eight

NICOLE

"How did it go?" Hawk asks as I collapse into the passenger seat of the Jeep. "Here. I know it's late for caffeine, but I figured you could use a coffee."

Gratefully, I warm my hands on the paper cup and take a sip of deliciously hot, perfectly sweetened latte, stalling for time. I don't want to tell Hawk that I totally blew the operation, that Kent has my phone and I've got nothing.

"Well, Timothy thinks I'm a star," I begin.

"And Kent?"

"He said every incriminating thing we could hope for."

"That's fantastic!"

I keep my eyes on my coffee. "Well, it would be. But Kent took my phone."

"We expected he might do that. We planned for it."

Tears begin to surface and I blink them back, determined not to let Kent make me cry. "You don't understand. He kept it. I didn't get the recording."

"Nickle." Hawk flashes a brilliant smile at me. "Give me some cred for being smarter than Kent. That conversation, and any conversation in the phone's vicinity, is uploading to the cloud until he powers it off. You are not getting on that witness stand. And you are not going to prison."

"Oh, Hawk!" I fling myself across the Jeep and try to hug him, coffee cup and all. His arm goes around me, his cheek pressing against my hair.

"That bastard is done screwing up your life. We'll quash the subpoena. We'll threaten to expose him if he carries out any of his threats. It's over, Nicole. You're safe now."

And now I am crying after all, but it's not Kent who made me do it. It's Hawk. It's this unmatched and novel feeling of being protected and understood. We sit there for a long time while I cry and he holds me, and then he says, "Your coffee is getting cold," and I suddenly feel self-conscious again.

I wipe my face with my hands and sit up. "Andrea will be wondering where I'm at." I reach for my phone to text her, and remember all over again that Kent has it. I can't check messages or call anybody. A small, panicky feeling washes over me. "Can I use your phone?"

"Of course. Tomorrow we'll get you a new one, okay?"

"Okay."

He dials Andrea's number and hands me the phone as it rings, but she doesn't answer. "I'm sure she's fine," Hawk reassures me. "Maybe she's taking a nap. But we'll drive directly over and check on her."

Wrung out, limp, exhausted by a long and difficult day, I lean my head back and close my eyes, drifting on the edges of sleep. An exclamation from Hawk wakes me.

"Uh-oh. This looks like trouble."

I jolt upright in my seat, eyes open, a whole new adrenaline spike running through me. There are cars parked in Andrea's usually empty driveway. More cars on the street. I recognize them all. Roberta's Subaru. Warner's minivan. Brina's Prius.

Déjà vu. I feel like a ton of cement has fallen from the sky directly onto my head.

"Maybe Andrea invited them all over for pizza and ice cream," Hawk offers.

"Right. And the Easter Bunny and Santa Claus are here to hand out treats and toys. Can we just keep driving? I don't want to do this."

"There's a spare room at Mom's. You want me to keep driving, I keep driving."

The offer is tempting. Peace. Acceptance. But Andrea's words from earlier today come back to me. I want to be the woman she thinks I am. The one who faces up to her problems, not the one who runs away.

I sigh. "Can't avoid them forever. I might as well get it over with. You could come in, if you want. Although if I were you, I'd flee for the hills."

"You couldn't keep me out," Hawk says. "I'm your bodyguard, remember? I've got your back."

He parks the Jeep, then comes around and opens my door, holding out his hand. He doesn't let go after he's tugged me up and out, and we walk together up to the house, my cold hand warmed by his, my courage reinforced by his calm strength. When we enter, I can hear the rise and fall of familiar voices in the living room.

In silence, Hawk and I remove our shoes and set them with the others. Then he holds his hand out to me again, and we walk together into the living room. Everybody falls silent, staring at us as we stand there side by side.

None of the kids are here, or even the spouses. Just my mom and my siblings and Andrea, with Sylvester purring in her lap, wearing a smile that is more frightening on her usually serious face than a glower or a frown.

"Oh good. You're home," she says. "And you brought Hawk. Perfect. Come in and have a seat."

Looking around the room, it's immediately clear that trouble is brewing.

Mom wears her brave martyr expression. The faces of the others, even Warner's, are cold and closed. I wonder what lies Kent has told them, what kind of damage he's done, and for an instant, I once more think about turning around and running—somewhere. Anywhere. Hawk squeezes my hand, and that holds me steady and reminds me to breathe.

"This," Andrea announces, "is an intervention."

"Waste of time and breath," Brina mutters. Mom's tears get away from her and she sobs quietly. Warner runs a hand through his hair. Roberta rolls her eyes. I wait for the sensation of crushing shame and despair that I have always felt in these situations, but it doesn't come.

I feel different. Stronger. I am not the same woman I was when I was dragged before the family tribunal just a few weeks ago. For one thing, I have Hawk, but it's more than that. I've learned some things about myself. I'm brave. I'm honest. And maybe moving objects around has hurt people, but it's also helped people. It's helped me, even, by exposing Kent for what he is. By bringing me Hawk. By teaching me that I have agency and control over many aspects of my life.

Instead of spouting sarcastic defiance, I say, with barely a quaver, "I'm glad you're all here. There are some things you need to know about Kent."

"Exactly," Andrea says. "Come sit over here by me, Nickle, and we'll explain together, shall we?"

She nods at me, and I slowly cross the room to sit beside her. Hawk walks behind the sofa and stands there protectively at my back. It feels like he's guarding my heart and soul and not just my body, and I'm able to meet the collective stare of my family members straight on.

"Thank you to Roberta for rounding everybody up and getting them here," Andrea says. "But I will confess first thing that you have all been misled as to the purpose of this gathering. The intervention is for you, not for your sister, because your behavior toward her has been reprehensible."

"Oh my God," Brina says. "You've bought into Nicole's bullshit."

Andrea stiffens. "Nicole's 'bullshit,' as you call it, got a killer off the streets and saved a woman's life. Could you confirm that, please, Hawk?"

"True," he rumbles.

Roberta glares at him. "Pardon me for being rude, but we don't even know who you are."

Hawk digs out his PI license and a business card and crosses the room to hand them to her. "If you require additional confirmation, I can get a statement for you from the lead detective on the case Andrea mentioned," he says.

Roberta's expression remains stubbornly set in denial. "Coincidence."

"Is it also a coincidence that the book she moved into this house forced me to stop running away from my past and is bringing the resolution of old wounds?" Andrea is warming up, her voice louder and stronger. "Now let's talk about that piece of shit that calls himself her husband. I know, you all are so enamored with him that you can't see past the surface. Do any of you have the slightest idea that the money Nicole relocated was dirty money meant to put a criminal back on the street? And that Kent has been using all of you as leverage to force her to perjure herself in court as a false witness? Roberta. Do you really believe in your heart that Nicole would go out of her way to sabotage your business?"

Her gaze travels over my family, all of whom stare back at her with varying expressions of shock and disbelief.

"Have you ever known Nickle to tell a lie?" Andrea continues. "Kent stole something from my house and tried to tell me it was Nicole who did it. He's threatened to disrupt Ash's living situation and have her child taken away from her. And all of you?" Her voice drips with scorn. "You all just keep on believing the word of an abusive narcissistic liar over that of your daughter. Your sister."

Mom looks stricken. Warner serious. Roberta's mouth has fallen open slightly. Brina's face is flushed nearly crimson.

"You want to know why I called this meeting, really?" Andrea demands. "Nicole and Hawk are helping me search for a baby—my baby—that disappeared thirty years ago. And Nicole wondered if that lost child might be her. That's how much you've all made her feel that she belongs in your family. How much you've excluded her. You all should be ashamed of yourselves. I lost my baby, but you still have yours. And this is how you treat her? Shame on all of you."

"Well, of course she's not adopted," Mom exclaims. "Nickle. Honey. You don't really believe that, do you?"

I clear my throat. "I'll admit I did wonder."

"But why?" Mom quavers. She looks small and bewildered, and I want to go and comfort her, but Andrea rests her hand on my knee and keeps me where I am.

"Tell her, Nickle."

So I tell her the fear that has been locked away in my heart since I was a child. "Because I'm not like any of you. I don't look like you. I certainly don't act like you."

Brina clears her throat. "I remember when they brought you home from the hospital. I was jealous. I wanted you to go away."

"You used to tell me I was adopted."

"Jealous, like I said." And then, words I never ever dreamed I'd hear from her cross her lips. "I'm sorry. For that and . . . other things."

"You look just like your father's sister," Mom says. "Alma. She died before you were born. Your dad wanted to name you after her, but I said no."

"I remember Mom being pregnant with you," Warner adds. "This is crazy, Nicole."

Roberta hasn't moved or spoken. I can almost see the wheels turning. Finally, she shakes her head and looks directly at Andrea. "It's really helped you, Nicole moving that book?"

"It did."

"And the money she took from Kent was dirty money?"

"Yes. Which got relocated and ended up helping a single mom get out of a bad situation," Hawk answers.

"But Kent," Mom says. "I . . . He's so very believable."

"I should know. I married him," I answer.

"You're my baby girl, Nickle, no matter what. I thought I was . . . I didn't want to . . ." Her body begins to shake with sobs. I get up and walk across the room to her, then kneel and put my head in her lap, as though I'm a child again. She strokes my hair.

"It's okay, Mom. Don't cry."

"It's not okay." I've never heard Warner sound so angry. He's the most peaceful, easygoing guy I've ever met, always the family mediator. He gets out of his chair and starts pacing. "Can Kent get away with this? Put Nicole in prison, get Ash evicted, trash Roberta's business? Can't you do something?"

"We're going to quash the subpoena," Hawk says. "We recorded a conversation between him and Nickle this afternoon that puts the power back in our hands."

"And then what?" Roberta asks. "What happens to him then?"

"Well, he doesn't have a witness, and I'd guess he'll be in trouble with the people who paid him to procure one," Hawk answers.

"That's it?" Brina squawks. "That's not good enough. He needs to pay for what he's done."

"Vengeance belongs to God," my mother remonstrates. "Kent will reap his just rewards."

Roberta says, "But he could still do all of those things, right? Even if we quash the subpoena, he can still do the things you say he's threatened to do."

"True," Hawk says, "but it's unlikely. I'm thinking about a little reverse blackmail. He leaves Nicole and everybody else alone, and we don't tell anybody what he's done."

"But then he's still getting away with it," Brina argues. "No offense, Mom, but I don't want to just sit around and wait for God to judge him. Besides, what's to stop him from doing the same thing again?"

"I suspect," Hawk says, "that there could be some wrath descending upon him from the party who paid him the bribe."

"He'll just wiggle his way out of that somehow," Brina scoffs. "He needs to be punished and exposed."

"He definitely needs to know he doesn't get to break apart our family like this," Warner says. "I'm sick about this, Nickle. He's been spewing poison about you ever since I met him, only it sounded so much like concern and love for you, I totally missed it."

"Maybe we just talk to him?" Mom asks. "Surely he's not beyond hope."

"I, for one, don't ever want to see his face again," Roberta snarls.

"Well, then, Miss Know Everything, what do you suggest?" Brina throws back at her. "He needs to know we're onto him."

"Easy, girls," Warner says. "Calm heads need to prevail here."

I stay where I am, my arms around my mother and hers around me, my cheek pressed against the softness of her breast, listening and thinking. Brina's outrage about Kent getting away without penalty strikes a chord with me. As much as I am basking in this love and support, I don't want anybody to fight this battle for me. And I do want Kent to have consequences for his actions, and to stop him from hurting anybody else.

"I guess I could stand to see his face one more time while we all tell him what we think of him," Roberta concedes. "But I still don't like it."

"Talking to Kent won't change anything. I've got a better idea." I wriggle out of Mom's arms, get to my feet, and move behind the sofa to stand beside Hawk, hoping he'll back me on what I've decided to do. Also, I figure he might help command a little respect from a group of people not used to listening to anything I have to say.

But for once in my life, they all listen without even interrupting. And when I'm done, still nobody says anything, all of them thinking about my plan. Hawk breaks the silence first. "I don't like it. There must be an easier way."

"Agreed," Roberta snaps. "You are not getting on that witness stand, Nickle. Why would you even do that?"

I meet each pair of eyes with my own, one at a time. "I want to do this. Actually, I need to do this. I'm asking all of you to work with me. Please."

"But it's unnecessary pain and suffering for you," Hawk protests. "I'd rather you never see the man again."

"It will be hard on all of us," Mom says. "You're asking us to pretend we don't know what Kent has done. To continue having you cut out of our lives. Just for a little revenge?"

"It's only two weeks," I answer. "And it's not revenge. It's justice. And I need to face him. Publicly. In court. But this plan will only work if everybody plays along."

Brina makes a face. "I'd be in favor of a nice quiet assassination, myself, but I get it, Nickle. I'm in."

"I'll do it," Roberta says.

"Me, too," Warner says. "But I hate for you to go through this, Nickle."

"Well, then," Roberta says. "I guess that's settled." She yawns and stretches. "I need to get home to the kids." She turns to me, her brow furrowed, her manner unusually tentative. "I still can't say I understand why you move things, Nickle. And I can't come around to believing that it's a good thing. I mean, taking other people's belongings is against the law, for heaven's sake. But you're my sister and I'm sorry that I didn't listen to you. And I forgive you for stealing Andrea away from me."

I laugh and fling my arms around her shoulders. She hugs me back, a little stiffly, but I don't blame her. If I don't understand why I do what I do, how can I possibly expect a practical person like Roberta to get it?

Warner sweeps me up off the ground and swings me around. "You're one of a kind, Nickle. I will say that."

Brina lingers in the entryway, dawdling with her boots and her coat, until the rest of the family is gone. And then she blurts out, "I always thought I was the adopted one." Before I can respond to that, she's out the door, leaving me alone in the entryway with Hawk.

"You can stay for dinner," I say. "If you want. But only if you stop glowering."

"Am I glowering?"

"You are. Let me guess, you don't like my plan."

"Wow, you're a mind reader." He rubs the back of his neck with one hand and tries for a smile. "Did I tell you about my hero complex? Big strong man not want little woman to suffer."

I laugh. "This little woman is on a mission. Agent Nickle out to balance the scales of justice and reclaim her self-esteem."

His expression shifts, his jaw softens, his eyes focus on mine. My breath hitches, my heart starts racing, there's a wobbliness in my knees. I forget everything I've been telling myself about how things would never work between us. I am willing to let us both be swept away into a disastrous relationship.

He takes a step toward me, clears his throat, and says, very low, "We have to talk to Ronda again."

I blink up at him in confusion, feeling like he's dumped a bucket of freezing water over my head. "We do? Why?"

"Quiet," he warns in an almost whisper. "Andrea will hear."

I glance back over my shoulder to make sure she hasn't silently materialized, crutches and all.

"Ronda was lying through her teeth," Hawk says, his lips close to my ear. "She knows more than she's saying."

"Well, okay, but—"

"You saw Andrea tonight, and how she went all mama bear for you. Do you really believe she would have abandoned or harmed a baby? I'm thinking we owe it to her to find out what Ronda is hiding."

I grab my hair with both hands and tug, just a little, to try to shift from where I thought we were going to where we apparently are. "Maybe we should just leave it alone," I suggest. "I mean, she was young and maybe psychotic. It's better to leave some things in the shadows, don't you think? Is this you going all hero complex again?"

"Maybe," Hawk says. "Doesn't matter. I'm going in the morning. If I find out something that will help her and Graham, then I'll tell them. If not, I'll keep it to myself. Are you coming or not?"

Looking into his determined face in that moment, I know I'll go with him into hell and back if he'll only let me tag along.

Chapter Thirty-Nine

HAWK

God, I hope this isn't a mistake.

I know Nickle thinks it is. She's been restless for the entire drive, her fingers tapping, her leg jiggling, her eyes big with worry. Which makes me worry. What if we discover something absolutely horrible, like that Andrea abandoned or killed her baby while she was psychotic? On the other hand, what if Ronda has information that will give Andrea and Graham some peace after all of these years, even if it's just the bread crumb of knowing their child was safe when last seen?

By the time I pull into the parking lot of Mama's Kitchen, I'm wound up every bit as tight as Nicole.

"We cannot do this," she says, quietly. "Turn around and go back."

At that moment, Ronda emerges from a side door and leans up against the building to light up a smoke.

"Oh, damn it," Nicole says. "Since we're already here and all." She squares her shoulders and tilts up her chin in that way she does when she's faking bravado. It's all I can do not to lean over and kiss her, and maybe I would, anyway, but she opens her door and gets out before my willpower entirely crumbles.

"Not you again." Ronda exhales a stream of smoke, casually, as if she's not at all surprised to see us. But her body tenses, her eyes dart from me to the door beside her to the parking lot, and I know she's thinking about making a run for it. Before I can move to block her, Nicole does it, positioning herself directly in front of the door. I stand in front of Ronda, not close enough to break her personal boundaries, but enough to be intimidating. For once, I welcome the shadow of fear that moves across her face.

"This is harassment," she says. "Leave me alone or I'll call the cops."

"By all means, go ahead. They might find the conversation we are about to have very interesting." It's a bluff. I have no connections with the Pasco cops, and they're likely to send me packing. But my gamble pays off.

Ronda doesn't make the call. She lifts the cigarette to her lips and takes a long drag, as if she hasn't a care in the world. She's gone deathly pale, though, the blush on her cheekbones standing out in garish contrast to the pallor of her skin.

"You know," Nicole says casually, "when you don't tell the truth the first time, there are bound to be annoying follow-up questions."

"I have no idea what you're talking about."

"Oh, I think you do." I step closer, crowding her. Ronda shrinks back against the railing, eyes wide and pupils dilated. "We know you took Andi to a psych hospital. What we want to know—"

"No good deed goes unpunished!" she exclaims. "Try to help somebody and you get accused of kidnapping and—"

"Nobody has accused you of anything. Yet," I say. "Although it's interesting to hear the word 'kidnapping' from you. Is that what happened?"

"No! Oh my God. Is that what Andi told you? I'm not a bad person. She was my friend and I tried to help her." She might just be playing the victim now, but there's a small tremble in her voice, and I change tactics.

I lower my voice, hunch my shoulders, make my body as small and soft and sympathetic as I can. "God, I need a smoke," I say. "You want one, Nickle?"

"No, thanks, I'm good." She's a natural, rolling right along with me as if she's seen me smoke a hundred times and isn't remotely surprised by this request. I pull out the pack I keep in my pocket for moments like this and tap a cigarette into my hand.

"You got a light?" I ask, and Ronda relaxes a little as she lights me up.

I wait, watching her posture and body language until I see the sheen of tears in her eyes. Then I say, "How about you tell us how you helped Andi. You must have been terrified, your friend gone crazy and with a baby and all."

Ronda drops her cigarette butt and grinds it out with her heel. Lights up another. I think maybe I've misjudged and she's not going to take the bait, but finally she says, "We were young, you know? I was only twenty, for fuck's sake. I didn't know anything about babies or depression or any of that shit. I figured Andi had the baby blues, right? Like everybody gets. So I took her out to get her mind off things, lift her spirits. We ended up taking off on a little road trip, and then she flipped out and went totally psycho on me. What was I supposed to do?"

"Can't imagine," I say sympathetically. "What a cluster, right?"

"We were in fucking Canada when she lost her marbles. Her parents were dead, and Tag . . . well, she kept telling me he was out to get her, so it wasn't like I could call him for help. She was scaring the shit out of me and I didn't know what to do. So I took her to a hospital and they admitted her. If that makes me an evil bitch, then sue me."

"Great story," Nicole says. "But you left out the good part. You know, the bit about what actually happened to the baby."

Ronda glares at her. "Maybe you should ask Andi that. Could you move away from that door? I need to get back to work."

"If you could give us just another minute of your time," I say, keeping my voice as easygoing and sympathetic as I can. "Here's our problem. We have talked to Andi. And we found Tag and talked to him, too. Funny thing. Andi admits her memories are pretty broken leading up to the hospital, but when the psychosis cleared, she couldn't remember what happened to the baby. She remembers freaking out in a motel room, and then being in the hospital. Her memory of what happened in between is missing. So if you could just fill in that blank, we'll get out of your hair."

"I wish I could help." But she's clammed up again and her tone is anything but helpful. "The truth is, I have no idea. I went out to get us some food, and when I came back, the baby was gone. I asked Andi what happened, and all I got was gibberish. So I took her to the hospital—"

"Before or after you called the cops?" I keep my voice casual.

Ronda freezes, seeing the trap. "Look, I don't have to talk to you," she says. "You're not a cop, and I need to—"

"You need to answer the question. I can certainly call the police and tell them you were the last person to see a missing child."

"It was thirty years ago!" Her voice rises, tight and high.

I shrug. "No statute of limitations on kidnapping. Or murder, for that matter."

"I didn't—"

"So when did you notify the cops that there was a missing baby? Before or after you took your friend to the hospital?"

Stricken, trapped, she licks her lips. Shuffles her feet. "I didn't," she finally whispers. "I never called the cops."

"Because you know exactly what happened to the baby. How about you just tell us? It's about time you got this off your chest. You'll feel better. Your friend will have some closure."

Ronda hesitates. My gut twists as her eyes search my face, half frantic. I hate this part, bullying somebody into a confession, especially a woman. I remind myself that she probably really will feel better if she tells the truth after keeping this secret.

A long breath escapes her, carrying her defiance with it. Her shoulders sag. "Andi had totally freaked out, like I said. I thought maybe it was my fault. I—well, I gave her some ecstasy. I figured it would help with the depression, you know? And she was better for a bit, but when she crashed . . . well, she just went batshit crazy. And all the time the baby was screaming, and I didn't know how to shut her up. I tried holding her and changed her diaper, but I guess maybe she was hungry. Andi was breastfeeding, but she didn't want to feed Lelia. So anyway, I was scared about both of them, that the baby was maybe going to starve.

"So I drove them to the nearest ER, and when they took Andi back to a room, I went with her. I was holding the baby, who was still crying, and a nurse looked at me and said, 'Could you please take the baby out to the waiting room? It will make this assessment so much easier.'

"I stayed in the waiting room for, like, hours. Nobody came out, and the crying wouldn't stop. I'm not gonna lie, I'd taken more pills and I was coming down hard. And then, this other woman who was waiting, she had a baby, too, and she said, 'I think your baby is hungry.' And I said, 'I know, but I don't have a bottle with me,' and she said, 'I've got a spare and some extra formula,' and then . . . and then I asked her if she would just hold Lelia for a minute so I could go to the bathroom . . ."

Tears fill her eyes and track down her cheeks.

She inhales smoke as if her life depends on it.

I finish it for her. "So you left the woman holding the baby and never came back."

"I was freaked." Her voice, her face, are pleading. "Coming off X is harsh, you know? And I was young and terrified and, so, yeah. I ran out of there. Got in my car and hightailed it home. I mean, Andi was safe, right? And the woman was a good person. I figured she'd take the baby to the nurses at some point, and they'd figure out it was Andi's and they'd be reunited and everything would be okay.

"But then, like two weeks later, Andi called. And asked what happened to the baby. And I realized they didn't know, had no way of knowing, who the baby belonged to. The birth certificate was in my car. They must have thought Lelia belonged to me. That I was the one who left her."

"You *were* the one who left her." Nickle's voice is ice.

"But she wasn't *mine*. She wasn't my problem." Ronda's voice rises again.

"She was your responsibility." My momentary qualms about hurting her have vanished and I'm done softening my words. "You abandoned your friend and her baby. I see how it could have happened. You were young and stupid and you panicked. But when Andi called? You realize that if you'd told her what happened then, they might have found Lelia? She was probably in emergency foster care. They were probably searching for her mother."

Ronda's mascara has smeared black circles around her eyes and tracked down her cheeks. "I don't know why I didn't tell her. I thought she'd hate me. It's been horrible, living with this," she sobs. "You have no idea. Andi could have called me again when she got out of the psych ward. She could have—"

"It's been horrible for *you*?" Nicole is incandescent with rage. "What about Andi, never knowing what happened to her baby? What about Tag, for God's sake? The poor man never knew what happened to either one of them." She puts her hands on Ronda's chest and shoves. "You're a selfish, narcissistic—"

I grab her shoulders from behind and hold her back. "Easy, Nickle."

Ronda's chin rises defiantly. "Easy enough for you to call names. You weren't there. You don't know."

"I know I would never have abandoned my friend's baby and then lied about it! Who does that?"

"Are you calling the cops?" Ronda sniffles. "Am I getting arrested for this now?"

"Nickle and I aren't calling the cops. But if Andi or Tag choose to press charges, that's certainly their prerogative."

"Last time I ever try to help somebody out," Ronda says.

Nicole lunges forward, and I loop my arms around her body and drag her backward toward the Jeep. She twists and struggles to get free. "Let me go! I'm going to—"

"What? Beat her up? Then she gets to call the cops on you and feel even more self-righteous and martyred. Nothing is accomplished. Come on. Get in the car."

"And do what? Go tell Andrea and Graham that Ronda abandoned their baby?"

"Better than Andrea believing that she did it herself."

Still stiff with absolute outrage, she climbs into the Jeep, and I peel out of there before she can change her mind.

"Now what?" she asks. "Ronda just gets away with what she did and the baby is still missing. This is fucked six ways to Sunday."

"We're PIs, Nickle. Now we investigate. Maybe Ronda gets off, but we do our best to find Lelia. Although I admit I know nothing about the Canadian system."

"Wait. You said *we* are PIs."

"You were born for this," I say. "Brilliant. We could really work together."

"But my record. Or, what if we're on a case together and then I feel compelled to move something . . ." Even as she spouts all of the disclaimers, her face radiates excitement. If I weren't driving, I would absolutely kiss her in this minute, scruples be damned.

"I've been thinking about that," I say carefully. "I'm not sure exactly how your object-relocation thing works, I'll confess."

"Me neither," she says, collapsing back in her seat.

"But," I say, with a side glance, "I'm wondering if it could be, I don't know, controlled and directed. Like, we could use it to find missing people or something. And while we're trying to figure that out, you could sign on to Team Hawkeye and let me teach you the ropes. What do you say?"

"I'd work like a psychic, you mean?"

"Sure. Something like that."

"And you'd teach me? Fingerprints and interview techniques and everything?"

"Absolutely. All the sleuthing that I know shall be yours. And writing. Sleuthing and writing. Deal?" I hold out my right hand and we shake on it. When I close my fingers around hers and don't let go, she doesn't try to pull away. After a moment, she leans over and rests her head on my shoulder.

Chapter Forty

NICOLE

"Hawk's here. Are you ready?" Andrea taps at my door, and then comes in when I give her the okay.

I'm standing in front of the mirror, dressed in the ensemble Karen picked out for me, wrestling with a wave of panic. I look like Kent's Nicole, the one he groomed and manipulated and belittled and controlled. In this moment, I also *feel* like that Nicole and am wondering why the hell I ever thought going through with this court thing was a good idea.

"Breathe," Andrea says. "This is not the time for a meltdown. You're beautiful and your slip is not showing. Come on."

Her stitches came out nearly two weeks ago, and though I know her feet must still be tender, she walks without flinching. Something that had already begun to change in her shifted permanently the night Hawk and I told her what really happened to her baby. She'd wept again, for a long time. And she's seemed softer ever since. Calmer.

Now she sits down on the edge of the bed and says, "You're doing the right thing. If I'd been as brave as you are, I wouldn't have spent my whole life looking back over my shoulder. You'll feel better, trust me."

"You think?"

"I know. You'll also feel better when you and that big hunky hulk of yours finally get it on."

"Oh my God. I can't believe you just said that. He's not into me that way." I busy myself slipping into a pair of shoes that hurt my feet, using the excuse to hide my face.

"Oh please," Andrea says. "For someone so smart, sometimes you're very dense. He can't stop looking at you. His heart is hanging out of his eyeballs. You don't see that?"

"He's always very sweet and nice and friendly. And now we're working together. But—"

"But nothing," she says. "The man suffers from a surfeit of decency. You're his client until this whole mess with Kent is over, and he'll be professional if it kills him."

"You think?"

"I know. Now. It's time. You've come this far. You can't back out now."

I hug her, and she hugs me back.

"You keep doing this, soon you'll hug like a human being instead of a mannequin," I tease.

"Ha. Funny girl. Go on now."

I hobble down the stairs in my clip-clop shoes and find Hawk pacing in the entryway, muttering to himself.

"You okay?" I ask.

"I should be asking you that." Then he adds, with an intensity that makes my heart ricochet like a pinball, "I'd take a bullet for you. But in this case, I can't do anything except watch, and it's making me crazy."

"I've got this," I tell him, looking up into his face. "Agent Nickle is prepared and ready. No rescuing required."

He salutes. "Yes, ma'am. Let's go."

In the car, both of us are self-contained and quiet. He turns on the radio and tunes it to classical, knowing that's my go-to for calm and focus. When he stops the car near the courthouse, we sit looking at each other for a long moment.

He tries to smile. "Remember, this evening the whole gang is meeting for pizza and celebration. You've got this."

There are so many things I'd like to say to him that I don't say any of them, just slide out the door and click-click toward my fate in the ridiculous heels.

Karen is waiting for me outside the courthouse. "You look . . . presentable," she says with a little sniff. I look like a bad imitation of her, is how I look, but I bite back a sarcastic retort.

"Timothy wants to meet with you for a moment," Karen says. "Come this way." We go through the metal detectors together. Then she guides me into a pretrial conference room. It's claustrophobic and small. No windows. A Formica table runs down the center, flanked by folding metal chairs with padded plastic seats. The all-too-familiar smells of disinfectant, industrial carpet, and despair resurrect old memories and insecurities.

Before I have time to work up a panic, Timothy bustles in, Kent at his heels.

"There's our star witness," Timothy says, settling into a chair and opening his briefcase. He gives me a thorough once-over, his head tilted to one side.

"You look perfect. How do you feel? Can we get you anything? Water, tea, a protein bar?" Before I can answer, his eyes slide away again and his brow furrows over something in the case file.

"I'm fine." I rest my hands loosely on the table. My gaze settles on Kent. I take in every detail to remember for later. The arrogant set of his shoulders, the smug little smirk on his face as he stares back at me. *Right where I want you,* his eyes say.

And in that moment, looking squarely into his face, I smile. I make a production out of it. A tuck of amusement at the corners of my lips, gradually forming into a little pucker, growing into a full-fledged grin. Uncertainty flickers across his features.

"I think we're all set," Timothy says, oblivious. "We'll be starting with you. The prosecution finished presenting their case yesterday. They established the time and cause of death and linked it to Brian. Your testimony is the key to our case, because it blows the timing apart."

He glances at his watch and returns the file to his briefcase. "Court's about to begin. Nicole, Karen will take you to a seat in the gallery. You have no reason at all to be nervous. The jury will love you, and you're about to save your friend from being falsely convicted." He beams at me. Kent glowers. Both of them get up and leave the room ahead of us. Kent looks back once, not at Karen, who is looking expectantly at him, but at me.

"Word of advice," I say as she escorts me down the hallway, "you might want to watch out for that other chick I saw in the office when I was there."

"Who, Wendy?" Her eyes register shock first, and then recognition.

"If Wendy is the brunette that I saw scoot through with the files, yes. She's exactly his type. Oh, and another thing? Get your diamonds tested to see if they're real." Head high, I speed up. I know this courthouse and don't need a guide to find the courtroom. Karen runs a few steps to catch up with me, her poise shattered.

I stop at the back of the hearing room, the nauseating miasma of varnished wood, industrial carpeting, sweat, cologne, and dry-cleaning chemicals solidifying the reality of what I'm about to do. Karen keeps moving, and I steady myself and follow her to a seat in the front row of the gallery, right behind the low wall that separates spectators, witnesses, reporters, and family members from the actual proceedings.

We're just in the nick of time. Almost immediately, the bailiff calls the court to order. We all stand while Judge Albers walks in and takes the bench. She reminds me of Judge Judy. Severe gray hair. No makeup.

Keen eyes survey the gallery, the defendant at his table with Kent and Timothy, the two lawyers at the prosecution table.

She sits. The members of the jury file solemnly in and take their seats. Timothy gets to his feet. He briefly refreshes the jury on the prosecution's case and pokes some holes in it.

"The prosecution wants you to believe that the defendant shot three innocent people in cold blood, allegedly because he was high on methamphetamines, and then robbed them. What you are going to hear today will prove beyond a shadow of any doubt that it was impossible for the defendant to have been in that place at that time. I would like to call my first witness, Nicole Brandenburg, to the stand."

A surge of adrenaline floods through me. This is it. I've spent enough time running from Kent. I get to my feet and walk steadily up the aisle.

The bailiff swears me in. I hear my own voice, clear and loud, ringing out into the silence. "I swear to tell the truth, the whole truth, and nothing but the truth."

Once I'm seated, Timothy makes a play for time, letting the jury look me over while he sifts through papers and whispers something in his client's ear. Kent glares, his expression clearly conveying the message that I'd better get this right. The prosecutor, Nancy Whitfield, glances up at me briefly, smiles, then returns to her papers. The jury's faces are all a blur.

Hawk and Andrea sit together at the back of the gallery, telegraphing support and courage. I know my family would be here if they weren't all pretending they were still mad at me. My eyes mist over with a rush of gratitude and love. I am not alone.

Timothy gets to his feet. *Here we go.*

"Could you state your name for the court, please?"

"Nicole Angelica Marie Wood Brandenburg." My voice is clear and steady. As coached, I hold my head high and look at the jury as I speak before shifting my attention back to Timothy.

"Now, Nicole. I want you to take a good look around the court-room. Do you recognize anybody here?"

"You." I smile at him, and he smiles back. We rehearsed this. A little humor, to warm the jury up to me. Making me likable and relatable. "And my soon-to-be ex-husband, who is assisting you in the defense."

"Yes. And I know it was especially difficult for you to be here today because of his presence. Thank you for contributing to the cause of justice. Now, is there anybody else that you recognize?"

"Him." I point at the defendant. "Brian Hazleton."

Brian has the gall to smile at me. His face wears an expression that matches Kent's. Privilege. Power. Control.

Timothy lowers his voice to sound confidential and apologetic. "Now, Nicole, can you please tell the jury how you know Mr. Hazleton?"

"Well, I've seen his photo. You've shown it to me several times since I received your subpoena requiring me to testify."

My eyes are on Kent as I say the words. I've waited for this moment. Dreamed about his reaction. He stiffens; his eyes widen as the first pre-sentiment of disaster strikes him. I'd been instructed not to mention the subpoena, to let the jury believe I'm here of my own free will, and I've already moved off script. Timothy smiles, as if this is all part of our plan, and moves a little closer to the stand, ramping up his reassuring manner.

"Could you please describe your relationship with Brian Hazleton?"

This is the moment. The air seems to swirl around me. I close my eyes. When I open them, I fix my gaze on the gallery. Andrea gives me a thumbs-up. Hawk nods and mouths, "You've got this." I turn my eyes back to Timothy and say clearly and distinctly, "I have no relationship with Brian Hazleton. I've never met the man, or even talked to him."

A murmur ripples through the courtroom. Kent looks like he's been shot, his face gone bloodless and slack. Hazleton, on the other hand, is almost purple with rage. He turns to whisper in Kent's ear, and I can see perfectly well from here that they are words the judge would not deem appropriate for the courtroom.

Judge Albers frowns, leaning forward over her desk and sweeping the courtroom with a penetrating gaze. "That's enough. You will come to order."

When all is quiet, Timothy fixes me with a commanding stare and sharpens his voice.

"Nicole, I know I do not need to remind you that you have sworn an oath to tell the truth, the whole truth, and nothing but the truth. Now, can you tell the jury what you told me in your witness statement?"

The worst is over now that I've taken the plunge. My breathing is steady, my heart racing only a little.

"Yes, of course. I told you that Brian and I were high school sweethearts. And I told you that we ran into each other at Starbucks, and that on the evening of January nineteenth of last year, we went out for dinner, and that I went home with him afterward and spent the night."

Timothy smiles and nods, a little of the tension going out of his shoulders. Kent knows me better. He's slumped at the table, his hand wiping his face repeatedly as if there's something on his skin that won't come off.

The prosecutor watches all of us, a cat eying a particularly fat and juicy mouse. The faces of the jury register varying degrees of confusion. Judge Albers's frown creeps toward a scowl.

"So, then, you are saying that you not only knew the defendant but had a relationship with him," Timothy nudges.

"No. I am under oath to tell the truth to the court, and I am saying that I have never met Brian Hazleton, and can only identify him because of the pictures you showed me."

Again, murmurs erupt in the courtroom, and again, the judge calls for order.

"Your Honor," Timothy says, "I request a brief recess in which to consult with my client."

"Objection," the prosecutor says. "I see no need for a recess. The witness was prepared by the defense previously. I am ready to cross."

Judge Albers turns an x-ray gaze in my direction, eyes narrowed. "Mrs. Brandenburg, I will remind you again that you are under oath."

"Yes, Your Honor. I understand. That's why I'm telling the truth."

"And do you clearly understand the questions that are being asked of you?"

"I do."

She nods and releases me from scrutiny, glaring at Timothy. "I see no reason to take up the court's time with a recess, when the witness clearly understands the proceedings and you have had plenty of time for discovery and preparation. You will proceed with questioning or allow the prosecution to cross-examine."

Timothy shoots me a reproachful look. "I have no further questions, Your Honor," he says.

"What the hell?" Brian half rises from his seat. Kent drags him back down as the prosecutor stands.

"Mrs. Brandenburg, let me get this clear. You are saying that you have never met the defendant."

"Yes, that's what I'm saying. I do not know him and have never seen his face before today."

"Except in photos."

"Yes."

"Which you were shown by the defense."

"Yes."

Ms. Whitfield looks not at me but at the jury as she asks the next question. "And can you tell the court in your own words how you came to receive a subpoena to come here today and testify that you did know Brian Hazleton, that you had a relationship with him, and that you were with him on the night when the victims were so brutally shot down?"

"I was asked by a member of the defense team to provide a false alibi."

"This person knew the alibi would be false?"

"Yes."

"And you agreed to do this."

"No. I did not agree."

Ms. Whitfield turns back to me, her tone incisive. "Mrs. Brandenburg. Your credibility is in question already with the court. I strongly advise that you tell the truth."

"I am telling the truth." I keep my eyes on her while I speak, the safest place to look. "When Kent first asked me, I said no. But then he threatened me, and then he threatened my friends and family. I received a subpoena. I was afraid of what would happen if I refused to testify, but I didn't want to come here and lie to the court."

"And you gave a statement that you did know the defendant and were with him the night of the murder. Why is that?" she asks.

"Like I said, I was afraid of what would happen if I didn't. I had to move out of my apartment, because he told my roommate's landlord that I was a drug addict and—"

"Objection—hearsay!" Timothy sputters.

"Sustained," the judge says. "Counselor, you are on a very slippery slope. Watch your step."

"Yes, Your Honor. Mrs. Brandenburg, did you speak to the landlord?"

"No, but—"

"I believe you," she says warmly, eyes on the jury. "And I believe your roommate. But let's focus on things the defendant, or his attorneys, said to you directly."

"Kent said I had stolen money that was a bribe from a client, meant to buy an alibi. And he said that if I didn't give him back the money, I would need to provide the alibi myself."

"Your Honor." Timothy is on his feet, his voice raised. "That recess that I asked for?"

"Perhaps you shouldn't have suborned perjury," Ms. Whitfield retorts.

"Your Honor," Timothy shouts. "The prosecution is—"

"Enough! Both of you." Judge Albers's voice lashes like a whip. "Ladies and gentlemen of the jury, I am going to call a brief recess while I get to the bottom of this matter. Bailiff, please escort the jurors to the jury room. And clear the court. Counsel, Mrs. Brandenburg, stay where you are."

The jury files out, and the observers clear the gallery, murmuring and shooting side glances in my direction. When only the lawyers, the judge, the defendant, and I remain, we sit in silence until the bailiff returns and closes the heavy wooden door with a click that reverberates in the empty room.

"Your Honor," Timothy says immediately. "This whole line of questioning is irrelevant."

"On the contrary, Your Honor," Ms. Whitfield argues. "It speaks to the credibility of the witness."

"I agree," the judge says. "However, we will take the precaution of proceeding without the jury. Continue, Counselor."

All three men at the defense table glare at me. My support team in the gallery is gone. I'm on my own. My mouth is dry; my legs are trembling, but they are fortunately out of sight.

I can do this.

Ms. Whitfield smiles at me encouragingly. "Let's clarify. You said that you were asked to provide an alibi for the defendant."

"Yes, that's right."

"And what would happen if you refused?"

"Objection!" Timothy snarls. "Conjecture. Your Honor, I really—"

"I'll rephrase," Ms. Whitfield smoothly interrupts. "What did you believe would happen if you refused to provide the testimony requested by the defense?"

"I believed my family and friends would be emotionally and financially harmed, and that I would be sent to prison because of the money I took from my husband."

"Money that he later told you was meant to be used to buy an alibi."

"That's correct."

Timothy scribbles furiously on a legal pad and shoves it under Kent's nose. Kent's mouth opens and closes soundlessly. He adjusts his tie, pulling as if it's suddenly become too tight.

The prosecutor softens her voice. "Now, Nicole, I know this has all been difficult for you, and we are almost through. I have one last question. You say you have no knowledge of the defendant. That you have never met him or seen him prior to today, outside of the photos that were shown to you by the defense. What made the defense team so confident that you could persuade a jury that you were speaking the truth?"

"Objection!" Timothy barks. "Speculation."

"I'll reframe," Ms. Whitfield says smoothly. "Can you tell the court in your own words where the story of your relationship with the defendant came from?"

"I was told exactly what to say."

"By whom?"

I point at Kent.

"She's lying, Your Honor!" Kent rises from his seat. "She's a diagnosed kleptomaniac with an extensive legal record. You can't believe a word she's saying."

"Sit down!" Judge Albers orders. "One more outburst like that, and I'll fine you for contempt."

The prosecutor goes on as if there has been no interruption. "And yet the defense relied on her for an alibi." She shakes her head dramatically and turns to the judge. "Your Honor, I believe that Mrs. Brandenburg's testimony is admissible, and relevant."

"This is outrageous," Timothy objects.

Judge Albers's expression offers him no mercy. "Perhaps you should have thought of that before. Bring the jury back in."

I try not to fidget while the members of the jury file solemnly back into their seats, and the spectators return to the gallery. When everybody is settled, the judge nods to the prosecutor. "Counselor. You may resume your cross-examination, but if you stray outside of the parameters, I will have no tolerance."

"Understood. Now, Mrs. Brandenburg." Ms. Whitfield keeps her expression neutral, but a hint of triumph bleeds through in her voice. "Can you tell the court in your own words what you were going to testify to today in court?"

"That Brian Hazleton and I were involved in a relationship, and that I spent the evening and the night with him on the night of the murders."

"And were you with him at that time?"

I shake my head. "No. I have never met the defendant."

"Do you know anything about his whereabouts that night?"

"I do not."

She smiles. "Thank you for your honest and courageous testimony today, Mrs. Brandenburg. The prosecution rests, Your Honor." She takes a seat.

"Does the defense wish to redirect?" Judge Albers asks.

Timothy gets to his feet. "The defense requests a continuance, Your Honor."

"I bet it does," the judge says. "Denied. However, we will break early for lunch."

"Your Honor—"

"Lunch, Counselor. Don't be late."

And just like that, it's over.

Kent tries to burn holes in me with his eyes, but I'm barely even aware of him. Hawk is waiting for me at the front of the gallery. I fling myself against him, pressing my cheek to his chest. He wraps his arms around me, murmuring softly against my hair, "You were brilliant."

"The two of you will pay for this little stunt," Kent growls. "Everybody will pay."

"Is that a threat?" Hawk asks. "It certainly sounded like a threat."

I turn to face my husband, Hawk's steadying arm around my waist. "This time, Kent, you're the person who is going to pay."

"Dream on," he snarls. "One more of your little delusions."

"Oh, I'm dreaming all right." I smile up at him. "But there's nothing delusional about this. We've been working hard. We've got witness statements. Hawk has built a whole case against you."

He laughs. "You're bad at bluffing." But he looks uncertain. I know him well enough to guess what he's thinking. Are we just messing with him? Or is this a real threat?

"You know that phone you stole from me?" I smile sweetly. "It was uploading to the cloud. We have that whole conversation recorded. Blackmail. Perjury. We've got you for so many things."

On cue, Hawk's aunt joins us. She's in uniform, accompanied by another officer. "Kent Brandenburg," she intones, "you're under arrest for suborning perjury." The officer moves behind him and snaps a handcuff on one wrist. "You have the right to remain silent—"

Kent struggles. "Stop. What are you doing? This is outrageous. I'll get you for this, Nicole."

"Sounds like another threat," Hawk says.

"We could add resisting arrest, obstruction of justice, and threats of bodily harm if you like," Detective Hansen suggests. Kent's expression is murderous, but he stops fighting and the cop finishes handcuffing him and goes on with reciting his Miranda rights.

Hawk steers me away. Out of the courtroom, down the hall, outside into a sunlit morning. I blink against the brightness of the light, draw in a bracing breath of cold February air.

"That was a beautiful thing," Hawk says, his arm still protectively around me as he pilots me away from the courthouse. "Hazleton is going down. Kent is going down. He can't hurt you anymore, Nicole."

I stop and look up into his face. "Are you sure about that?"

"He'll be disbarred and do time. Timothy would be an idiot if he doesn't fire him, like, yesterday. And after that . . . well, you have me. And my mother. And my aunt. And your family. Not to mention Andrea and Graham and Ash and Penelope Lane. It's quite an army."

A warm glow starts in my belly and spreads outward through every inch of my body.

Hawk opens the door of the Jeep for me.

"Pizza, right?" I ask.

"In a bit. I have a surprise for you first. Victory celebration."

We stand there, so close, looking into each other's eyes, and I feel like I can read his soul. I summon all of my courage and say, "Can I ask one more favor?"

"Name it." His voice is low, gravelly.

I rest my palms on his chest and whisper, "Would you maybe please kiss me?"

"God, Nicole." The words come out half strangled, and I think maybe I've read him wrong, but then his arms go around my waist and his lips are pressed against mine and my doubts are swept away. A long time later, when I pull away to catch my breath, grateful for his strength supporting my shaky knees, he says, "Get in the Jeep. I still have that surprise for you."

Hawk holds my hand but drives in silence, looking like the cat who has eaten the canary, snagged a bowl of cream, and is now monitoring a busy mousehole. We dart stealthy side glances at each other, me trying to guess what he's up to while he attempts to keep his secrets.

My first thought, and hope, when he parks the Jeep at his mother's and leads me into his basement lair is that he'll carry me into his room, throw me down on the bed, and ravish me.

Instead, he sits me down in front of one of the computers and covers my eyes with one hand while tapping at the keys with the other.

"There we go." Triumphant, he uncovers my eyes and waits for my reaction.

It takes a minute. My vision is blurry from the pressure of his palm. And when I finally get focused on the screen, it still takes me a few minutes to register what I'm seeing. Some sort of chart. Words pop out at me.

Shared DNA—50%.

Daughter

Hope creeps in through all of the cracks in my armor, but I can't let myself believe that this is what I so much want it to be.

"What am I looking at?" I ask.

"That, my magical mover of things, is a match to Andrea's DNA from a woman looking for her birth parents. And here is Graham's."

"Oh, Hawk. You found her?"

He taps a few more keys and opens another screen. "Meet Michaela Olafson."

A Facebook page shows a serious dark-haired woman holding a laughing toddler on her hip. A man stands behind her, his arm around her shoulders, face radiating love and pride. The woman's eyes are Graham's, her face a younger version of Andrea's. Hawk scrolls a little to the post at the top of his feed, which reads:

Friends, I am blown away. Remember my wild idea to try 23andMe? Looks like I may have located my birth parents. Both of them, can you believe it? Still reeling. More to come.

The screen blurs. My body heaves with sobs. Hawk's hands are on my shoulders, then smoothing my hair. "Nickle? I thought you'd be happy. I—"

"I *am* happy," I try to say, but my voice comes out all distorted. Hawk drops to his knees and swivels my chair toward him. I fling both arms around his neck and bury my face against his chest while I'm shaken by a fit of weeping entirely beyond my ability to control.

"It's just all so . . . so big . . . ," I try to explain when I'm remotely able to speak again. He fetches a box of tissues. Disappears for a minute and comes back with a warm washcloth. When I've blown my nose and wiped my face, he says, "I think I might understand. All of these years, everybody's told you you're broken because you move things, and now that very thing has helped you find Graham and Andrea's daughter."

His understanding very nearly sends me off again, but this time, I blink back the tears and snuggle into his arms. "Helped *us*," I clarify. "None of it would have happened without you. Not this. Not finding the kidnapped girl, none of it."

He strokes my hair, silent for a moment, then says, "I never told you. When I saw you—that very first time I got close to you at the Goodwill store—I felt like I already knew you. That we were somehow *meant*. Does that make any sense?"

"Totally."

"I need to tell you something else," he says. But then he doesn't.

"Well?" I say. "Spill it."

"It's . . . hard to say."

I gaze up at him, trying to guess what he could possibly be so hung up over. He swallows. Takes a breath. "I . . . love you," he says, his voice breaking on the words.

Hope is no longer a tentative thing. It's a blinding, blazing incandescent light that fills me to the brim. It's too much, it's going to sweep me away.

"Thank God," I say, clinging to the last fragments of my defenses. "Now you've got that out of the way, maybe you could get to the ravishing."

He makes a sound somewhere between laughter and tears and lifts me off my feet. His kiss steals my breath away, and apparently his own, because he sounds kind of strangled when he says, "Your wish is my command," and carries me off to the bedroom.

"There are people waiting at the pizza restaurant," he says, laying me down on the bed.

"Which means they aren't here," I point out. "Since I'm giving instructions, would you maybe take your clothes off? I've been imagining you naked for weeks."

"God, Nicole." He starts to lift his shirt over his head. Pauses. "You're sure?"

I sit up and place both hands over my heart. "I love you, Hawk. You're my holy grail of objects. And where you belong is with me."

"That's exactly it," he says. And then he's on the bed and kissing me, and for once I stop thinking and trust that somehow everything will turn out right.

Chapter Forty-One

ANDREA

Tag and I sit side by side on the park bench, looking for all the world like we're a couple enjoying the spring sunshine. We picked up coffee on the way—mine a half-caf latte made with coconut milk, his a salted caramel Frappuccino with whipped cream—but mine is cooling and his is melting, untouched. So far, we've used the drinks only as props, something to hold on to. We look at the river, grateful for the opportunity to avoid each other's eyes.

In the months since Hawk and Nicole discovered the truth of what happened to our daughter, we've begun, very gradually, to reconnect with each other, mostly through text messages and email. Tag says that what happened wasn't my fault, that I was not in a position to be able to make decisions. I think he believes it. On good days, I believe it, too, but shedding so many years of guilt and self-hatred is a long, slow journey. I've been going to counseling, and it helps more than I thought it would.

I cry so easily these days, over the smallest thing, good or bad. Sylvester curling up in my lap. A sunrise. All the opportunities for love and connection that I've lost and can never get back. It's amazing how quickly the empty spaces in my life are filling up now that the walls have come down. Nicole and Hawk come over at least once a week for dinner. I've been introduced to Ash and Arya and have even been trusted to babysit that adorable child.

The first time she was left alone with me, I literally froze in terror, all of the old what-ifs clamoring through my brain. But we both survived and now I'm on the babysitting roster. I still react with wonder and, yes, inevitable tears, when she reaches up those chubby little arms to be picked up or hugs them around my neck.

"Do you think they're coming?" Tag asks, drawing me back to the present moment of impossible waiting. Today, we are going to meet Michaela. We've all exchanged brief messages and emails and pictures. She declined a video chat, saying she wanted to meet us really in person or not at all. Hawk has facilitated a meeting, and she's flying into Spokane today from her home in Vancouver.

"Maybe her flight was delayed," I say, fidgeting. It's after eleven. Michaela's flight was supposed to come in at ten, and Hawk and Nicole went to meet the plane.

Tag starts tapping out a rhythm on his leg, and I can't repress a smile. "You always used to do that when you were nervous."

"And you always said it felt like marbles rattling in your skull."

Five minutes pass. Ten. Tag starts tapping again, and I feel like I'm going to explode. I put my hand over his to stop him. At my touch, he goes perfectly still. I feel his tension in my own body, and realization washes over me that this is the first time we've touched in thirty years. Unexpectedly, like a gift, he turns his hand palm up and laces his fingers through mine.

"Andi," he says, his voice a little husky. I turn my head to look into his eyes, the only part of his face that hasn't changed at all, and feel the years fall away.

"Hey! Sorry we're late!"

Our eye contact breaks as we both turn to see Nicole waving from down the bike path. Hawk walks on one side of her. On the other is the dark-haired woman our lost baby has grown into. A choked cry escapes me. Tag squeezes my hand, and I anchor myself to him as the three approach.

I don't know what to do. Should I get up or stay seated? Do we shake hands? Can I hug her? There's no established protocol for a meeting such as this.

"Andrea. Graham," Nicole says, without any ceremony at all, "this is Michaela." We all stare at each other in silence until I realize that our daughter might be even more nervous than we are. I let go of Tag and get to my feet. Holding out my hand to Michaela may be the most difficult thing I've ever done. I'm terrified that she'll stare at it in disgust and disdain. She has every reason to hate me. She has every reason to—

Michaela ignores the hand and hugs me.

Breathless, I hug her back. When we let go, there are tears on both of our faces. Michaela hugs Tag, too, and then in some sort of emotional confusion, Tag hugs me and I bury my face in a shoulder both familiar and strange, but only for a moment, because I can't get enough of looking at my daughter.

Impossible to believe that this tall, beautiful, self-possessed woman was once that tiny baby that blew my life apart. She's a stranger, yet at the same time, her face is familiar, as is the way she moves, the gestures she makes with her hands.

"Wow," she says. "This is just mind blowing to meet you in person. I don't know what to say."

"Same on this end." Tag reaches for my hand again, and the act of solidarity makes my tears flow.

"I'm so sorry," I tell her. "It would mean everything if you could forgive me."

"You weren't yourself." She stops there. Dashes away new tears and goes on, "I only had a touch of the baby blues, myself, but I can imagine it. Even sleep deprivation made me kind of crazy."

"But I didn't hunt for you when I got out of the psych ward," I say, because as difficult as the words are, I know she needs to hear them. "And that has to feel like I didn't love you. I did. I can only explain that by saying I felt ashamed and guilty. And I was terrified that I might have . . . hurt you . . . while I was psychotic. But before that, before you were born, you were . . . wanted."

Tag's fingers squeeze my hand tighter. "Andi was almost obsessed with health during her pregnancy," he says. "She stopped all caffeine. Everything she ate, you knew she was thinking, 'Will this be good for the baby?' So much love went into decorating the nursery and buying baby clothes."

Tears flow down Michaela's face, and this time she doesn't scrub them away. Tag clears his throat again. "I never stopped looking for you. Please don't feel like we didn't . . . like we didn't . . ." He stops, his breathing ragged, wiping his own eyes.

"I know," she says. "I understand. And my adopted parents are fantastic. I couldn't have been more lucky." She smiles through her tears, revealing a dimple in her right cheek, and I wonder which ancestor that bit of DNA came from. "Only thing is, my whole adopted family is Norwegian. All blonde and so Scandinavian looking. I got teased in high school—lots of jokes about my mother and the mailman, that sort of thing. And I knew nothing about my past, except that I was dropped off in a hospital ER. I don't even know my birthday."

"June 7," I say. "It was a Sunday. You were born at eight thirteen a.m. and you weighed seven pounds and seven ounces."

Her face lights up, and I want to capture that expression, a moment caught out of time to keep with me always.

"That's so amazing. They guessed at how many days old I was and put June 8 on my birth certificate."

"Now you get two birthdays," Nicole says. "More is better, right?"

"Funny thing, but I suspect I'm always going to feel like today is my real birthday," Michaela says, a slight flush creeping into her cheeks, her expression gone shy. "Because today is the day I met my parents."

I'm completely choked up again. In all of my imaginings, I never dreamed of such a kind, compassionate, put-together young woman. But I should have, because she is so much like her father.

"And your life now?" Tag asks. "Do you like teaching? Chemistry, right?"

"Love it," she says, lighting up. "I'm a card-carrying nerd, so it's super cool to get to make a living playing with chemicals. And I actually kinda love the high school kids, too, especially the ones who are awkward like me."

"You are so not awkward," I object, wondering how someone so obviously perfect could even entertain self-doubt.

She laughs. "Oh yes, I am. But Jace makes up for all of that with social skills and practical stuff and being utterly gorgeous besides. We've been married for five years. And . . ." She hesitates, then comes to some sort of decision. "You have a granddaughter. Trina. She'll be two in a couple of weeks now. She's a total handful. Every word she says is no, even when she means yes, but of course we absolutely adore her . . ."

She breaks off there, kind of frozen, some of the light going out of her face. Because the adoration is not an "of course" at all, she of all human beings knows that. I wish there was some way, any way, to change the past, to go back and undo everything I did, to love her the way she deserved to be loved. To have her grow up with me and Tag.

But there is no going back. Only forward.

"Sorry," Michaela says. "I get carried away on the topic of Trina. It's why I did the DNA search, really. I wanted to find out my family history. Hereditary health conditions. Or, you know, genius-level talents!"

"Not much of either on my side of the family," I tell her. "But your father is a brilliant poet."

He clears his throat. "Haven't written poetry in years. I'm a psychologist now."

Michaela's gaze lingers on his face, then mine. "So the two of you aren't . . . together . . . then?"

Tag gives me a half smile, then says, "We lost each other when we lost you. We've only recently reconnected."

"Someday," I say hesitantly, "I . . . we . . . would love to meet your daughter."

Michaela twists her hands together, a mirror of something I often do when I'm nervous. "Sometime. Maybe. We'll see."

My heart aches with equal parts pain and pleasure. She's a good mother. Protective, as she should be.

"But I definitely want to see you again," Michaela says. "And maybe we can do video calls, now that we've met. And, you know, email and text and whatever."

"I couldn't begin to ask for more," I say. My eyes sweep over the faces gathered here, my heart full of love and gratitude. Hawk's arm rests on Nicole's shoulders, and her head leans against him, her face radiant. I look back at my daughter and ask, "Has anybody told you the story of how we came to find you after all these years?"

She shakes her head, her lips curving into a questioning smile.

So I begin. "Nicole, here, has this Object Relocation Program . . ."

~

Penelope: Pizza at the Hut? Arya wants Auntie Nickle. Also Ash says it's been a week.

Nickle: Can't, we're on a case. 😎. 😊. 😍 Kiss that cute face for me.

Penelope: Ha. I'll have to catch her first. Tell me about the case!

Nickle: Missing person thing. Hush hush. Can't say more.

Penelope: Ooh, covert operation. ⭐ Please tell me there's an object involved . . .

Nickle: Well, there was this bottle opener in the parking lot at Target. Gotta go. Subject on the move. 💜 Agent Nickle out for now.

ACKNOWLEDGMENTS

First and foremost, thank you to the elusive creative forces that drop story ideas into my brain, even though they have a tendency to then run off and leave me to hash out all of the complicated details for myself. This story was born of a random thought—*What if a woman cleaning houses could sense energy left behind on objects?*—and ran amok from there. Special thanks to the character Hawk, who not only helped to save Nicole but saved me and the book by turning up in the shower to volunteer for service when the manuscript was half written and hopelessly stuck.

Thank you again and again and again to my Viking, who makes sense of scrambled plot segments, offers up brilliant suggestions, and anchors my flights of fantasy to the logistical requirements of the real world. Much gratitude to my son Brandon for his insights into the life of a cleaner of other people's houses, and for helping me ground the story in Spokane.

Barbara and Sandi—our MFM meetings not only helped keep me sane but also inspired, energized, and positive during this bizarre year of writing during COVID-19. And, Marcella, our consistent writing-together times kept me honest and helped to keep the words flowing. Thank you. So much love to Heather Webb and Kristina Martin for the early read and the excellent suggestions you offered. Barbara Davis, thanks ever so much for educating me about diamonds.

To the wonderfully interactive and supportive readers of my newsletter—thank you for not only reading my books but for also giving feedback and suggestions and even offering up your names on the altar of the storytelling gods. Michaela and Lelia, your names are beautiful, your name stories made me happy, and thank you for naming Andrea's missing daughter.

Deidre, you are so much more than a fabulous agent. I am privileged to count you as a friend.

To my editorial team—you ladies are pure magic. Jodi, thank you for loving my crazy book ideas and for asking such excellent and insightful questions about plot and character. Jenna, bless you for pushing me, even when I thought I was already done. Michelle, your sharp eyes and sense of phrasing add so much during the copyediting stage. This book owes so much to all of you, and so do I.

And to every reader everywhere, whether you read this book or not, thank you for keeping the world of books alive for all of us.

ABOUT THE AUTHOR

Photo © Diane Maehl

Kerry Anne King is the *Washington Post* and Amazon Charts bestselling author of *Whisper Me This*; *Everything You Are*, a finalist for the Nancy Pearl Book Awards hosted by the Pacific Northwest Writers Association; and *A Borrowed Life*, a best women's fiction nominee in the 2020 Authors on the Air Book of the Year Awards. Voted the 2020 Writer of the Year by the Rocky Mountain Fiction Writers, Kerry writes compelling and transformational stories about family and personal growth with elements of mystery, humor, and an undercurrent of romance.

When she's not absorbed in creative pursuits, you'll find Kerry hanging out with her real-life Viking on their little piece of heaven in rural northeastern Washington. For more information visit www.kerryanneking.com.